Richard R. De Hampole, Richard Morris

The pricke of conscience, Stimulus conscientiae

A Northumbrian poem

SALZWASSER
VERLAG

Richard R. De Hampole, Richard Morris

The pricke of conscience, Stimulus conscientiae

A Northumbrian poem

Reprint of the original, first published in 1863.

1st Edition 2022 | ISBN: 978-3-37500-447-7

Verlag (Publisher): Salzwasser Verlag GmbH, Zeilweg 44, 60439 Frankfurt, Deutschland
Vertretungsberechtigt (Authorized to represent): E. Roepke, Zeilweg 44, 60439 Frankfurt, Deutschland
Druck (Print): Books on Demand GmbH, In de Tarpen 42, 22848 Norderstedt, Deutschland

THE PRICKE OF CONSCIENCE

(STIMULUS CONSCIENTIÆ)

A NORTHUMBRIAN POEM

RICHARD ROLLE DE HAMPOLE.

WITH

AN INTRODUCTION, NOTES, AND GLOSSARIAL INDEX

BY

RICHARD MORRIS.

1863.

PREFACE.

Among the manuscript-collections of the British Museum there are no less than ten copies of the 'Pricke of Conscience' and though all of them have been carefully examined for the purpose of obtaining a good text, yet one has seemed of so much greater philological value to the students of Old English literature than the others that I have made it the basis of the following text.— The ten copies, a description of which will be found in the printed catalogues of Manuscripts, are:—

Additional MSS., Nos. 11305, 22283;
Cottonian MS., Galba E. ix;
Harleian MSS., Nos. 106, 1731, 2377, 2394, 4196, 6923;
Lansdowne MS., No. 348.

The present volume is printed from the Cottonian MS., Galba E. ix, a fine folio volume of Northumbrian poetry, containing the romance of Ywaine and Gawaine, the Seven Sages, Minot's poems, a few short treatises on the deadly sins, shrift &c., the Gospel of Nichodemus, together with the Pricke of Conscience which forms the concluding portion of the manuscript.

My choice of this MS. in preference to the others has been influenced by the following considerations:—

1. The reputed author RICHARD ROLLE de Hampole more commonly called Hampole, lived in the priory of Hampole, four miles from Doncaster in Yorkshire. He was one of the most popular divines of the fourteenth century. Writing as he tells us he did for the *unlered and lewed*, it is not at all likely that he would have employed any other mode of communication than the

dialect of the district in which he lived; this as we well know was Northumbrian, the

'Language of the Northin lede
That can nan other Inglis rede'.[1]

2. Six manuscripts[2] out of the ten already enumerated are evidently transcriptions of a Northern copy adapted more or less skilfully to the southern, western and midland dialects. This is easily proved by the way in which the several transcribers have endeavoured to *translate* pure Northumbrian words into their own South-, West- and Midland-English.

One example must suffice to explain our meaning.—In the Cottonian manuscript Hampole speaks of the conception of man in the following terms:—

"He was consayved synfully
Within his awen moder body,
Þar duellid man in a myrk dungeon,
And in a foul sted of corupcion,
Whar he had na other fode,
Bot wlatsom glet and *loper blode.*" (p. 13, l. 446—459.)

A north countryman would have known that loper (more commonly *loperd, lopered)* meant curdled, coagulated, but the word was evidently unknown in the south for instead of

"Bot wlatsom glet and loper blode."

Addit. MS. 11305 reads:—

"Bot lothsom glotte and *filthede of blode.*"

The transcriber of MS. Y.[3] shews still more ingenuity in ren-

[1] Cursor Mundi (Northumbrian version) a MS. in the College of Physicians at Edinburgh, fol. 43b, col. 2. Quoted by J. Small M. A. in Metrical Homilies p. xxi.

[2] Harl. MSS., Nos. 106, 1731, 2377 (all very imperfect).
Addit. MSS. Nos. 11305, 22283 (perfect).
Lansd. MS. No. 348 (imperfect).

The Harl. MSS. 2394, 6923 (all very imperfect) and 4196 (imperfect) are in the Northumbrian dialect and have been collated so far as was possible with the Cott. MS.—The Harl. MS. 4196 is the best of these Northern copies and differs but slightly from the copy which has supplied the present text.

[3] I take this opportunity of acknowledging the kindness of James Yates Esq. who, unsolicited, placed a fine MS. copy of the 'Pricke of Conscience' (xivth century) at my disposal, as soon as he heard that an

dering the uncouth term by one easily intelligible and which at the same time bears no slight resemblance to it, as the following reading will shew:—

"He was conceyved synfully
Wiþ-inne his owen moder body
Þanne dwelleþ man in a foule dungeoune,
And in a foule stede of corrupcioune,
Where he haþ non oþer fode,
Bot glette and *lepres foule blode.*" (fol. 14.)

It need hardly be said that between '*lepres* blode' and '*loper* blode' there is not the slightest connection.

Lopered, Sc. *lopperit,* like many other northern terms has gradually travelled southwards, for we find it in Forby and other collectors of provincialisms.

This example is sufficient to show how far the numerous transcribers of Hampole are to be trusted in their translations of Northumbrian words. In some instances however the various readings are useful and a few of them from Addit. MSS. 11305, 22283; Lansd. MS. 348, are worthy of notice:—

coldness	for	dasednes, (Northern)
droubelonde	,,	domland,
pees	,,	saghtel,
lowryng	,,	merryng,
riche	,,	bigg,
roryng	,,	romyng,
slouh	,,	rym,
strangly	,,	worow.

From these remarks it may be inferred that the Cottonian manuscript supplies us with a text, which if we have a knowledge of its vocabulary, is far more intelligible than any of the copies written for readers of the South of England. The language too is more archaic, while the length of the poem furnishes us with material for the study of a most important English dialect, the published vocabulary of which is confessedly very meagre; and the influence of which upon the classical or written language has as yet received but little attention.

edition of that poem was forthcoming. This copy I have marked as MS. Y., and from it is printed the very full table of contents contained in the present volume.

Most writers upon the English language, and even those who have treated their subject historically, seem to have been ignorant of the existence of any material for the illustration of English dialects from the latter part of the xiiith to the middle of the xvth century. Mr Marsh in his new volume on the English language produces passages from the Northumbrian Psalms, along with many extracts from southern writers, as illustrating the progress of our language in the latter part of the xiiith century, while in treating of the literature of the xivth century he refuses to give credit to Minot's poems on account of their Scotch accent!

The hand-writing of the Cottonian Manuscript is generally assigned to the reign of Henry V, but there are good reasons for placing it not later than the commencement of the xvth century. The language of Hampole is of course much earlier than this, being that of the North of England towards the end of the first half of the xivth century[1]. Towards the latter half of this period we find the Northumbrian yielding to the influence of the Southern dialects; thus in undoubted specimens of this idiom in the latter part of the xivth century we find that *bath, mare, ma, na, ar* and *twa* have become also, both, more, mo, no, or, two. We even find the *a* in the preterites *wrang, sang &c.* becoming *o* in wrong and song &c.

The Cottonian MS. is unfortunately imperfect, but this was not discovered until a great portion of it had been transcribed and in print. The text of the poem in the present volume is however complete, the deficiency being supplied by a Northumbrian MS. (Harl. 4196) of the same date which is also imperfect.

THE NORTHUMBRIAN DIALECT.

In discussing the peculiarities of the Northumbrian dialect[2] most writers have confined their remarks to that portion of it spoken

[1] There are MSS. (southern) of the 'Pricke of Conscience' as old as the middle of the xivth century, but their language is comparatively modern as compared with the Northumbrian ones of a later date.

The fact of not finding MSS. older than the middle of the xivth century would seem to show that Hampole compiled the 'Pricke of Conscience' but a few years before his death (A. D. 1349).

[2] The following is a list of works which have furnished material for determining the characteristics of the Northumbrian dialect:—

in the North of England, forgetting that the same form of speech was also spoken in the Lowlands of Scotland.

In the literary documents of the xiv[th] and xv[th] centuries there is very little difference between Scottish and this N. English dialect, in fact, so little that critics have been sadly at fault in determining the locality of certain Northumbrian writings, ascribing a Scottish origin to many works composed South of the Tweed. Minot's poems and Barbour's Bruce have many points of resemblance, together with some few of difference, the latter being chiefly confined to orthography, and to a number of words peculiar to the Lowland Scotch. Otherwise in Grammar and Vocabulary the idioms North and South of the Tweed belong to one and the same dialect.

As regards orthography the Lowland Scotch has an advantage over its sister-dialect, in giving stress to the syllable which marks inflexion as:—

1. *-is* or *-ys* for *-es*, *-s* in the plural number, possessive case of nouns, and in the person endings of the Indicative mood present tense.

 Thar sper*is*, pennoun*is* and thar scheld*is*,
 Of licht enlumynit all the feld*is*.
 (Barbour. The Bruce, p. 181.)

2. *-it*, *-yt* for *-ed*, *-d* in the preterites and passive participles of regular verbs:

 "Bath he and law the land was then
 All occupy*it* with Inglismen
 That disput*it* atour all thing. (The Bruce p. 96.)

The Early English Psalter. Edited by the Rev. J. Stevenson, for the Surtees Society.
English Metrical Homilies. Edited by John Small, M. A. 1862.
The Romance of Ywaine and Gawaine, in Ritson's Metrical Romances.
The Cursor Mundi. Cottonian MS. Vespasian A. iii.
Metrical Homilies in Harleian MS. 4196 and Cottonian MS. Tiberius E. vii.
The Seven Sages &c. Cott. MS. Galba E. ix.
Barbour's Bruce. Edited for the Spalding Club.
The Morte Arthure and Thornton Romances (edited by Halliwell), have been *very sparingly* used. — There is good reason for believing that a Lincolnshire scribe has tampered with the texts. The fine romance of Sir Tristem (Ed. Scott.) originally composed in the Northumbrian dialect, has been rendered nearly worthless by the alterations of a midland scribe.

"In carrik sone arriv*it* he,
And pass*it* throu all the cuntre." (Ibid. p. 95.)

Other orthographical differences occur of which the following are the most marked:—

I. a) *-icht*, *-echt*, *ocht* for *-ight*, *-eght*, *-oght:*
ficht for fight,
hecht for heght = height,
licht for light,
ocht for oght = aught,
wicht for wight = active;

b) *-aucht* for *-aght:*
aucht for aght = eight, possession,
saucht for saght = reconciliation,
straucht for straght = stretched;

c) *-euch* for *-ogh:*
beuch for bogh,
dreuch (drew) for drogh (drow) = drew,
eneuch (enew) for enogh (enow) = enough,
leuch for logh = laughed,
pleuch for plogh (plow) = plough,
sleuch (slew) for slogh (slow) = slew.

II. *a* for *e:*
na for ne = nor,
skar for sker = rock,
warld for werld = world,
wary for wery = curse,
yharn for yhern = yearn.

III. *e* for *a:*
threll for thrall,
wes for was,
ger for gar.

IV. *o* for *a:*
mony for many,
ony for any,

V. *u* for *o:*
cluke for cloke = claw,
ruse for rose = boast,
tume for tome = empty,
wuke for woke.

VI. *gif* for *yf*, if.

Yef occurs in the Metrical Homilies for 'if' and is worthy of notice on account of its likeness to the Fris. *jef* (A.Sax. if = *gif*).

Among grammatical differences the following are the most important: —

I. *Begouth* and occasionally *couth* for *began* or *bigan*.

Dr. Latham[1] calls *begouth* a present tense supposing it to be another form of *beginneth*, an almost impossible word in Scotch, the usual form of it being *beginnes*.

Begouth or *couth* is however a preterite and always used as a principal, whereas *gan* (= began) is employed only as an auxiliary verb.

II. *a* or *o* for *e* in the following preterities: —

claf for clef = clave, cleft.
grat for gret = wept,
lap for lep = leapt,
wox for wex = increased.

III. The use of *syne* as a preposition and an adverb.

Barbour and Wyntown frequently use *syne* as a preposition in the sense of 'after', and as an adverb = afterwards, while Hampole and other Northumbrian writers employ *syn* or *sen* as a conjunction only and never as a time-word, for which they employ *sithen*. — The dialect North of the Tweed has made a distinction between *syn* and *sen*, employing the former as an adverb and preposition, the latter as a conjunction.

IV. *Set* (= seth = sithen) in Scotch means 'since' and is only employed as a conjunction, while writers South of the Tweed always employ *sythen* as an adverb in the sense of 'afterwards, since'.

V. *Bot* (but) as a preposition meaning 'without' is confined to Scottish writers[2]. It never takes this meaning in Hampole,

[1] English Language 2nd edition.

[2] *Southern* writers of the xiiith and xivth centuries use *but* (butan) as a preposition but never as a conjunction, in the sense of *but* (adversative) for which they employ *ac*. Barbour uses *bot (but)* as an adverb, a conjunction or a preposition.

Psalms &c. where it is employed as a conjunction or an adverb in the sense of 'but, except, only'.

The vocabulary of the Lowland Scotch is substantially one with the Northumbrian South of the Tweed; there are however terms peculiar to each, as for instance; in the former we never find *layt* to seek, *amell (emell, omell)* among, *forwit* before, *slike* (such), while in the latter we never meet *anerly, forouten, gretumly, inkerly, sic &c.*

The forms *sic, slike,* and *swilk* signifying 'such' are worthy of notice as they seem to indicate, wherever they occur in literary documents, three distinct localities of composition.

Sic is Scottish and is perhaps a contracted form of *slike.* The latter word marks a border dialect and is evidently the Icelandic *slik* = such, the like, *(slikt, slik'r, slik). Swilk* A.S. *swilc* is the usual Yorkshire form.[1]

Sic for *slike* is perhaps the earliest instance of dropping the *l*, a practice which became very common, at a much later period, among Scottish writers.

Wherever we find the form *slike,* we find also a marked resemblance to forms which have been looked upon as peculiarly Scottish; thus in the Cursor Mundi, Metrical Homilies and Minot's Poems where *slike* so frequently occurs we meet with *sa* and *thoru* (Sc. *sa* and *thorow*) which in the Psalms and Hampole are represented by *swa* and *thurgh.*[2] (*Thoru* is the Anglian *thorh* while *thurgh* is the West Saxon *thurh.*)

In the former works we meet with a larger number of words of Scandinavian origin, a few of which have hitherto been noticed as occurring only in the Local-names of the North of England, as *sker,* rock, *hogh* (Sc. *heuch*), hill, *stank, stang,* pond, *fell,* hill, *keld,* a well. *Gar* or *ger* [pret. *gart, gert*] common enough in Barbour, the Cursor Mundi and Met. Hom. never occurs either in the Psalms or in Hampole.

[1] It must not be supposed that *swilk* is unknown where *sic* and *slike* occur; its employment however in Scotch is only occasional. It is somewhat strange that *sic* is *now* used South of the Tweed while in the xiii^th^ and xiv^th^ centuries it was unknown.

[2] *Swa* or *sua* is not unfamiliar to Scottish writers of the xiv^th^ and xv^th^ centuries.

As the Cursor Mundi is frequently quoted in the present volume as an authority for certain words and forms of words, the following short poem entitled 'De Penis' is transcribed from it as a specimen of the Northumbrian dialect (of Northumberland) in the latter part of the xiiith century. It may perhaps throw some light upon the material employed by Hampole in the compilation of the 'Pricke of Conscience'.

VIIII paines principale es þar, [in helle]
Crist lat us never þider far.
þe first, it es þe fire sa hatte,
þat al þe mikel se sa wate,[1]
þof þat it casten war þar-in,
Suld it never-þe-less brin;
Sua þat ur fire ne mai na mare
Again þat fire þat [sal] brin þar,
þan painted fire gain[2] urs moght
þat apon a wagh[3] war wroght.
Ever it brennes dai and night
Bot never mare it castes light.
þe toþer paine is tald sa kene,
þat mans muth it mai noght mene.
þat þof a fer[e]n felle war made,
And þoru a chance þar-in it gladd[4]
Quils þou moght turn þi hand abute,
It suld worth [f]rese[a] wituten dute.
þe thrid pine es hard to drei,
O wormes þat sal never dei,
Ffelle draguns and tades bath,
þat ar apon to lok ful lath,
Fful wlatsum on to here or se,
Fful wa es þam þat þare sal be;
Als we se fixs in water suim,
Sua live þai in þat lou[5] sa dim.
þe ferth paine it es o stinc,
þat mai na man sa mikel thinc.
þe fifte es undemnes dint,
þat þaa wreches þare sal hint,
Als it war dintes on a steþi,
þat smythes smittes in a smeþey.

[1] wet [2] against [3] wall [4] glided [5] pit.

[a] As the MS. is rather indistinct *yse* may have been the original reading.

Þaa diutes ar ful fers and felle
Herder þan es here irinn melle.
Þe sext paine, es noght to scape,
Es suilk mercknes men mai it grape;
Sua wonder think[a] þar sal it be,
Þat nan ne mai on oþer se.
Þe sevend scenscip al for þair sin,
Ai scam lastand þat never sal blin,
Ffor þar-tille sal ilkan ha sight
To se þe scenscip on oþer plight.[6]
Þe aghtand pine it es ful grise[7]
To se þaa warlaus in þait wise,
Strang paine es it on þam to loke,
And namli laght until þair crok;
Þat dreri din, þat balful bere,[8]
Þat þai wit-uten stint sal here,
O þaa wepand in þat waa,
Þat sal þam last for ever and ai.
Ffirend bandes es þe nind,
Als in hali writt we find,
Þat al þair limes ar bunden wit,
Wituten leth[9] of ani lith[10].
Bot a point es þar [þat] þam pines mare,
Þan elles al þair oþer fare[11].
Þai wat þair pine sal ha nan end,
Ffor þai mai haf na might to mend.
And qui þar es þaa paines nine
Here nu þe skil of ilk pine;
Nine orders of angels þai forsok,
Quen þai þam to þe warlau tok,
Þarfor sal þai pined be,
Wit þaa pines, sex and thre;
Ffor þat þai war won to brin
In catel wit covetise to win,
To-quils þai in þis werld war
Ai sal þai brin *al þar for þar*.[b]
And þaa men þat sa starck[12] war her,
Stilli[13] þair wickedhed to ster
And brint þar-in sa war þai bald,
Þai sal have ever þat water cald.
Þai þat war fild wit enst and hete
Þat iþenli[14] þair hertes ete,

[a] *thick?* [b] al þar for þar = always there for that (sin).
[6] misfortune [7] terrible [8] noise [9] loosening [10] limb
[11] sorrow [12] stubborn [13] secretly [14] frequently.

þar wormes sal þam underwrote[15]
In bale wituten hope and bote,
And for-þi þai her war wont to li
In þair stincand licheri,
Ne wald noght here bot þair delites,
þat drogh þam until oþer vices,
þai sal haf iþen[16] stinc iwiss
þat þai sal never mar mis.
And for þai wald na disciplin,
Thole for luve of ur drightin[17]
þai sal be beft[18] wit-uten hove[19],
Ne merci nan to þair behove;
And for þai wald noght þe light,
þat gis of sothfastnes þe sight,
þat es godd self at understand,
þai sal haf mircknes ai lastand;
And for þai wald noght scrive þair sake[20],
Ne fore þair ending mendes make,
Ilkan sal se wit sight o scam
Quat blenck[21] on oþer es to blam;
And þai þat wald na spelling here
O godd, ne of his laghes lere
Ffor-þi þan sal þai here þe sunes
O nedders bath and of draguns,
þat reuful bere, þat waful cri
þat wa es þam sted þar-bi.
And for-þi þai gilderd were,
Wit in þis liif wit lustes sere,
þai sal suffer soru ai þar,
Apon þair membres ai-quare;
Ai[22] wend þai here to live in sin,
þar sal þai dei wit-uten blin,
Deiand ai and never ded,
Ffor ded sal fle þam als þair fede[23];
þai sal be sett in þair prisun,
Upward þair fete, þair hefdes dun
þair backes til war oþer[*] bete
Wit pine on ilk side umsete.
þe rightwismen sal se þaa pines
Apon ur laverd wiþerwines[24],
þat þair blis mai be þe mare,
þat þai er scaped o þat care.

[15] under-root [16] frequent [17] lord [18] beaten [19] cessation [20] fault [21] fault [22] = wened = thought [23] enemy [24] adversary. [*] *over?*

þe wicked alsua þe gode sal se,
Wit-in þair gammen stad and gle,
þat þai þe sorfuller sal be,
þat losen folili has þat le;*
To domesdai sua sal þai fare,
Bot efter domesdai na mar
Ffor to þam se þaa maledight;
Bot þe seli sal o þam ha sight.
Bot þof þai se þam, wiit þou wele,
O þaim þai sal noght reu a dele;
If fader sagh his son þare,
Or sun his fader in þat care,
þe wiif hir man, or man his wiif,
Or freind he luved als his liif,
Ffor þair misfar suld þai not murn,
Ne ans for þair skathes skurn.[25]
Bot suld þai haf a gret delite
To se þam seclid[26] in þair site,
Als we haf here on summers dai,
To se fixs in a water plai;
Ffor-qui, þe rightwis blith sal be,
Quen he sal wrak[27] on sinful se.
If þai suld for þaa feluns prai,
It war gain godd and gret derai;
Ffor þai til him sal be sa queme,
Al sal þam like þat he sal deme.
To deme us mot þat drightin sua
þat we com never unto þat wa.

* *gle?*
[25] shun [26] *setlid?* [27] vengeance.

GRAMMATICAL DETAILS.

I. Nouns.

The genitive singular ends in *-es*, *-s*, occasionally in *-is*, *-ys*, as in Scotch.

Very frequently the sign of the case is omitted as,

Fader house = father's house,
Hefd hare = head's hair, hair of the head,
Man son = man's son, son of man,
Moder kne = mother's kne.

The plural number ends in *-es*, *-s*.

Eghen (eyes), *oxen* and *schon* (shoes) are examples of plurals in *-en*, *-n*, and the only ones I have been able to meet with.

Child and *ka* (or *cu* = cow) make the plurals *childer* and *ky*.

Brother is in the plural *brether, brethir* just as the Icelandic *brothir* makes *brœthir*, Dan. *bröder*. *Hend*, the plural of *hand*, is the Icelandic *hender* (the plural of *hönd*) and is of very frequent occurence.[1]

Harn, brain, makes the plural *hern*. Cf. the Dan. *haand, hænder; vaand, vænder*.

Frend is both singular and plural. This may have arisen from the A. Saxon plural *frýnd* not being very differently pronounced from the singular *freond*. *Frend* occurs also as a plural in the Ormulum. The use of *freond* as a plural in the Owl and Nightingale (but not noticed in Coleridge's Glossarial Index) would lead us to suppose that the singular had acquired a collective sense. Hampole always uses *gayte* (goat)[2] as a collective noun, a practice peculiarly Northern though not confined to Northumbrian writers.

The nouns *winter, yhere* (year), *pund* (pound), *thing*, which were of the neuter gender in Anglo Saxon, are frequently used as plurals without any change of form as:

> 'fyve hundred *wynter*',
> 'fyve thowsand *yhere*',
> 'five hundreth *pund*',
> 'alle *thing*'.

Myle feminine in A.S. is also used as a plural as 'fourty *myle*'.

All words ending in *-yng*, *-ing* (derived from verbs) are substantives and not participles:

> *geting*, conception; *gretyng*, cry; *kepyng*, custody; *knawyng*, knowledge; *movyng*, motion; *removyng*, removal.

We find traces of the Scandinavian suffix *-leik* (O.N. *leikr*) in:

> ferdlayk fear,
> hendlaic politeness,
> revelaic robbery,
> wedlayk wedlock.

Tinsel = perdition contains the Dan. *-sel* in *födsel*, birth; *inforsel*, importation.

[1] In the Northumbrian Gospels ed. Bouterwek, *feder* occurs as the pl. of *fader*. (Mt. 10, 32.) Cf. Icel. *faðir*, pl. *feðir*.

[2] Cf. 'a tryppe of gayte.' (Thornton Romances.) Wiclif also uses *gayt* as a collective noun.

The A. Sax. suffix *-ræden*[2] is preserved without much change in:

fa-reden enmity,
felaw-reden fellowship,
hat-reden hatred,
luf-reden love,
man-reden homage,
sib-reden relationship.

The ending *-hede, -hed* = -hood is not the A. Sax. *-hád,* preserved by the Scotch in *-hade*, but the Frisian *-hed, -hede* in

dwalikhed, error; *dweshed,* folly; *werhed,* truth; *falschede.* falsehood. Cf. Dan. *-hed* in *frihed,* freedom; *hvidhed,* whiteness,

II. Adjectives.

Adjectives have no sign to mark the plural, unless the *e* in hise and thise (before plural nouns) be examples of the final *-e* which is so frequently employed in Southern English, as late as the middle of the xvth century, to mark the plural of adjectives.

We often find *this* = *these*, the final *-e* having been dropped in writing but perhaps pronounced in reading.[2]

Fone or *fune,* a form unknown to Barbour or Wyntown, occurs in Hampole as the plural of *few.*[3]

Þ*a* (A. Sax. *thá*) is generally used as a demonstrative adjective before plural nouns as:

'þ*a* clerkes', 'þ*a* bokes', 'þ*a* wardes'.

It is also used pronominally before the relative þ*at,* and after the prepositions *of* and *to*, as:—

'of tha' = of them, theirs; *'to tha'* = to them.

In þ*ir,* þ*er,* these, we have the Icelandic þ*ær* (þ*au,* þ*eir,* þ*ær*) = these.

Þ*as* = those. A. Saxon þ*æs.*

The Numerals preserve much of the A. Sax. orthography e. g.

An, ane = one. A. Sax. án.
Twa, twin = two. A. Sax. twá (Ac. twám).
Thrin = three. A. S. threo (Ac. thrym).

[1] This forms of the ending *-red* is not found in Scottish writers.

[2] It may be stated once for all that the final *e* is not of any value (either as a number or case ending) in Northumbrian Manuscripts. This was pointed out long ago by Dr. Guest.

[3] *Bothen* is the plural of *both* in the Promptorium Parvulorum.

Aght, eght = eight. A. Sax. eahta.

Neghen = nine. A. Sax. nigon.

An, ane, one like our article *an* sometimes changes to *a* before a noun commencing with a consonant. This will explain the expression: —

'a manere is' = '*one* manere is'.

Aghtend or *achtande* = eighth is note worthy because it is not the A. Saxon *eatoða*, but the Frisian *achtenda, achtanda*, both forms being preserved in the Northumbrian dialect.[1]

The comparative degree is formed by *-er* or *-ere*, occasionally by *-ar* or *-are*; and the superlative ends in *-est, -este; -ast* or *-aste.*

Scottish writers more frequently employ the endings *-ar*, *-are*, *-ast*, or *-aste*. This is an instance perhaps of Scandinavian influence.

In *lenger* the comp. of *lang* we have an example of vowel change as in A. Saxon: —

lang, lengre, lengest,

strang, strengre, strengest.

And modern English old, elder, eldest.

The long vowel of the positive often appears shortened in the comparative and superlative[2] as in the modern English late, latter, last (A. Sax. *læt, lator, latost*).

Brade, bradder, braddest.

Depe, depper, deppest.

Grete, gretter, grettest.

Hate, hatter, hattest.

Swete, swetter, swettest.

The following forms are very common: —

Mikelle, mykel, great; comp. *ma,* or *mare*; superl. *mast.*

Yvel, ill, bad; comp. *wers;* superl. *werst.*

Fer (far); comp. *ferrer;* superl. *ferrest.*

Are, early; superl. *arst.*

[1] The numerals *sevend*, *aghtend*, *neghend (nind)*, *tend* &c. may be compared with the Dan. *syvende*, *attende*, *niende*, *tiende* &c. The Southern forms are *sevethe*, *eiȝteothe*, *nythe*, *teothe (tethe)*. The Kentish dialect however prefers *-nd* to *-th*.

[2] The doubling of the consonant generally marks the shortening of the preceding vowel.

Form, first, in composition only; superl. *form-ast.*[1] (*formast* barn, *formast* fader &c,)

Wer, werr, Sc. *war*, occasionally occurs for *wers;* O.N. *vérr*, Dan. *værre*, Sw. *värre.*

The only case endings to be met with are:—

1. *-er*, a remnant of the A.Saxon genitive plural (*-re*) in *aller, alder* or *alther*, 'of all', and in *bother*, 'of both'.
2. *-um*, sign of the dative, in *ferrum*, 'afar', which occurs in the Cursor Mundi and Met. Homilies. It enters perhaps into the Scotch adverb *greatumly*, greatly, the *-ly* being superfluous.

Such phrases as *wel ald, wel lang*,[2] = very old, very long; *al clere, al rede, al blak, alle warme*[3] = very clear or quite clear, quite red, quite black, very warm, are evidently modelled upon the Icelandic phrases *vel heitt*, quite warm or very warm; *vel mikit*, very large; *all goðr*, very good; *all vitr*, very wise.

Wel is not only employed before the positive but also before the comparative, as *wel better, wel the bet* = much better; *wel war*, much worse; *wel mar, wel the mar*, much more.

The adjectives *ald, brade, hate, wate, wrathe* (i. e. old, broad, hot, wet, wroth) are always distinguished from their corresponding substantives *eld, brede, hete, wete, wrethe* (i. e. age, breadth, heat, wet, wrath).

Modern English has preserved only the double forms *hot* and *heat, wroth* and *wrath.*

The following adjectives are nearly always employed with the dative of the personal pronouns:—

lyke (like), *lefe* (lief), comp. lever, *dere* (dear), *lath* (loth).

The participial ending *-and* is often used as a termination for adjectives as *mightand*, mighty, *boghand*, obedient, *semande*, apparent.

Kyn, kind, is frequently incorporated with its adjective forming a compound word as:—

alkin, nankin, nakin, ilkin, sumkin, whatkin i. e. all kind of, no kind of &c.

[1] Cf. *form*-dais, *form*-birth, *form*-tide with the Icelandic *frum*-móthir, *frum*-getin (first born), *frum*-rit, original (of a book).

[2] Metrical Homilies. [3] Cursor Mundi.

We find a large number of adjectives derived from Nouns with the suffix *-in, -en:*

almandin wand, an almond wand,
boken lare, book learning,
cluden piler, a cloud pillar,
firen piler, a fire pillar,
rochen stan, a rocky stone,
wildrin way, a desert way,[1]
stelene wapyns,
sylverene disches.[2]

In the phrases, *thrid half yere, half fierth eln,* two and a half years, three and a half ells, we have perhaps the latest examples of a very common construction in Anglo Saxon and one still in use among modern Teutonic dialects.

III. Pronouns.

The Northumbrian pronouns *sco, sho, thai, thair, tham,* are less archaic than the Southern forms *heo, hi, heor* (*her, hor*), *hem* (*heom, hom*).

The following tables exhibit the declension of the personal and relative pronouns:—

1.	Nom.	Ic, I.	We.
	Poss.	My, myne, mine.	Ur, our, urs, ours.
	Obj.	Me.	Us.
2.	Nom.	þu, þou, þow.	Yhe[3] or yhou, yhow, you.
	Poss.	þy, þyne, þine.	Yhour, your, yhours, yours.
	Obj.	þee, þe.	Yhow, yhou, you.
3.	Nom.	He.	þai.
	Poss.	His.	þair, þairs.
	Obj.	Him,	þam, þaim.
	Nom.	Sco, sho.	
	Poss.	Hir, hirs.	
	Obj.	Him.	
Relative.	Nom.	Wha (= who).	
	Poss.	Whas, whase.	
	Obj.	Wham.	

[1] Cursor Mundi. [2] Morte Arthure. [3] *Yhe* is occasionally used as an *objective* case.

The relative *that* undergoes no change to express number, gender or case, and connects *adjective* clauses with the principal sentence; while *noun* clauses are connected by *wha, wha-swa. That* is often employed as equivalent to *what.*

That and *it* are frequently used before the third person singul. indicative of the verb 'to be' where we employ the adverb 'there', as:—*That* es na clerc, *that* es na man, for 'there is no clerc' &c. *It* es na man for 'there is no man'.

The interrogative pronouns are *wha, wha-swa,* and *whilk* or *qwilk* (which). The phrase *'alswa* say'= *'als wha* say' i. e. 'as *one* may say', also frequently occurs.

The dative of the pronouns is nearly always used with the adjectives *like,lefe, lath, dere,* and the impersonal verbs

aw, pret. *aght* (ought), *behove, lyke* (please), *list, thar* (need), *think*(seem), pret. thought, *want* (is missing, is absent), *fail, rew.*

Self or *selven* is frequently employed after nouns as well as pronouns as: *Godd self, man self.* It is also used as an adjective with the sense of 'same'.

Me self, us self &c. are found along with *thi self, hir self* &c.

The modern *sen* = self, seems to be a corruption of *selven.*

IV. Verbs.

The conjugation of the Northumbrian verb is extremely simple, one form in *s* being used for every person in the present tense Indic. Mood. It is moreover a test by which Northumbrian may be distinguished from other dialects of the North of England.

The verb *to love* is thus inflected.

Indicative Mood.

Present Tense.

Singular.		Plural.	
	(I) loves.		(We) loves.
	(Thou) loves.		(Yhou) loves.
	(He) loves.		(Thai) loves.

We have occasionally (thai) *loven* instead of (thai) *loves.*

Preterite.

Singular.	Plural.
(I) loved, gaf (gave)	(We) loved, gaf
(thou) loved, gaf	(yhou) loved, gaf
(he) loved, gaf	(thai) loved, gaf.

We find (thai) *loveden* for (thai) *loved*, but it is not of frequent occurrence.

Imperative Mood.

Singular.	Plural.
2d pers. loves (thou)	loves (yhe or yhou).

The Northumbrian has what may be called an uninflected imperative, conjugated as follows:—

Ga I[1] = let me go
Ga thou = do thou go
Ga he = let him go
Ga we = let us go
Ga yhou = do you go
Ga thai = let them go.

On page 96 of the present volume there are no less than five examples of the 3d pers. sing., while such phrases as *gæ we, lat we* &c. for let us go, let us, occur often elsewhere.

This uninflected imperative survived to a very late period in our literature, and examples of the 3d pers. sing. and 1st and 3d plural may be found in Pope, Thomson and Goldsmith.[2]

Participles.

Imperfect.	Perfect.
lovand	loved.

The A. Sax. prefix *ge* never occurs in Northumbrian MSS. of the xiiith and xivth centuries, whereas the dialects of the Southern counties retained it to a comparatively late period.[3]

Infinitives in *-en* are seldom employed. The Cursor Mundi contains *lasten,* to last, *wenden,* to walk, *wacken,* to wake, *fasten,* to make fast, and in Hampole we have *enden,* to end, *heghen,* to exalt, *clensen,* to cleanse, *wedden,* to wed, used after the verb *sal.*[4]

The Scandinavian *at*, to, as the sign of the infinitive is not un-

[1] I have not come across any instances of the first pers. sing.

[2] Fall he (Pope). Be my tongue mute (Thomson). Turn we (Goldsmith).

[3] Garnett quotes the solitary form *ihaten* (called or named) as the only example of this prefix, but I have not been able to find any Northumbrian MS. that contains this or any other verb having the prefixal element *i* or *y*.

[4] The *-en* after all may be the verbal suffix *-en* as in *ripen &c.*

common as '*at* drink, *at* eat' &c. Scottish writers use *till* as well as *at*, as *till* drink, *till* eat &c.

The preterites and passive participles of the so-called strong verbs are more archaic than the Southern forms of the same period.

	1st pers.	pret.	passive participle.
	Bind	band	bunden
A. Sax.	binde	band	(ge)bunden
	sing	sang	sungen
A. Sax.	singe	sang	(ge)sungen
	shine	shane	—
A. Sax.	scine	scán	(ge)scinen.

The preterites *drave, shane, wrate &c.* are valuable because they account for the double forms found in our language. Dr. Latham has explained the preterites *sang,* sung, *swam,* swum, *smate,* smit, *wrate,* writ, but leaves unexplained *smate, wrote &c.*

The forms *drove, shone, smote, wrote* are Southern, while *drave, shane, smate, wrate &c.* are Northern preterites.

The influence of the Northumbrian upon the written dialect is best estimated by the large number of such preterites as *drave, brast &c.* which are so often met with in classical literature as late as the middle of the xviith century.

It is to this Northern dialect that we owe the preservation of the passive participles in *-en, -n;* the tendency of the Southern and Western dialects was to drop the p. participial ending and to retain the prefix *y* (or *ge*), the Northumbrian on the other hand dropped the prefix but tenaciously clung to the suffix.

TABLE OF VERBS.

A. Simple Order.

	Present.	Preterite.	P. participle.
Class I.	Hate	hated	hated.
Class II.	Bede (offer)	bedde	bedde.
	Bete (beat)	bette	bette.
	Bete (amend)	bette	—
	Cleth (clothe)	cled	cled (clad).
	Ken (teach)	kend	kend.
	Kythe (show)	kydde	kydde, kyd.
	Lede (lead)	ledde	ledde, lad.

	Present.	Preterite.	P. participle.
	Mete (measure)	mette	—
	Rede (advise)	redde	redde.
	Send	send	send, sent.
	Shed	shedde	—
	Spend	spend	spend, spent.
	Stede	stedde	stedde, stad.
	Wene (suppose)	wend	—
Class III.	By (buy)	boght	boght.
	Leche (take)	laght	—
	Reche (reach)	raght	—
	Reck	roght	—
	Seke	soght	soght.
	Selle	salde	salde.
	Telle	talde	talde.
	Teche	taght	taght.
	Wille	wald	—

B. Complex Order.

Division I.

Class I. *a*)	Bere	bare	born.
	Breke	brake	broken.
	Brest	brast	brusten (brosten).
	Help	halp	holpen.
	Kerve	karve	korven.
	Leke	—	loken.
	Shere (cut)	share	shorn.
	Steke (shut)	stake	stoken.
	Stele	stale	stolen.
	Swere	sware	sworn.
	Threst	thrast	thrusten.
	Wreke (avenge)	wrake	wroken.
	Yhelde	yhald	yholden.
b)	Chese (choose)	ches	chosen.
	Cleve	clef (claf)	cloven.
	Crepe	crep	cropen.
	Delve (dig)	delf (dalf)	dolven.
	Grete (weep)	gret (grat)	—

	Present.	Preterite.	P. participle.
	Lepe	lep (lap)	lopen.
	Lese	les	losen, lorn.
	Melt	melt (malt)	molten.
	Wepe	wep	—
	Slepe	slep	—
	Swepe	—	swopen.
	Yhete (pour out)	yhet	yhotten.
c)	Bete	bete	beten.
	Ete	ete	eten.
	Forbid (forbede)	forbed (forbad)	forbeden.
	Forget	forgat	forgeten.
	Frete (eat)	—	freten.
	Get	gat	geten.
	Sit	sete, sate	seten.
Class II.	Blaw (blow)	blew	blawen.
	Cast	kest	casten.
	Fall	felle	fallen.
	Fast	fest	fasten.
	Ga, gang	yhede, yhode	gane, went.
	Gnaw	—	gnawen.
	Hate	hete	hatt, hatyn.
	Late, lete	lette	leten, laten.
	Saw	sew	sawen.
	Snaw	snew	—
	Start	stert	—
	Walk	welk	walken.
	Wash	wesh	washen (weschyn).
	Wax	wex (wox Sc.)	waxen (woxen Sc.).
Class III.	Bake	—	baken.
	Draw	drogh, droh, drow	drawen.
	Fare (to go)	for, ferd	faren, farn.
	Fla (flay)	flogh	flane.
	Laghe (laugh)	lughe, loghe	laghen.
	Qwake	qwoke	qwaken.
	Shape	shope	shapen.
	Stand	stode	standen.
	Sla	slogh, sloh, slow	slane.

Present.	Preterite.	P. participle.
Take	toke	tane.
Wake	wokè	waken.

In Scottish *qwuke, shupe, tuke* and *wuke* occur for *qwoke, shope, toke* and *woke.*

Division II.

	Present.	Preterite.	P. participle.
Class I.	Bigin	bigan	bigunnen.
	Bind	band	bunden, bonden.
	Blin (cease)	blan	blunnen.
	Climb	clamb	clumben, clummen.
	Cling	clang	clungen.
	Ding	dang	dungen.
	Drink	drank	drunken.
	Fight	fight	foghten.
	Find	fand	funden (fonden).
	Fling	flang	flungen.
	Grind	—	grunden.
	Nim (take)	nam	nomen, numen.
	Rin (run)	ran	runnen.
	Sing	sang	sungen.
	Sink	sank	sunken.
	Spin	span	sponnen.
	Swing	swang	swungen (swongen).
	Swink	swanc	swonken.
	Threst	thrast	thrusten.
	Win	wan	wonnen.
	Wring	wrang	wrungen.
	Come	come	comen, cumen.
Class II.	Bite	bate	bitten.
	Drive	drave	driven.
	Give	gave	given.
	Glide	glade	glidden.
	Ride	rade	ridd en.
	Rise	rase	risen.
	Shine	shane	—
	Shrive	shrave	shriven.
	Smite	smate	smiten.

	Present.	Preterite,	P. participle.
	Strike	strake	striken.
	Swike	swake	swiken.
	Write	wrate	writen.
	Writhe	wrathe	—
Class III.	Flegh (fly)	flegh, flaw (Sc.)	flown.
	Lie (speak falsely)	leigh	—
	See	segh, sagh	seen.
	Stegh (ascend)	stey, stegh	—

Anomalous Verbs.

Agh, aw, pret. aght.
Can, (infin. kun) pret. couth.
Dur (dare) pret. durst.
May, mow, pret. might, mught, moght.
Mot (may, must) pret. most.
Sal (shall) pret. suld. Cf. Dan. *skal, skulde.*
Thar (need) pret. thurt.
Wate (know) pret. wist.
Wille, pret. wilde. (Dan. *vil, vilde.*)

The verbs *sal, wille &c.* take no inflexion e. g.

I sal,	wille &c.	We sal,	wille &c.
Thou sal,	wille &c.	Yhou sal,	wille &c.
He sal,	wille &c.	Thai sal,	wille &c.

The substantive verb *to be* is thus conjugated:—

I es,	am.	We er,	es.
Thou es,	ert.	Yhou er,	es.
He es,	es, bes.	Thai er,	es.
I was		We war	(ware)
Thou was		Yhou war	(ware)
He was		Thai war	(ware).

Occasionally we have the Norse *war* for was, e. g. he *war* = he was.

The following contractions occasionally occur:—

bus = behoves, *ha* = have, *ma* = make, *ta* = take; *mase* = makes, *tase* = takes, *tane* = taken.

V. Adverbs.

The adverbs *hethen* (hence), *thethen* (thence), *whethen* (whence) are worthy of notice on account of their Scandinavian origin.

The A. S. forms are *hĕnan, þonan, hvonan,* corresponding to the O. Norse *hĕðan, þaðan, hvaðan.*

The adverb *sum, som* is often used as in Danish, in the sense of 'as', e. g. 'black *sum* ani cole' = 'black as any coal'.

It occurs also as an adverbial suffix with the sense of 'so' in *whare-sum, quat-sum, how-som &c.*

The termination *-gatĕ* (also employed as an adverbial ending in O. Norse) = wise is a common adverbial suffix in the Cursor Mundi, Met: Hom., the Bruce, but it does not occur in Hampole or in the Psalms (*thus-gate, swagate, algate, howgate &c.*)

The Scottish ending *-sis* is a contraction of the Northumbrian *sythes,* times, as *oftsis* = oftsythes. It occurs once only in the Cursor Mundi.

By than = by that time; *fra than, fra thine* = from that time.
To-when = how long; *to-whiles,* whilst; *to-forn* = before.
Outwith = outwards; *forwit* (*forwith*) = before.

VI. Prepositions.

Fra, from, *at,* to, *til,* to, *amell* (*emell*), among, *emid,* amid, at intervals, are of Norse origin (*frá, at, til, á milli, á medal*).

The prefixes *again, ogain* (= against), *dun, down, forth, in, on, out, over, up* are used as *separable* particles; thus we have *dun light* and *dun tham light; on luke* and *on to luke &c.*

The prefix *um* in *umset, umlap, umloke* is a good criterion of a Northern dialect.

VII. The only conjunction peculiar to the Northumbrian is *warn* or *warne,* unless. It occurs in the Metrical Homilies MS. Harl. 4196 and in the present poem, where it is found two or three times.— I have not met with it however in the Cursor Mundi. I take it to be cognate with the Old High German and Middle Dutch *ne-ware,* Old Saxon *ne wari,* unless, literally 'if-not'. The Northumbrian has placed the negative *ne* after the conjunction *war* instead of 'before it'. *War* in the sense of 'if' is not found in A. Saxon, but we have the Old Frisic *wara, were, wera* (*sondern, aber, ausser*) which seems to offer a satisfactory solution of *warne.* *If* forms the compounds *bot-if,* unless; *alle-if,* although.

VIII. The interjection *quin,* O that! deserves some notice. The earliest instance of its use is in the Cursor Mundi fol. 46:—

"He wok and thoght al on that sight
And said 'our laverd god alle-might,
Sua hale *quin* war i and swa light,
Als me thoght i was to night."

Quin is merely another form of the A. Saxon *hwý ne*, lit. *why not.* Hampole employs it two or three times under the forms *whyn, whine.* I am inclined to think that *hwý ne* had this sense in Anglo Saxon and that it has escaped the notice of Bosworth and other lexicographers. — In Alfred's translation of Boëthius Ch. xxiv, 10 we have the following passage:—

> "*Hwý ne* miht þú on-gitan þætte ælc wuht cwices býð innan-weard hnescost and útan-weard heardost?"

The editor by placing the mark of interrogation after the passage renders the meaning obscure. His translation would be:

> "Why might thou not understand that each living thing is softest inwardly and hardest outwardly?"

I would suggest that we should drop the interrogatory mark and read:

> "O that thou might understand &c.,

the writer evidently desiring that the person addressed had the power to understand the mystery of things being soft and hard, and not questioning any ignorance upon the subject.

Characteristics of the Northumbrian Dialect from the latter half of the xiii[th] to the end of the xiv[th] century:

1. The most striking peculiarity perhaps is the preservation of the long *a* in words of A. Sax. origin containing this vowel, which the Southern dialects changed into a long *o*.

A. Saxon.	Northumb.	Southern form.
Áld	ald	old.
Án	ane	one, oon.
Bán	báne	bone, boon.
Cláth	clathe	cloth.
Cráwan	craw	crow.
Gást	gast	gost, ghost.
Grápian	grape	grope.
Hám	hame	home.
Hláf	lafe	loaf, loof.
Láng	lang	long.
Lám	lame	loam.
Lár	lare	lore.
Láth	lath	loth.

A. Saxon.	Northumb.	Southern form.
Má	ma	mo.
Nán	nan	none.
Rá	ra	roe.
Ráp	rape	rope.
Sár	sare	sore.
Sárig	sari	sorry.
Snáw	snaw	snow.
Stán	stan	stone, stoon.
Twá	twa	two.
Wá	wa	woe, wo.
Wáh	wagh	wow (=wall).

Many words once peculiar to the Northumbrian gradually got further South but we observe still the same change of vowel, e.g. and, ond (breath); bla, blo (blue, livid); wath (evil, harm), woth, fra, fro.

2. The adjectives *ilk*, *swilk* (slike, sic), *thir* (*ther*), *tha*.

3. The pronouns *wha, whilk* (qwilk).

4. The adverb *sum, som* (= so, as), *swa*, and the adverbial ending *-gate*.

5. The prepositions *at, fra, til, amel, emid*.

6. The inflection of the verb in the present Indicative. The verb *sal, suld* and the want of inflection in the preterite. The absence of the prefix *ge* or *y*, and the disappearance of the infinitive ending *-en*.

7. The conjunctions *at* (= that); *warn, warne*, unless. The interjection *quin, quine*, (*whyn, whine*).

8. A large Norse element in the vocabulary.

9. The Northumbrian seems to have preferred the guttural *k* to the softer sound of *ch*. This will account for the double forms still in use as *poke* and *pouch*, *skirt* and *shirt*.

The following double forms are also very common:

Northern.	Southern.
ask	ash,
bink	bench,
birk	birch,
blak	blotch,
blink	blench,

Northern.	Southern.
brek	breach,
brekes	breeches,
cloke	clouch (clutch),
hak	hatch-et,
kirk	church,
kist	chest,
mickel	muchel,
pik	pitch,
reke	reach,
rike	rich,
scake	schake,
scrill	shrill,
skift	shift,
skirt	shirt,
skenke	schenche (= to pour out),
skriek	shriek,
spek	speech,
sterck	sterch (= stiff),
thak	thatch,
think	thenche
wrenk	wrench (= trick).

10. The following forms are worthy of notice indicating, as they seem to do, a vowel change:—

	Northern.	Southern.
1.	sla	sle (= to kill),
	stra	stre (= straw),
2.	bra (= bro)	breye (= brow),
	clai	clei (= clay),
	dai	dei (= day),
	rayke	reke (= spread),
	wayke	weke (= weak),
3.	trayst	trist (= trust),
4.	lither	luther (= bad),
	rig	rug (= back),
5.	sĕk	sack,
6.	seke	sike (= sick).

Hampole often writes *th* for *t*, as *thechyng* for techyng, *feth* for fet. Whether *th* at the beginning of words had the sound of *t*, I cannot say, but that it had this sound at the end of words is extremely probable.

1. In the Cursor Mundi *with* is always written *wit*.

2. In Hampole *Judith* rhymes with *writt*, but what is still more curious is that *David* rhymes with *Judith*. It would thus appear that *d* at the end of words was pronounced as *t*. Cf. *servand, sembland, avenand,* for *servant, semblant, avenant.*

We have an instance of a final *b* being pronounced as *p* for *Iob* is made to rhyme with *hope,* and in one instance it is written *Iope.*

In a poem of such considerable length as is the 'Pricke of Conscience we might expect to find many incidental allusions to the manners and customs of the age in which Hampole lived, but we find only a passing notice of that wretched state of affairs so well described in the poem on the 'evil times of Edward II', in which we are told that

"Knytes schuld were clothes
Ischape in dewe manere,
As his order wold aske,
As wel as schuld a frere:
Now thei beth disgysed
So diverselych i diȝt
That no man may knowe
A mynstrel from a knyȝt wel ny:
So is mekenes falt a down
And pride aryse an hye."

(Poem on the Times of Edward II,
published by the Percy Society 1849.)

Not very different are the words of Hampole when he complains that

"Of bathe þer worldes gret outrage we se
In pompe and pride and vanité,
In selcouthe maners and sere degyse,
Þat now es used of many wyse.
In worldis havyng and beryng,
In vayn apparail and in weryng,
Þat tas over mykel vayn costage.
And tornes al until outrage,
For swilk degises and suilk maners,
Als yhong men now hauntes and lers,

And ilk day es comonly sen,
Byfor þis tyme ne has noght ben. — — —
Now many men se ofte chaungyng
Of sere maners of gys of clethyng;
For now wers men short and now syde,
For now uses men narow and now wyde;
Som has þair clethyng hyngand als stoles,
Som gas tatird als tatird foles. — — —
Swa mykelle pryde als now es I wene,
Was never byfore þis tyme sene. (p. 43, l. 1516-1545.)

Valuable as is the *language* of Hampole to the student of our early literature, the matter will be found to be almost as interesting.

The reader, who is on the look out for what is curious, can learn how to tell by the *cry* of the new born babe 'whether it be man or woman' (p, 14):

"If it be man it says 'a a'
And if the child a woman be
When it is born it says 'e e'.

He can read about the *lynx* that, 'with its sharp sight and clear eyes', sees 'through thick stone walls' (p. 17), He will find the miseries consequent upon 'Old Age' most minutely enumerated (p. 22-23). He may learn, from 'men that are sly', the signs of approaching death, how the left eye of the dying man is narrower than the right, and how

"His nose at the point is sharp and small,
Then begins his chin to fall;
His pulse is still without stirings,
His feet get cold, his belly clings." (p. 23.)

Those who have been accustomed to death bed scenes may have observed perhaps that

"If near the death be a young man
He always wakes and may not sleep than,
And an old man to death drawing
May not wake but is always sleeping."[1] (p. 23.)

[1] Hampole here seems to have followed the authorities of his time, as the following extract from a Medical MS. will show:—

"For to wete yf a seke man sal lyve or dy—Qwen his broues hildes doune; the right eigh mare than the lefte ye; neyse ende waxes sharp; his eres waxes calde; his eighen waxes holle; the chyn falles; his eighen and his mouth es open when he slepes, bot he be wont thar-to; his

The reader will find, whatever may be said to the contrary, that *death* is exceedingly painful, much worse than the wrenching from their roots 'each vein, sinew and limb' of our bodies (p. 53). Not only is there physical pain at the approach of death, but mental torture, for the soul of the dying man is disquieted by 'the sight of fiends', ramping, scowling, grinning and staring like 'mad beasts' (p. 61). The devils are very 'ugly' and are only permitted to appear in their 'proper shape' to the dying (p. 63).

If any Protestant reader should not believe in the existence of Purgatory, our author will give him as trustworthy information upon it as if he had travelled through the country and seen its 'sights'. He may learn 'what it is' (p. 64); 'where it is' (p. 76); 'what pains are there' (p. 79-89; 'what souls go thither and for what sin' (p. 89-96); and 'what may help to slake their pain' (p. 96-108).

If any one desires information upon future punishments he will find an interesting question raised at p. 82.—'How may the soul feel pain?' Hampole answers it by showing that all *feeling* is in the soul and not in the body. The soul shall feel the pain, but 'each one shall appear to another as possessing shape of body of man' (p. 83). But some clerks, our author tells us, 'maintain that the soul that is in purgatory, or in hell, has of the air a body for to suffer pain in various limbs' (p. 84).

About Antichrist, 'the man of sin' there is no lack of information,

"He shall be called the child that is lorn,
And in Chorazin he shall be born,
Of a woman of the kindred of Dan." (p. 113.)

And of Gog and Magog, in a passing allusion, we are told that they are the 'worst folk in the world', and the general opinion concerning them is that they live beyond the mountains of the Caspian Sea, and are kept quiet by the queen of the Amazons. At the end of the world however 'they shall break out and de-

ere-lappes waxes lethy; his fete waxes calde; his wambe falles away; if he pulle at the straes or the clathes; if he pyke at his nese thrilles; his forhede waxes rede; yonge man ay wakand, alde man ay slepand; his twa membres waxes calde agayns kynne, and hydes tham; if he rutills; thir er the takenynges of dethe, forsothe witte thu wele he sal noght leve thre dayes." (Reliq. Antiq. p. 54.)

stroy many lands about' (p. 121). A curious piece of information is given too, about the *resurrection,* when the age of old and young shall be the same i. e. thirty two years and three months (p. 135). The reason of this is, that Christ, when he rose from the dead,

"Was of thirty three years and two
And of three months therewith also."

The reader who is ignorant of the whereabouts of hell, can learn that it is in the middle of the earth, like the hollow in the yolk of an egg. According to Hampole an egg 'hard boiled' exactly represents the relative positions of heaven, earth and hell.

"And as the *yolk* amidst the egg lies,
And the *white* about on the same wise,
Right so is the earth without a doubt,
Amidst the heavens that go about." (p. 174.)

Hell too is an 'ugly hole' (p. 180) full of boiling brimstone and pitch (p. 181). 'There the devils shall stuff the sinful in the fire so that they shall glow as fire brands' (p. 198). So Burns had pretty good authority for addressing the 'deil' as one

"Wha in yon cavern grim and sootie
closed under hatches,
Spairges about the brunstane clootie
to scaud poor wretches."

Our author in the seventh and last part of his work treats us to an *astronomical* lesson, far more amusing than instructive. He tells us (p. 206) that

"From the earth until the circle of the moon, es
The way of five hundred winters and no less."
— — — — — — — — — — — — — —
"And from the point of the earth to Saturnus
The highest planet may be guessed thus,
The way of seven thousand years
And three hundred" (p. 207).

For these, and some few other points of this sort, Hampole relies upon the authority of Rabbi Moses; he seldom advances statements of his own, and it is only in describing the 'city of heaven' that he ventures, as he tells his readers, to 'imagine on his own head' (p. 239). For other points of interest the reader must consult the volume itself.

Since Warton prophesied that he would be the last transcriber of any part of the Pricke of Conscience, it has been the fashion for subsequent writers upon English literature to speak of Hampole as prosy and prolix. But to writers of the xv[th] century, many of whom however were above making any acknowledgement of their original, the Pricke of Conscience furnished abundant material for sermons and homilies.

The Rev. John Pery, Canon of Holy Trinity without Aldgate, who lived a century later than Hampole, wrote for the instruction of his parishioners, a little treatise on Heaven and Hell[1], the leading ideas of which are taken from the Pricke of Conscience. Pery was so great an admirer of Hampole as to use the Northern dialect in preference to that of his own, in addressing his Southern flock. That the Canon of Aldgate was really indebted to our author will easily be seen from the following parallel passages, which occur in the description of Heaven.

"Þare es alkyn delyces and eese,
And syker *peysibilnes* and pees;
Þare es *peysebelle ioy* ay lastand,
And *ioyful selynes* ay lykand;
Þare es *sely endeles* beyng,
And *endeles blysfulhede* in alle thyng;
Þare es ay *blysfulle certaynté*,
And *certayne* dwellyng ay fre." (Pricke of Consc. p. 211.)

"There is ay gret fulnesse of lyght,
And largesse of roume withouten pros,
And merthes that passith alle menys syght;
There is soverayn *sikernesse* dight,
And *siker peisibilnesse* with pees,
Peisable joye with lykyng of sight,
And *joyful* silence with ees;
There is *sely endeles* beyng
And *endeles* blys in that place." (MS. Addit. 10053, f. 141.)

To bring this somewhat rambling preface to a conclusion, the Editor of the present volume would remark that he has endeavoured to make the text of the poem as correct as possible, the proof sheets in every case having been read *twice* with the Manuscript. It is hoped that the Glossary will be found useful for lexicographical purposes, since no pains have been spared to make it complete, both as an index of Northern words, and as supplying also a reference to many others (of Romance origin) which appear perhaps for the first time in the language of the North.

[1] See MS. Addit. 10053 (British Museum).

TABLE OF CONTENTS.

(From Mr. Yates' Southern MS. of the xiv[th] century.)

Here bigynneþ þe boke whiche is iclepid
þe Prick of Conscience . þe whiche is
dyvised in vii parties.

Here bigynneþ þe chapitles of þe first part of þis boke.

Here bigynneþ þe chapitles of þe secunde part of þis boke
þat telleþ of þe world.

Here bigynneþ þe chapitles of þe vi. part of þis boke þat telleþ of helle.

Here bigynneþ þe chapitles of þe vii. part and þe last of þis boke. þe whiche spekes of þe ioyes of heven.

THE PRICKE OF CONSCIENCE.

Þe myght of þe Fader almyghty,
Þe witte of þe Son alwytty,
And þe gudnes of þe Haligast,
A Godde and Lorde of myght mast,
Be wyth us and us help and spede,
Now and ever, in al our nede;
And specialy at this bygynnyng,
And bryng us alle til gude endyng. Amen.

Before ar any thyng was wroght,
And ar any bygynnyng was of oght,
And befor al tymes, als we sal trow,
Þe sam God ay was þat es now,
Þat woned ever in his godhede,
And in thre persons and anhede.
For God wald ay with þe Fader and þe Son
And wyth þe Haligast in anhede won,
Als God in a substance and beyng
With-outen any bygynnyng;
Bygynnyng of hym, myght never nan be,
He was ay God in trinité,
Þat was ay als wys and ful of wytte,
And als myghty als he es yhitte,
W[h]as[1] myght and wytte of him-selve was tan,
For never na God was bot he alan.
Þe sam God sythyn was þe bygynnyng,
And þe first maker of alle thyng;

[1] whose.

And als he is bygynnyng of alle,
Wyth-outen bygynnyng swa we him call,
Ende of al wyth-outen ende,
Þus es in haly bokes contende;
For als he was ay God in trinité
Swa he es, and ay God sal be;
And als he first bygan alle thing,
Swa sal he, at þe last, mak endyng
Of alle þing bot of heven and helle,
And of man, and fende, and aungelle,
Þat aftir þis lyfe sal lyf ay,
And na qwik creature bot þai,
Als men may se in þis boke contende,
Þat wille it se or here to þe ende.
And God that mad man sal ay be þan,
Als he is now, God and man.
Alle thyng thurgh his myght made he,
For with-outen hym myght nathing be.
Alle thyng þat he bygan and wroght
Was byfor þe bygynnyng noght.
Alle thing he ordaynd aftir is wille
In sere kyndes, for certayn skylle;
Whar-for þe creatours þat er dom,
And na witt ne skille has, er bughsom
To lof hym, als þe boke beres wytnesse,
On þair maner als þair kynd esse.
For ilk a thyng þat God has wroght,
Þat folowes þe kynd and passes it noght,
Loves his maker and hym worshepes,
In þat at he þe kynd right kepes;
Sen þe creatures þat skill has nane,
Hym loves in þe kynde þat þai haf tane;
Þan aght man þat has skille and mynde
Hys creatur worshepe in his kynde,
And noght to be of wers condicion
Þan þe creatours with-outen reson.
Mans kynd es to folow Goddes wille
And alle hys comandmentes to fulfille;

For of alle þat God made, mare and les,
Man mast principal creature es,
And alle þat he made was for man done,
Als yhe sal here aftirward sone.
God to mans kynd had grete lufe
When he ordaynd, for mans byhufe,
Heven and herth and þe werld brade,
And al other thyng, and man last made
Til hys lyknes and semely stature;
And made hym mast digne creature
Of al other creaturs of kynde;
And gaf hym wytte, skille and mynde,
For to knaw gude and ille;
And þare-with he gaf hym a fre wille
For to chese, and for to halde
Gude or ille, wethir he walde;
And alswa he ordaynd man to dwelle
And to lyf in erthe, in flesshe and felle,
To knaw his werkes and him worshepe,
And his comandmentes to kepe;
And if he be til God bousom,
Til endeles blis at þe last to com;
And, if he fraward be, to wende
Til pyne of helle, þat has nan ende.
Ilk man þat here lyves, mare and lesse,
God made til his awen lyknesse;
Til wham he has gyven witte and skille
For to knaw bothe gude and ille,
And fre wille to chese, als he vouches save,
Gude or ille whether he wil have;
Bot he þat his wille til God wil sette,
Grete mede þarfor mon he gette;
And he þat til ille settes his wille
Grete payne sal have for þat ille;
Whar-for þat man may be halden wode,
Þat cheses þe ille and leves þe gude.
Sen God made man of maste dignité
Of alle creatures, and mast fre,

And made him til his awen liknes,
In fair stature, als befor sayde es,
And maste has gyven him, and yhit gyves
Þan til any other creature þat lyves,
And has hight him yit þar to
Þe blise of heven, if he uele do;
And yhit when he had done mys,
And thurgh syn was prived of blys,
God tok mans kynd for his sake
And for his love þe dede wald take,
And with his blode boght him agayne
Til þat blisse fra endeles payne;
Þus grete lufe God til man kydde,
And many benyfices he him dydde;
Whar-for ilk man, bathe lered and lewed,
Suld thynk on þat love þat he man shewed,
And alle þier[1] benefice hald in mynde,
Þat he þus dyd til mans kynde,
And love hym and thank him als he can,
And elles es he an unkynd man,
And serve him, bathe day and nyght,
And þat he has gyven him, use it ryght
And his wittes despende in his service,
Elles es he a fole and noght wise;
And knaw kyndly what God es
And what man self es þat es les;
How wake man es in saul and body,
And how stalworth God es, and how myghty;
How man God greves þat dose noght wele,
And what man es worthi þar-for to fele,
How mercyful and gracyouse God es,
And how ful he es of gudenes;
How rightwes God es and how sothefast,
And what he has done and sal do at þe last,
And ilk day dos to man-kynde;
Þis suld ilk man knaw and haf in mynde.

[1] þir (Harl. MS. 4196).

For þe right way þat lyggus til blys,
And þat ledys a man theder, es þys;
þe way of mekenes principaly,
And of drede, and luf of God almyghty,
þat may be cald þe way of wysdom;
In-tyl whilk way na man may com
Wyth-outen knawyng of God here,
And of his myght, and his werkes sere,
Bot here he may til þat knawyng wynne.
Hym byhoves knaw him-self with-inne,
Elles may he haf na knawing to come
In-til þe forsayde way of wysdome.
Bot som men has wytte to understand,
And yhit þai er ful unkunand,
And of som thyng has na knawing
þat myght styrre þam to gude lyfyng;
Swylk men had nede to lere ilk day
Of other men, þat can mare þan þay;
To knaw þat, myght þam stir and lede
Til mekenes, and til lufe, and drede;
þe whilk es way, als befor sayde es,
Til þe blis of heven þat es endeles.
In grete perille of saul es þat man
þat has witt and mynde and na gude can,
And wil noght lere for to knaw
þe werkes of God and gode law,
Ne what hym-self es þat es lest;
Bot lyves als an unskylwys best,
þat nother has skil, witt, ne mynde;
þat man lyfes agayn his kynde.
For a man excuses noght his unkunnyng,
þat his wittes uses noght in leryng,
Namly, of þat at hym fel to knaw
þat myght meke his hert and make it law,
Bot he þat can noght, suld haf wille
To lere to knaw bathe gude and ille;
And he þat can oght, suld lere mare
To knaw alle þat hym nedeful ware;

For an unkunnand man, thurgh leryng,
May be broght til undirstandyng
Of many thynges, to knaw and se
þat has bene, and es, and yhit sal be,
þat til mekenes myght stir his wille,
And til lufe, and drede, and to fle alle ille.
Many has lykyng trofels to here,
And vanités wille blethly lere,
And er bysy in wille and thoght
To lere þat þe saul helpes noght;
Bot þat ne[de]ful war to kun and knaw,
To listen and lere þai er ful slaw;
For-þi þai can noght knaw ne se
þe peryls þat þai suld drede and fle,
And whilk way þai suld chese and take,
And whilk way þai suld lef and forsake.
Bot na wonder es, yf þai ga wrang
For in myrknes of unknawyng þai gang,
With-outen lyght of understandyng
Of þat, þat falles til ryght knawyng.
þar-for ilk cristen man and weman
þat has witte and mynd, and skille can,
þat knaws noght þe ryght way to chese,
Ne þe perils þat ilk wise man flese,
Suld be bughsom ay, and bysy
To here and lere of þam, namely,
þat understands and knawes by skille,
Wilk es gude way and wilk es ille.
He þat right ordir of lyfyng wil luke
Suld bygyn þus, als says þe boke;
To knaw first what hym-self es,
Swa may he tyttest come to mekenes,
þat es grund of al vertus to last,
On whilk al vertus may be sette fast;
For he þat knawes wele, and can se
What him-self was, and es, and sal be,
A wyser man may he be talde,
Wether he be yhung man or alde,

Þan he þat can alle other thyng,
And of him-self has na knawyng.
For he may noght right God knaw ne fele,
Bot he can first him-self wele:
Þar-for a man suld first lere
To knaw him-self propely here;
For if he hym-self knew kyndely,
He suld haf knawyng of God almyghty,
And of his endyng thynk suld he
And of þe day þat last sal be.
He suld knaw what þis worlde es,
Þat es ful of pompe and lythernes,
And lere to knaw and thynk wyth-alle
What sal after þis lyf falle.
For, knawyng of all þis shuld hym lede
And mynd with-alle, til mekenes and drede,
And swa may he com to gude lyvyng,
And atte þe last til a gode endyng;
And when he sal out of þis world wende,
Be broght til þe lyfe, þat has na ende.
Þe bygynnyng of alle þis proces
Ryght knawyng of a man self es.
Bot som men has mykel lettyng,
Þat lettes þam to haf right knawyng
Of þam-selfe, þat þai first suld knaw,
Þat þam til mekenes first suld draw.
And of þat, four thynges I find
Þat mase a mans wytt ofte blynd,
And knawyng of hym-self lettes,
Thurgh wilk four, he hym-self forgettes.
Of þis Saynt Bernard witnes bers
And er þa four wryten in þis vers.
Forma, favor populi, fervor juvenilis, opesque
Surripuere tibi noscere quid sit homo.
Þat es "favor of þe folk and fayrnes,
And fervor of thoght[1] and riches,

[1] yhouthe.

Reves a man sight, skylle and mynde,
To knaw hym-self, what he es of kynde."
Þus þer four lettes his insight
Þat he knaws noght him-selfe right,
And mas his hert ful hawtayne
And ful fraward til his soverayne.
Þir four norisches ofte pompe and pride,
And other vices þat men can noght hyde.
For in him, in wham ane of þer four es,
Es selden sen any mekenes;
Alswa þai lette a man þat he noght sese
Þe perils of þe werld, ne vanitese,
Ne of þe tyme of þe dede þat es to come;
Thynkes noght ne of þe day of dom,
Ne he can noght undirstand ne se
Þe paynes, þat after þis lyfe sal be
To synful men þat here lofes foly,
Ne þe blise þat gude men er worthy;
Bot in his delytis settes his hert fast,
And fares als þis lyfe suld ay last,
And gyffes him noght bot to vanité,
And to al þat lykyng to hym myght be.
Swylk men er noght led with skylle,
Bot þai folow, ay, þair awen wille
And of noght elles thynkes, ne tas hede.
What wonder es yf þai haf na drede;
For what þai suld drede, þai knaw noght,
Þarfor þai can haf na drede in thoght,
Of þat þat myght þam to drede bryng,
And þat es thurgh defaut of knawyng.
Yhit som men wille noght understande
Þat þat mught mak þam dredande,
For þai wald noght here, bot þat þam pays,
Þarfor þe prophet in psauter says:
Noluit intelligere
ut bene ageret.
He says "he has no wille to fele,
Ne to understand for to do wele".

þis wordes by þam may be sayd here,
þat wil noght understand ne lere
To drede God and to do his wille,
Bot folowes þair likyng and lyves ille.
Som understandes als þai here telle,
Bot na drede in þair hertes may dwellé,
And thurgh defaut of trouthe þat may be;
For þai trow nathyng bot þat þai se,
But groches when þai dredful thyng here;
þarfor þe prophet says on þis manere:
Non crediderunt
et murmuraverunt.
þe prophet sayd "þai trowed noght,
And groched" and was angred, in thoght;
þus er many þat trowes na thyng
þat men þam says ogayn þair likyng,
Bot groches gretly and waxes fraward,
When men says oght, þat þam thynk hard.
Som can se in buk swilk thyng and rede,
Bot lightnes of hert reves þam drede,
Swa þat it may noght with þam dwelle
And þarfor says God þus in þe gospelle:
Quia ad tempus credunt, et in tempore
temptacionis recedunt.
"Til a tyme", he says, "some trowes a thyng
And passes þar-fra in þe tyme of fandyng."
Alswa þos says þe prophet David,
In a psalme þat cordes þar-wyth:
Et crediderunt in verbis eius. et lau-
daverunt laudem eius, cito, fecerunt
et obliti sunt opera eius.
He says, "in his wordes, trowed þai
And loved his lovyng als þai couth say,
But tyte þai had don, and forgat
His werkes, and thoght na mar of þat;"
Swilk men er ay swa unstedfast,
þat na drede may with þam last,

For þai er swa wilde, when þai haf quert,
Þat na drede þai can hald in hert;
328 Bot wha-swa can noght drede may lere,
Þat þis tretice wil rede or here;
Yf þai rede or here, til þe hende,
Þe maters þat er þar-in contende,
332 And undirstand þam al and trow,
Parchaunce þair hertes þan sal bow,
Thurgh drede þat þai sal consayve þar by,
To wirk gude werkes and fle foli.
336 Þarfor þis buke es on Ynglese drawen,
Of sere maters, þat er unknawen
Til laude men þat er unkunnand,
Þat can na latyn understand,
340 To make þam þam-self first knaw
And fra syn and vanytese þam draw,
And for to stir þam til right drede,
When þai þis tretisce here or rede,
344 Þat sal prikke þair conscience with-yn,
And of þat drede may a lofe bygyn
Thurgh comfort of ioyes of heven sere,
Þat men may aftirwar[d] rede and here.
348 Þis buk, als it-self bers wittenes,
In seven partes divised es.
I. Þe first party, to knaw and hafe in mynde,
Es of þe wrechednes of mans kynde.
II. Þe secunde es of þe condicions sere
353 And of þe unstabelnes of þis werld here.
Þe thred parte es in þis buke to rede
III. Of þe dede and whi it es to drede.
IV. Þe ferthe part es of purgatory,
357 Whar saules er clensed of alle foly.
V. Þe fift es of þe day of dome,
And of taknes þat befor sal come.
VI. Þe sext es of þe payns of helle
361 Þar þe dampned sal ever-mare dwelle.
VII. Þe sevend es of þe ioys of heven.
Þer er þe partes of þis buk seven,

And of ilka parte fynd men may
Sere maters in þis buk to say.
Ga we now til þat parte þat first es,
Þat spekes of mans wrechednes;
For alle þat byfor es wryten to luk,
Es bot als an entré of þis buk.

Here bygynnes þe first part
þat es of mans wrechednes.

First whan God made al thyng of noght,
Of the foulest matere man he wroght
Þat was of erthe; for twa skyls to halde;
Þe tane es forthy þat God walde
Of foul matere, mak man in despite[1]
Of Lucifer þat fel als tyte
Til helle, als he had synned thurgh pride,
And of alle þat with him fel þat tyde;
For þai suld have þan þe mare shenshepe,
And þe mare sorow when þai tuk kepe,
Þat men of swa foul matere suld duelle
In þat place fra whilk þai felle.
Þe tother skille es þis to se;
For man suld here þe meker be
Ay, when he sese and thynkes in thoght,
Of how foul mater he is wroght;
For God, thurgh his gudnes and his myght,
Wald, þat sen þat place in heven bright
Was made voyde thurgh þe syn of pride,
It war filled ogayne on ilka syde
Thurgh þe vertu of mekenes,
Þat even contrary til pryde es;
Þan may na man þider come
Bot he þat meke es, and boghsome;
Þat proves þe gospelle þat says us,
How God sayd til his disciples þus:

The two reasons why God made man of earth.

[1] MS. Addit reads:
"Of so foule matere man make, as in despite
Of the foule fende, him therwith to edwyte."

Nisi efficiamini sicut parvulus, non intrabitis in regnum celorum.

"Bot yhe", he sayde, "be als a childe,
þat es to say, bathe meke and mylde,
Yhe sal noght entre, be na way
Hevenryke þat sal last ay."
þan byhoves a man ay here seke,
þat may tittest make him meke;
Bot nathyng here may meke him mare
þan to thynk in hert, als I sayde are,
How he was made of a foul matere,
And es noght elles, bot herthe here.
For-þi says a clerk, als I now say,
'What es man bot herth and clay,
And poudre þat with þe wynd brekes?'
And þarfor Iob þus to God spekes:

Memento, queso, quod sicut lutum feceris me, et in pulverem reduces me.

He says, "thynk, Laverd, þat als þow made me
Foul erthe and clay here to be,
Right swa þou sal turne me agayne
Til erthe and poudre"; þis es certayn.
þan says our Laverd God almyghty
Agayne til man, þus shortly:

Memento, homo, quod cinis es, et in cinerem reverteris.

"Thynk man", he says, "askes er-tow now,
And in to askes agayn turn sal-tow."
þan es a man noght elles to say
Bot askes and pouder, erthe and clay;
Of þis suld ilk man here haf mynde
And knawe þe wrechednes of mans kynde,
þat may be sene, als I shewe can,
In al þe partys of þe lyfe of man.
Alle mans lyfe casten may be,

Of the three parts of the life of man.

Principaly, in þis partes thre,
þat er þir to our understandyng;
Bygynnyng, midward, and endyng.

Þer þre partes er þre spaces talde
Of þe lyf of ilk man, yhung and alde.
Bygynnyng of mans lyf, þat first es,
Contenes mykel wrechednes;

The beginning of man's life.

Þarfor I wille, ar [I] forthir pas,
Shew yhou what a man first was;
Some tyme was when a man was noght,
Befor þat he was geten and forth broght.
He was geten aftir, als es knawen,
Of vile sede of man with syn sawen;
He was consayved synfully
With-in his awen moder body,
Whar his herber with-in was dight,
Als David says in þe psauter right:
Ecce in inquitatibus conceptus sum, et in peccatis concepit me mater mea.
"Lo", he says, "als man-kynd es
I am consayved in wykkednes,
And my moder has consayved me
In syn and in caytefté."
Þar duellid man in a myrk dungeon,
And in a foul sted of corupcion,
Whar he had na other fode
Bot wlatsom glet, and loper blode,[1]
And stynk and filthe, als I sayde ar,
With þer he was first norisshed þar.
Aftir-warde, when he out came
From þat dungeon, his moder wame,

Man's feebleness.

And was born til þis werldys light,
He ne had nouther strenthe ne myght,
Nouther to ga ne yhit to stand,
Ne to crepe with fote, ne with hand.
Þan has a man les myght þan a beste
When he es born, and es sene leste:

Man is less than a beast.

For a best when it es born, may ga
Als tite aftir, and ryn to and fra;

[1] 'Bot lothsom glette and filthede of blode.' MS. Addit. 11305.

Bot a man has na myght þar-to,
When he es born, swa to do;
For þan may he noght stande ne crepe
Bot ligge and sprawel, and cry and wepe.
For unnethes es a child born fully
Þat it ne bygynnes to goule and cry;

A male child at its birth says a. a, and a female child e. e.

And by þat cry men knaw þan
Whether it be man or weman,
For when it es born it cryes swa:[1]

a. denotes Adam, and e. stands for Eve.

If it be man it says "a. a",
Þat þe first letter es of þe nam
Of our forme-fader Adam.
And if þe child a woman be,
When it es born it says "e. e."
E. es þe first letter and þe hede
Of þe name of Eve þat bygan our dede.
Þarfor a clerk made on þis manere
Þis vers of metre þat es wreten here:
Dicentes E. vel A. quot-quot nascuntur ab Eva.
"Alle þas", he says, "þat comes of Eve,
Þat es al men þat here byhoves leve,
When þai er born what-swa þai be,
Þai say outher a. a, or e. e."

The reason why man's life commences with crying.

Þus es here þe bygynnyng
Of our lyfe sorow and gretyng,
Til whilk our wrechednes stirres us;
And þarfor Innocent says þus:
Omnes nascimur eiulantes,
ut nature nostre miseriam
exprimamus.
He says, "al er we born gretand,[2]
And makand a sorowful sembland,
For to shew þe grete wrechednes
Of our kynd þat in us es."

[1] MSS. Addit 22283, 11305 read 'wa'.

[2] He saith: "we ben ybore everichone
Making sorwe and reuly mone." MS. Addit 11305

Man brings nothing into the world with him.

þus when þe tyme come of our birthe,
Al made sorow and na mirthe;
Naked we come hider, and bare
And pure, swa sal we hethen fare;
Of þis twa tymes we suld thynk þan,
For þus says Iob, þe rightwes man:
Nudus egressus sum de utero matris
mee, et nudus revertar illuc.
"Naked", he says, "first I cam
Hyder, out of my moder wam,
And naked I sal turne away."
Swa sal we al at our last day.
þus a man es, at þe first comyng,
Naked, and bringes with him nathyng;
Bot a rym[1] þat es ful wlatsome,
Es his garment when he forth sal com,
þat es noght bot a blody skyn
þat he byfor was lapped in,
Whils he in his moder wam lay,
þe whilk es a foul thyng to say,
And fouler to here, als says þe buke,
And aldir-foules[2] on to loke;

Man is born to trouble and sorrow.

þus es a man, als we may se,
In wrechednes borne and caytefté,
And for to life here a fon dayse,
þar-for Iob þus openly sayse;
Homo, natus de muliere, brevi vivens
tempore, repletur multis miseriis.
He says, "Man þat born es of woman[3]
Lyfand short time to[4] ful-fild es þan
Of many maners of wrechednes."
þus says Iob, and swa it es,

[1] MS. Lansd. 348 reads 'slow'. MS. Addit 22283 reads 'slouh'. MS. Addit 11305 reads 'reme'. [2] aldir foulest (MS. Harl. 4196)
[3] He saith: "after that a man is bor of a woman
He lyveth but short tyme, and sone bicometh wan." MS. Addit 11305.
[4] *to* is superfluous?

Alswa man es borne til noght elles
Bot to travayle, als Iob yhit telles:
Homo nascitur ad laborem,
sicut avis ad volatum.
He says, "man es born to travaile right
Als a foul es to þe flight."
For littel rest in þis lyf es,
Bot gret travayle and bysynes;

Man at his birth is the devil's son.

Yhit a man es, when he es born,
Þe fendes son, and fra God es lorn
Ay, til he thurgh grace may com
Til baptem and til cristendom;
Þus may a man his bygynnyng se
Ful of wrechednes and of caytifté.

The second or middle period of man's life.

Þe tother part of þe lyf, men calles
Þe mydward, aftir þat it falles,
Þe wilk reches fra þe bygynnyng
Of mans lyfe un-til þe endyng.
Þe bygynnyng of man, als I talde,
Es vile and wreched to behalde;
Bot how foule es man aftir-warde

Man is full of corruption.

Tels þus, openly, saynt Bernarde:
Homo nihil aliud est, quam sperma
fetidum, saccus stercorum et esca vermium.
Saynt Bernard says als þe buke telles,
Þat "man here es nathyng elles
Bot a foule slyme, wlatsome til men,
And a sekful of stynkand fen,
And wormes fode" þat þai wald have,
When he es dede and layde in grave.
Bot som men and women fayre semes
To þe syght with-outen, als men demes,
And þat shewes noght elles bot a skyn;
Bot wha-swa moght se þam with-in,
Fouler carion moght never be
Þan he suld þan of þam se.
Þarfor he þat had als sharp syght,
And cler eghen and als bright

Als has a best þat men Lynx calles,[1]
þat may se thurgh thik stane walles,
Littel lykyng suld a man haf þan
For to behald a faire woman,
For þan mught he se, with-outen doute,
Als wele with-in als with-oute,
And if he with-in saw hir right,
Sho war ful wlatsom til his sight;
þus foul with-in ilk man es,
Als þe buk says and bers witnes.
þan may we se on þis manere,
How foul þe kynd of man es here;
Whar-for I hald a man noght witty
þat here es over-prowde and ioly,
When he may ilk day here and se
What he es, and was, and sal be.
Bot proud man of þis tas na hede
For hym wantes skille, þat hym suld lede,
When he es yhung and luffes laykyng,
Or has ese, and welth, and his lykyng;
Or if he be at grete worshepe,
What hym-self es þan, he tas na kepe;
Whar-for him-self þan knawes he leste
And fares als an unresonabel beste,
þat his awen wille folowes, and noght elles,
And þar-for þe prophet in þe psauter telles:
Homo, cum in honore esset, non intellexit, comparatus est iumentis insipientibus, et similis factus est illis.
"Man when he is til worshepe broght
Right understandyng has he noght:
He may be likend and he es lyke þan
Til bestes, þat na skylle ne witte can;"
þarfor ilk man þat has witte and mynde,
Suld thynk of þe wrechednes of his kynde,
þat es foul, and vile, and wlatsom;
For he may se fra his body com,

The lynx sees through thick stone walls.

The proud man has no thought about himself.

Of the foulness of man's body.

[1] 'As hath a beste that men lynx calles,
That may se thurgh *nyne stoon walles.* MS. Addit 11305.

Bathe fra aboven and fra bynethe,
Alkyn filthe with stynkand brethe;
For mar filthe es nane, hard ne nesshe,
Þan es þat comes fra a mans flesshe;
And þat may a man bathe se and fele,
Þat wil byhald him-self wele,
How foul he es to mans syght,
And þarfor says Saynt Bernard right:
Si diligenter cansideres quid per os,
quid per nares, ceterosque meatus
corporis egreditur, vilius sterquilinium
nunquam vidisti.
"If þow wille", he says, "ententyfly se,
And by-hald what comes fra þe

What comes from man.

What thurgh mouthe, what thurgh nese, commonly,
[1]And thurgh other overtes of his [2] body,
A fouler myddyng saw þow never nane,"
Þan a man es, with flesche and bane.
Al þe tyme þat a man here lyves,
His kynd na other fruyt gyfes,
Whether he lyf lang or short while,
Bot thyng that es wlatsome and vile,
Als filth and stynk and nathynge elles,
Als Innocent þus in a boke telles:

Man as compared with trees, plants &c.

Herbas et arbores, inquit, investiga: Ille de se
producunt flores, frondes et fructus; et
tu de te lendes, pediculos et lumbricos.
Ille diffundunt oleum, vinum, et balsamum; et
tu de te sputum, urinam, et stercus: Ille
de se spirant suavitatem odoris; et tu
de te reddis abhominationem fetoris.
Qualis est arbor, talis est fructus.
Þis gret clerk telles þus in a buke:

Herbs and trees bring forth flowers and fruit, but man only nits, lice and vermin.

"Behalde", he says, "graythely and loke,
Herbes and trese þat þou sees spryng,
And take gude kepe what þai forth bryng;

[1] 'And other issues of the body:
A fouler dongehull sawe thou never none.' MS. Addit 11305.

[2] þe (MS. Harl. 4196).

Herbes forth bringes floures and sede,
And tres fair fruyt and braunches to spede,[1]
And þou forth bringes of þi-self here
Nites, lyse, and other vermyn sere.
Of herbes and tres, springes baum ful gude,
And oyle and wyne for mans fude;
And of þe comes mykel foul thyng,
Als fen, and uryn and spyttyng;
Of herbes and tres comes swete savour,
And of þe comes wlatsome stynk, and sour;
Swilk als þe tre es with bowes,
Swilk es þe fruyt þat on it growes."
An ille tre may na gude fruyt bere,
And þat knawes ilk gude gardynere.
A man es a tre, þat standes noght harde,
Of whilk þe crop es turned donward,
And þe rote to-ward þe firmament,
Als says þe grete clerk Innocent:
Quid est homo, secundum formam, nisi quedam
arbor eversa, cujus radices sunt crines;
truncus est caput cum collo; stipis est pectus cum
alvo, rami sunt ulne cum tibiis; frondes sunt
digiti cum articulis; hoc est folium quod a ven-
to rapitur, et stipula a sole siccatur.
He says, "what es man in shap bot a tre
Turned up þat es doun, als men may se,
Of whilk þe rotes þat of it springes,
Er þe hares þat on þe heved hynges;
þe stok nest þe rot growand
Es þe heved with nek folowand;
þe body of þat tre þar-by
Es þe brest with þe bely;
þe bughes er þe armes with þe handes
And þe legges with þe fete þat standes:
þe braunches men may by skille call
þe tas and þe fyngers alle;
þis es þe leef þat hanges noght faste,
þat es blawen away thurgh a wynd blaste.

Man is like a tree inverted: the roots are the hair, the stock is the head, the boughs are the arms and hands, with the legs and feet; the branches are the toes and fingers.

[1] Sprede (MS. Harl. 4196).

And þe body alswa of þe tre,
Þat thurgh þe son may dried be."

Man, like a flower, soon fades.

A man þat es yhung and light,
Be he never swa stalworth and wyght,
And comly of shap, lufly and fayre,
Angers and yvels may hym appayre,
And his beuté and his streng[th] abate,
And mak hym in ful wayk state,
And chaunge alle fayre colour,
Þat son fayles and fades, als dos þe flour.
For a flour þat semes fayre and bright,
Thurgh stormes fades, and tynes þe myght.

Man's strength is weakened by disease.

Many yvels, angers, and mescheefes
Oft comes til man þat here lyves,
Als fevyr, dropsy, and Iaunys,
Tysyk, goute, and other maladys,
Þat hym mas streng[th] and fayrnes tyne,
Als grete stormes dose a flour to dwyne;
Þarfor a man may likend be
Til a flour, þat es fayre to se,
Þan son aftir þat it es forth broght,

Man fades as a flower.

Welkes and dwynes til it be noght;
Þis aught to be ensample til us;
For-whi Iob, in a boke, says þus:
Homo, quasi flos, egreditur et conteritur, et fugit velud umbra et nunquam in eodem statu permanet.
"Man", he says, "als a flour bright,
First forth comes here til þis light,
And es sone broken and passes away,
Als a shadu on þe somers day;
And never mare in þe same state duelles,"
Bot ay passand, als Iob telles;
Of þis þe prophet witnes beres,
In a psalme of þe psauter, thurgh þis vers
Mane, sicut herba, transeat, mane floreat et transeat; vespere decidat, indurat[1] et arescat.

[1] induréscat?

The prophet says þus, als writen es,
"Arely a man passes als þe gres,
Arely at þe bygynnyng of þe day,
He floresshe and passes away;
At even late he is doun broght,
And fayles, and dries, and dwynes to noght.
In þe first bygynnyng of þe kynd of man
Neghen hundreth wynter man lyfed þan,
Als clerkes in bukes bers witnes;
Bot sythen bycom mans lyf les
And swa wald God at it suld be;
For-whi he sayd þus til Noe:
Non permanebit spiritus meus
in homine in eternum, quia caro
est, erunt dies illius centum
viginti annorum.
"My gast," he says, "sal noght ay dwelle
In man, for he is flesshe and felle;
Hys days sal be for to life here
An hundreth and twenti yhere."
Bot swa grete elde may nane now bere,
For sythen mans lyfe bycom shortere.
For-whi þe complection of ilk man
Was sythen febler þan it was þan;
Now es it alther-feblest to se,
Þarfor mans life short byhoves be;
For ay þe langer þat man may lyfe,
Þe mare his lyfe sal hym now griefe,
And þe les him sal thynk his lyf swete,
Als in a psalme, says þe prophete:
Si autem in potentatibus octogynta an-
ni, et amplius eorum labor et dolor.
"If in myghtfulnes four scor yhere falle,
Mare es þair swynk and sorow with-alle."
For seldom a man þat has þat held,[1]
Hele has, and him-self may weld;

Of the length of man's life, and the reason why it is shortened.

Of the shortness of man's life.

[1] held = 'eld'.

Bot now falles yhit shorter mans dayes,
Als Iob, þe haly man, þus says:
Nunc paucitas dierum meorum
finietur brevi.
"Now," he says, "my fon days sere
Sal enden with a short tyme here."

Of the changes wrought in man by old age; and of the properties of 'eld'.

Fone men may now fourty yhere pas,
And foner fifty als in somtym was;
Bot als tyte als a man waxes alde,
þan waxes his kynde wayke and calde,
þan chaunges his complexcion
And his maners and his condicion;
Than waxes his hert hard and hevy,
And his heved feble and dysy;
þan waxes his gaste seke and sare,
And his face rouncles, ay mare and mare;

Bodily infirmities caused by old age.

His mynde es short when he oght thynkes,
His nese ofte droppes, his hand[1] stynkes,
His sight wax dym þat he has,
His bak waxes croked, stoupand he gas
Fyngers and taes, fote and hande,
Alle his touches[2] er tremblande:
His werkes for-worthes þat he bygynnes,[3]
His haire moutes, his eghen rynnes;
His eres waxes deef, and hard to here,
His tung fayles, his speche is noght clere.

Mental infirmities.

His mouthe slavers, his tethe rotes,
His wyttes fayles, and he ofte dotes;
He is lyghtly wrath, and waxes fraward,
Bot to turne hym fra wrethe it es hard;
He souches and trowes sone a thyng,
Bot ful late he turnes fra þat trowyng;
He es covatous and hard haldand,
His chere es drery and his sembland;

[1] i. e. *and* = breath.
[2] MS. Lansd. 348 reads 'lymmes'.
[3] 'His werkes forweren that he bygynneth'. MS. Addit 11305.

He es swyft to spek on his manere
And latsom and slaw for to here;
He prayses ald men and haldes þam wyse,
And yhung men list him oft despyse;
He loves men þat in ald tyme has bene,
He lakes þa men þat now are sene;
He is ofte seke and ay granand,
And ofte angerd, and ay pleynand;
Alle þir, thurgh kynd, to an ald man falles,
Þat clerkes propertés of eld calles.
Yhit er þar ma þan I haf talde,
Þat falles to a man þat es alde.
Þus may men se, wha-so can,
What þe condicions er of an ald man.
Þe last ende of mans lyfe es hard,
Þat es, when he drawes to ded-ward.
For when he is seke, and bedreden lys,
And swa feble þat he may noght rys,
Þan er men in dout and noght certayn,
Wethir he sal ever cover agayn.

How to tell whether an old man will recover from his sickness.

Bot yhit can som men, þat er sleghe,
Witte if he sal of þat yvel deghe
By certayne takens, als yhe sal here,
Þat byfalles when þe ded es nere;
Þan bygynnes his frount dounward falle,
And his browes heldes doun wyth-alle;
Þe lefte eghe of hym þan semes les,
And narower þan þe right eghe es;
Hys nese, at þe poynt, es sharp and smalle,
Þan bygynnes his chyn to falle;
His pouce es stille, with-outen styringes,
His fete waxes calde, his bely clynges.

How to tell whether a young man will recover from his sickness.

And if nere þe dede be a yhung man,
He ay wakes, and may noght slepe þan;
And an aldeman to dede drawand
May noght wake, bot es ay slepand;
Men says, al þir takens sere
Er of a man þat þe dede es nere.

What's a man like when he is dead?

Whiles a man lyves he is lyke a man;
When he es dede what es he lyke þan?
Þan may men his liknes se
Chaunged, als it had never bene he;
And when his lyf es broght to þe ende,
Þan sal he on þe same wys hethen wende,
Pure and naked, right als he cam
Þe first day fra his moder wam.
For he broght with him nathyng þat day,
And noght sal he bere with him away,
Bot it be a wyndyng clathe anely,
Þat sal be lapped obout his body;
Þus wrechedly endes þe lyf of man.
And if we behalde what he es þan,

A dead body is but earth and clay.

When þe lyfe of hym passes oway,
Þan es he noght bot erthe and clay
Þat turnes til mare corrupcion,
Þan ever had stynkand carion.

A dead body pollutes the atmosphere.

For þe corrupcion of his body,
Yf it suld lang oboven erthe ly,
It myght þe ayr swa corrumpud mak,
Þat men þarof þe dede suld take,
Swa vile it es and violent;
Þarfor þe gret clerk says, Innocent:
Quid enim fetidius humano cadavere,
quid horibilius homine mortuo.
He says, "What-kyn thyng may fouler be
Þan a mans carion es to se:
And what es mar horibel in stede
Þan a man es when he es dede?"
Alswa [I] say, nathyng es swa ugly,
Als here es a mans dede body;
And when it es in erth layd lawe,[1]

Man's body shall be eaten by worms.

Wormes þan sal it al to-gnaw,
Til þe flesshe be gnawen oway and byten;
For-why we fynde þos in buk writen:

[1] 'And whan it es in erthe bywounde,
Wormes wol him gnawe on every stounde'. MS. Addit 11305.

Cum autem morietur homo, heredita-
bit vermes et serpentes.
Þe buk says þus, "þat when a man
Sal dighe he sal enherite þan
Wormes and nedders," ugly in sight,
Til wham falles mans flessh, thurgh right,
Þarfor in erthe man sal slepe,
Oman[g] wormes, þat on hym sal crepe,
And gnaw on þat stynkand carcays,
Als es wryten in a bok þat says:
Omnes in pulvere dormient, et
vermes operient eos.
Þat es "in pouder sal slepe ilk man,
And wormes sal cover hym þan;"
For in þis world es nane swa witty,
Swa fair, swa strang, ne swa myghty,
Emperour, kyng, duke, ne caysere,
Ne other þat bers grete state here,
Ne riche, ne pure, bond ne fre,
Lered or lawed, what-swa he be,
Þat he ne sal turne at þe last oway,
Til poudre and erthe and vyle clay;
And wormes sal ryve hym in sondre;
And þarfor haf I mykel wondere
Þat unnethes any man wille se
What he was, and what he sal be.
Bot wha-so wald in hert cast
What he was, and sal be at þe last,
And what he es, whyles he lyves here,
He suld fynd ful litel matere
To mak ioy whilles he here duelles,
Als a versifiour in metre þus telles:
Si quis sentiret, quo tendit, et unde veniret,
Nunquam gauderet, sed in omne tempore fleret.
He says, "wha-so wille fele and se,
Wethen he com and whider sal he,
Suld never be blythe bot ioy forsake,
And alle tyme grete and sorow make."

Emperor, king, duke and kayser, all shall worms rive asunder.

Man has little cause to rejoice here.

Why is man so tender of his vile body?

904 Whar-to þan es man here swa myry,
And swa tendre of his vile body,
Þat sal rote and with wormes be gnawen,
And swa ugly to syght may be knawen?
908 Loverd wha-so of him þan had syght,
Aftir þat wormes him swa had dight,
And gnawen his flesshe un to þe bane,
Swa grysly a sight saw he never nane,

A grisly sight his vile carcass shall be.

912 Als he myght se of þat vile carcays:
For Saynt Bernard þos in metre says:
Post hominem vermis, post vermem, fetor et horror,
Et sic, in non hominem vertitur omnis homo.
916 "Aftir man", he says, "vermyn es,
And aftir vermyn stynkand uglynes;
And swa sal ilk man turned be þan
Fra a man intil na man."
920 Þos may ilk man in þis parte se,
What he was, and what he sal be,
And what he es ay whils he here lyfes,
And whatkyn fruyt his kynd here gyves.
924 Here may men se, als writen es,
Mikel of mans wrechednes,
And mykel mare yhit may men telle;
Bot here-on wille I na langer duelle.
928 Ga we now forther-mar and luke,
To þe secund part of þis buke,
In whilk men may haf understandyng
Of þe world, and of worldysshe lyfyng.

932 Here bygynnes þe secunde part þat
es of þe world.

Of 'worldish' men.

Alle þe world so wyde and brade,
Our Lord speciali for man made,
936 And al other thynge, als clerkes can profe,
He made anly to mans by-hove.
Sen he al þe world and alle thynge wroght
Til mans by-hove, þan man aght noght
940 Lufe nowther worldisshe thyng ne bodily,
Mare þan our Lord God almyghty,

Ne als mykel as God, þogh þat war les;
And wha-so dos, unkynd he es;
944 For God war worthy mare to be lufed
Þan any creature, and swa byhufed,
Syn he es maker of althynge,
And of alle creatures þe bygynnynge.
948 Þis say [I] by men þat gyves þam mykel
Til þis world, þat es fals and fikel,
And lufes alle thynge þat til it falles;
Swilk men worldisshe men, men calles

Of those who set their love most on this world.

952 Þat þair luf mast on þe world settes,
And þat luf, þe luf of God lettes.
Þarfor gude it es þat a man him kepe,
Fra worldisshe luf and vany worshepe.
956 For thurgh luf of þis world and vanité,
A man at þe last forbard may be,
Of þe blisful world þar al ioy es,
Whar þe lyfe of man sal be endles,
960 Þat dos to God here þat hym falles,
Þat world þer clerkes 'world of world' calles.
Whi [1] alle þe world þat God walde make
For man, of whilk I byfor spake,
964 Þat swa generaly here is tane,
May be undirstanden ma worldes þan ane;

More worlds than one; the one visible, the other invisible.

For a grete clerk says, þat hight Berthelmewe,
Þat twa worldes er principaly to shewe,
968 Þat þe elementes and al þe hevens
Contenes, als he þam in boke nevens,
And alle þe creatures þat God wroght,
Swa þat withouten þa worldes es noght.
972 Þe tan es gastly, invisile and clene,
Þe tother es bodyly and may be sene.
Þe gastly world, þat na man may se,
Es heven, whar God syttes in trinité,
976 And þe neghen ordres of angels,
And haly spirytes in þat world duelles,

The spiritual world is heaven, where dwell God, the nine orders of angels and holy spirits.

[1] For-whi?

And þider sal we com and þar lyf ay,
If we þederward hald þe right way.
Þat world was made for mans wonnyng
Omang angels in ioy and lykyng,
Evermare þar-in for to duelle,
As men may here þer clerkes telle.
Now heir-on wille I na langer stand,
For after-ward commes þis matere til hand.

The visible world is divided into two parts; the one is high, the other low.

Þe tother world þat men may se,
In twa partes divised may be,
Þe whilk alle bodily thyng may hald,
And ayther part may a world be cald,
And bathe men may se and knawe;
Bot þe tan es heghe, and þe tother lawe;

The higher world contains the planets and stars.

Þe hegher reches fra þe mon even
Til þe heghest of þe sterned heven;
Þat werld is ful bright and fayre,
For þar es na corrupcion, bot cler ayre,
And þe planettes and sternes shynand,
And sere signes and noght elles þar wonand.

The lower world contains the earth and man.

Þe lawer werld, þat lawest may falle,
Contenes haly þe elementes alle,
Þat on þe erthe and about þe erthe standes,
Whar sere manere of men wonnes in sere landes.
In þis werld es bothe wele and wa,
Þat es ofte chaunged to and fra,
Þat til som es softe and til sum harde,
Als yhe may here or se aftirwarde.
Þir worldes byfor als was Goddes wille,
For man was made for certayn skille;

The highest world was made for man's endless abode.

Þe heghest world, þat passes alle thyng,
Was made for mans endles wonnyng;
For ilk man sal hafe þar a place
To wone ay in ioy, þat here has grace.
Þat world was made to our most avantage,
For þar falles to be our right heritage.
Þe tother world, þat is lawer,
Whare þe sternes and planets er,

God ord[a]ynd anly for our byhufe,
By þis skille, als I can prufe.
Þe ayre fra þeþen, and þe heat of þe son
Sustayns þe erthe here, þar we won,
And nurisshes alle thyng þat fruyt gyves,
And confortes best, and man, and alle þat lyves;
And tempers our kynde and our complexioun,
And settes þe tymes of yhere in seson,
And gyfes us light here, whar we duelle,
Elles war þis world myrk als helle;
Yhit þe bodys of þe world in þair kynde,
Shewes us for bisens to haf in mynde,
How we suld serve God in our kynde here,
Als þai do þar, on þair manere.

The air from the higher portion of the visible world, together with the sun, sustains the earth and produces fruit &c.

Þe lawest world was alswa made for man,
For þis skylle, als clerkes shew can;
For þat man suld be þar-in wonnand,
Goddes werkes to se and undirstand,
And his commandmentes and his wille
To knawe, and kepe, and to fulfille,
And to be proved here in gastly batayls,
Of gastly enmys þat man oft assayls;
Swa þat þurgh gastly strenth and victori,
He may be made in þis world worthy
To haf þe coroun of blisse endeles
In þe blisful world þat heghest es.

God made man to dwell on the earth that he might see and understand the works, and do the will of the Creator, and be proved here, by spiritual conflicts.

Twa worldes here to-gyder may falle
Þat men may erthely worldes calle.
An es þis dale, whar we er wonnand,
Another es man þar-in lyfand;
Þis dale whar we won thurgh, clerkes caldes
Þe mare world, and þe man þe les.
Of þe les world wil I noght speke yhit,
For aftirward I sal speke of it;
Bot of þe mare world yhit wil I mare say,
Ar I pas fra þis matir away;
Þan wil I after shew, als falles,
Skille why men a man world calles.

There are two earthly worlds: 1. the world we live on, 2. man who lives thereon.

The earth is the greater world, man is the lesser.

Þe mare world God wald law on erth sett,
For it suld be til man suggette,
For to serve man, and man noght it;
And þus ordand God, for mans profit.

The world waxes wicked.

Bot now þis world þat man lyfes in,
Waxes swa lither and ful of syn,
And of welthes þat are bot wayn,
Þat many mas þe world þair soverayn,
And gyves þam þar-to al þat þai may,
And serves it bysily, nyght and day,
And mas þam-selfe þe worldes tharlles.

Of worldish men.

Þas men worldesshe men men calles,
For about worldisshe thynges þai here travaile
Ful bysily, þat at þe last sal fayle;
Bot wald þai do half swilk bysines
About goddes[1] of heven, þar al gude es,
Þai suld haf alle þat gude es þare,
Þat never sal faille, bot last ever mare.

By the world that waxes wicked is meant the different kinds of people who herein dwell.

Þe world þat es here, es noght elles,
Bot þe maners of men þat þar-in dwelles;
For þis world men may noght ken,
Bot by þe condicions of þe worldis men.
For what mught men by þe world understand
If na worldishmen war þar-in dwelland?
Alle þas men þat þe world mast dauntes,
Mast bisily þe world here hauntes;
And þas þat þe world serves and loves,
Serves þe devel, as þe buk proves;

The world is the devil's servant, and therefore is he called the prince of the world.

For þe world here, es þe devels servand,
Þat brynges his servauntes til his hand;
Þarfor God him prince of þe world calles,
Þat es of worldismen þat to him falles;
For-þi þis world es perillius to lufe,
By many skilles, as clerkes prove.

It is perilous to love the world, for it is fickle and deceptive.

Þis worlde es fikel and desayvable,
And fals and unsiker and unstabel.
Many men þe world here fraistes,
Bot he is noght wise þat þar-in traystes:

[1] gudes (MS. Harl. 4196).

For þe world laghes on man and smyles,
Bot at þe last it him bygyles;
þarfor I hald þat man noght witty
þat about þe world is over bysy;
For a man may noght Goddes servand be,
Bot he þe maners of þe world fle,
Ne lofe God, bot [he] þe world despise,
For þe godspel says on þis wyse:
Nemo potest duobus dominis ser-
vire, quia aut enim unum odio ha-
bebit et alterum diliget, aut unum
sustinebit et alterum contempnet.
He says "na man may serve rightly
Twa lordes to-gedir, þat er contrary,
For outher he sal þe tane hate
And þe tother luf aftir his state,
Or he sal þe tane of þam mayntene,
And þe tother despyse", þus es ofte sene.
þe world es Goddes enmy by skille, The world is opposed to God.
þat contrarius es to Goddes wille;
And swa er al þat þe world lufes,
Als þe apostel says þus and profes:
Qui vnlt esse amicus hujus mundi,
inimicus dei constituitur.
He says, "wha-so þe werldes frend wil be,
Goddes enemy þan es he;"
þan suld we noght assent þar-to,
Ne nathyng þat lykes til þe world do;
For worldisshe men here God mysprays,
þarfor þe apostel yhit, þus says:
Nolite diligere mundum, nec ea
que sunt in mundo.
"Lufes noght þe world here", says he,
"Ne þat, þat yhe in world may se;"
For al þat in world men tel can,
Es outher yhernyng of þe flesshe of man,
Or yhernyng of eghe, þat may luke,
Or pride of lyfe, als says þe buke:

Omne quod est in mundo, aut
est concupiscencia carnis, aut
concupiscencia oculorum, aut
superbia vite.

What is meant by 'lust of the flesh', 'lust of the eye' and the 'pride of life'.

"Yhernyng of flesshe es a thyng
Þat falles til lust and flesshe lykyng;
Yhernyng of eghe, als I can gese
Falles to worldes rychese;
Pride of lyf þat some in hert kepes,
Falles to honours and worshepes;
Lust and lykyng, þat es flesshely,
Engendres þe syn of lychery;
Worldes riches of grete pryse
Engendres the syn of covatyse;
Honours nuryshes, als men may se,
Vayn glory, vauntyng and vanité.

De Eremita qui quidem sequebatur[1]
mundum a se fugientem, et postea
fugiebat mundum tunc se sequentem;
munde vale! tibi ve! fugiens me, dum
sequerer te, Tu sequeris modo me,
iam respuo despiciens te.

God made the world to serve man, and not man to serve the world.

Sen God made þe world, als says haly writ,
To serve man, and noght man to serve it,
Whar-to serves man þe world þan,
And mas hym þe worldes bondman,
When he may serve God and be fre,
And oute of servage of þe world bę?
Bot wald a man ryght knaw and fele
What þe world es, and byhald it wele,
Hym suld noght lyst, als I understand,
Make þe world na glade sembland,
For lo! what says Barthelmew
Þat spekes of þe world, als I wil shew:

Bartholomew says, the world is like a dull vale full of sorrow, and a place of exile.

He says, "þe world es na thyng elles
Bot an hard exil, in qwilk men duelles,"

[1] This quotation is absent from most of the MSS.

And alswa a dym dulful dale,
Þat es ful of sorow and bale,
1168 And a sted of mykel wrechednes,
Of travail and angers, þat here ay es,
Of payne, of syn and of foly,
Of shens[h]epe and of velany,
1172 Of lettyng and of tarying,
Of frawardnes and of strivyng,
Of filthe and of corrupcion,
Of violence and of oppression,
1176 Of gilry and of falshede,
Of treson, discorde and of drede;
In þe world, he says, noght elles we se
Bot wrechednes and vanité,
1180 Pride and pompe and covatyse,
And vayn sleghtes, and qwayntyse;
Þe world, he says, tyl hym drawes [1]
And tilles, and lufes þam, þat him knawes;
1184 And many he nuyes and fon avayles.
His lufers he desayves and fayles;
His despisers he waytes ay,
Als shadow to tak to his pray;
1188 Bot þa þat wille him folow, he ledes
And þam scornes and taries in his nedes;
Þe whilk a while he here socours,
And þam heghes with ryches and honours.
1192 Bot he waytes to bygille þam at þe laste;
And in to povert agayn þam cast;
Whar-for worldes worshepe may be cald
Noght elles but vanité, and swa I it hald.
1196 And worlisshe riches, how-swa þai come,
I hald noght elles bot filth and fantome.
Þe world has many with vanité filed,
And with pride and pompe þam ofte bygyled,

The world is no support in time of need.

[1] 'Thus þe world draweth in to his route,
All men that to him wol allowte,
And many greveth and fewe availeth·
For his lovyers he deceyveth and failith.' MS. Addit. 11305.

þarfor an haly man, als yhe may here,
Spekes to þe world on þis manere:
O munde immmunde, utinam esses ita immundus, ut me
non tangeres, aut ita mundus, ut
me non coinquinares!
þis es on Inglishe þus to bymene:
"O þou world", he says, "unclene,
Whyn mught þou swa unclen be,[1]
þat suld never mare neghe me,
Or be swa clene and noght vile,
þat þou suld never mare me file."
þe world here who-so wille
Un-to four thinges may liken by skille.[2]

The world is like the sea.

First þe world may lykend be,
Mast properly, unto þe se;
For þe se, aftir þe tydes certayn,
Ebbes and flowes, and falles agayn,
And waxes fulken, thurgh stormes þat blawes,
And castes up and doun many gret wawes;
Swa castes þe world, thurgh favour,
A man to riches and honour.
And fra þat agayn he castes hym doun
Til povert and to tribulacioun.
And þa er þe grete stormes kene
And þe wawes, þat in þe world er sene.

The world is like a wilderness.

Yhit may þe world here þat wyde es,
Be likend to a wildernes,
þat ful of wild bestes es sene,[3]
Als lyons, libardes and wolwes kene,
þat wald worow men bylyve,
And rogg þam in sonder and ryve;
Swa þe world es ful of mysdoers
And of tyrauntes þat men ofte ders,

[1] 'Whyne moght þou swa unclene be.' MS. Harl. 4196.
[2] 'Unto four thinges may lykend be, bi skyll.' MS. Harl. 4196.
[3] 'The whilk is ful of bestes unmylde,
The whilke wol a man strangly and destrye.' MS. Addit 11305.

Þe whilk er bisy, nyght and day,
To nuye men in alle þat þai may.
Þe world alswa may lykend be
Til a forest, in a wilde cuntré,
Þat es ful of thefs and outlawes,
Þat, commonly, til forestes drawes,
Þat hald pases, and robbes and reves
Men of þat þai have, and noght þam leves;
Swa es þe world here þar we duelle,
Ful of thefs, þat er devels of helle;
Þat ay us waytes, and er bysy
To robbe us of our gudes gastly.
Þe world may yhit, als yhe sal here,
Be lykend, on þe fierth manere,
To a feld ful of batailles
Of enemys, þat ilk day men assayles.
For-why here we er on many wyse
Alle umset with sere enmys,
And, speciali, with enmys thre,
Agaynes wham us byhoves armed be:
Þa er þe world, þe fende, our flesshe,
Þat, to assayle us here, er ay freshe;
And þar-for byhoves us, day and nyght,
Whilles we lif here, agayn þam fight.
Þe world, als clerkes understandes,
Agayn us fightes with twa handes,
With þe right hand and þe left; þere twa
May be taken, bathe wele and wa;
Þe right hand es welthe, als I halde,
And þe lefte hand es angre calde;
For þe worlde assayles sum men awhile,
With þe right hand þam to bygile;
Þat es welth, als I sayde before,
Of worldly riches and tresore;
And assayles men, nyght and day,
With þe left hand þam to flay;
Þat es with angre and tribulacion,
And povert, and persecucion,

The world is like a forest.

The world is like a battle-field.

The world fights against us with two hands.

The right hand of the world is wealth, the left is sorrow, poverty, &c.

Þe whilk þer clerkes þe left hand calles
Of þe world, þat ofte sythes falles.
Bot with þe world comes dam fortone,
Þat ayther hand may chaung sone;
For sho turnes about ay hir whele,
Up and doune, als many may fele;
When sho hir whele lates obout ga,
Sho turnes sum doune fra wele to wa,
And, eft agaynward, fra wa to wele;[1]
Þus turnes sho obout oft hir whele,
Þe whilk þir clerkes noght elles calles,
Bot happe or chaunce, þat sodanli falles,
And þat men haldes here noght elles,
Bot welthe and angre in whilk men dwelles.
Þarfor worldly happe es ay in dout,
Whilles dam fortune turnes hir whele about.
Angre men dredes and walde it fle,
And in welthe men wald ay be;
Bot parfit men, þat þair lif right ledes,
Welthe of þe worlde ay flese and dredes;
For welthe drawes a man fra þe right way
Þat ledes til þe blisse þat lastes ay,
Us aght to drede worldly welthe þan
For Saynt Ierom says, þe haly man:
Quanto in virtutibus crescimus,
tanto amplius timere debea-
mus, ne de sublimiori corruamus.
"Þe mare", he says, "þat we wax upright
In welthe, and in worldly myght,
Þe mare we suld have drede in thoght,
Þat we fra þe hegher fal noght;"
Tyl þis acordes þe wordes of Senek,
Þat says þus, als yhe here me spek:
Tunc tibi salubria consilia advoca,
cum tibi alludit prosperitas mundi.

Dame Fortune helps the world to fight against man.

Wealth draws a man from the right way.

Worldly success is to be dreaded.

[1] 'And efte sone from wo in-to much blisse
So þat hir whele hath never lysse. MS. Addit 11305.

Senek on þis maner says:
"When welthe of þe worlde with þe plays,
Sek þan gude consayl wyth-alle."
For welthe mas men in perils falle,
Þan es worldes welthe to drede þarfor,
Als says þe grete clerk, Saynt Gregor:
Si omnis fortuna timenda est, ma-
gis tamen prospera quam adversa.
Saint Gregor says on þis manere:
"If ilka chaunce be to drede here,
Yhit es happe of welthe to drede mare
Þan chaunce of angre," þat smertes sare.
For angres mans lyf clenses, and proves,
And welthes his lif trobles and droves,
And þe saul of man may lightly spille;
For welthes, þat men has here at wille,
Semes tokenyng of endeles pyn.
For lo! what says here Saynt Austyn:
Sanitas continua et rerum habundan-
cia, sunt eterne dampnacionis indicia.
He says, "continuel hele here
And plenté of worldly gudes sere,
Er taknes, als in boke writen es,
Of þe dampnacion þat es endles."
And to þis[1] wordes, þat sum men myspays,
Acordes Saynt Gregor, þat þus says:
Continuus successus temporalium, fu-
ture dampnacionis est indicium.
He says, "continuel happy commyng
Of worldly gudes, es a takenyng
Of þe dampnacion þat sal be,"
At þe last day, with-outen pité.
Bot þe world prayses nan, bot þa anly
Þat til alle worldes welthes er happy,
And on worldly thynges settes þair hert,
And flese ay þe state of povert;

Sorrow cleanses man of sin.

Worldly success is a sign of eternal damnation.

The world praises only the rich.

[1] Þes. MS. Harl. 4196.

Swilk men purchaces and gaders fast,
And fares als þis lyfe suld ay last;
Til þam þe world es favorabel
In alle þat þam thynk profitabel.
Þe world þam lofes, and þai luf it,
And for þai folow þe worldes wit,
And mykel can of worldes qwayntys,
Þe world þam haldes gude men and wys,
Til þam commes gudes here many-falde
To þair dampnacion, als I talde.
For-why til heven may na man come,
Þat folowes þe worlde and worldes wysdome,
Þe quilk, als says wyse men and witty,
Onence God es bot foly.
Sapiencia huius mundi est
stultitia apud Deum.
Many men þe world here fraystes,

The wise man will not trust in the world.

Bot he es noght wyse þat þar-in traistes;
For it ledes a man with wrenkes and wyles,
And at the last it hym bygyles;
Bot he may be called witty and wyse,
Þat þe world can fle and dispise,
And hates þe maners þat it loffes,
And thynkes ay whyder hym byhoves;
And on þis lyfe here traystes noght,
Bot on þe tother settes his thoght.

Man has no sure dwelling place on earth.

For na syker duellyng fynde we here,
Als þe apostel says on þis manere:
Non habemus manentem civitatem,
sed futurum inquirimus.
"Na syker wonnyng-sted here haf we,
Bot we seke ane, þat sal ay be."
For als gestes we here soiourne
Awhile, til we sal hethen tourne;
Þat may fal soner þan som wenes,
For we duelle here als aliens,
To travail, here in þe way, our lyms,
Til our countré-warde, als pilgryms.

Þarfor þe prophet says til God thus,
Als þis vers in þe psauter shewes us:
Ne sileas, quoniam advena ego sum apud
te et peregrinus, sicut omnes patres mei.
"Be noght stille Loverd" says he,
"For I am a commelyng towarde þe,
And pilgrym, als alle my faders was."
Þus may al say þat in þis world sal pas,
Þat es to say, be noght swa stille,
Þat þow ne make me here knaw þi wille;
And swilk comfort to my saul shew swythe,
Þat mught make it in þe glade and blythe:
And say thos to it: "I am thy hele,
For þou ert my pilgrim lele."
Þis world es þe way and passage,
Þurgh whilk lyes our pilgrimage;
By þis way byhoves us al gang,
Bot be we war we ga noght wrang.
For in þis world liggis twa ways,
Als men may fynd þat þam assays;
Þe tane es way of the dede calde,
Þe tother es way of lyfe to halde,
Þe way of dede semes large and eesy,
And þat may lede us over-lightly,
Until þe grysly land of mirknes,
Þar sorow and pyn ever-mare es.
Þe way of lyfe semes narow and harde
Þat ledes us til our contré-warde
Þat es þe kyngdom of heven bright,
Whare we sal won ay in Goddes sight
And Goddes awen sons þan be calde,
If we þe way of lyfe here halde.
Þe life of þis world es ful unstable,
And ful variand and chaungeable
Als es sene in contrarius manere,
By the tymes and vedirs and sesons here.
For þe world and worldis life to-gider,
Chaunges and turnes ofte hider and þider,

Man is a pilgrim.

Of the way of life and death.

The life of this world is full of change and as variable as the seasons.]

And in a state duelles ful short while,
Unnethes, þe space of a myle.
And for-þi þat þe worlde is swa unstable,
Alle þat men sese þar-in es chaungeable;

The changes of the times and seasons are tokens of the variableness of worldly things.

For God ordayns here, als es his wille,
Sere variaunce, for certayn skille,
Of þe tyms and wedirs and sesons,
In taken of þe worldes condicions,
Þat swa unstable er and variande,
Þat ful short while may in a state stande.
For God wille men se, thurgh swilk takens sere,
How unstable þis world es here,
Swa þat men suld mare drede and be abayste,
Over mykel in þe world here to trayste.
Ofte chaunges þe tymes here, als men wele wate,

Of the change in the times and seasons.

Als thus, now es arly, now es late,
Now es day, now es nyght,
Now es myrk, now es light,
And þe wedirs chaunges and þe sesons,
Þus aftir þe worldes condicions;
For now es cald, now es hete,
Now es dry, and now es wete.
For now es snaw, hail or rayn,
And now es fair wedir agayn;
Now es þe wedir bright and shynand,
And now waxes it alle douiland;[1]
Now se we þe lyfte clere and faire,
Now gadirs mystes and cloudes in þe ayre.
Alle þer variance to understande
May be takens of þis world swa variande;
And yhit er þar other ma takens sere
Of þe unstablenes of þis life here.

Of the changes in man's life.

For now es mirthe, now es murnyng,
Now es laghter and now es gretyng;

[1] MS. Harl. reads *domland.*—MS. Lands. 348 has the following reading:
'Now is wedir bryght and schinonde
Now is dym *droubelonde.*'

Now er men wele, now er men wa,
Now es a man frende, now es he faa;
Now es a man light, now es [he] hevy,
Now es he blithe, now es he drery;
Now haf we ioy, now haf we pyn,
Now we wyn, now we tyn;
Now er we ryche, now er we pur,
Now haf we or litel, now pas we mesur;
Now er we bigg, now er we bare, [1]
Now er we hale, now seke and sare;
Now haf we rest and now travail,
Now we fande our force, now we fail;
Now er we smert, now er we slawe,
Now er we heghe, now er we lawe;
Now haf we ynogh, now haf we noght,
Now er we aboven, and now doun broght;
Now haf we pees, now haf we were,
Now eese us a thyng, now fele we it dere;
Now lofe we, now hate, now saghtel, now strife.
Þer er þe maners here of þis lyfe,
Þe whilk er takens of [þe] unstabelnes
Of þis worldis lyfe, þat chaungeable es.
Bot als þis lyfe es ay passand,
Swa es þe worlde, ilk day, apayrand;
For þe world til þe endewarde fast drawes,
Als clerkes by many takens knawes.
Þarfor þe world, þat clerkes sees þus helde,
Es als mykel to say als þe wer elde.[2]

The world is drawing to an end.

Twa erthely worldes til þis life falles,
Als es sayd by-for, þat clerkes calles
Þe mare world of erthe, and þe les;
Ful chaungeable ayther world es.

There are two 'earthly' worlds, a greater and a less.

Þe mare world es þis world brade,
And þe les es man, for wham it es made,

The greater world is the *earth* and the less is *man*.

[1] 'Now es he *riche* and now es he bare.' MS. Addit 11305.

[2] 'Þis world þat we seo þus helde
Is not but þis worldes elde.' MS. Addit 11305.

And als the marc world es round sette,
Swa es þe les world man round for to mette,

Of the breadth and length of man.

For in þe brede of man.es contende,
Als lang space fra þe lang fynger ende
Of þe right hande, with armes outspredande,
Til þe same fynger ende of þe left hande,
Als fra þe haterel oboven þe croun,
Es sene tyl þe sole of þe fot doun.
Þan if a man [h]is armes out sprede
Na mar es þe lengthe, þan þe brede;
Swa may men mette a man with-oute,[1]
Als a compas round aboute.

Man has the shape and likeness of the greater world.

Þos has þe les world þat man es,
Shap of þe mare world and liknes;
Bathe þer worldes, I dar wele say,
Sal fail atte þe last and passe away;
For ay þe mare elde þat þai bere,
Þe mare þai appair and er feblere,
Als men sees þat til þam tas tent,
And þarfor says þus Innocent:
Senuit iam mundus, uterque macrocosmus [et]
major mundus, et microcosmus et minor mun-
dus, et quanto prolixius utriusque senectus producitur,
tanto dexterius utriusque natura turbatur.
He says þus, als in Latyn es talde,
"Ayther worlde now waxes alde,
And þe langer þat þair tym es soght,
And þe elde of ayther of þam forth broght,
Þe mare in malys and febelnes
Þe kynd of ayther trobled es."

Of the great outrage that is seen in both worlds.

Of bathe þer worldes gret outrage we se
In pompe and pride and vanité,
In selcouthe maners and sere degyse
Þat now es used of many wyse,
In worldis havyng and beryng,
In vayn apparail and in weryng,

[1] And so may a man be yemed without.
Right as a compas is. rownd aboute. MS. Addit 11305.

þas tas over mykel vayn costage,
And tornes al until outrage.
1524 For swilk degises and suilk maners,
Als yhong men now hauntes and lers
And ilk day es comonly sen,
Byfor þis tyme ne has noght ben; Of the change in the manners and customs.
1528 For þat somtyme men held velany
Now yhung men haldes curtasy;
And þat som tyme was curtasy cald,
Now wille yhong men velany hald.
1532 Now many men se ofte chaungyng
Of sere maners of gys of clethyng;
For now wers men short and now syde,
Now uses men narow and now wyde;
1536 Som has þair clethyng hyngand als stoles, Of clothing.
Som gas tatird als tatird foles;
Some gase wrynchand to and fra,
And some gas hypand als a ka;
1540 Þus uses yhong men all new gett,
And þe world þai all awkeward sett,
Thurgh swylk uncomly pomp and pryde,
Þat þai schew wheþer þai gang or ryde;
1544 Swa mykell pryde, als now es, I wene,
Was never bifore þis tyme sene,
Of swilk comes þir gyses þat we se.
Bot I dred þat þai may takens be
1548 Of gret hasty myscheves to understand
Þat tyll þe world er nere command.
Þarfore in þair gyses þai sall fall,
Ffor þare-wyth þai wreth God þat sese all;
1552 And his wreth at þe last sall with þam mete,
Wharfore þus says David þe prophete:
Et irritaverunt eum in advencionibus suis,
et multiplicata est in eis ruina,
1556 "And þai styrd God tyll wreth", sais he, The wicked move God to wrath.
In þair new fyndynges of vanité,
And in þam is fallyng many-fald,"
And þat es thurgh pryde þat I of tald;

þis may be said, als þe boke proves
Be þam þat new gyses controves.
Ffor þai do swa þe worlde to plese,
Ffor pryde mare þan for þair eese.
And þa, þat with swylk gyses God greves,
Sall fall in many grevos myscheves;
And for þai will noght be led with skyll,
God lates þam awhile have þair will;
Bot at þe last on þam will sende
Veng[e]aunce, bot if þai þam here amende:
þan most þai bifore schew som taken,
þat God has þam left and forsaken;
And þat may be knawen bi sere gyse.
þarfor says David in þis wyse:
Et dimisi eos secundum desideria cordis eorum,
ibunt in advencionibus suis.
þe prophet David here spekes þus,
In Godes name, als þes verses shewes us.
"I left þam", he says, "out of covert,
After þe yhernynges of þair hert,
In þair fyndynges sall þai ga."
þis may be said be all þa
þat God suffers folow vanytese,
After þair lykyng þat þai chese;
þe whilk tyll þe world mase þam gay,
And turnes þam al fra God oway,
þai sall at þe last fro hethen wende
In þair syn, tyll pyne with-outen ende,
Bot þai swylk vanytese forsake
And amendes here be tyme make;
Yhit has þe world, als men sese and heres,
Ma other contrarius maneres;
For now es vertow turned to vyce,
And play and bourd untyll malice;
Now es devocyon, on som syde,
Turned tyll pomp and to pryde;
Now es wysdom halden foly
And turned intyll trechery.

And foly is halden [now] wysdome,
With proud men and unbowsome.
Now es luff turned tyll lychery,
And ryghtwisnes tyll tyrauntry;
Þus es þis world turned up þat es doune,
Tyll many mans dampnacyoune,
Þe wilk folowes þe worlde swa fraward;
And þarfore þai mon fele payne ful hard,
After þis lyfe þat þai here lede,
And þat aght þam gretly to drede.

Concerning those who call good evil, and evil good.

Bot it semes þat swilk men er wode,
For þai hald gud thing evell and evell gude;
Wa sall þam be, als we here clerkes tell,
Fforwhi Crist says in þe gospell:
Ve vobis qui dicitis malum bonum,
et bonum malum!
He says: "wa till yhow þat says with will
Þat ille es gud and gud es ill;"
Þat es to say þam sall be wa
Þat here mysturnes þair lyfe swa.
Þus es þe world, and þe lyfe þare-in,
Fful of vanyté and of syn.
Bot som men lufes þis lyfe swa mykell
And þe world þat is swa fykell,
Þat þai wald never part þar-fra,
Bot lyfe here ay, if it moght be swa;
For þai luf swa þis worldes vanyté
Þat þai wald never other lyfe suld be.
Þai will noght knaw þe peryls all
Of þis lyfe, ne what after sall fall;
Bot for þai life here in delices sere
Þai think no hevene es bot here,
Bot at þe last, when þair lyfe sall stynt,
Þan sall all ioy be fra þam tynt.
Bot wald a man understand wele
What þis world es and what he sall fele,
When he sall wend fra þis world oway,
Him suld noght lyst, nouther nyght ne day,

Myrthe here ne blythe chere make,
Bot all þe welthes of þis world forsake,
And lyf in penaunce and in povert,
Ffor þe dred þat he suld hafe in hert,
If he wald knaw and trow how hard
Him bihoved suffer afterward;
Bot ogayne þat dred yhit moght he,
Thurgh hope of hert, conforted be,
If he think wele of heven bryght,
Whare he sall won if he here lyf ryght,
Þus may ilk man do and thynk,
In whase hert grace of God may synk.
And he þat will noght thynk of this
And yhernes to have nane other blys,
Bot þis wreched lyfe þat him thynk gude,
He es outher clomsed,[1] or wode;
Or it es a signe of suspecyon
Þat he es in way of dampnacyon.
Here have I shewed on sere manere
Þe condicyons of þis world here,
And of þe worldes unstabilnes,
And of þe maners þat in þe world es;
And now will I pass, forther-mare
To þe thred part and se what es þare;
Ffor þat part now will I begyn
To shew yhow maters þat er within,
Þat specialy spekes, as I sall rede
Of þe ded, and whi it es to drede.

Of death and why it is to be dreaded.

Here bigynnes þe thred part
þat es of þe ded.
Ded es þe mast dred thing þat es
In all þis world, als þe boke witnes;
Ffor here es na qwyk creature lyfand
Þat it ne es for þe ded dredand

[1] For clomsed. Harl. MS. 6923 reads: *glomsede*. MSS. Lands. 348, Addit 22283 read *cursed* for *clomsede*.

And flese þe ded ay whils it may
Bot at þe last he most be þe dedes pray.
Ded, of all þat it comes to, abates
And chaunges all myghtes and states,
No man may wele ogayn it stand;
Whare þat it comes in any land,
Þat es to say, bodily ded,
Ogayns þe whilk no man may help ne red,
Ffor all þat lyf has bihoves it fele,
Þat aght ilk man to knaw wele.
Bot bi þe name of ded may be tane,
And understanden ma dedes þan ane,
Ffor als þir clerkes fyndes writen and redes,
Thre maners of dedes er þat men dredes.
Ane es bodily ded, þat thurgh kynd es,
Ane other gastely, þe thred endeles.
Bodily ded, þat is kyndely,
Es twynyng betwene þe saule and þe body;
And þat ded es full bytter and hard,
More kinds of death than one.
Of whilk I sall schew yhow afterward.
Gastely ded es twynyng thurgh synne,
Bitwene God and man saule within;
Ffor als þe saule es lyf of þe body,
Swa þe lyfe of þe saule es God allmyghty;
And als þe body, with-outen dout,
Of bodily death.
Es ded when þe saule es passed out,
Þe saule of man es ded ryght swa.
When God es departed þarefra;
For whare syn es, es þe devell of hell,
Of spiritual death.
And þare whare þai er, will God noght dwell.
For dedely syn and þe devell and he
In a stede may noght to-gyder be;
Þarfor when þe saule es wounded with syn,
God passes out, and þe fende gase in;
The devil passes into the souls of the sinful.
Þan es þe saule onence God ded,
Ay whils syn and þe devell dwelles in þat stede;
And als þe body may be slayne
Thurgh wapen þat men may ordayne,

Swa es þe saule slane thurgh syn;
Wharfor God and it bihoves twyn.
Þan es gastly ded to dred wele mare,
Þan bodily ded þat nane will spare,
In-als-mykell as þe saule namely
Es better and mare worthy þan þe body;
Ffor all-if þe saule thurgh syn be dede
Fra God allmyghty þat es the hede,
Yhit may it ay lyf and be pyned,
Bot þe body es dedly here thurgh kynde.
Of bodily ded es no gayn-turnyng,
Ffor of erthly lyf it es endyng,
And ryght entré and way it es
Till ioy or payn þat es endeles.
Yhit if þe saule thurgh syn be slayne.
It may thurgh grace qwyken ogayne,
And þe gastly woundes of syn
Thurgh penaunce may be heled within;
Ffor all-if God be ryghtwyse and myghty

God is full of mercy and desires not the death of the sinner.

He es full of gudenes and of mercy,
And to turne him tyll man mare redy es he
Þan any man till him will be;
For all-if he þe dede of body that greves
Ordaynd til alle þat here lyfes,
Þe dede of saul wild noght he
Of na man þogh he synful be;
For þe life of þe saule mare him pays
Þan þe dede, for þus him-self says:
Nolo mortem peccatoris, sed ut magis convertatur et vivat.
"I wille noght þe ded of synful man,
Bot þat he may be turned and lyf þan;"
Þan may þe synful þat his saul has slayn
Be turned þurgh grace, and lyf ogayn.

Of endless death.

Endles dede es þe dede of helle
That es mast bitter and mast felle.

Hell is a horrible place.

Helle es halden a full hidos stede,
Þe whilk es full of endeles dede,

And of paynes and sorow þat never sal blyn,
And yhit may nan dighe þat es þar-in;
Bot if þai mught dighe, als body here may,
Of alle sorow þan delyverd war þay;
Þai sal fele þar many a ded brayde,
Bot þai sal ay lyf þar-with, als I sayde;
For þe ded of helle es a lif ay dyand,
And a ded þat es ay lifand.
Dede of helle es noght elles to say,
Bot payns and sorow þat sal last ay,
Þe whilk saules sal fele with-outen ende,
Þat tille þat grisely sted sal wende.
Of þis ded may men rede and luke
Ynoghe, in þe sexte part of þis buke,
Þat spekes of þe payns of helle;
Þarfor here-on I wille na langer duelle,
Bot of bodily dede I wille spek mare
Þat es entré and way, als I sayd are,
Til lyf or ded þat has nan hende,
Als es aftirward in þis part contende.
Bodily dede here dredes ful many,
For twa skilles principaly;
Ane es for þe payne þat a man has,
When þe dede hym assayls, and slas.
Þe tother es, for when his lif sal here ende,
He what never whider he sal wende;
For in dout he es and uncertayn
Whether he sal til ioy or payn;
Bot how-swa he sal aftir fare,
Þe payn of dede here es bitter and sare;
Þarfor ilk man þat of dede has mynde
Dredes gretely þe dede here thurgh kynde;
And swa it semed, als says þe boke
Þat Crist did in manhede þat he toke,
For he byfor, ar he deyghed on þe rode,
For drede of dede he swet blode;
For he wyst, ar he til þe dede suld passe,
What þe payn of þe dede wasse,

Of bodily death

Death is dreadful for two reasons.

The pain of death is bitter and sore.

Þan may we þarby trow right wele
Þat þe payn of þe dede es hard to fele.

Death parts all things.

Of þe dede here men may thynk wonder,
For alle thyng it brestes in sonder,
Als it sculkes[1] by diverse ways;
Þarfor þe haly man in boke þus says:
Mors omnia
Solvit.
"Þe dede", he says, "louses alle thyng
And of ilk mans lif mas endyng."
Þe dede es swa sutil and pryvé,
Þat na man may it properly se;

No man knows what death is.

And for-þy þat na man may se it,
Þarfor may na man knaw ne witt,
Ne ymagyn thurgh witte what it es,
Ne what shappe it has and lyknes.
Bot what dede es properly to say,
Wha-swa wille, shortly wite he may.

Death is a separation between soul and body.

Dede es noght elles to telle shortly,[2]
Bot a partyng of þe saul and body,
Als I byfor aparty sayde.
Þis may be calde þe dedis brayde,
And a privacion of þe life,
When it partes fra þe body in strife.
And als yhe may se and wate wele,
Þat myrknes kyndly es noght to fele,
Bot overalle whar na light es
Þar es properly myrknes;
Right swa þe dede es noght elles
Bot a pryvyng of lyf, als clerkes telles;
For whar-swa-ever þe lyf fayles
Þar es þe dede þat þan assayles.
Þus þe dede þat men dredes mast,
When þe lyf fayles men byhoves tast.

[1] stalkes (Lands. MS. 348).
[2] Dethe is nothing elles to telle sothly,
Bot a departyng of the soule and the body. (MS. Addit 11305.)

Of the four special reasons why death is feared.

Four skilles I fynd writen in som stede,
Why men suld specialy drede þe dede:

I. The death struggle is full of pain.

An es for þe dede stoure swa felle
Þat es mare payne þan man can telle,
Þe whilk ilk man sal fele with-in,
When þe body and þe saule salle twyn.

II. Devils appear to the dying man (p. 61, l. 2216).

Another es for þe sight þat he sal se
Of devels, þat about hym þan sal be.

III. Man will have to yield account of the whole of his life.

Þe thred es for þe acount þat he sal yheld
Of alle his lyf, of yhouthe and elde.

IV. Man is uncertain of his future state.

Þe ferth es, for he es uncertayne
Whether he sal wend til ioy or payne;
Wha-swa wil of þer four take hede,
Hym aght gretely here þe dede to drede.
Of twa of þere four, byfore I spake,
Now wil I other twa til þam take;
For of twa I spak first generaly,
Now I wille with other twa þam specify.

Of the death conflict.

First aght men drede þe ded in hert,
For þe payn of þe dede þat es swa smert,
Þat es þe hard stour at þe last ende,
When þe saule sal fra þe body wende;
A doleful partyng es þat to telle,
For þai luf ay togyder to duelle;
Nouther of þam wald other forga
Swa mykel lof es bytwen þam twa;
And þe mare þat twa togyder lufes,
Als a man and his wyfe oft pruves,
Þe mare sorow and murnyng
Byhoves be at þair departyng.

Four reasons why soul and body are so closely united.

Bot þe body and þe saul with þe lyfe
Lufes mare samen þan man and hys wyfe,
Whether þai be in gude way or ille,
And þat es for many sere skylle.

First reason.

A skylle es, als yhe sal now se,
Why þai wald ay togyder be;
For-þy þat God, als says haly writ,
First body and saul togyder knyt;

Second reason.

Another for the tane may noght do
Bot if þe tother help þar-to;

Third reason.

Þe thred for þai bathe togider sal come
Byfor God at þe day of dome;

Fourth reason.

Þe ferthe, for when þai er comen theder,
Þai sal ay after duel togider.
Þarfor þair payne and sorow es mare
When þe tane sal fra þe tother fare.

Death spares none.

Þis twynnyng may be cald þe dede,
Þat fleyghes about fra sted til stede,
Thurgh alle landes, fer and nere,
And spares nan of wham he has powere,
For prayer ne gyfte þat men may gyfe.
Whare he comes he lattes nane lyfe,
Ne for luf ne awe er nane sparde;
For þe dede til na man tas rewarde,
Ne riche ne pover he spars, hegh ne law,
Þat he ne þe lyf wil fra þam draw,
Þe dede has mercy of na wight,
Als Saynt Bernard þus shewes right:
Non miseretur mors inopie,
non reveretur diviciis, non sa-
piencie, non moribus,
non etati.

Death has no respect for poverty or riches, wisdom, age or good manners.

He says "þe dede of povert na mercy has,
Ne to ryches ne[1] reward tas,
Ne til wysdom þat wyse men schewes,
Ne til elde of man ne til gude thewes."
Dede wil na frendshepe do ne favour,
Ne reverence til kyng ne til emperour,
Ne til pape, ne til bisshope, ne na prelate,
Ne til nan other man of heghe estate,
Ne til na religiouse, ne til na seculere,
For dede over al men has powere.
And thurgh þe dede hand al sal pas,
Als Salamon says, þat wyse was:
Communionem
mortis scito.

[1] No (MS. Harl. 4196).

"Knaw þow," he says, þat þe dede es
Comon to al men, bathe mare and les."
Þus sal dede visite ilk man,
And yhit na man discryve it can,
For here lyves nan, under hevenryke,
Þat can telle til what þe ded es lyke.
Bot þe payn of dede þat al sal fele
A philosopher þus discrived wele;
For he lykend mans lyf til a tre
Þat war growand, if it swa mught be,
Thurgh a mans hert and swa shuld sprynge,
Þat obout war lapped with þe hert stryngе,
And þe croppe out at his mouth mught[1] shote,
And to ilka ioynt war fested a rote;
And ilka vayne of þe mans body
Had a rote festend fast þarby,
And in ilka taa and fynger of hand
War a rote fra þat tre growand;
And ilka lym on ilka syde
With rotes of þat tre war occupyde;
Yf þat tre war tite pulled oute
At a titte with al þe rotes oboute,
Þe rotes suld þan rayse þar-with
Ilka vayn and ilka synoghe and lith.
A mare payne couthe na man in hert cast
Þan þis war, als lang als it suld last.
And yhit halde I þe payne of dede mare
And mare strang and hard, þan þis payn ware;
Þos a philosopher when he lyfed,
Þe payn of þe dede here discrived.
Þarfor ilk man, als I byfor sayde,
Aght to drede þe bitter dedes brayde,
For bathe gode and ille sal it taste;
Bot ille men aght drede it maste,
For dred of ded mast pyns wythin
A man þat here es ful of syn,
Þarfor þe prophet says in a stede,
And spekes þus un-til þe dede:

Of the pain of death and what it is like.

Bad men fear death most.

[1] The MS. reads: 'And þe croppe out at his *mught mught* shote'.

O mors quam amara memoria
tua homini iniusto.
"O þou grysely dede," says he,
"Ful bitter es þe mynde of þe,
Until þe synful man" namly,
Þat for his syn es paynworthy;
Þarfor me thynk he es unsleghe
Þat mas hym noght here redy to deghe;
Death comes unexpectedly. For þe dede es privy and sodayne,
And þe tyme of his commyng uncertayne.
A man for certayne sal dighe at þe last,
For his lyf is noght bot als a wynd blast,
Bot he wayte never what tyme ne whan;
For swa certayne es here na man
Þat can þe tyme of þe dede forluke,
Forþi says Saynt Bernard in a boke:
Quid in rebus humanis cercius est
morte; quid incercius hora mortis invenitur.
He says: "What es til man mare certayn
Þan þe dede es þat es swa sodayn;
And what es mare uncertayn thyng,
Þan es þe tyme of the dede commyng",
Alswa say nathyng þat may be [1];
Þan may na man here þe dede fle.
Man should prepare himself for death. Þarfor a man hym suld redy make,
Byfor ar þe dede com hym to take,
And put hym byfor and ded byhynde,
Swa þat ded may hym redy fynde;
Þarfor Saynt Austyn þe haly man
Says þus, als I shew yhow can:
Nescis qua hora veniat mors,
semper vigila, ut, quod nescis quando
veniat, paratum te inveniat
cum venerit, et adhoc forte
nescis quando veniat, ut semper
sis paratus.
"Man þan knawes noght," says he,
"What tyme þe dedes comyng sal be;

[1] *Als wha* say na thyng that may be. (MS. Harl. 6923.)

Wake ay als þou had na knawyng
Watch for death.
Of þe tyme of dedys commyng,
Þat þe dede may fynd þe, when it sal com,
Ay redy til God and bugh[so]m;
And to þat perchaunce knaw þou ne may
Þe commyng, for þou shuld be redy ay."
Þan byhoved us our lyf swa cast
Als ilk day of our lif war þe last;
And ilk day be redy and lif wele,
Als we suld ilk day þe ded fele,
And byde noght til þe dede us vyset,
Þarfor þos says Saynt Austyn yhet:
Latet ultimus dies, ut observentur
omnes dies, sero parantur reme-
dia cum mortis imminent
pericula.
"Þe last day of man is hyd", he says,
Man's last day is hidden from him.
"For he shuld kepe wele al þe other dayes,
For over late men ordayns remedy,
When perels of dede comes sodanly."
For if a man þat unredy es,
Be tane with dede in his wykednes,
Turne agayne þan may he noght
For to amend þat he has myswroght;
In þat state, þat he es in tane,
He sal be demed when he es gane;
Wharfor a man for drede of lettyng
Shuld noght abyde þe dedes commyng,
Bot make hym redy, ar he fel harde,
And kepe hym ay wele aftirwarde,
For when þe dede es at þe yhate,
Þan es he warned over late.
Þe dede fra a man his mynd reves
Death deprives man of his mind.
And na kyndely witte with hym leves,
For þan sal he fele swilk payn and drede,
Þat he ne may thynk of na mysdede,
Bot of his payn and of noght elles,
Als þis grete clerk Saynt Austyn telles:

Tymor mortis totam animam sibi vendicat,
ut nec de peccatis tunc libeat cogitare.

The dread of death occupies the soul wholly.

Þe drede of þe ded when it fayles a man,
Chalanges al þe saul tyl it þan;
Swa þat hym liste þan haf na thoght
Of his synnes þat he here has wroght.
Þan folowes þat man na wys rede
Þat abydes þe commyng of þe dede,
And hastes hym noght to clense hym sone
Of al his syns þat [he] has done;
For when þe dede comes til a man
It es over late to bygyn þan;
Bot I rede a man he amend hym here,
Or þe dede come, or his messangere;[1]
For if he wille swa byfor be war.

Sickness is death's messenger.

Þe dede þan wele les drede hym þar;
His messangere may be called sekenes,
Þat comes byfor als ofte felled es;
For sekenes ofte a man swa pynes

The dying man loses his senses.

Þat thurgh þat payn hys mynd he tynes,
For he may þan thynk on noght elles
Bot of þe payn þat with hym duelles.
Bot when þe ded comes aftirward
And hym byhoves fele mare hard,
Þan sal he be in swylk drede sette,
Þat he sal God and hymself forget,
And þat es skylle for he wil noght,
Whyles he has hele, haf God in thoght,
Þarfor he sal þan his mynde tyne
And þarfor þus says Saynt Austyne:
Hac animaversione percutitur
peccator, ut moriens obliviscatur
sui, qui dum viveret oblitus
est Dei.
"Þe synful", he says, als es writen,
"With pyne of þe dede es smyten,
Þat he thurgh payn þat him byhoves drighe,
Hym-self forgetis when he sal dighe,

[1] The MS. reads *mensangere.*

þat whylles he mught lif here bodyly,
Forgatte his God þat es almyghty."
Many synful has here na grace
To haf tyme of repentance, ne space;
For whiles þai lyf þai have na mynde
Of God, bot forgettes hym, als ay unkynde.
Me thyn[k] þan þat it es skille and right
þat thurgh dede God reve þam mynd and myght;
þus sal þai dyghe and heven blis tyne
And be putted til endeles pyne,
þat til God here er swa uncurtays,
þarfor David in þe psauter says:
Vos sicut homines moriemini, et
sicut unus de principibus cadetis.
He says: "Als men yhe sal digh alle,
And als ane of þe princes yhe sal falle."
þat es yhe sal dighe of þe same manere,
Als men dighes in þis world here,
And als þe spyrites þat fra heven felle,
Be casten don intille helle.
þarfor til a man it war wysdome
To repente hym or þe dede come,
And haf God in mynde whyles he lyfes here,
Als þe prophet biddes on þis manere:
Memento creatoris tui antequam ve-
niat tempus visitacionis sue.
"Thynk," he says, "and haf in þi thoght
Of hym þat made þe first of noght,
Whilles þou lyffes, ar þe tyme sal be,
When he with þe dede sal viset þe."
For when dede here assayles a man
He may noght thynk wele on God þan,
For þe dede his mynde away þan brekes,
And þarfor David þos til God spekes:
Quoniam non est in morte
qui memor sit tui.
"Lord", he says, "þat man es noght
In dede, þat of þe here has thoght."

Many men never think of God.

'Ye shall die as one of the princes.'

'Think of God while thou livest.'

Bot men may understand hereby
Dede of saule thurgh syn namly;
For he þat has ay God in thoght,
In dede of saul semes he noght;
And he þat of God es myndles
It semes þat he in saul dede es.
God visites us in ilka stede

Of the tokens of death.

Whare we may fele takens of dede,
And if we couthe understand wele,
Ilk day we may takens of dede fele;
Þarfor me thynk alle this lif here semes
Mar dede þan lyf, þus wysmen demes;
For þe boke says, als it beres wyttenes,
Þat a man, when he first borne es,
Bygynnes towarde þe dede to drawe
And feles here many a dede thraw,
Als sere yvels and angers when þai byfalle,
Þat men may þe dede thrawes calle,
And other perils and quathes many,
Þat commes to men ofte sodanly.
Þan es our birthe here bygynnyng
Of þe dede þat es our endyng;
For ay þe mare þat we wax alde
Þe mare our lif may be ded talde.
Þarfor whylles we er here lyffand
Ilk day er we þos dighand;

Life is but death.

Þan semes our lyf nathyng elles
Bot als a dede, als þe bok telles,
And til other lyf wyn we noght,
Til þe dede þis life til ende haf broght;
Bot when þe dede has made ende,
Þan wate we never whyder we sal wende;
Wether we sal til wele or wa,
Bot til þe tane byhoves us ga.
For-why til gude men þe dede es way
Til þe blisse of heven þat lastes ay,
And til ille men yhate and entree
Til þe pyn of helle þat ay sal be;

Þarfor David, þat was swa haly,
Spekes þus til God almyghty:
Qui exaltas me de portis mortis, ut an-
nunciem omnes laudaciones tuas, in portis filie Syon.
"Loverd", says David, "þou ert he
Þat fra þe yhates of dede liftes me,
Þat I may shew over alle thynges
Specialy alle þi lovynges,
In þe yhates of doghter Syon."
Þat, als clerkes says þat can þar-on,
The gates of the daughter of Sion denote Holy Church.
Es haly kyrk þat God first ches,
Thurgh whilk men commes to þe sight of pes.
By þe yhates of dede, als men may se,
The gates of death denote the death of Hell.
Þe dede of helle may understanden be
Fra wilk God liftes us day and nyght,
To shewe his lovynges with alle our myght,
And to serve hym and his werkes to wyrk
In stedfast trouthe of haly kyrk,
Swa þat we may afterwarde wende
Til þe sight of pees þat has nan ende.
Heghe in heven es þat fair sight,
Þat alle sal se þat here lyves ryght;
Bot alle þat sal com til þat stede
Byhoves passe hethen thurgh bodily dede;
For þat dede to þam es noght ille
Þat lyffes here after Goddes wille,
And in þat lif stedfastly duelles;
And þarfor Saynt Austyn þus telles:
Mala mors putanda non est quam
bona vita precessit, neque enim facit
malam mortem, nisi quod sequitur
ipsam mortem.
He says: "na man ille dede shuld wene
Death preceded by a good life, is not to be dreaded.
Þar, whar gude lyf byfor has bene;
For nathyng mas ille dede to tast,
Bot þat þat folows þe dede mast",
Þat es dedely dedes þat sum wille do,
And yhit says Sayn[t] Austyn þos parto:

Non potest male mori qui bene vixit,
Et vix bene moritur qui male vixit.

Good men do not fear death.

He says: "he may noght ille dede fele
Þat in Goddes laghe has lyfed wele;
And unnethes may men se by skille,
Þat he dyghes wele þat hafes lyfed ille."
Bot he þat hates þis lyfes lykyng
Thar noght drede þe dedes commyng;
For aftir his dede na payn hym ders,
Þarfor says Caton þus in a vers:
Non metuit mortem,
qui sit contempnere vitam.
He says: "he þat þis lif despyse
Thar dred þe dede here on na wyse;"
Swa did martirs þat þe dede soght,[1]
For by þis lyf sette þai right noght;

Holy men desire to die.

And other halymen yherned to dyghe
For to be with God in heven hyghe,
Als þe boke of þair lyfes shewes us,
And swa did Saynt Paul þat says þus:
Cupio dissolvi
et esse cum Cristo.
"I yhern", he says. "be loused away
Fra þis life and be with Crist ay."
Haly men thogh[t] þis lyf bot wast,
Þarfor þair yhernyng til God was mast;
And for-þi þat þam thoght alle þis lyfe
Noght bot travail, angre, and strife,
Þai yherned þe ende of þair lyf days,
And þarfor þe haly man þos says:
Melius est dies mortis
quam dies nativitatis.

The day of death is better than the day of one's birth.

He says: "better es þe day of dede
Þan þe day of burthe", and mare standes in stede.
For-why a gude man dighes to wend to rest,
Whare his lyf sal be alther-best

[1] The MS. reads *soghot*.

2196 When þe saul fra þe body swippes,
Als Saynt Johan says in þe Appocalippes:
Beati mortui qui in domino
moriuntur.
2200 "Blessed be alle þas þat in body
Dighes here in God alle-myghty."

> 'Blessed are those who die in the Lord.'

For þas þat men sese in gude lyfe ende
Dighes in God, and þai sal wende
2204 Til þe blisse of heven þat es swa hyghe,
Wele es hym þan þat swa may dighe.
Bot alle-yf haly men may digh wele,
Yhit þe payn of dede byhoves þam fele,
2208 Þat es mare þan man can ymagyn
When þe body and þe saule sal twyn;
Þe wilk þam aght dred aparty,
Thurgh manskynd or elles war ferly:
2212 For sen Crist, als I sayd befor, had dred
Of the ded, thurgh kynd of his manhed,
Þan aght ilkman, bathe mare and les,
Drede þe dede here þat swa bitter es.
2216 Þe secund skil, als byfor es redde,
Why þe dede es swa gretely drede,
Es for þe grisly syght of fendes
Þat a man sal se when his lyf endes.

> The second reason why death is feared (see p. 51, l. 1824.)

2220 For when þe lyf sal pas fra a man
Devels sal gadir obout hym þan,
To ravissche þe saul with þam away
Tyl pyne of helle, if þai may.

> Devils shall gather about the dying man.

2224 Als wode lyons þai sal þan fare
And raumpe on hym, and skoul, and stare,
And grymly gryn on hym and blere,
And hydus braydes mak hym to fere;
2228 Þai sal fande at his last endyng
Hym in-to wanhope for to bring,
Thurgh thretynges þat þai sal mak,
And thurgh þe ferdnes þat he sal tak.
2232 Ful hydus sightes þai sal shew hym
Þat his chere sal make grisly and grym.

Þat sight he sal se with gastly eghe
With payn of dede þat he most dreghe.
Here-of þe prophet Ieremy
Spekes þus in his prophecy:
Omnes inimici eius apprehenderunt
eum inter angustias.
He says: "omang his grete anguys
Hym þai sal tak al hys enmys."
Na vonder es if þe devels com þan
In þe ende obout a synful man,

How the devil came to St. Martin when he was dying.

For to flay hym and tempte and pyn,
When þe devel com to Saynt Martyn
In þe tyme of dede at his last day
Hym for to tempte and for to flay:

St. Bernard and the devil.

And in þe life of Saynt Bernard
We rede þat when he drogh til dedeward,
Þat þe devel þat es grisely and grym,
Til hym come and asked hym,
By what skille he wald, and bi [1] what ryght
Chalange þe kyngdom of heven bright;
Þan answerd Bernard þus mekely,
And sayd: "I knaw þat I am unworthy,
Thurgh myn-awen desert, to haf it
When I sal out of þis world flit.
Bot my Lorde Ihesu Crist ful of myght,
Þat it has and weldes thurgh doble ryght,
Thurgh right of his faders heritage,
And alswa for our grete avauntage,
Thurgh right of hys hard passion,
Þat he tholed for our raunson,
Þe ta right frely he graunted me,
And þe tother til hym-self held he;
Of was gyfte I chala[n]ge it by skille,
Als þe lagh of his mercy wille."
And when þe devel herd hym þus say,
Alle skomfit he vanyst oway;
And þe halyman when þis was done
Torned ogayne til hym-self sone,

[1] The MS. reads *be*.

And he yhelded þe gast to God and dyghed,
And swa þe saul til heven flyghed.
And yhit es mare wonder to telle
Þat God wald suffer þe devel of helle,
Apere til hymself þat es of myght mast,
When he suld dygh and yheld þe gast,
Als docturs says of haly writ,
In bukes thurgh whilk men may knaw it.
Þan semes it wele þat God wil þus
Suffer þe devel apere til us
In tyme of dede, at our last ende,
When we sal out of þis world wende,
Sen haly men þat here liffed right
Mught noght dygh with-outen þat sight,
Ne godys moder þat he loffed mare,
Wald noght fra þat syght spare,
Bot þat he graunted at hir askyng
Þat in þe tyme of hir passyng
Þai suld na power haf hir to dere,
Ne þat þe syght of þam shuld hir fere;
And yhit sen God hymself spard noght,
For at his dede þe devel til hym soght
In his manhede for swa þan he walde,
Als men says þat er gret clerkes calde.
Þan er we certayn, with-outen were
Þat at our last ende þai sal apere.
Bot a gret payne þan til us sal þis be
Þe sight of þam when we þam se;
For þai er swa grisely, als says þe buke,
And swa blak and foule on to loke,
Þat al þe men here of mydlerd
Of þat sight mught be aferd;
For al þe men here of þis lyfe
Swa grysely a sight couth noght descryfe,
Ne thurgh wyt ymagyn ne deme,
Als þai sal in tyme of dede seme,
Ne swa sleygh payntur never nan was,
Þogh his sleght mught alle other pas,

Good men as wel as bad, will be tempted by devils on their deathbed.

Of the horrible appearance of the devils that are seen by the dying man.

Þat couthe ymagyn of þair gryslynes
Or paynt a poynt aftir þair liknes;

The devil does not appear in his proper form to living men.

For in þis lif here may na man
Se þam in þe fourme þat þai haf þan,
For if þai had swa large powere,
In swilk forme to shew þam here,
Out of witte þan þai shuld men flay,
Swa orrible and swa foul er þai;
For-why swa hardy man here es nane
Ne þat ever was liffand in flesshe and bane,
Þat saghe a devel in his fygur right,
Þat he ne for ferdnes of þat sight
Shuld dighe, or at þe leste tyn his witt,
Als son after als he had sene it;
Bot in swilk fourme, als I undirstand,
Þai shew þam til na man liffand,
Bot til þam til wham þe dede es nere;
For God has restreyned þai[r] powere
Þat þai may na man tempte ne greve,
Ferrer forthe, þan þai hafe leve.
Bot when þe ded assaylles a man,
In þe foulest figure þai apere þan;
Þarfor aght ilk man dredand be
Agayne þe tyme when he sal þam se.

The devils are horribly disfigured through sin.

Bot I wille shew yhow aparty
Why þai er swa foul and grisly,
For sum tyme þai war bright angels,
Als þa er þat now in heven duels,
Fra þat blisful place thurgh syn þai felle,
And bycome þan foule devels of helle,
And horribely defygurd, thurgh syn
Þat þai war wyth-fild and hardened þarin.
For warne syn war þai had ay bene
Bright aungels, als þai war first sene;
And now er þai made foule and ugly
Thurgh fylyng of þair syn anly,

Sin is more horrible than any devil.

Þan es syn mar foule and wlatsome,
Þan any devel þat out of helle may come;

For a thyng es fouler þat may file,
þan þe thyng þat it fyles, and mare vile,
þarfor says clerkes of grete cunnyng,
þat syn es swa foule and swa grisly thyng,
þat if a man mught properly se his syn
In þe kynd lyknes þat it falles be in,
He shuld for ferdnes titter it fle
þan any devel þat he mught se;
Here may men se and undirstande
How foul es syn and how fylande:
Bot men sese noght ne knawes what it es,
þarfor men dredes it wele þe les.
Bot if a synful myght se with-oute
How foul þe syn es, þat he bers oboute,
He suld never make ioy ne haf lykyng,
Until he war delyverd of þat foul thyng.
Sen[1] þe devel þus has tane his uglines
Of þe filth of syn, þat swa filand es,
þan aght þe saul of synful with-in
Be ful foule þat es alle slotered in syn;
þarfor a man aght, war-so he wendes,
Mare drede syn þan þe syght of fendes,
þat sal aper til hym at his dede day.
Bot his syn he sal se fouler þan þay,
Of whilk he wald noght hym right shrife.
Ne repent hym here in his lyfe.
þe thred skill til our undirstandyng
Why us aght drede þe dede commyng,
Es for þe acont ful strayt and harde,
Of alle our lif þat has bene frawarde,
þat us byhoves yheld in God sight
Als wele of wrang als of right,
Of alle thyng þat ever we wroght,
In werk, in worde, in wille, in thoght,
And of alle þe tymes þat passes oway
Fra our bygynnyng to our last day,
Alle sal þan be shewed and sene,
Bathe gude and ille, foul and clene,

Could we see sin we should flee from it faster than from any devil.

Sin is the cause of the devil's ugliness.

The third 'skill' why death is feared, is the strict account which we shall have to give of the whole of our lives.

[1] The MS. reads *Syn*.

Devils and angels shall rehearse the events of our lives.

And be reherced als þe buke telles,
Bytwene grysely fendes and bright angels;
Þai sal dispute þan of our life
With grete discorde and grete strife.
Þe aungels sal reherce þe gude,
And þe devels þe yvel, with grete mude.[1]
Alle þe werkes þat we here haf wroght,
Bytwene þam þan sal be out soght,
And ilka thoght and ilka wille,
Als wele þe gude als þe ille;
And ilka worde þat spoken haf we
Gude or ille whether þai be,
Alle sal be reherced, als I sayde are.

They shall spare none.

Bytwen þam þan þai sal nan spare,
Bot anly syn þat es wele clensed here,
And gude dede þat es don on right manere.
Þan sal we bathe here and se
Al þe privetese þat ever did we,
Þarfor says God in þe godspelle,
On þis manere, als I wille yow telle:
Nichil est opertum quod non reveletur, nec occultum quod non sciatur.

Nothing shall be left 'undiscussed'.

Nathyng here swa covered and hydde,
Þat sal noght þan be shewed and kydde,
Ne swa privé es nathyng þat touches man,
Þat sal noght be knawen þan.
Þan most us abyde, we may noght fle,
Until al our lyf examynd be,
And alle our dedys, bathe gude and ille,
Be discussed, after Goddes wille;
Þan sal we se alle our syn halely
And what we er for our syn worthy.
And alle our dedys þat gud here semed
Þan sal be discussed haly and demed,
Swa þat we may se and knaw by sight,
Whether we þam dide wrang or ryght;
And wilk was don on wrang manere,
And wilk we dyd parfitely here;

[1] 'eger mode' (MS. Harl. 6923).

þarfor Seynt Anselme, als þe buke shewes us,
Spekes tyl þe saul and says þus:
"Wreched saul," he says, "what may thou say
When þou partes fra þe body away,

What may the wretched soul say when it parts from the body.

þan þe byhoves acounte yhelde
Of alle þi lyf of youthe and elde,
How þow has here led þi lyfe,
And how þow has spendyd þi wittes fife,
Fra þe first day þat [þou] had witte
Unto þe last day þow shuld hethen flite.
þan sal walaway be þi sang,
For þou here dispended þi tym wrang,
Bathe in werk and word, in thogh[t] and wille,
And yhit when þou mught helpe, þou held the stille.
þou has done many synful dede,
To greve God þou had na drede;
Bot when you sese alle þi trespas
þan sal þou say 'allas! allas!'
When alle þi life sal be thurgh soght
Unto þe lest thyng, þat ever þou wroght,
Whether þou be lered or þou be lewed;
þi syns sal þan be many shewed,
þat þow has done here in þe life
Of whilk þou couthe þe never shrife;

The soul will see all its sins that have been left unshriven.

And þa sal be shewed byfor þe
Ful foule and ugly syns to se,
Of whilk þou sal haf mare drede and awe,
þan of þa þat þou mught here knawe.
Yhit som dedys þat þe thoght here don wele
þou sal þan se foul syns and fele,
þan byhoves þe resayve sone
Efter þi werkes þat þou has done;
þat es to say outher ioy or payne,
þou may on nawyse be þar agayne."
þos sal ilk man, at his endyng,
Be putted til an hard rekenyng,
And be aresoned, als right es
Of alle his mysdedys, mare and les.

Some deeds that we thought good, will appear sinful.

Na syn þan unrekend sal be,
þogh it war never swa privé.

Our good deeds will seem few in comparison with our evil ones.

Alle þe gud dedys þat we haf done
Onence our syns sal þan sem fone;
And yhit we er unsyker in thoght
Wether þai sal be alowed or noght;

The three 'skilles' why man should not place confidence in good deeds.

For I fynd wryten thre skills why
þat na man may trayste sikerly
In hys gude dedys, þat he dus here.
þir thre skils er gude to lere,
Ane es forthy þat alle thynges

I. Good deeds only spring from God.

þat gude er, anly of God springes,
þan er al gude dedys þat er wroght
Goddes awen dedys and ours noght;
Bot alle our syns þat may be knawen,
Commes of our-selven þa er our-awen,
For-why, with-outen God we syn sone,
Bot na gude with-outen God es done.

II. We are always more ready to sin than to do what is right.

Another skille es alswa forþi,
þat we er comonly mare redy
An hondreth sythes here for to syn,
þan anes a gude dede for to bygyn;
Swa may we ay rekken and rede
An hondreth syns agayne a gude dede.

III. Good deeds are often performed wrongly.

þe thred skille es þis to shew omang,
For our gude dedys er ofte done wrang,
Noght of right maner als þai suld be
Or parchaunce done oute of charité.
Alle our syns er here certayne
And by right and skille er worthy payne:
Bot for our gude dedys certanly
We wate noght what we er worthy;
Wharfor our gude dedys we shuld noght prayse
And þarfor þus Saynt Austyn sayse:

Our good deeds are not perfectly good, but our bad ones are thoroughly evil.

Mala nostra non sunt pura mala, sed bona nostra non sunt pura bona.
He says "our ille dedys er pur ille wroght,
Bot our gud dedis pur gud er noght."

Here to acordes, als þe buk telles us.
Ysidre þe grete clerk, þat says þus:
Omnes iusticie nostre quasi pannus
menstruale.
He says "alle our ryghtwysnes er sene
Als a clathe, filed of thyng unclene;"
Wharfor certanly here wate nane
How he sal fare, when he es hethen gane.
Bot comfort of gud hope may he fele,
Þat here lyves wele, to fare wele;
For we awe to trow, with-outen were.
Þat God sal hym yhelde þat dose wele here.
Bot yhit es he noght syker in þir days.
For-why, þe haly man þos says,
Nescit homo utrum dignus sit
odio vel amore.
For certayn, he says, "a men what noght,"
Þogh he had never swa mykel gude wroght,
"Whether he war worthy after his dede
To hafe luf of God or hatrede."
And Isidre, als a buke shewes us.
Acordes þar-to, þat says þus:
Servus dei dum bonum agit, utrum
sit ei ad bonum incertus est.
He says, "he þat es God servand.
When he gude dus, outher with tung or hand.
He es noght certayne yhit in thoght,
Wether it be gude til hym or noght."
Wharfor our lyfyng here es harde,
Als þe haly man says, Saynt Bernarde:
Quis, sine trepidacione et timore,
hanc vitam ducere potest?
"Wha," he says, "may þis lyfe here lede
With-outen tremblyng and drede?"
Alswa[1] say here, may lyf na man
With-outen drede, þat witte can;
For al-if a man here afforce him ay
For to do alle þe gude þat he may,

Isidore says that our righteousness is like an 'unclean cloth.'

No man knows whether he is worthy of God's love or hatred

'Who may lead this life without trembling?'

[1] 'Als wha' (MS. Harl. 6923).

Yhit may his gude dedis be swa wroght,
Þat parchaunce God allowes þam noght;
And þarfor Saint Bernard pleyned him here
Of his lyf, þat says þus on þis manere.

'St. Bernard' says that he is frightened by a review of his life, for it is wholly sinful.

Terret me tota vita mea, qua diligenter discussa,
apparet mihi aut peccatum aut sterilitas;
Et si quis in ea fructus videtur, sic est
aut simulatum, aut imperfectum, aut alio
modo corruptum, ut possit aut non placere
deo aut displicere.

Þer er Bernard wordes þat says:
"Al my lyfe here me flays,
For if it ententyfly discussed be,
It semes noght elles here until me
Bot owther syn, þat þe saul mast deres,
Or barran thyng, þat na fruyt beres;
And if any fruyt þar-in seme,
It may be þus be[1] skil to deme,
Outher feyned thyng to shew in syght,
Or thyng, þat es noght alle done ryght,
Or, on other wyse, corrumped with-in,
Þat es to say, filed with syn;
Swa þat outher þan may it noght
Pay God almyghty, þat es swa wroght,
Or paraunter it hym myspays;"
Þos þe haly man, Saynt Barnard, says.

Life is barren.

What may a synful man say þan,
When he, þat was swa haly a man,
Couth na fruyt here in his life se?
Þan aght þe synful dredand be
Of [th]is life here, þat es unclene,
In whilk na fruyt may be sene.

What may a sinful man say of his life?

Þe ferth skille and þe last to telle,
Why man dredis þe dede swa felle,
Es for he wate noght whether he sal wende
Tylle ioy or payne aftir his lyfes ende.
For swa wyse and witty man es nane,
Þat wate, when þe dede him has tane,

IV. Man is uncertain of his future state.

[1] 'bi' (Harl. MS. 4196).

For certayn, whederward he sal ga,
Whether he sal wend til wele or wa.
Þan aght ilk man, bathe yong and alde,
Haf drede for þis skille þat I talde.
For when þe devels and þe angels
Has desputed our lif, als þe buk telles,
And discucion made, als fals to be,
Þan sal we certanly here and se
Our certayne dome, þat we sal have;
Wether we sal be dampned or save,
And outher þan wend to ioy or pyne;
Þarfor þe haly man says, Saynt Austyne:

The discussion of our deeds shall be followed by the judgment.

Bene unusquisque de die novissimo
formidare debet, quia unum quemque
in quo invenerit suus novissimus dies,
cum de hoc seculo egreditur, talis in die
novissimo indicatur.

"Ilk man" he says, "þat sal pas away
Shuld haf drede of hys last day;
For in what state swa he be þan,
Swilk als his last day fyndes a man,
When he sal out of þis werld wende,
Swilk mon he be demed at þe ende."
Þarfor our last day þat sal falle,
Our day of dome we may calle.
Bot at þe general day of dome
With our bodys we sal come,
Byfor Ihesu Cryst allemyghty kyng,
Þat sal þat day deme alle thyng.
Þan sal he deme ilka nacyon,
And mak a fynal declaracyon
Of alle þe domes byfor shewed,
In tyme of dede, to lered and lewed.
For þe bodys sal wend to þe same stede
Til whilk þe saul es demed aftir þe dede;
And outher þan have ful ioy togyder,
Or ful sorow when þai com thyder,
And ever-mare aftir togyder duelle,
Whethir þai wend to heven or helle.

Each man should live in fear of his last day.

After the 'dome' the soul and body shall dwell together.

Bot in erthe sal duelle þe bodis alle.
Until þat dredful day sal falle,
When þe dome sal be mast strayt and harde,
Als þis buke shewes aftirwarde.

The soul is 'demed' as soon as it leaves the body.

Bot first, als sone als þe saul namly,
Thurgh þe dede es passed fra þe body,
It sal be demed, aftir his werkes,
Til ioy or payne, als says þer clerkes.
Þe synful saul þan gas strik to helle,
In pyne withouten ende to duelle;
Þe clene saul þan gas up even,
With-outen lettyng, til þe blis of hevene.

Many go to Purgatory before they can reach Heaven.

Bot many saules, þat er save,
Ar þai com to blis, payne byhoves have
In purgatori, and duelle þar-in
Until þai be clensid of al syn,
Þat er schrywen and noght clensed here,
And þar be fyned als gold þat shynes clere.
For in heven may na saul be sene,
Unto it be fyned and clensed clene,
Outher here thurgh penaunce, als clerkes wate
Or in purgatori thurgh fire hate.

Some few who have been purified by penance and almsdeed go straight to heaven.

Wharfor þe saul þat es clensed wele
Of al dedely syn and of veniele,
Thurgh penaunce here and almusdede,
Þe angels als tit þan sal lede,
When it es passed fra þe body away,
Til þe blis of heven þat sal last ay;
Þarfor whaswa wille folow wysdome,
He suld before, ar he saw þe dede come,
Mak him redy and clense hym clene
Of al spottes of syn þat mught be sene,
Thurgh shryfte of mouthe and repentance,
And thurgh almusdede and penaunce;
Swa þat dede fynd hym clene of syn,
When þe body and þe saul sal twyn.
And whyles he lyffes til he hethen wende,
Thynk he suld ay of his lyfes hende,

Swa may he hym kepe fra alle folys.
And þarfor says þus Salamon þe wys:
In omnibus operibus tuis, memorare
novissima tua, et non peccabis
ineternum.
Þat es on Inglis þos to say;
He says "Thynk on þi endyng day,
Ay when þou sal any werk bygyn
And þan sal þou never mare syn."
And þarfor þou man[1] in þi werk be slyghe,
And thynk ay wele þat þou sal dighe;
Thynk þou sal dyghe, þou wate never whan,
Ne in what state þou sal be þan,
Ne þou whate never in what stede
Þou sal dyghe, ne of what dede.
Þarfor at morne, when þou sese lyght,
Thynk als þou sal dygh ar nyght;
When þou gas to slep, if þou be wyse,
Thynk als þou suld noght with þe[2] lyf ryse.
For Saynt Austyn says þus in a buke,
"Let ay þi hert on þi last day luke."
Wha-swa wille thynk ay on þis manere,
And be war, and make hym redy here,
And of alle hys syn clense hym wele,
Ar þe dede com þat hym byhoves fele,
Þan may he eschape and passe lightly
Þe bitter payn of purgatory,
And com til þe blisse of heven bright;
Þar ay es day, and never nyght.
Here es þe thred parte of þis buke spedde
Þat spekes of þe dede, als I haf redde.
On þis part I wille na langer stand,
Bot passe to another neghest folowand;
Þat es þe ferthe part for to specify,
Þe whilk spekes of purgatory,
Whar many saules feles ful harde,
Als yhe sal here sone aftirwarde.

Think of thy last day.

In the morning think that thou shalt die before night.

[1] *mon?* [2] *þi?*

Here bygynnes þe ferth part
þat es of purgatory.

Of Purgatory.

Many spekes, and in buke redes
Of purgatory, but fon it dredes;
For many wate noght what it es,
þarfor þai drede it wele þe les.
Bot if þai knew wele what it ware,
Or trowed, þai walde drede it þe mare.
And forthy þat sum has na knawyng
Of purgatory ne undirstandyng,
þarfor I wille now speke aparty,
In þis buke of purgatory.

What Purgatory is.

And first shew yhow what it es,
And whare it es, als þe buke wittenes;
And whatkyn payns er þar-in,
And whilk saules gas þeder, and for what syn;
And alswa what thyng es mast certayn,
þat þam mught help and slake þair payn.
Of þir sex poyntes I wil spek and rede,
And swa I sal þis ferth part spede.

Purgatory is a place for the purification of sinful souls.

Purgatory es nathyng elles
Bot a clensyng sted þar saules duelles,
þat has synned, and had contricyon,
And er in þe way of salvacion,
And er noght parfytly clensed here
Of al veniel syns sere.
Bot þar byhoves þam payne fele,
Til þai be clensed parfytely and wele
Of alkyn syn þat þai ever wroght,
In worde, in dede, in wille or thoght.
For swa pured and fyned never gold was,
Als þai sal be, ar þai þethen pas.

The pains of Purgatory are more severe than all the sufferings of martyrs.

Wharfor þe payn þat þe saul þar hentes
Er mare bitter þan alle þe tourmentes
þat alle þe marters in erthe tholed,
Sen God was for us boght and sold.
For þe lest payn of þe payns þar sere
Es mare þan es þe mast payn here,

Als says a grete clerk þus shortly,
In a buke of þe payns of purgatory:
Minima pena purgatorii est major
maxima pena mundi.
He says, "þe lest payn þat es þare
In purgatori, es wele mare
þan þe mast payn þat may be
In al þis werld, to fele or se."

'The least pain in Purgatory is more severe than the greatest earthly pain.

For þe payne þar, es mare bitter and felle
þan hert may thynk, or tung telle,
Als þe buke says, trow wha swa wille.
For sum clerkes says, and pruves by skille
þat bytwen þe payne of helle namly
And þe payn of purgatory
Es na difference bot at þe tane
Has ende, and þe tother has nane.
þe payns of helle sal never sees,
Ne þe saules þar-in never haf relees;

'The pain of Hell shall never cease.'

Bot in purgatori saules dueles stille
Until þai be clensed of alle ille,
And mare payn fele, als I understande,
þan ever feled man here lyfande;
For þai sal haf a day þare
Als mykel bitter payn or mare,
Als a man mught thole here of penaunce
A yhere and fele als mykel grevaunce;
And als mykel drighe þar fourty days,
Als fourty yhere here; þus clerkes says;
Swa es þe payn þar a day to se
Als mykel als here a yhere may be.

One *day's* pain in Purgatory is as great as a *year* of penance on earth.

Bot ever a day of penaunce here
May stand in-stede þar for a yhere,
Als God says openly and wele,
Thurgh þe prophet Ezechyele:
Diem pro anno
dedi tibi.
þat es on Inglys þus to say,
"For a yhere I gyf þe day."

The pain endured in Purgatory obtains no reward in Heaven.

Þe payn þar þe saules avayles noght
When þai til purgatori er broght,
Bot for to clense þe saul of syn,
And for na mede in heven to wyn;
Þogh þai a thousand yhere war þare,
Þair mede in heven shuld never be þe mare.
Þan serves þat payne þar, of noght elles
Bot to clense þam of syn, þat þare-in duelles.

Penance is useful in two ways.

Bot penaunce to thole here with gude wille,
Serves here til twa thynges by skille.

1. It cleanses the soul of sin.

Ane es to clense here þe saule wele
Of dedly syn and of veniele;

2. It obtains a greater reward in heaven.

Another to haf in heven mare mede;
Til þer twa may penaunce us lede.
For þe saul for ilka penaunce here,
Sal haf specyel ioy in heven swa clere,
Þat with-outen ende sal laste,
If þai thole payne here with hert stedfast.
Here may men se, als þe buke wittenes,
And understand what purgatori es.
Now wil I shew yow shortly

Where Purgatory is.

Whar, als clerkes says, es purgatory.
Þe stede, þat purgatory es calde,

It is under the earth, above the place where unbaptized children dwell.

Under þe erthe es, als I halde,
Aboven þe stede, als som clerkes telles,
Þar crysom [1] dede childer duells,
Þat fra þe sight of Goddes face
Er putted for ever, with-outen grace.
Þat place es neghest aboven hel pitte,
Bytwen purgatory and itte.
Þus standes þe stede of purgatory,
Oboven þam bathe in þat party.
Alle þat er þar payn byhoves hafe,
Bot þai haf grace and er save.
Bot fra þe other stedes, til þe day of dome,
Sal never mare saule out come;

[1] uncristen (MS. Harl. 6923).

For þan sal þai come til þe last iugement,
And with þe bodys agayn til helle be hent.
Bot fra purgatory saules may wynne
Til blisse when þai er clensed of synne.

The soul may pass out of Purgatory.

Aboven þat yhit es þe ferthe stede,
Þat Crist visited when he was dede;
And þa þat þar war with hym out tuke
And left nane þaryn, als says þe buke.

Above Purgatory is the place that Christ visited when he descended into Hell.

Ne fra þat tyme als we here clerkes telle
Com never nan yhit þeder to duelle,
Ne never nan forthward sal com;
And þat stede clerkes calles *lymbus patrum*
Þe whilk a fre preson on Inglys es,
Whare þe haly faders duelled in myrknes.

Limbus patrum.

Alle þir four stedes men may helle calle,
For þai er closed with-in þe erthe alle;

These four places are within the earth.

And for helle þai may alle be tane,
Of whilk four purgatory es ane.
Þarfor haly kyrk þat for saules prays,
Calles purgatory helle, þat þus says:
Domine Ihesu Criste libera animas
omnium fidelium defunctorum, de
manu inferni!
"Loverd deliver out of helles hande
Alle crysten saules þat þar er duellande;"
Þat es to say, out [of] purgatory
Þar þe saules er clensed parfytely.
Bot fra þe lawest helle, with-outen dout,
Na saul may be delyverd out;

No soul may leave Hell.

For of mercy þar es na hope;
Þarfor þus says þe haly man Iobe.
Quia in inferno nulla est redempcio.
"In helle", he says, "es na raunceon."
For na helpe may be in þat dungeon,
Þat es to say, in þe lawest helle,
Whar þe dampned saules sal ay duelle,
Whar messe ne prayer helpes noght,
Til þam þat er þeder broght.

Nothing may avail the souls in hell.

For na thyng may abate þair pyne,
And þarfor þus says Saynt Austyne,
Si scirem patrem meum aut matrem
in inferno, pro eis non orarem.
He says, "if my fader or moder ware
In helle, and I wist þam þare,
I wald nouther nyght ne day,
For þam byd bede here, ne pray."
For-why, almusdede, ne messe, ne prayers
Helpes na saul þar, bot parchaûnce ders,
Þe twa lawest stedes, þat I nevend ar,
Er þe helles þat sal last ever mar.

Purgatory lasts only till Domesday.

Bot purgatory sal noght last ay;
It lastes na langer þan to domesday,
For aftir þat day, als clerkes can se,
Na stede of purgatory sal be,
Bot helle, ful of devels with in,
Sal ay last, for vengeaunce of syn.
Now som has wonder, and may ask why

Why Purgatory is in the middle of the earth.

God has swa ordayned purgatory,
And helle ymyddes þe erthe swa law;
Þe skylle why may be þis to knaw;
Þe syn þat es in erthe wroght
Fra erthe unpunyst passes noght.
Þan nedly byhoves be punyst syn,
Outher opon erthe or with-in,
Þat es outher here þar we duelle,
Or in purgatory or in helle;

Sin drags the soul downwards.

For syn es swa hevy and swa harde,
Þat it drawes þe saul ay dunwarde;
Until payn and penaunce haf wasted þat syn
Þe saul may never tylle heven wyn;

Some say, there are two kinds of Purgatory.

Yhit says þir grete clerkes namly,
Þat twa stedes er of purgatory;

1. common.

Þe tane es comon, als yhe herd me telle,
Þat with-in erthe es, oboven helle;

2. special.

And þe tother es speciele, thurgh grace,
Þat es oboven erthe, in sere place.

For in þe comon stede som er noght ay, *The 'stedes' of Purgatory.*
Bot er here punyst, outher nyght or day,
In sere stedes specialy in gast,
Whar þai haf synned in body mast.
And þat may be thurgh helpe and spede
Of prayer of frendes and almusdede,
Til wham þai ofte in gast apere,
Thurgh speciel grace, in sere stedes here,
For to hast þair deliverance
Out of þair payn and þair penaunce,
Þat, als I ar sayde, gretely greves,
And for warnyng of frendes þat lyefes.
Here may men properly by skille se
What purgatory falles to be.
Now wille I rede forthermare,
And shew yhow of sum paynes þat er þare. *The pains of Purgatory.*
In purgatory, als þe buke wittenes,
Es diverse payns, som mar, som les,
And many mare þan I can neven;
Bot I fynd wryten payns seven, *They are seven in number.*
Þat may be called payns of purgatory;
And þa seven I wille here specefy,
Of whilk men sal som fele and se,
Als tite als þe ded-comyng sal be.
Þe first payn es of þa seven, *First pain 'sight' of Devils.*
Als yhe herd me byfor neven,
Þe grete drede þat þe saul es in
When þe body at[1] it sal twyn;
For þe saul sese þan about it stande
Grysly devels agayn it raumpande,
Als wode lyons to wayt þair pray,
And to ravisshe it with þam away.
And þat syght es a payn ful grevous;
For þe devels er swa foul and ydous,
Þat swa hardy man was never nane
Lyfand here in flesshe and bane,

[1] And it (MS. Harl. 6923).

þat saw þe syght þat þe saul þan sese,
þat ne he for ferdelayk is witte shuld lese,
Thogh he war never of hert swa balde,
Als in þe thred parte of þis boke was talde.
A grete payn aght þis syght to be
Til þe saule þan, þat it sal se.

Second pain: The soul's doubts about its future state..

þe secunde payn neghest folowande
Es þe grete drede, to understande,
þat þe saul sal hafe wyth dole and care,
Until þe dome be gyfen, how he sal fare.
For þe angels sal þare redy be
And þe devels swa grisly to se,
þat sal disput of alle his lyfe
Bytwen þam þar, with grete stryfe.
His syns sal þan be shewed ful many,
Als I tald byfor in þe thred part namly.
þe saul þan sal bytwene þam stande,

Dispute between devils and angels.

And þe angels on his ryght hande,
And devels on þe lefte syde.
þan mot þe saul in grete dred abyde,
Until þat stryfe be broght to ende,
And til it witte whyder it sal wende,
And whether it sal be dampned or save;
þan sal þe saul a grete drede have,
Als a man þat es in myddes þe se
In grete perille, and may noght fle,

The soul then, is like a man on the sea in a storm.

When tempestes falles and stormes smert,
þan has þat man grete drede in hert;
He mas þan vowes, and cryes on Crist,
For, he es afered þat he sal be peryst;
And þat drede til hym es a grete payn;
For of his lyf he es uncertayn;

The soul is in bodily fear, like one accused of felony.

And als a man has drede bodily,
When he es acouped of felony
Byfor kynges iustice, and þe cuntré,
þat charged es if he gilty be,
He wate noght whether he sal be spilt,
Or be delyvered of þat gilt.

Until þai have gyven þair verdite,
And outher þar-of made hym qwyte
Als þe laghe walde, or made hym gilty.
If he þan haf drede, it es na ferly,
For in grete dout of lyfe es þat man.
Bot yhit has the saul mare drede þan,
Til þe dome be[1] gyven and it may se
Whether it sal dampned or saufe be.
For if it dome of damp[na]cion here,
It gas til helle with-outen recoverere;
And þe saul þat es dampned til þat place
Thar never hope to haf mercy ne grace.
What wonder es þan if þe saule drede have
Þat doutes whethir he sal be dampned or save.
Of þes twa maners of payns of drede
Yhe herd me aparty byfor rede,
Þe whilk es declared in a stede,
In þe thred part þat spekes of þe dede.
Alle þis matere men may se þare,
Þarfor here I wil spek þar-of na mare.

The souls of the damned go to hell without hope of ever leaving it.

Þe thred payn es a maner of exil
When þe saules here agayn þair wil
Er exild fra þis lyf til payn,
With-outen any turnyng agayn;
For þan sal þai haf grete murnyng,
When þai er flemed fra þair lykyng,
Fra alle þair frendes lefe and dere,
And fra alle þe delyces þat þai had here.
Þe murnyng þat þai haf on þis wyse,
Til þam sal be grete payn and anguyse.

The third pain of Purgatory is a kind of exile.

Þe fereth payn es sere malady,
Þat þe sauls sal haf in purgatory.
For þai sal haf þar yvels sere,
For sere syns, þat er unclensed here;
Som for pride þat þai haf here-in bene,
Sal haf þar als a fever cotidiene,

The fourth pain is disease of various kinds.

[1] The MS. reads *by*.

þat þe saule sal pyn mar bitterly
þan ever fyver pyned here mans body.
Som sal haf þar, for covatyse,
Dropsy.
Als þe dropsy to grege[1] þair angwyse.
Som sal haf in alle þair lymmes obout,
Gout.
For sleuthe, als þe potagre and þe gout.
Som, for envy, sal haf in þair lyms,
Ulcers and boils.
Als kylles and felouns and apostyms.
Palsy.
Som for ire sal have als þe parlesy,
þat yvel þe saul sal grefe gretely.
Som for glotoni sal haf þare,
Quinsey.
Als þe swynacy, þat greves ful sare.
And som, for þe syn of lechery,
Leprosy.
Sal haf als þe yvel of meselry.
þus sal þe saules, als God vouches save,
For sere syñs, sere maledys have,
þat here has hadde repentance
And has noght ful-filed here þair penaunce.
These maladies grieve the soul very much.
þir maladies þar þe saul mar greves,
þan it dos any body þat here lyves.
Thynk we what payn has þe body,
þat has here bot a malady
In þis lif, lastand alle a yhere,
Or noght bot thre days, or four here.
þat malady greves þe body sare,
Bot yhit it greves þe saul vele mare
In purgatory, þar es it pynde,
For þe saul es of mare tender kynde;
For als a lytel thynd[2] þin eghe lokand
May greve mare þan it may þi hand,
Swa feles þe saule mare penaunce
þan þe body, when it has grevaunce.
Bot now may som say here agayne,
How can the soul feel pain since it is spiritual?
And aske how þe saul may fele payne,
þat es noght elles bot a spirit,
þat may noght be feled, swylk es it;

[1] 'eche' (Lands. MS. 348). agrege (Harl. 6923).
[2] thyng (Harl. MS. 6923).

For it es swa sutil, þat aftir þe dede,
It may occupy na stede.
Til þis, þus men answer may,
Als men may here grete clerkes say.
Þe saule þe lyfe of þe body es
Of ilk man here, bathe mare and les.
And with-outen þe lyfe is na felyng,
For felyng may be in na dede thyng.
Þan es alle þe felyng halely
In þe saul, and noght in þe body;
For when þe saul es passed away,
Þe body es noght bot erthe and clay,
Þat es a dede thyng, als a stane;
Þe whilk may fele na thyng be[1] it ane.
Alswa yhit may som þos aske mare,
How may þe saule þat duelles þare,
Be pyned with sere maledy
Þat falles til sere lymes of þe body,
Sen it has nouther body ne hede,
Ne lym þat may occupy stede.
Til þis, men may answer þus shortly:
Þe saul, al-if it haf na body,
It sal be pyned als in lyms sere,
Thurgh whilk it has mast synned here.
Swa sal þe saul, fele payn and wa,
And til other saules it sal seme swa.
For ilkan til other sal seme þan,
Als þai had shap of body of man;
Þus sal ilka saul other se,
For nan of þam may feled be.
Na mar þan here a man ande may,
When it passes fra his mouthe away.
And þis may be pruved be[1] þe godspelle,
Thurgh þe ensampel of þe ryche man in helle,
And of Lazar þat he ward[2] mete
Þat in Abraham bosom had his sete.

The soul is the life of the body.

The body without the soul is as dead as a stone.

How may the soul suffer maladies proper to the body?

Souls in Purgatory appear to one another as if they had bodily forms.

[1] by?

[2] And of þe lazar þat he *warned* mete. (MSS. Lands. 348, Addit 22283.)

Abraham's bosom denotes heaven.

Abraham bosom es nathyng elles,
Bot heven þar haly spyrites duelles.
When þe ryche man, þat in helle sat lawe,
Lazar in Abraham bosom sawe,
He cryed til Abraham and prayed with-alle
Þat a drope of calde water mught falle
Til his tung, fra Lazar fynger ende,
Als es in þe godspel contende.

Lazarus had no tongue nor finger, foot or hand in reality.

Bot al-if he þus spak to hym,
Yhit had he na tung ne[1] other lym,
Ne Lazar, als yhe sal understande,
Had nouther fynger, ne fote, ne hande,
For þai bathe war spirites anly,
Þat nouther had lymmes ne body.
Þe tane was in blis soverayne,
Þe tother was in endles payne.
Bot þe ryche man saule feled in helle
Payne, als he had bene in flesshe and felle;
And Lazar saule til him semed þan
Als he had body and lymes of man.

Some 'clerks' say that the soul in Purgatory 'has of the air a body'.

Yhit has men herd som clerkes maynte[ne]
Swilk an opinion, als I wene,
Þat a saule, þat es in purgatory
Or in helle, has of þe ayre a body
For to thole payne, in lyms sere,
After þat he has synned here.
Bot whether þe saul haf body or noght,
He sal fele payne, after he has wroght.

The fifth pain of Purgatory is fire, the heat of which may be mitigated by almsdeed, mass and prayer.

Þe fifte payne es þe fire hate,
Þat na maner of thing may abate,
Bot almusdede and messe and prayere,
Þat frendes dus for þe saul here.
To abate þat fire, þa thre er best,
For þa thre may bring þe saul to rest.
Þat fire is hatter and mare kene,
Þan al þe fire þat here es sene;

[1] The MS. reads *no*.

For als þe fire of erthe, þar we won,
Es hatter þan þe beme of þe son,
Ryght swa þat fire on þe same manere,
Es hatter þan þe fire es here.
Alle þe waters, þat men may rekken,
A spark þar-of may noght sleken.
We se þe fire þat here es, greves sare
Þe body, þat standes þar-in bare;
Bot mare greves þe fire of purgatory
Þe saul, þan þis fire dus þe body.
For þe fire here, of strenthe es les
Þan þe fire of purgatory es;
And þe body with flesshe and bane,
Es harder þan þe saul by it ane;
And þe saul mare tender and nesshe
Þan es þe body with þe flesshe.

The body is not so tender as the soul.

Sen þat fire es mare hate þare
Þan þe fire es here, als I sayd are,
And þe saul es swa tender of kynde,
Þan semes it þat it es mare pynde
Thurgh þat fire, þan þe body mught be
With alle þe fire of Cristianté;
For a spark of þat fire es mare hate
Þan al þe fire of erthe, als clerkes wate.
Many saules duells in þat fire strang.
Bot sum duelles short wyle, and sum lang,
Aftir þair syn es mare or les,
And aftir þair penaunce fulfild es,
Bot na saul may þethen pas,
Until it be als clene als it first was,
When he was hoven at funtstane
And his crestendome þar had tane.

A spark of the fire of Purgatory is hotter than all the fire of earth.

Som clerkes, þat spekes of purgatory,
Says þat þe fire þare is bodily,
And noght gastly als þe saule es;
For þe saule, als þe boke bers wytnes,
May be pyned with fire bodily,
Als it may be with þe[1] awen body.

Some 'clerks' say that the fire of Purgatory is 'bodily'.

[1] þy?

Bot þat fire wirkes noght thurgh kynde
In þe saule, þat þar-with es pynde,
Als dos þe fire þat brinnes here,
Bot it wirkes on wonderful manere,
Als God has ordaynd, forwhy, it es
An instrument of Goddes ryghtwysnes,
Thurgh wilk þe saule most clensed be
In purgatory, ar it may God se.

The fire of Purgatory destroys sin.

Alle þe fire þat es þar-in,
Es bot a maner of fyre to wast syn,
And noght divers fires, les and mare,
Bot a maner of fire, als I sayd are,
Þat alle veniel syns þan sal waste,
Þat es unclensed here, lest and maste.

The stay in Purgatory is of long or short duration.

For als fyre þat caffe son may bryn,
Gold may melt þat es lang þar-in,
Ryght swa þe fyre þar thurgh lang hete
Þat wastes smale syns, may wast grete,
And als þe hete of þe son þat comon es,
Som men greves mare, and som men les,
Right swa þe fyre þat es þare,
Som sawles pyns les, and som mare;
For þe sawles byhoves duelle þar-in,
Aftir þe charge es of þair syn.
Bot som sawles þar sal be delyver[d] sone,
Þat large penaunce here has done;
Som sal duel þar many a yhere,
Þat litel penaunce has don here.
And lang lygyn in þair syn;
And þarfor says þus Saynt Austyn:
Necesse est quod tantum urat dolor,
quantum erat amor; tanto enim quisquis
torquetur diucius, quanto affectus eius
venialibus ahherebat forcius.
Saynt Austyn says "nedeful it es,
Þat sorow war als mykel and na les

Pain is in proportion to sin.

For ilka syn and ilka trespas,

Als luf and delyte in syn was."
And alswa he says on þis manere,
Þat ay þe styther þat ilk man here
Gyves his lykyng and wille
Til veniel syns, outher loud or stille,
Þe langer sal he pyned be
In purgatory;" þus says he.
Þis fire, als byfore wryten es,
Som saules pynes mare, and sum les,
Aftir þat þai þat commes þar-in,
Brynges ought with þam þat may bryn.

Some souls are tormented more than others.

For byfor ar þai may God se
Byhoves als thre thynges brinned be,
Þat es at say, als wodde, and hay,
And stubble, þat may sone wast away;

Venial sins burn as hay, wood and stubble.

Þa er veniel synnes þat may falle,
Bathe grete and smale, and men with-alle,
Þe mast veniel syns sal þar bryn langly,
Als wodde brinnes, þat es sadde and hevy,

The greatest as wood, the least as stubble.

Þe lest veniel syns sal brin sone,
Als stobble, þat son brinnes and son es done.
Bot swa son brinnes noght þe mene synnes;
Þai brin mar slawly als hay brynnes.

Moderate sins burn as hay.

Þus sal be brynned and wasted þare,
Als veniel syns, bathe les and mare;
And al dedly syns of wilk men er shryven,
And þe gilt God has forgyven,.
For whilk þe penaunce es noght fulfilled here,
Sal þare be wasted on þe sam manere
And þe saules in þat fire be pyned
Unto þai be als clene als gold fyned.
And when þai er fyned and made bright
Þai sal be broght befor Goddes sight,
Til hey Paraydise, þat blisful place
Whar ay es rest, ioy and solace.
Þe sext payne es þis to telle;
Þat þe saules unclensed, þat sal duelle

The sixth pain of Purgatory is bonds of sin.

In purgatory, sal be bunden faste
With bandes of syn, whilles þai may laste,
Als men þat er bonden in pryson,
Þat na man may for gyf[t] ne raunson,
Out of þat hard payn þam wyn,
Until þe fire haf wasted þair bandes of syn.

The souls in Purgatory are bound hand and foot.

Þus er þai bunden by hend and fete,
Allen bydonen[1], in þat brinnand hete.
Me thynk þat na payne may be mare
Þan þa saules has, whyles þai er þare.
Grete dole þay mak, somtyme, and sarowe;
For þai may nathyng begg ne borowe,
To help þam, þat þai war out broght,
Ne þair awen prayer help þam noght;
For þar es nouther stede ne space,
Helpe ne frenshepe to purchace;

Souls in Purgatory shall feel the good they did on earth.

Bot þe gude þat þai did here, þai sal þar fele;
Or if þair frendes, þat luffes þam wele,
For þam here pray or do almus de[de];
Alle þat may help þam in þair nede.
Ful hard payn þar þai fele,
Bot at þai er save þai wate wele;
Bot sum tyme swa mykel pay[n] þai hafe,
Þat þai tak na kepe þat þai er save;
Wharfor we shuld thynk, þat lyves here,
What payn it es, on þis manere,
To be swa pyned, and fele swa sare
Fourty wynter, outher les or mare,
Omang devels, þat þan has leve
Som tyme to turment þe saules and greve,
Ay whiles þai haf any spot of syn;

They remain in Purgatory till they are cleansed.

For are, may þai noght out of payn wyn,
Til þai be clensed and made right clene
Of alle spottes of syn þat may be sene.
And when þai er þus clensed wele
Þan sal þai namare payn fele,

[1] Albedene (MS. Harl. 6923).

Bot als tite þar-efter þai sal wende
Tille þe blis þat es with-outen ende.
Þe sevend payn of purgatory es
Þat þe saules er als in wildernes,
Þar defaut es of alkyn thyng
Of wilk man mught haf lykyng;
Þair payn es turned manyfalde.
Now er þai in hete, and now in calde;

The seventh pain of Purgatory is the absence of all kinds of pleasure.

For sumtyme þai sal be pyned lang
With hete, and som tyme with cald omang.
Þai sal haf þare bathe hunger and threst,
And travayl grete, with-outen rest.

Cold and heat, by turns, torment the soul.

Þai er dungen þare, to eke þaire payn,
With smert stormes als of wynd and rayn,
And with stormes of hayle, sharpe and kene,
Swylk stormes was never here sene,
Als þe sauls sal þar here and se.
Þus sal þai on sere-wyse pyned be,
Sum many wynter for þair syn,
Ar þai til þe sight of God may wyn.
Swilk maner of payns þai sal have þare,
With other ma, þat sal greve sare.
Bot a grete payn yhit þis sal be,
Þe grete yhernyng þat þai haf to se
Þe face of God, þat es swa bright,
And þe lang tariyng fra þat syght.
Bot til þat sight þai may never wyn,
Until þai be clensed þar of al syn.

The great yearning of the sight of God torments the soul.

Here haf I talde yhow aparty,
Of sum payns of purgatory.
Now I wille shew, als þe boke telles,
Whilk sauls in purgatory duelles.
Þe saules þat to purgatory most wend
Aftir þe dede, when þis life has end,
Nedly byhoves dwelle þar-in,
Unto þai be clensed of al syn,
Thurgh bitter paynes þat er þare.
Bot sum sal fele les, and sum mare,

What souls go to Purgatory.

Aftir þair syn es mare or les,
Als in þis part byfor wryten es,
Or aftir þair syns er many or fone,
And aftir þai haf here penaunce done.
Bot alle saules sal noght duelle in þat stede,

Some, after death go straight to heaven while others go to hell.

For sum here þat als tite aftir þair dede,
Sal wend strykly til heven blis,
Als Innocentes þat never dyd mys,
And other saules of men parfite,
Þat in nathyng here has delyte,
Bot anly in God þat boght þam dere,
In[1] lyffed ay in penaunce here.
Som þat þe dede here sodanly tas.
In dedely syn strik til helle gas;
And þat me thynk es na ferly,

Deadly sin will draw a man down to hell, unless penance is done for it.

Forwhy dedely syn es swa hevy
Þat it may with-in a litel stonde
A saul draw doun til helle grounde.
Bot þe saul þat of dedly syn es shryven,
Swa þat þe gilt be here forgyven,
If þe penaunce þat es here aioynt
Be noght fulfilled at þe dedes poynt,
And þe saul þat es noght clensed wele

And for venial sins, bitter pain must be suffered.

Of smale syns þat er veniele;
Þis twa maners of saules er save,
Bot in purgatory þam byhoves have
Ful bitter payn, and duel stil þare
Unto þai be clen, als I sayd are,
Als þai war first when þai had tane
Haly baptem at þe font stane.
Yhit says som clerkes on þis manere,
Þat swa clen of syn es naman here,
Ne swa parfite in þe law of Crist,
Ne yhit a childe, þat es new baptist,
Þat til heven sal wend aftir þe dede,
Þat he ne sal pas forth by þat stede,

[1] And (MS. Harl. 6923).

And se þe payns þar ilkan.
Bot yhong Innocentes sal fele nan,
For þai couthe never na syn wirk,
And passes[1] in þe trouthe of haly kyrk.
Þarfor þai swippe þurgh purgatory
Als a foul þat flyes smertly,
With-outen payn þat may dere,
Or any sight þat may þam fere,
Bot unnethes any other may
Passe qwyte thurgh purgatory away,
Þat þe fire ne sal noght fynd in þam to bryn,
Ar þai passe thurgh som veniel syn,
Swa strayt þai sal be examynd þan;
For it es nan swa parfite man
Þat he ne thynkes, some tyme, som vayn thoght
Þat he lattes par and charges it noght;
Of swilk hym byhoves clensed be
Or[2] he may þe bright face of God se;
For als gold, þat shynes clere and bright,
Semes fyned clene ynoghe til mans sight,
Whar it put in fire to fyn mare
Yhit suld it leve sum dros þare;
Right swa þe saules, on þe same manere,
Of parfit men, þat semes clene here
Of al syn, and es to God redy,
Yhit when þai sal pas thurgh purgatory,
Þe fire þar, þat es with in,
Sal fynd in þam sum dros of syn,
Als light speche, or thoght in vayn,
For whilk þam byhoves fele sum payn,
For swa fyned never na gold here was
Thurgh fire, als þai sal be ar þai pas.
Here haf I shewed swilk[3] saules sal be
In purgatory, als clerkes can se.
Now wille I som syns here specify
For whilk þai duelle in purgatory.

Young innocents shall feel no pain, but fly smartly through Purgatory like a bird.

No others are so perfect as to escape.

However pure the soul may seem, the fire of Purgatory will find in it some sin.

[1] passede (MS. Harl. 6923). [2] ar? [3] wilk.

The sins which send the soul to hell are called deadly sins.

Many maners of syns, þat greves,
Regnes omang men þat leves;
Of wilk sum er dedly to fele
And sum er noght bot veniele,
Þa syns þat er cald dedly
Sal noght be purged in purgatory,
Bot þai sal be punyst ay in helle;
And whilk þas er I wil yow telle.
Þir er þa hede syns þat er dedely;

Pride, hatred, gluttony, sloth, lechery, covetousness, sacrilege, false witness, perjury, murder, theft.

Pride, hatreden, and envy;
Glotony and sleuthe in Goddes servise,
And lychery and covatyse,
Sacrilege, and fals wyttenessyng,
And slaghter and forsweryng,
Thefte alswa and ravyn,
Ilkan of þir es a dedly syn.
And wreth es dedly syn omang,
If it be halden in hert lang;
And yhit drunkenes es dedly to fele,
If it be over continuele;
Wha-swa feles hym here gylty
In any of þir syns dedly,
Bot-if he hym amende, ar he hethen wende,
He sal noght aftir his lyfes ende
Wend strek til purgatory,
Bot even til helle with-outen mercy.
Bot if he wille hym repent and shrife
Of alle swilk syns here in his lyfe,
Fra helle pyne þan es he save;

Penance must be performed on earth or else in Purgatory.

Bot payn and penaunce hym byhoves have
In purgatory, als I wene,
Until he be made of alle syn clene;
Forwhy penaunce for syn, als I sayd are,
Most be fulfilled outher here or þare.
Syns þat er veniele may dere,
Bot þai er noght swa hevy to bere,
Als er dedly, for þai may be here
Fordon on light manere.

For als men heres þer clerkes say,
Ilk man here lyghtly may
Swilk remedys thurgh grace wyn,
Þat may fordo al veniel syn;
Þat es to say, if he clene be
Of dedly syn, and wil it fle;
For I fynd writen ten thynges sere,
Þat veniel syns fordus here.

Ten things destroy venial sins.

Þas ten er þir þat I now rede;
Haly water and almusdede,
Fastyng, and housil of Goddes body,
Prayer of þe *Pater Noster* namly,
General shrifte, þat ilk day may be,
Benyssoun of bisshope of his dignité;
And benyssoun of prest, þat gyyen es
Namly, in þe end of þe mes;
Knokyng of[1] þe brest of man þat es meke,
Last enoyntyng gyven to þe seke.
Þer ten puttes veniel syns away,
Als men may here þer clerkes say.

1. Holy water, 2. almsdeed, 3. fasting, 4. the sacrament, 5. the Pater Noster, 6. shrift, 7 and 8. blessing of the bishop and priest, 9. knocking on the breast of a meek man, 10. anointing of the sick.

Bot swa many veniel syns sere
May be gadyrd atans togyder here,
Þat þai may weghe on þe saul als hevy
Als a syn dus þat es dedly,
Þat slas þe saul and God myspays;
And þarfor þe poet on þis wyse says:
De minimis granis fit
maxima summa caballo.

Many venial sins press heavily on the soul.

"Als of many smale cornes es made
Til a hors bak a mykel lade,"
Right swa may veniel syns many
Mak a mykel syn dedly.
For þai gadir on þe saul ful thyk,
And cleves togyder als dos pyk,
Bot if þat swythe be done oway,
Ay als þai com, with-outen delay;

A deadly sin may arise out of many venial ones.

[1] On (MS. Harl. 6923).

For swa parfitely may nane lyf here,
With-outen veniel syns sere.
For a man syns alday þat here duels
Als þe boke says þat þus tels.
Septies in die cadit
iustus

Seven times a day the righteous man sins.

"Seven sythes at þe lest o[f] þe day
Þe ryghtwys falles," þat es to say,
In sere syns þat er veniel,
Bot som er mare, and som les to fel.

The various kinds of venial sins.

In swa many veniel syns we falle,
Þat na man can reken þam alle;
Bot sum of þam reherce I can,
Als Saynt Austyn telles, þe haly men.
For in a boke he reherces som,
Þat mast es used of custom,
And to telle þat[1] syns he þus bygyns,
And says þat þer er veniel syns.

Excess in eating and drinking.

First when a man etes or drinkes mare
Anytime, þan myster ware;

Uncharitableness.

When þou may vaile thurgh wytte and skille
And wille noght help bot haldes þe stylle;

Speaking sharply to the poor.

When þou spekes sharppely til þe pure,
Þat sum gode askes at þi dore;

Eating at fasting time.

When þou erte hale and may wele last
And etes when tym es to fast;
When þe lyst slepe and wil noght ryse,

Coming late to church.

And comes overlate tyl Goddes servise;
Or when þou ert in gude state

Saying prayers late.

And says þi praers ever late;
Or when þou says praier or orison

Want of devotion.

With over litel devocion;
When a man list dele in bed
With his wyfe þat he has wed,

Lust.

Hys lust anly for to fulfille,
And to gette a child es noght in wille;

[1] þas?

When þou visites men overlate
Leaving the sick unvisited.
Þat sek er and in febel state,
Or men þat lyes in prison,
Or in any tribulacion,
Or men þat er synful and sary,
Or saules þat er in purgatory;
For to visite þam it war grete nede,
Thurgh praier and thurgh almusdede;
When þou paynes þe noght aftir þi state
Neglecting to act the part of the peace-maker.
To accorde þam þat er at debate;
When þou spekes over bitterly
Til any man with noyse or cry;
When þou prayses any man mare
Thurgh flateryng, þan mister ware;
Flattery.
When þou in kirk makes ianglyng,
Or thynkes in vayn anythyng;
Jangling in church, and idle thoughts.
Be it with-outen, be it with-in,
Yhit it es a veniel syn;
When þou ert over lyghtly wrathe,
Anger, swearing.
Or sweres and may noght hald þin athe;
When þou bannes any man,
Cursing.
In wham þou fyndes na gilt to ban;
When þou supposes any wykkednes,
Thurgh suspecion þar na es.
Suspicion.
Þir smale syns Saynt Austyn telles,
Thurgh whilk many saules duelles
In purgatory, in payne and wa.
Bot yhit þar er ful many ma
Of veniel syns, be[1] many a score,
Over þas þat I haf tald byfore.
Bot swa witty es nane erthely man,
Þat alle veniel syns reken can;
Venial sins are innumerable.
For ofte sythes of þe day men falles
In syns, þat clerkes veniel calles,
Thurgh werk, or worde, or thoght in vayn,
And ilka syn es worthy payn,
Each sin is pain worthy.

[1] by?

Þe whilk most be fordone clenly,
Outher here or in purgatory.
Þarfor I rede ilk man, whyles he lyffes here,
Þat he use þa ten thinges sere
Þat fordus, als I sayde are,
Alle veniel syns, bathe les and mare.
And if any fal in dedly syn

Deadly sin must be shriven by the priest.

Ryse he up, and ligg noght lang þar-in,
And ga to þe prest hym to shrife,
And tak his penaunce in his life,
And haf he forthynkyng ay in thoght,
For þas syns þat he has wroght,
And do he penance with al his myght,
And be in prayers, bathe day and night,
And fast and ga wolwarde, and wake,
And thole hardes[1] for Goddes sake;
For na man may to heven ga,
Bot-if he thole here anger and wa.
And when God sendes a man angwise
He suld thole it with-outen fayntise,
Be it sekenes, or oght elles þat greves,
Losse of catelle, or of fre[n]des þat lyves,
Or unkyndnes, fals[h]ed, or treson,

Tribulation should be patiently endured.

Or any other tribulacion,
Thole he it mekely and thynk in thoght
Þat with-outen cause commes it noght.
Bot God wate wele þe cause why,
Parchaunce it es for his foly,
To chasty hym on swilk manere,
For his syns þat he dyd here,
Or it may be hym here to pruve,
Or to make hym mar drede God and lufe.
Þarfor sen God ofte vouches save
Þat a man here swilk angers have,
Outher for his syn or hym to fande;
Love he him þan of alle his sande,

[1] hardnes (Harl. 6923).

And take mekely þat God him sendes,
And fle alle thyng þat he defendes.
For thurgh nuyes and angers sere,
He makes a man, als his preson here,
Payn to drighe for hys foly,
In þis lif als he es worthy.
And, if he it thole noght grotchand,
In-stede of penance it sal hym stand,
And yhit wille God him mare do,
He wil gif him mede þar-to,
Þat his ioy in heven sal heke,
If he thole angwyse with hert meke.
Als þe gude son tholes mekely
Þe fader, when he wille hym chasty,
Swa suld ilk man thole and love God ay,
And do alle þe gude þat he may,
And specialy almusdede,
Þe naked to clathe, and hungry to fede,
And other werkes of mercy wirke,
Als theches and preches haly kirke;
And kepe him clene, to his lyfes ende,
Fra syn, þan sal his saul wende
Til blis, and lyghtly pas alle payne
Of purgatori; þis es certayne.
Here haf I shewed yhow, on Inglys,
Som syns þat Saynt Austyn specifys.
Now wil I shew what help es certayne
For þam þat in purgatory has payne,
And what may mak þair payn cees
And þam of þair payn to haf relees.
Þe saules, þat til purgatory wendes,
May be helped thurgh help of frendes,
Þat almus for þam dus, and prays,
For þe haly man, Saynt Austyn says:
Non est negandum spiritus defunctorum, pietate
suorum viventium, posse relevari.
He says "men shuld not denye on na manere,
Þat þe saules of þam þat er dede here,

Sorrow serves instead of penance.

The means by which the pains of Purgatory may be alleviated and shortened.

Help of friends.

Of payn may relesed be
Thurgh frendes lyfand þat has pyté."
For als þas þat passed, als I sayd are,
Til purgatory er pyned þare
For weniel syns, mare and lesse,
Aparty, thurgh Goddes rightwisnesse,
Right swa thurgh help þai may aparty,
Be relesed þar, thurgh Goddes mercy.
Alle þat men dus here, bathe les and mare,
For þe saules þat duelles þare
Avayles þam noght als to heven mede,
Bot for þair deliverance fra payn to spede.

Of the four kinds of help that assists the souls in Purgatory.

Four maners of helpes er general,
Þat in purgatory availes þam al,
Þat es to say, prayer and fastyng,
And almus dede and messyng.
On twa maners, als clerkes can se,
Þe saule fra payn deliverd may be;
Þe tane by way of grace es,
And þe tother by way of rightwisnes,
By way of grace on twyn manere
Als es writen in þis boke here.

1. Prayer.

First thurgh prayer of Crist þat es hede,
When he es offerd in fourme of brede,
Thurgh prestes hande here at þe mes,
When þe sacrament swa made es.
Alswa thurgh prayer of his lyms,
Þat es, of gude men þat toward heven clyms.
Þan may þe saules in purgatory,
By way of grace specialy,
Be delivered of pyn þat ders,
Thurgh messes and rightwis men prayers.
By way of rightwysnes help may be
On twyn maners, als yhe may se.

2. Almsdeed.

First, through byhyng of paynes þat greves,
With almus, þat men to the pure gyves.
Another es here thurgh assethe makyng,

3. Fasting.

Als thurgh penance of fre[n]des and fastyng.

Þus may saules, als þe buke beres wytnes,
By helpyd by way of rightwysnes,
Þat es to say, þai may in þat nede
Be boght fra payn thurgh almusdede;
And thurgh penance for þam here don,
Þe dette of payn may be qwitte son,
Right als a man, þat duelles in prison
Til he haf payed a certayn raunson;
May be delyverd and broght away
Thurgh a frende, þat wille it for hym pay.
On þis wyse may þe saules þat wendes
Til purgatory, be helped thurgh fre[n]des.
Bot sum frende may help, and som noght,
Þe saules þat til purgatory er broght.
Thurgh þas frendes may þai helped be
Þat here lyves thurgh ryght charité.

Some friends are of service to those in Purgatory, and some are not.

Bot þe help of þam, þat charité failles
Til þe saules þat er þar noght availles,
For alle er als lymes of a body,
Þat here er, and in purgatory;
And als we may se properly here
A body hafe many lymmes sere,
And ilkan of þam, bathe les and mare,
May help other þat feles sare;
Bot if a lym dighe, and þe myght faile,
Þat lym may noght til þe others availe.
Right swa it fars on þe same wyse,
By þam [þat] in purgatory lyese,
And þat er here; for men may þam calle
Als lyms of a body alle.
Wha-swa in dedly syn es broght
And charité in his hert has noght,
He es als dede in saul with-in;
Ay, whiles he es in dedly syn,
His help vailles noght, bot es in vayne
Als to þe saules þat er in payne.
His help thurgh hym-selfe standes in na stede,
For he es als a lym þat es dede;

Those in deadly sin, have no power to help their friends.

Bot never-þe-latter, alle-if he swa be
In syn and out of charité,
Yhit may he helpe þe saales þus,
If he til pure men gyf almus,
Þat þai for þe saules pray specialy
And helpes þe saules in purgatory.
Yhit may þe help and þe travaile
Of sum synful men þe saules avayle,

The help of the sinful may be of service.

If it thurgh biddyng done be
Of a frende þat es in charité;
Or of[1] þe dede self þat has mast nede
Of help of prayer and almusdede;
Þat help may avayle þe saules son
For his sake, þat biddes it be don,
Þat charity in hert has knytt
And noght for his sake þat dos it,
For-why God wille noght do for his sake
Þat charité wille noght in hert take.
Þis case ofte falles, als I understande,
Bytwen a loverd and his servande,
Whare þe loverd es gude and rightwys,
And þe servand ille and uses folys.
If þe servand do anythyng
Þat es gude at his loverdys bydyng,
Yhit may it availle to a gude use,
Alle-if he be ille þat it duse;
And þat by reson of þe gudenes
Of hym of wham þe bygynnyng es.
For alle be it onence þe doer dede[2],
Onence þe bidder it standes in stede;
Bot if þai bathe in charité ware
Þe helpe til þe dede war wele þe mare.

A sinful priest is still the minister of God and holy church.

Alswa a prest alle-if he be
Synful and out of charité,
He es Goddes minister and haly kirkes,
Þat þe sacrament of þe auter wirkes;

[1] The MS. has 'if'.

[2] Anence the doer if it be dede. (MS. Harl. 6923.)

Þe wilk es never-þe-les of myght,
Alle-if þe prest here lyf noght right.
For if a prest þat synges mes
Be never swa ful of wykednes,
Þe sacrament, þat es swa haly,
May noght apayred be thurgh his foly.
Þan may mes saules fra payn bring,
Alle-if a synful prest it syng.
For in Goddes name he synges þe mes,
Under wham in order he es.
Bot speciel prayers with gude entente,
Þat es made besyde þe sacramente.
Of a gude prest er wele better
Þan of an ille, and to God swetter;
Bot þe offeryng of Goddis body
Helpes þe saules principaly;
Wharfor it semes þat mes syngyng
May titest þe saul out of payn bryng,
Þat passes hethen in charité,
And in purgatory clensed suld be.
Bot til þam þat er dampned for ay
Na gude dede avayle ne help may,
Nouther almus dede, prayer, ne messe,
For þai er, als þe buke bers witnesse,
Departed halely fra þe body of Criste,
And þe saules for ever er periste,
For als lymmes, þat er dede, er þai
Þat er hewed fra þe body oway.
And als nathyng may help kyndely
Þe lymes þat er cutted fra þe body,
Right swa alle helpes þat men can telle,
Availles þam noght þat er in helle.
Yhit help of frendes here on sum wyse,
Availles þam þat er in paradise,
And alswa þam þat in helle duelles,
Als a grete clerk in boke telles.
Þan availles almus, messe, and bedes,
To þe saules þat er in alle þre stedes;

The sin of the priest does not destroy the efficacy of the Sacrament.

4. Mass.

The souls in hell, are not assisted by any of the four aids that are of service to those in Purgatory.

How the help of friends serves those in Paradise as well as those in Hell.

Þai availe þe saules in purgatory
To spede þam out mare hastily.
Þai vaile þam þat in heven er;
For þai multiplie þar þe titter,
And þe ma þat gaders to þat place,
Þe mare þair ioy es, and solace.
Þai avail til þam þat er in helle,
For þe foner shuld com þider to duelle,
And þe foner þat þider commes for syn,
Þe les payn þai have þat duelles þar-in;

The fewer that go to hell, the less pain those feel who dwell there.

And ay þe ma saules þat þider wendes,
Þe mare þair payne es, þat never endes.
Þus may help here and availe be skille
Til þe saules þat duelles ay in helle stille;
And til þe saules þat er in heven namly,
And til þam þat er in purgatory.
Bot help may na saules out of payn spede,
Bot þam þat has charité and nede.

No charity exists in hell or need in heaven.

For in helle es na charité,
And in heven na ned may be.
Bot bathe þa twa þe saules has
Þat fra hethen til purgatory gas.
And als a man may here with his hande,
Make asethe for another lyfande,
Þe whilk es noght of power þar-to,
Right swa may a man for þe ded do.
Þe saules þat til paradise er gane
Nede of help here haf þai nane;
Bot if for þam war don any gude dede,
It may availe þam, þat of help has nede.
Þe help þat es don here specialy
Availles til þe saules in purgatory,
Bot to som mare and til som les,
Aftir þai er of worthynes;
And aftir þe charité es clere
Of þam þat er lyffand here,
Þat mast er bysy, and dus mare
For sum þan for other þat er þare.

Bot when a man fra þis world sal flitte
Na man for certayn here may wytte
Whether he sal þan-til purgatory wende,
Or to blisse or to payn with-outen ende.
For som semes gude here and parfite,
Þat, after þe dede, er dampned als-tite;
For parchaunce þai er ille with-in,
And passes away in dedely syn.
Some semes synful, als þai lyfed mys,
Þat er save and er in þe way til blisse,
For parchaunce byfor þair endyng,
Þai er amended of þair myslyvyng.
Of þis may na man certayn be,
For it es Goddes pryveté.
Bot we shuld trow, and suppose ay
Þat alle er save and in gude way,
Þat we se here gude werkes wirk,
And has þe sacramentes of halikyrk.
Bot whether it be or noght þus,
We suld do þat es in us;
We suld pray, bathe loud and stille,
For al cristen saules; þus charité wille.
Now sum may aske why synges men mes
For a yhong child when it dede es,
Þat of prayer, ne mes has na nede,
For it couth never do synful dede.
Þis may be þe right skille why,
For þe lovyng of God principaly
And for usage of haly kyrk,
And for þe dedes use þat office to wirk.
And yhit may þe mes in sum case
Help þam in purgatory þat ned hase.
Here haf yhe herde, als þe buke bers witnes,
How almus, penance, praier and mes,
Þat er done thurgh fre[n]des certayne,
May help þe saules þat[1] er in payne.
Now wille I shew yhow yhit mare þarto,
What pardon may to þe saules do,

No man is certain of his future state.

Why mass is sung for a young child.

On the use of pardon to the soul.

[1] The MS. reads 'þar'.

Þe whilk þai purchaced, on right manere
In clene lif whilles þai liffed here.
Pardon helpes þam, als clerkes says,
Þat it has purchased in þair lif days;
For pardon of papes and bisschopes,
Þat es granted here als men hopes,
May availe þair saules in purgatory,
Þat has purchaced it here worthyly,
If þai of þair syn had contricion
And war shrifen byfor þat pardon,
Þan may pardon after þair dede
In purgatory þam stand in stede.

Pardon releases the soul from the 'debt of pain.'

For pardon here, þat es certayn,
May þam relese of þe dede[1] of payn,
Als fer-forthe als pardon may reche,
Þus haf I herd grete clerkes preche.
Pardon properly noght elles es
Bot of payne, þat es dette, forgyfnes.

Pardon is a part of the treasure of holy church.

Pardon may nane hafe bot he wil wirke,
For it es of þe tresur of haly kirke,
Þat es gadirde for nede of pardon,
Of þe vertu of Crestes passion,
And of þe worthines of þe dedys
Of his halowes and of þair medys;
And [it] es gaderd on many maners;
First als of marterdom of martires;
Of penance and travail of confessours,
And of þe thechyng of docturs;
And of chastité of virgyns clene,
Þat chast and haly ay has bene;
Of þe fruyt of haly kirk werkes,
And of þe prayers of gude prestes and clerkes;
Of alle þis, als I shewed byfor,
Es gadird haly kirkes tresor;

The Pope bears the keys of this treasure.

Of wilk þe pape þe kays bers,
Whar-with he bathe opens and spers.

[1] dette (MS. Harl. 6923).

Þat falles hym of office to halde,
For he es in erthe, Godes vicar calde.
The Pope is God's vicar.
Þa cays er noght elles to se
Bot playn power of his dignité,
Thurgh whilk he may, be law and skille,
Louse and bynde at his wille.
For þe sam power hym falles to have,
Þat Crist til Peter in erthe gave.
For Crist gave to Peter playn powere,
And says to hym on þis manere.
Quodcunque ligaveris super terram
erit ligatum et in celis, Et quodcunque
solveris super terram, erit solutum
et in celis.
"Alle þat þou byndes in erthe," says he,
"Sal in heven bunden be
And alle þat þou lowses in erthe right
Sal be loused in heven bright."
Þis power til alle papes gaf he,
Þat aftir Petre in erthe shuld be,
The power given to St. Peter, is given to all the Popes after him.
Als shewes an exposicion
Of þe haly godspelle in a lesson.
Þan semes it wele by þis skille here,
Þat þe pape has swa large powere
To assoyle a man, and hym forgyfe,
Alle þe dette of payn þat may greve,
Swa þat he, þat þe pape assoyles, fulfille
Þat, þat þe laghe of þe gospelle wille,[1]
And yheld agayn, if he be myghty,
Alle þat he tas wrangwysly;
For when þe pape, þat grace wil do,
He byndes hym and alle haly kirk þarto
For hym til wham þat grace avayles
To fulfille alle þat in hym failles,
Bot bischopes here of lagher state,
And has les power, als clerkes wate,
The bishop has less power than the Pope.

[1] Yf he þat es assoilede fulfylle
Als þe lawe and þe godespelle wille. (Harl. 6923.)

For-why þair dignité here es les
And þarfor þair powere restreyned es;
Bot if it be noght swa suffishaunt
Als þe papes es, yhit may þai graunt
Of þair power pardon aparty
Til þair hawen underloutes[1] anly;
And yhit most þat, als I sayd befor,
Be gyfen of haly kirkes tresor.

No man may obtain pardon unless he be out of deadly sin.

Bot na man may here pardon wyn,
Bot he be out of dedly syn;
For he, þat kepyng of þat fair tresour has,
May noght it dele til haly kyrk fas;
And swilk er þai and nan elles
Þat here in dedly syn duelles;
For out of haly kirk er þai,
Þarfor na pardon whyn þai may.
Bot þe frendes of haly kirk may wyn
Pardon, for þai er with-in;
And swilk er þas þat here er fre
Of dedly syns and er in charité;
Til wham pardon sal noght fail,
Bot in purgatory it sal þam avail,
To allege þair saules of payne,
Als fer als it reches of certayne,
Þe whilk, als sum says, falles to be sett

Of the 'remnant of the debt of pain'.

For þe [r]emenand of payns, þat es, dett
Þat parchaunce es lefte undon here;
And þat may falle on sere manere.
Aparty for penance þat es [en]ioynt,
Þat es noght done at þe dedes poynt;
Aparty for veniel syns sere;
Aparty for syns þat er forgeten here;
Aparty for over litelle penance,
And for over littelle repentance;
Aparty, for penance enioint, and done
Parchaunce over reklesly and over sone;
Aparty, for penance þat enioynt es,
And es forgeten thurgh reklesnes.

[1] underlynges (MS. Y).

Alle þis may be cald þe remenand,
Of þe dette of payn, als I understand
Þe whilk felle to be fulfylled haly,
Outher here or in purgatory,
Bot alle þis dett may þar be qwytt
Thurgh large pardon, wha-swa has itt,
In forgyvenes of alle penance soght,
Whethir it be here enioynt or noght.
For swa mykel pardoun may a man
Purches here, þat he may þan
In purgatory qwyte alle þe dett,
Þat hym fra blis may tary or lett;
For swa large es haly kirkes tresor,
Þat it es ynogh to pay þarfor,
And for alle þe paynes þat dett may be
Of alle þe men of cristanté.
Þus pardon in purgatory availles,
Als I tald; bot som clerkes counsailles
Þat we it spare and reserve halely,
Until we com til purgatory,
And do here penance whilles we lyf may,
For a man sal thynk þare a day
Lenger þan hever thogh[t] him here,
Þe space of alle ane hale yhere;
Þan es a day of pardon to gesce
Mare worthy þan alle þis worldis riches,
For þe saule had lever, þat in payn dueles,
A day of pardon þan anythyng elles;
For alle þe werld, [if] it his ware,
He wald gyf for rest a day þare.
Of þis maters, þat þus mas mencion
Of help of frendes and of pardon
Þat vailles þam þat er in purgatory,
Als I shewed byfor openly,
Spekes Innocent and Austyn
In bukes, whar þair[1] maters er sen;
And Raymu[n]d spekes of þe same
In a boke, þat es called his name;

The treasure of holy church is sufficiently large, to release from 'the debt of pain' all the men in christendom.

A day in Purgatory will seem longer than a year on earth.

Of the authors who have written about Purgatory.

[1] þir?

And Thomas Alqwyn spekes alswa
Of þis mater, and of other ma
In a boke, þe whilk made he,
Þat[1] hat Veritas Theologie.
Here I have many maters redde,
And þe ferthe parte of þis boke spede,
The subjects discussed in Book IV. In þe qwilk yhe hafe herd me specify
Þe condicions of purgatory.
First what it es to fele and se,
And whar God has ordaynd it to be;
And what paynes falles þar-to, les and mare,
And whilk saules byhoves be pyned þare;
And alswa for what manere of syn,
And what may þam help þat er þar-in.
Of al þis haf I spoken til þe ende,
And now wille I til þe fifte part wende,
Þat spekes of þe day of dome,
And of takens þat byfor sal come.

Here bygyns þe fifte part þat es of
þe day of dome and of takens þat sal cum byfor.

In þis part men may of ten þinges rede,
Signa ante Judicium. Þat touches þe grete day of drede,
Of whilk sum byfor þat day sal be,
And at þe day, als men sal se.
I. Þe first es of the wonderful takens sere,
Þat byfor þat day sal be shewed here.
II. Þe secunde es of þe fire þat sal bryn
Þe world and al þat es þar-in.
III. Þe thred es of þe rysyng generale
Of alle men, bathe grete and smale.
IV. Þe ferthe es of crystes commyng don
Til þe dome, in proper parson.
V. Þe fifthe es þe certayn stede
Whar Crist sal deme bathe qwik and dede.
VI. Þe sexte es of þe fourme of man,
In whilk Crist sal shew hym þan.

[1] 'And' (Harl. 6923).

Þe sevend, of þe accusers many, VII.
Þat þe synful saul sal accuse þar openly.
Þe aghtynd, of þe acunt and þe rekennyng, VIII.
Þat þai sal yheld of alle þair lyfyng.
Þe neghend, of al men aftir þai haf wroght, IX.
Of wilk som sal be demed, and som noght,
Þe tend es of þe grete dome final, X.
Þat Crist sal gyf and mak ende of al.
Of þir sal som falle, als yhe herd me say,
Byfor þat day and sum at þe day. The tokens of the day of doom.
Byfor þe day sere takens sal com,
Of whilk men may here fynd wreten some,
Als of ancrist[1] commyng, and his pousté,
And of other ma þat byfor þat day sal be,
Þe whilk takens men sal thynk ful harde,
Als yhe may se and here afterwarde.
And wha-swa wille avise hym wele,
He may ilk day here, se, and fele
Takens, war-thurgh he may understande,
Þat þe day of dome es fast comande.
For wonders þat shuld falle, als I trow,
Agayn þe worldes hende er sene now,
Thurgh whilk wondres grete clerkes knawes
Þat þe worlde fast to þe endeward drawes.
Wharfor we shuld make us redy here,
Als þe day of dome war command nere.
Crist disciples, þat yherned haf knawyng,
Of sum takens agayns his last commyng, Of the tokens of Christ's last coming.
Spak to Crist, als yhe may here,
In þe godspelle on þis manere:
Dic nobis signum adventus tui et
consummacionem seculi; Et respondens,
Ihesus Christus dixit eis, Videte ne quis vos sedu-
cat; multi enim venient in nomine
meo dicentes, Ego sum Cristus, et multos
seducent &c. Consurget enim gens

[1] 'Antecrist' (Harl. 6923).

contra gentem et regnum in regnum,
et erunt pestulencie et fames, et terre
motus per loca. Hec autem omnia
inicia sunt dolorum, et habundabit
iniquitas, et refrigescet caritas multorum.
"Says us", cryed þai, "of þi commyng
Som taken and of þe world endyng.

The answer given by Christ to the inquiry about the signs of his last coming.

Crist als tite answerd þam þan,
And sayd lukes þat yhow desayve na man,
For many sal com in my name,
Þat sal say þus, 'Crist I am,'
And many a man þai sal bygilo
Bot þai sal regne here bot a while;
And rewme ogayne rewme, on þe same wyse
Men ogayne men, thurgh strength, sal ryse;
Pestilences and hungers sal be,
And erthedyns in many contré.
And al þis sal be bygynnyng hard
Of þe sorows þat sal com aftirward;
Wykkednesse sal wax many falde,
And charité of many sal wax calde."
Þir takens til his disciples tald he
Þat ogayn þe worldes ende shuld be.
Bot sum of þir takens has bene,
And sum of þam sal yhit be sene.
And of takens þat yhit sal com,
If yhe wille, I sal tel yhow som.

Of Antichrist who shall come before doomsday.

And first of ancrist wille I say
Þat sal com befor domesday,
Aftir þe destruccion sal be
Of þe empyre of Rome, þat es yhit fre.
Som tyme al landes of þe world obout
Was sugette til Rome and underlout,
Þat at certayn teremes [1] gaf it trowage,
Als þe custom þan was and þe usage;
Þat custom alle landes þan byhoved do,
Bot Saynt Paule says þus þarto:

[1] termes (Harl. 4196).

Quoniam nisi venerit dissencio primum etc.,
id est, nisi prius dissenserint omnia regna
a Romano Imperio, que prius erant sub-
dita, non antea veniet antichristus.
He says "bot if dissencion come,
Before the coming of Antichrist Rome must be destroyed.
Þat es, bot-if alle landes hald agayn Rome,
Swa þat it be put til destruccion
Thurgh þam þat first was in subieccion,
Of the destruction of Rome.
Anticrist ar þat tyme sal noght com
Þat sal com byfor þe day of dom.
Þat destrucion, als says haly writt,
Sal be, bot þat tyme com noght yhitt.
Fra þat tyme sal na land ne contré
In subieccion of Rome langer be;
Ne fra þan sal na man be bughsome,
Ne obedient to þe kirk of Rome.
Men sese þat þe empire, þat was swa myghty,
Es now destruyed a grete party;
Bot at þe last, als I sayd are,
It sal be destruyed wele mare,
Bot þe dignité þat til it sal falle,
Sal noght in þat tyme perysshe alle.
It sal stand and duelle with-outen dout
In alle his regyons obout.
Þos sal þe first taken bygyn at Rome;
The first token of the day of doom shall begin at Rome.
For it es heved of al cristendome;
For when it es put til destrucion
Alle haly kyrk sal be put don.
Some clerkes says þat an sal come
Þat sal hald þe empire of Rome
Alle halely and his croun bere
Wele, and in pees with-outen were.
He sal be last emparour þat þare sal be,
Of the last emperor of Rome.
And mast of alle kynges of pousté;
Þe whilk sal wele maynten his state
And þe empire, with-outen debate,
And it governe thurgh laghe and witte,
Als lang als he sal hald itte.

Bot afterwarde at þe last ende
Until Ierusalem he sal wende;
And on þe mount of Olyvette
He sal þe septre of Rome sette,
And his coron he sal lay don alswa,
And lef þam þar and fra þam ga.
Þus sal ende þe dignité of Rome;
And als sone aftir sal anticrist come,
Als clerkes says, þat has understandyng
Of Daniel and of Saynt Paul saying;
Þan sal anticrist þat tyme bygyn,

St. Paul speaks of Antichrist as the 'man of sin'.

Þat Saynt Paul calles þe man of syn.
For alle-if he be man, never-þe-les,
He sal be welle of alle wykkednes.
Þe devels son he sal be cald;
Bot thurgh kynd men shuld him noght swa hald,
Bot thurgh his turnyng fra gode til ille;
For he sal þe devels wille fulfille.
Alle þe power of þe devel of helle
And alle his witte in hym sal duelle;
In wham al þe tresor of malice
Sal be hidde with alle maner of vice.
He sal til Criste contrarius be
And til alle his lyms þat he sal se;

Antichrist shall exalt himself above all the pagan deities.

And heghen hym thurgh pride, þat he sal halde,
Aboven al þat er paens goddes calde.
Þat es to say, Iubiter and Mercury,
And Appolyn and Herculy;
And noght anly oboven þa goddes alle,
Þat þe paens þair goddes sal calle,

He shall exalt himself above the holy Trinity.

Bot he sal heghe himself to be
Aboven þe haly trinité;
And alle þe creatours, bath mare and les,
Shuld honoure over alle thyng þat es,
Ful synful sal be his bygynnyng,
And wonderful sal be his lyvyng.
And his endyng sal be sodayn;
For thurgh myght of God he [sal] be slayn,

In his tyme sal be swylk tribulacion
And swa mykel parsecucion,
Þat unnethes any sal dur graunt
Þat he es cristen, and God servant.
For mare parsecucion sal be þan,
Þan ever was sythen þe world bygan.
Anticrist es, þos mykel at say,
Als he þat es ogayn Crist ay.

Antichrist signifies one who is against Christ.

Þan may ilk man be cald by skille
Anticrist þat dos ogayn Goddes wille.
Þan may alle þas anticristes be calde,
Þat ogaynes Goddes laghe will halde.
Bot ma[n]y swilk men may wele knawe
Þat mykel dus ogayns Goddes lawe.[1]
Bot anticrist, als says haly writ,
Sal com at þe last, þat com noght yhitt,
Als mast tyraunt with-outen pyté,
Þat ever was or ever sal be.
Wharfor I hald þir gret mysdoers
Als anticrist lyms and his forgangers.
Now wha-swa wille a whyle duelle
Aparty here I wille hym telle
Of þe maner of anticrist bygynnyng,
And of his lif and of hys endyng.
He sal be geten, als clerkes shew can,
Bytwen a synful man and a woman,
And aftir þat he consayved sal be
Þe fende sal entre, thurgh his pousté,
With-in his moder wambe sone;

He shall be begotten by a sinful man on a woman, into whose womb the devil shall enter;

Þus, sais a grete clerke, sal be done
Thurgh was myght he sal be forth-broght;
And wonders thurgh hym sal be wroght.
He sal be cald þe child þat es lorn;
And in Corozaym he sal be born
Of a woman of þe kynred of San[2];
Bot cristendome sal he have nan.

and shall be born at Chorazin and come of the tribe of Dan.

[1] Be many skill we may some knawe
Þat mekille dose agayne Goddes lawe. (MS. Harl. 6923.)

[2] Dane (MS. Harl. 6923) = of the tribe of Dan.

He sal be maliciouse and ful of envy,
Als of hym þus spekes þe prophecy:
Fiat Dan coluber in via, cerastes
in semita, mordens ungulas equi,
ut cadat ascensor eius retro, Hoc est [Anticristus] sicut
serpens, in via sedebit, et in semita erit,
ut eos, qui per semitam iusticie ambu-
lant, feriat et veneno sue malicie occidat.

For Dan, as the adder in the way, denotes Antichrist.

"Þe Dan" he says "sal þe nedder be
Sitand in þe way als men sal se;
And sal byte þe hors by þe hufe harde,
And mak þe upstegher fal bakwarde:
And þat es þus mykel at say,
Als[1] anticrist, als nedder, sal sit in þe way,
And smyte þam alle, bathe mare and les,
Þat walkes in þe way of rightwysnes,
And sla þam thurgh þe venym
Of þe malice þat sal cum of hym."
Yhit sal he be circumcid
And thurgh þat his malice a whyle sal hid.

And though a good angel shall be assigned him,

Alswa til hym sal assygned be
A gude angelle, þat he sal noght se,
Aftir his birthe in his bygynnyng,
Þat of him sal haf þe kepyng,
Bot for he agayn þe trouthe þat es,

It will be obliged to leave him to the devil.

Sal be hardend in wikkednes
His gude angelle sal fra hym wende,
And leve hym in þe kepyng of þe fende.

He shall be brought up in the city of Bethsaida,

He sal be lered, als I understand,
And nurist and mast conversand
In þe cité of Bethsayda;
In Capharnaum he sal regne alswa
Þe whilk Bethsayda, and Capharnaum,
And Corozaym God weried whilom;
For God spak til þas thre cites þos,
Als þe godspelle here shewes us:

[1] þat (Harl. 4196).

Ve tibi Corozayin! Ve tibi Bethsayda!
Ve tibi Capharnaum!
He says, "wa til þe Corozaym mot cum
4208 And til þe Bethsayda and Capharnaum."
For þus in þe first he sal be born and bredde,
And in þe secunde be nuryst, and regne in þe thredde.

And reign in Capernaum.

He sal gader fast til hym þan
4212 Alle þat of þe devels crafte can,
Als negremanciens and tregettours,
Wiches and false enchauntours,
Þat þe devels crafte sal hym ken
4216 Whar-thurgh he sal decayve þe men.

Antichrist shall gather around him necromancers, witches, magicians &c.

Afterwarde thurgh ledyng of þe fende
He sal even to Ierusalem wende;
And þar sal he duelle in þat cité
4220 And in myddes þe temple make his se,

He shall go up to Jerusalem,

And say til alle þat þar sal won,
Þat he es Crist, Goddes son,
And mak þe folk hym to honour;
4224 And sal say þat he es þair saveour.

and say that he is Christ,

He sal say þat na right cristen man
Was never byfor his tym bygan,
Bot fals anticristes he sal þam calle;
4228 And say þai lyved in fals trowthe alle
Þat has bene fra þe worldes bygynnyng
Until þe tyme of his commyng.
He sal be lusty and lycherous,
4232 And desayvabel and trecherous;

and be lusty and lecherous;

He sal hym feyn first als haly,
And shew þan appert ypocr[is]y,
To desayve cristen men and lele
4236 Als says þe prophet Danielle:
In aperto tum per ypocrisym simulabit sanctitatem, ut facilius decipere possit.
"First" he says "he sal apertely
4240 Feyn halynes thurgh ypocrisy,
Þat he mught lightlyer men bygile."
Bot þat time sal last bot a while,

though he shall at first, feign to be holy.

He sal al kynges and princes til hym drawe
And turne þam alle til his lawe;
And thurgh þam þe poples sal turned be
Of ilka land and ilka cuntré.
In alle stedes he sal walk and pas,
Þar Crist welk when he in erthe was.
In swylk a presumpcion he sal falle
Þat he sal thynk hym loverd of alle.
Thurgh pride he sal ogayn God ryse
And hym sclaunder and his law dispise,
And afforce hym and be bysy,

Antichrist shall afterwards turn all people to his law in four ways.

His laghe to chaunge and fordo haly;
He sal turne al poples to his lawe,
And til him on four maners þam drawe.
I. A manere sal be, thurgh fals prechyng
II. Another thurgh fals miracles shewyng,
III. Þe thred thurgh large gyftes to gyfe,
IV. And þe ferthe thurgh drede of turmentis griefe.
Thurgh fals prechyng in ilk cuntré
Many til hym sal turned be.
For he sal send thurgh alle þe world wyde
His prechours to preche on ilka side,

He shall proclaim the law of Christ to be false.

Þe qwilk sal preche undir fals colour,
And say Cristes lawe es not bot errour;
And anticristes lawe þai sal comend
And agayn suthfastnes it defend,
And forbede ilk man þat þai noght halde
Þe new lawe, þat es Cristes lawe calde,
And his ministres sal swa lette yhit
Þat na man sal expound haly writ,
Þat es to say, to right undirstandyng.
For þai sal say it es bot lesyng,
And make þe pople to trow haly

He shall bring the people into error.

Þat þai sal noght be saved þarby.
Þus sal þai bring þe folk in errour
Thurgh þair prechyng with false colour,
Swa his lawes sal pas and his powere
Fra þe est syde til þe west, thurgh þe world here;

And fra þe southe til þe north, alswa
His lawes and his power sal ga.
He sal turne men on another manere
Thurgh fals miracles and wonders sere;
For he sal þan shew wonders many
Thurgh enchauntementes and nygroma[n]cy.
Swa gretely, þat þe pople sal se,
And þat thurgh myght of þe devel sal be,
Of whilk wondirs I sal tel yhou sum,
He sal do fire fra þe heven don com,
And þat sal be noght bot an ille spirit,
Þat out of þe ayre sal com doun tite,
And omang his disciples don light,
And with sere tunges til þam spek ryght,
Als dyd til þe apostels þe haly gast
And þat sal be in mens sight mast,
For þa þat his disciples sal be cald
Sal þam avant, and þam self hald
Better of lif and to God mare dere,
Þan ever war Cristes appostels here.
Alswa thurgh þe devels crafte and myght,
He sal feyn him ded til mens syght,
And on þe thred day thurgh þe devels rede
He sal feyn hym to ryse fra dede,
And devels aftir sal bere hym up even
In-til þe ayre als he suld stey to heven;
And als he byfor sal be sene,
Als he fra dede rase, men sal wene
Þat he es til heven ravyst,
And trow þan þat he es verray crist.
Þus sal anticrist þan countrefette
Þe wondirs of God in erthe swa grete;
Ma wondirs yhit wirk sal he
Þat þe pople sal openly se.
He sal do tresė growe and florisshe fayre
And chace þe wyndes about and þe ayre.
Fra heven he sal do falle rayne-shours
And mak waters to ryn ogayn þair cours.

Antichrist shall perform miracles through the power of the devil.

An evil spirit shall come out of the air and descend upon his disciples.

He shall pretend to rise for the dead.

He shall cause rain to come down.

He sal trobel þe se when he wille,
And pees it and make it be stille.
He sal chaung on wonder manere
Divers kyndes in figures sere.

He shall cause images to speak.

He sal do dede ymages and dome
Speke of thynges þat er to come.

He shall raise the dead.

He sal alswa dede men uprays,
Þat sal gang obout, als þe boke says,
And þat sal be thurgh þe devels quayntis,

Devils shall enter into dead bodies.

For devels sal entre in-til þe dede bodys
And bere þa dede bodys obout,
Swa þat parfit men sal be in dout
Whether he es verray crist or noght,
And þus sal men be in errour broght.

Antichrist shall beguile the people through gifts.

On þe thred maner he sal bygille
Many thurgh gyftes within short whyle,
And turne þam til a fals belyefe
Thurgh large gyftes þat he þam sal gyfe.
For he sal fynde alle þe tresour
Þat es, or was ever hidde byfor
Under erthe, or ourwar elles
Þat may noght be gesced; for sum telles
Þat mar tresor under erthe es hidde
Þan oboven es knawen or kydde;
Of whilk he sal þam alle ryche make,
Þat þe lawe of Criste here wille forsake.
Þos sal he shew men welth worldly
For to desayve þam þan þarby.
Of þe ferthe maner aftir þan

He shall lead astray the people through torments and dread of death.

He sal turne til hym many a man;
And do þam haly folowe his trace
Thu[r]gh grete tourmentes and manace,
And thurgh drede of dede þat mast may grefe,
For elles he sal noght thole þam lyefe.
Ful grete tribulacions he sal þam shewe,
Als God in þe godspelle sayis thurgh Mathewe:
Tanta erit tribulacio, ut in errorem
inducantur, si fieri potest, eciam electi.

He says "mikel tribulacion
Sal be þan til ilka naçion,"
Thurgh out þe world, ferre and nere,
"Þat þas þat God has chosen here
Suld be broght in error sone
If God wild suffre þat it warre done."
Bot in þe appocalipse apparty
Es sayd þus ful mistyly,
Pedes eius sunt simules auricalco,
sicut in camino ardente.
He says "his fete er like latoun bright
Als in a chymné brynnand light."
And þis was þat Iohan saw in a vision
Of hym þat semed þe virgyn son.
By his fete þat als latoun was semand
Crist last lyms men may undirstand,
Þe whilk sal be parfite men in charité
Þat agayne þe worldes ende martird sal be,
Þat es to say, in tym of Anticrist,
Thurgh wham many saules sal be perist.
Þe chimné, brinand with þe het,
Bytakens þe tribulacion gret.
Þat sal be when anticrist sal come,
Thurgh wham many sal thole grete marterdome.
Anticrist sal be þe mast tyraunt
Þat ever was; for he sal haunt
Alle þe maners of turmentes kene
In whilk any martirs byfor has bene;
For on sere maners he sal þam turment
Þat wille noght til his law assent;
And put alle þa to þe dede at þe last
Þat ay duels in þe trouthe stedfast.
Bot alle cristen men in þat cuntré
Þar Crist welk, mast tourmented sal be.
And Haymo says, þat a grete clerk was,
Hys tyrauntry thurgh þe world sal pas.
Þe devels þat er now bunden swa,
Þat þai may noght about flegh ne ga,

Antichrist shall be the greatest tyrant that ever was.

Devils, that are now kept bound shall then be let loose.

Ne nuye als mykel als þai walde,
Sal þan be louse and nathyng þam halde.
Þat tyme sal preche na cresten man,
For þai sal be halden als cursed þan;
Ne nan sal bye with þam ne selle,
Ne felaghshepe hald with þam ne duelle,
Bot with þas þat had Criste forsaken

The mark of Antichrist shall be on men's forehead or in the right hand.

And þe merk of anticrist had taken,
Þat men mught knawe and understand
Þat þai til anticrist war assentand.
For al þas men sal bere his merk,
Þat sal forsake to wirk Cristes werk,
And sal folowe anticristes lawe,
By his merk men sal þam knawe,
Þe whilk þai sal ber, als I understande,
Outher in þe frount or in þe ryght hande.
Bot other þat wille noght do his rede
Sal be done to vilans dede.
On þis four maners, als I haf shewed,
He sal drawe til hym bathe lered and lewed,
And crysten law sal be doun layde,
Þarfor þus in appocalips es sayde:
Cauda eius tertiam partem stellarum
celi trahebat, et misit eas in terra.
He says, "with his tayle he droghe don even
Þe thred part of þe sternes of heven,
And into þe erthe sent þam ryght,"
Þar þai mught noght shyne ne gyf lyght.

The tail of the dragon is the fiend.

Þis was þe taille of þe dragon
Þat Saynt Johan saw in a vision.
Þe dragon es understanden þe fende
And his taille anticrist þat folowed at þe ende
And þe thred part of þe sternes bright

The stars of the heavens are those Christians led into sin by Antichrist.

Er cristen men undirstanden right,
Þe whilk he sal fra right trowthe draw,
And do þam in erthe to hald his law.
Þe men of þe worlde þat er covaytous
He sal turne thurgh gyftes precious,

For he sal gyf þam, þat turned wil be,
Of gold and silver grete plenté.
Alswa men of symple connyng
He sal turne thurgh miracles and prechyng.
Gude men, þat haldes Goddes commandmentes,
He sal turne thurgh manace and turmentes.
Many þat semes gude and rightwyse
Sal trow in hym, and Crystes trouth despyse.
First sal anticrist com in myldnes
And prech ogayn þe right trouth þat es,
And myracles sal thurgh hym be done;
Þan sal þe Iewes resayve hym sone
And be turned til hym al haly.
And þat tyme sal com Ennoc and Ely
Ogayn anticrist to preche ful harde,
Als yhe may se and here afterwarde.
Þan sal anticrist bygyn felly
To pursue men thurgh tyrauntry,
Gret parsecucion þan sal he wyrk
Agayn cristen men and haly kirk,
Þan sal he destroye cristen lawe,
And Gog and Magog til hym drawe,
Þe whilk er halden, als men telles,
Þe werst folk þat in þe world duels.
Som says þat þai er closed haly
By-yhonde þe mountes of Caspy;
Bot þai er noght swa closed obout
Þat þai ne mught lightly com out,
Yif a qwene ne war, þat haldes þam in,
Thurgh stre[n]gthe, þat þai may noght out wyn,
Þat es cald þe qwene of Amazons,
Under whas powere þat folk wons,
Bot at þe last þai sal breke out
And destroy many landes obout.
For þe Iewes has swylk a prophecy
And says þus omang þam commonly,
Þat þis folk ogayne þe worldes ende
Sal com out, and til Ierusalem wende

The Jews shall receive Antichrist.

Enoch and Elijah shall come from heaven to preach against Antichrist.

Concerning Gog and Magog,

who live beyond the Caspian sea,

and are ruled over by the queen of the Amazons.

With þair crist, þat wonders sal wirke,
And þan sal þai distroie haly kyrke.
Some clerkes says, als þe glose telles,

Gog and Magog according to some 'clerks' signify the host of Antichrist.

Þat Gog and Magog es noght elles
Bot þe host of onticrist [þat] sal come
Sodanly ogayn þe day of dome,
And ogayne haly kyrk werray
For to distroye it if þai may.
Þe glose of þe buke says alswa

By Gog are meant those who shall secretly persecute the christians.

Þat by Gog er understanden alle þa
Thurgh whilk þe devel, our mast enemy,
Sal cristen men pursue prively.

Magog denotes those who shall openly persecute the christians.

By Magog may þas understanden be
Thurgh wham openly pursue sal he,
Or þas er understanden þar-by,
Þat in anticrist tyme first pryvely
And aftirward openly, sal wyrk
Wykkedness ogayne haly kyrk.

Gog means *secret*, and Magog *open*.

Gog es als mykel at say, als covert,
And Magog es noght elles bot als apert.

Some say that Enoch and Elijah shall come upon earth,

Þir twa prophetes, als says som,
Ennok and Hely byfor sal com,
Bytwene þe tyme of þe commyng privé
Of anticrist, when he sal born be,
And þe tyme of his oppen commyng,
Þat sal be thurgh open prechyng
And thurgh open parsecucion,
Þat he sal do til diverse nacion.
Bytwen þa tymes þa prophetes twa

and preach, and convert the Jews to Christianity.

On sere partes sal preche swa,
Þat thurgh þair prechyng þai sal drawe
And convert þe Iewes til cristen lawe,
For þus spekes þe prophete Malachy,
In a boke of þe prophecy:
Convertent corda patrum
in filios.
He says "þai sal turne thurgh Goddes myght
Þe fadirs hertes intil þe sons right."

Þat es, þai sal turne þe Iewery
Until right cristendom halely.
Þan sal Iewes þe sam lawe halde,
Þat þai haf, þat er cristen men calde
And als cristen men dus swa sal þai do,
Als þe glose says þat acordes þar-to:
Percipient fidem quam
ipsi habuerunt.
"Þe Iewes sal tak þan with hert glade
Þe trouth þat cristen men byfor hadde."
Wharfor þe Iewes and cristen men,
Als þa twa prophetes sal þam ken,
Sal þan thurgh even entencion
Assent in Crist als a religion.
Þai sal preche als þe appocalips says, **Enoch and Elijah shall preach for 1260 days.**
A thousand and twa hundreth days
And sexti, als men sal se and here.
And als þe glose says; þat es, thre yhere,
Als Crist him-self did þat voched safe
To preche þe sam law þat we hafe.
Þai sal be als þe appocalips spekes,
In harde hayres clende[1] and in sekkes; **They shall be clothed in sack-cloth.**
Þat es þai sal þan penance preche
And thurgh ensaumple of penance teche,
Bot als tite als anticrist sal knawe
Þat þai turne Iewes til cristen lawe
Thurgh ensaumple þat þai shew, and sarmon[2],
Þan sal he shew grete parsecucion
And grevusly þam tourment,
Þat til his law wille noght assent,
And do þam to hard dede at þe last,
Yf þai in þe trouthe be stedfast.
Anticrist sal be þan ful wrathe, **Antichrist shall put Enoch and Elijah to death.**
He sal do tak þa prophetes bathe
And in Ierusalem, thurgh þe devels rede,
Hastyly do þam bathe to dede.

[1] Cled (MS. Harl. 4196).
[2] Thurgh þair ensample and þair sermone (MS. Harl. 6923).

þan sal þair bodys, als þe buke says,
In þe stretes ligg stille thre days
And an half, oboven erthe namly,
For na man sal þam dur biry,
For drede þat þai sal haf þan.
Of anticrist, þat wikked man.
þair enemys when þai er slayn
Of þair dede þai sal be fayn.

Enoch and Elijah after lying three days upon the earth shall rise again.

When þai haf liggen dede on þis wyse
Thre days and an half, þai sal ryse,
And þan þair enmys a voce sal here
Until þam spek, on þis manere:
'Ely and Ennok steyes up bathe,
For yhe er passed al maner of wathe.'
And als tyte, when þai haf herd þis steven,
In a cloude þai sal stey up til heven,
þat alle þe pople þan sal se.
A grete wondre tyl þam þat sal be.

After their death, Antichrist shall reign 15 days, but his reign of terror shall last altogether three and a half years.

Aftjr þair dede, als þe buke says,
Anticrist sal regne, yhit fiften days,
þan sal he turne alle til hym haly
þat war turned til Ennok and Hely;
And alle, þat til hym wille noght trow þan,
Sal þan be don til þe dede, ilk man.
Anticrist, in his grete tyrantry,
Sal regne thre yhere and an half fully;
þan sal God abrege his days,
Als Mathew in þe Godspel says:
Nisi breviati finissent dies, non
erit salva omnis caro.
"Bot his days war abreged," says he,
"Fone men fra þan sal save be."
Bot his tyme God abrege sal þan.
Til þis, says Saynt Gregore þe haly ma
Quia nos infirmos aspicit deus, dies
malos quos singulariter intulit, misericorditer breviabit.
He says "for-þi, þat God sese right
þat we er freyle and feble of myght,

þe days þat er ille and hevy,
þat er putted til sere men singulerly,[1]
Yhit, at þe last, abrege sal he,
Thurgh his gudenes and his pyté."
Anticrist sal be with-outen pere,
And he sal lyf twa and thretty yhere
And an half, als som clerkes says þai se;
Of swa many yhere his eld sal be
Fra þe tyme of his first bygynnyng,
Until þe tyme of his last endyng.
For sum says he sal lyf als many yhere
Als Crist lifed, in manskynd here,
And when he has þus lang lyfed,
þan sal na ma thurgh him by[2] greved.
He sal þan son fele Goddes vengeance
And with-outen any repentance,
He sal be slayn, ful sodanly,
Thurgh þe myght of God almyghty,
Opon þe mounte of Olyvett,
In þe stede whar Crist his fete sett,
When he stey up til heven bright,
And swa sal he ende thurgh Goddes might.
Som clerkes yhit says alswa,
þat Saynt Michael sal hym sla,
Thurgh Goddes byddyng in þe same stede,
In þe whilk he sal be funden dede.
And þe boke says, alswa, þat he,
Thurgh þe gast of Goddes mouthe slayn sal be.
Bot how swa it be þis es certayn,
Thurgh Goddes myght þar sal he be slayn.
Anticrist mynisters, when he es dede,
Sal mak ioy þan in ilka stede,
And haf þair delices nyght and day,
And wedden wyfes, and þus say:
'Alle-if our prince be dede þus
We haf pees and welthe plenteuus,'
And right als þai sal say þus alle
Sodanly ded þai sal doun falle,

Antichrist shall live for 32½ years,

he shall be slain upon the mount of Olivet,

and after his death his followers shall make great rejoicings,

but they shall be slain suddenly.

[1] singulary (MS. Harl. 4196).
[2] be?

Thurgh þe myght of God almyghty,
Þus sal þai enden sodanly.
Bot yhit when þai alle er þus fordone,
Þe grete dome sal noght be aftir alsone.
For þe glose of Danyel þus says:

Five and forty days shall be given for repentance.

"God sal graunt fyve and fourty days
Til alle þas þat desayved sal be,
Thurgh anticrist and his meyné,"
Þat þai may amende þam of þair syn,
And do penance, ar þe dome bygyn."
Þe Iewes sal þan al turned be
Til þat right trouthe, þe whilk haf we
Þan sal God fulfille in þe last days,
Þis worde þat he in þe godspel says,
Et fiet unum ovile
et unus pastor.
He sais "alle folkes to fald sal falle,
And a hirde sal be to kepe þam alle."
Þat folk Iewes and cristen men sal be talde
Under a trouthe in haly kirkes falde;
Fra þat tyme forthe sal hali kirke be
In pees and rest with-outen adversité.

The power of the devil shall cease.

For þan sal faile alle power of þe fende,
Fra þat tyme unto þe worldes ende,
Swa þat he sal nother tempte ne gryefe
Haly kirk, ne man þat þan sal lyefe.
Bot how mikel space sal be fra þan
Til þe day of dome, wate na man;
For of al þe prophetes, þat men may neven,
And alle þe halghes, and angels in heven,
Mught never nane witt þat privité,

The time of the doom has not been revealed to any.

What tyme þe day of dome sal be;
For God wille þat nane it byfor wytte,
Bot him-self þat has ordaynt itte;
Þarfor Crist til his disciples sayde þus,
Als þe boke of apostels werkes shewes us:
Non est vestrum nosse tempora vel momenta
que pater possuit in sua potestate.

"It falles noght yhow knaw þe time privé
Þat þe fadir has sette in his awen pousté,"
Þarfor na man suld aske, ne say
How mykel we hafe til domes day;
Ne we suld noght yherne it to lere,
Ne witte wether it be ferre or nere.
Bot we suld mak us redy alle,
Als þe day of dome to morn suld falle,
And thynk ay on þat drede-ful dome,
Als þe haly man dyd, Saynt Ierome.
Þat ay þar-on thoght, bathe nyght and days,
And þarfor þus in a boke he says:
Sine comedam, sine bibam, sine aliquid
aliud faciam, semper michi videtur illa
tuba resonare in auribus meis, 'sur-
gite mortui, venite ad iudicium.'
He says "whether I ette or I drynk,
Or oght elles do, ay me thynk
Þat þe beme þat blaw sal on domsday,
Sounes in myn eres, þat þus says ay:
'Ryse yhe þat er dede, and come
Un-to þe grete dredful dome'."
Now haf yhe herd of þe bygynnyng
Of anticrist, and of his lif and his endyng,
Þat men may a werray[1] taken calle,
Þat agayne þe day of dome sal falle.
Many ma takens yhit men sal se,
Byfor ar þat dreful day sal be,
Bathe in erthe and yhit in heven,
Als we here Crist in þe gospelle neven,
Whare he spekes of takens sere
Þat sal falle, And says on þis manere:
Erunt signa in sole, et luna, et stellis;
et in terris pressura gencium pre confusi-
ione sonitus maris et fluctuum, arescen-
tibus hominibus pre timore et expectacione, que
supervenient universo orbi. Nam virtutes

We should not seek to discover this secret, but strive to be always ready for the doom.

The words of St. Jerome.

Tokens of the day of doom shall be seen upon earth and in heaven.

[1] verray.

celorum movebuntur, Et tunc videbunt
filium hominis venientem in nubibus,
cum potestate magna et maiestate &c.
þir er þe wordes of þe gospelle,
þat Crist til his disciples gun telle.
He says þus als he ordaynd be done:

Signs shall be in the sun and moon,

"Takens sal be in þe son and in þe mone,
And in þe sternes þat in heven men may ken,
And in erthe sal be grete thrang of men,
For þe mengyng of þe noys of þe se
Of þe flodes, þat þan sal be;
And men sal wax dry in þat dyn
For drede and for lang bydyng þar-in,
þat til al þe world sal com" says he,

and the mights of heaven shall be stirred.

For þe myghtes of heven sal þan styrd be,
And þai sal se þe son of man
Comand doun in cloudes þan,
With his grete myght and magesté,"
And þat tyme sal þe grete dome be.
þir takens er tald aftir þe lettre here,
Bot þe exposicion may be on othir manere.
Alswa God, þat alle thynges knawes wele,
He says þus thurgh þe prophete Ioele:
Et dabo prodigia in celo sursum, et signa
in terra deorsum, sanguinem et ignem et
vaporem fumi; sol convertetur in tenebras et lu-
na in sanguinem, antequam veniat dies domini
magnus et manifestus.

The words of the prophet Joel as to doomsday.

He says "I sal gyfe wonders sere
Up in heven, als men sal here;
And takens doun in erthe ere-on to luke,
þat es blode and fire and brethe of smoke;
þe son sal be turned in-til mirknes,
And þe mone in-til blode, and be lyghtles,
Byfor or þe day of our lord sal falle,
þat sal be grete and openly shewed til alle.
þat grete day is þe grete day of dome,
Agayn whilk alle þir takens sal come;

Þan may men by swilk takens wytte
Þat it es þe mast day þat ever was yhitte,
And þe straytest and þe mast harde,
Als men may se and here aftirwarde.
Yhit spekes þe haly man Saynt Ierome
Of fiften takens þat sal come

The XV tokens of the Doom,

Byfor Cristes commyng, als he says,
Þe whilk sal falle in XV days;
Bot whether any other days sal falle
Bytwen þa days, or þai sal alle
Continuely falle, day aftir day,
Saynt Ierom says, he can noght say;
And yhit for certayn approves noght he
Þat þa fiften days of takens sal be,

are rehearsed by St. Jerome,

Bot he reherces þa takens fiftene
Als he þam fand, and writen had sene
In som bokes of þe Ebriens,
Þat þa XV days contens.
Bot Saynt Ierome shewes noght ne telles,
Þat he þam fand writen ourwhar elles,
Bot in þe Hebriens bokes he þam fande
And reherces þam, als he saw þam stande,

as he found them in the books of the Hebrews.

Ilka day aftir other even,
Als yhe may here me now neven.
Þe first day of þas fiften days,
Þe se sal ryse, als þe bukes says,

I. The rising of the sea.

Abowen þe heght of ilka mountayne,
Fully fourty cubyttes certayne,
And in his stede even upstande,
Als an heghe hille dus on þe lande.
Þe secunde day, þe se sal be swa law
Þat unnethes men sal it knaw.

II. The sinking of the sea.

Þe thred day, þe se sal seme playn
And stand even in his cours agay[n],
Als it stode first at þe bygynnyng,
With-outen mare rysyng or fallyng.

III. The sea becomes even and returns to its former course.

Þe fierth day, sal swilk a wonder be,
Þe mast wondreful fisshes of þe se

IV. The fishes of the sea make a dreadful noise.

Sal com to-gyder and mak swilk romyng[1]
Þat it sal be hydus til mans heryng.
Bot what þat romiyng[1] sal signify,
Na man may whit, bot God almyghty.

V. The sea shall burn.

Þe fift day, þe se sal brynne
And alle watters als þai sal rynne;
And þat sal last fra þe son rysyng
Til þe tyme of þe son doun gangyng.

VI. A bloody dew shall fall upon grass and trees:

Þe sext day, sal spryng a blody dewe
On grisse and tres, als it sal shewe.

VII. Buildings shall fall down.

Þe sevend day byggyns doun sal falle
And grete castels, and tours with-alle.

VIII. Rocks and stones shall 'hurtle' together.

Þe eght day, hard roches and stanes
Sal strik togyder, alle attanes.
An ilkan of þam sal other doun cast,
And ilkan agayn other hortel fast,
Swa þat ilka stan, on divers wyse,
Sal sonder other in thre partyse.

IX Earthquakes.

Þe neghend day, gret erthedyn sal be,
Generaly in ilka contré;
And swa gret erthdyn als sal be þan
Was never hard, sythen þe world bygan.

X. The earth shall be turned into one great plain.

Þe tend day þar-aftir to neven,
Þe erthe sal be made playn and even,
For hilles and valeis sal turned be
In-til playn, and made even to se.

XI. Men shall come forth from caves and holes, and roam about as if mad.

Þe ellevend day men sal com out
Of caves, and holes and wend about,
Als wode men, þat na witt can;
And nane sal spek til other þan.

XII. The stars shall fall from heaven.

Þe twelfte day aftir, þe sternes alle
And þo signes fra þe heven sal falle.

XIII. The dead shall rise.

Þe thredend day sal dede men banes
Be sett to-gyder, and ryse al attanes,
And aboven on þair graves stand;
Þis sal byfalle in ilka land.

[1] roryng (MS. Lands. 348).

XIV. The death of those still living.

Þe fourtend day, al þat lyves þan
Sal dighe, childe, man and woman;
For þai shalle with þam rys ogayn
Þat byfor war dede, outher til ioy or payn.

XV. The burning of the world.

Þe fiftend day, þos sal betyde,
Alle þe world sal bryn on ilk syde,
And þe erthe whar we now duelle,
Until þe utter end of alle helle.
Þus tels Ierom þer takens fiftene,
Als he in þe bokes of Ebriens had sene.
Bot for alle þa takens þat men sal se,
Yhit sal na man certayn be

The time of the Doom will be as sudden, as was the flood.

What tyme Crist sal come til þe dome,
Swa sodanly he sal doun come;
For als byfel in Noe and Loth days,
Swa sal he com, for Luke in þe godspel says:
Et sicut factum est in diebus Noe, ita
erit adventus filii hominis: edebant
et bibebant, uxores ducebant et
dabantur ad nupcias, usque ad diem,
qua intravit Noe in archam; et
venit diluvium et perdidit omnes: Si-
militer factum est in diebus Loth, ede-
bant et bibebant, emebant et vendebant,
plantabant et edificabant,
qua die autem exiit Loth a Sodomis, et subito
pluit ignem et sulphur de celo, et perdidit
omnes; secundum autem hoc erit
qua die filius hominis revelabitur.
Þir er þe wordes of þe godspelle,
Þat es on Inglissche þus to telle:

The days of Noah.

"Als was done in þe days of Noé,
Right swa mans son sal com" says he,
"Men ete and drank þan and war glade,
And wedded wyfes, and bridalles made
Until þe day, namly, þat Noe
Went in-to þe shippe þat made he,

And sodanly come þe flode þat tyde
And fordid alle þe world swa wyde.

The days of Lot.

Alswa in þe days of Loth byfelle,
Men ete and drank, shortly to telle,
Ilkan with other, and salde and boght,
And planted, and bygged, and houses wroght,
And þat day, þat Loth yhed out of Sodome,
Sodanly Goddes vengeance come;
It rayned fire fra heven and brunstane,
And tynt al þat þare was, and spard nane,
Right þus sal falle, als men sal se,
Þe day man son sal shewed be."
In þe ende of þe world, byfor þe dome,

A hideous fire shall burn the world and all that it contains.

An hydus fire sal sodanly come,
Þat alle þe world sal haly bryn,
And nathyng spare þat es þar-in,
For alle þe erthe sal bryn with-oute
And þe Elementes, and alle þe ayre oboute,
And alle þat God in þe world has wroght,
Sal þan be brynned and wasted to noght.
Þis fire þat thurgh þe world sal ryse,
Sal com þan fra sere partyse;

All the fire in, under, and above the earth shall meet together.

For alle þe fire þat es in þe spere,
And under erthe, and aboven erthe here,
Sal mete togyder attans þan,
And bryn alle þat lyves, best and man,
And alle þat growes in erthe and ayre,
Tille alle be clensed, and made fayre
Of alle þe corrupcions þat men may se,
Þe whilk in þe ayre or in þe erthe may be;

This fire shall burn in four ways.

Þis fire, als þe buk says als[1] lers,
Sal brin and wirk on four maneres.
It sal wirk als þe fir of helle
To punyssche þe synful þat þar sal duelle
It sal wirk als fire of purgatory
To clense men of veniel syn fully.

[1] And leres (Harl. 4196).

It sal wirk als fire of herth here,
þat over alle sal bryn far and nere,
To wast alle þat on erthe springes
Als gresse, and tres, and alle other thynges,
And alswa þe bodys of ilk man

The elements shall become clear.

To brin haly in-to askes þan;
It sal wirk als þe fire of þe spere,
To make þe elementes clene and clere
And alle þe ayre bright of hew,
And þe hevens, for to serve als new.
Thurgh þis fire þat þus sal rayke obout,
þe face of þe erth sal brin with-out,
And þe shappe of þe world sal for-done be
Als it was first thurgh þe flode of Noe;
And als þat flode passed cubites fiften
Over þe heyghest mount, þat ever was sen,
Right swa þe fire als heyghe sal pas

The world shall be purged by fire.

To fordo þe world als it þan was;
And als God byfor his first commyng
Wald here fordo, with-outen lettyng,
Alle þe world thurgh water anly
Agayn þe fire of lychery,
Right swa, byfor his last commyng,
He sal of þe world mak endyng,
Thurgh fire þat sal swa brinnand be,
Agayn þe dasednes[1] of charité.
þe wirkyng of þe fire swa brinnand
Sal contend[2] þir thre short tymes passand,

Three periods of this fire.

þat es bygynnyng, mydward, and ende,
Als in þis bok es here contende.
First þe fire, at þe bygynnyng,
Sal cum byfor Cristes commyng,
þat þe gude men sal þan clensen and fine,
And þe wikked men hard punnys and pyne,
þat here luffed syn and thoght it swete,
And þarfor says þus David þe prophete:
Ignis ante ipsum precedet, et inflammabit
incircuitu inimicos eius.

[1] coldnes (MS. Lands. 348). [2] contene?

"Þe fir byfor hym, on sere partys,
Sal ga and about brine his enemys;"

The fire shall burn mens bones to ashes.

Þat fire mens bodys to askes sal brin,
And þe world and alle þat es þar-ine;
Þus sal þe fire first byfor come,
Ar Crist com doun til þe dome.

When this fire has destroyed every thing, the dead shall rise to the Doom.

And when þe fire has wasted, als I talde,
Þan sal al men ryse, bathe yhong and alde,
Out of þair graves with saul and body,
And come til þe dome þan alle halely
And our Loverd Crist sal com doun þan,
And sit in dome, als domes man,
And deme þan, bathe gude and ille,
Als yhe may aftir-ward here, if yhe wille;

The fire shall burn about the Doomsman.

And yhit þe fire alle þat tyde
Sal brin obout hym, on ilka syde,
Als þe prophete David bers wytnes
In þe Psauter, þar þus writen es:
"Ignis, in conspectu eius, exardescet,
et incircuitu eius tempestas valida."
"Þe fyre sal brin in his sight," says he,
And obout hym grete tempest sal be."
And als lang als þat dome sal last
Þe fire sal brin, on ilk syde fast;

After the Doom, the wicked with this fire, and all kinds of filth shall be swept into hell.

And when þe dome es broght til ende,
Þa þat sal be dampned sal wende,
With alle þe fire þat swa sal brin,
Til helle pytt, and duelle ay þar-in.
Þan sal alle þe fire be sweped doune
In-til helle, with alkyn corrupcioune,
And alle þe filth of þe world, neshe and hard,
Als in þis bok es writen aftirward.
Þus thurgh alle þe world þe fire sal brin,
And clense it of al manere of syn,
And of alle corrupcions, bath hegh and, law
Þat men may now se, here, and knaw;
And when þe fire has wasted al erdly thyng,
Þan sal þe hevens sees of movyng.

Christ, before he comes to judge the world, shall send his angels to sound aloud their trumpets;

Our Lord yhit þan, or he com doun,
For to sytte in dome in proper parsoun,
Sal send byfor, als þe buke tels,
In four partys his angels,
With þair bemes þat þai sal blaw,
Þat alle þe world sal here and knaw;
Alle men þai sal þan upcalle
And byd þam cum til þe dome alle.

and then all shall rise,

Alle men sal ryse þan þat ever had life,
Man and woman, mayden and wyfe,
Gude and ille, with fleshe and felle,
In body and saul, als clerkes can telle;
And þat in als short whyle als hert may thynk,
Or mans eghe may open or wynk,
Fra þe tyme þat þai þe son sal here,
For þe apostel says on þis manere:
"Omnes resurgent in momento, in
ictu oculi, in novissima tuba."
He says "alle sal ryse in a tym movyng,

in the twinkling of an eye.

Als in þe space of an eghe twynklyng,
When þai here þe dredeful blast
Of þe beme, þat þan sal blaw last."
Alle men sal þan tite up-ryse
In þe same stature and þe same bodyse,
Þat þai had here in þair lifedays,
And in non other, als þe buk says.
Þan sal alle ryse in þe same eld þan,
Þat God had fully here als man,
Namly, when he upprayse thurgh myght
Fra dede, als says Saynt Austyn ryght;

The age of all shall be thirty two years and three months.

Þan was he of threty yhere elde and twa,
And of thre monethes þar-with alswa;
In þat elde alle sal ryse at þe last,
When þai here þe grete bemes blast,
With þair awen bodys alle hale
And with alle þair lymes, grete and smale.
For alle-if þe bodys of ilk man
Shulde alle be brynned til askes þan,

Though the bodies of men be reduced to ashes and scattered about, yet shall they appear perfect in all their limbs.

And yhit þogh alle þe askes of þair bodys
War strew[d] and skaterd in sere partys,
Thurgh ilka land and ilka cuntré,
Þai sal þan togyder alle gader[d] be.
And ilka body sal rise þan halely,
With alle þe lyms, þat falles til þe body,
And with alle þe hare of body and hede
Swa þat na hare sal want in na stede;
For þare sal na hare be peryste,
Als Saynt Luk says þe Evaungeli[s]tte:
Capillus de capite,
vestro non peribit.

Not even shall a single hair be missing.

"Na hare sal perishe, ne faile", says he,
"Þat falles on þe heved for to be."
And if any lyms be here unsemely,
Thurgh outragiousté of kynd namely,

All defects of the limbs of the good shall be corrected.

God sal abate þat outrage, thurgh myght,
And make þa lyms semely to sight;
And if any lym wanted, þat shuld falle
Til þe body, or any war over smalle,
Thurgh þe defaut here of kynd God þan wille
Alle þe defautes of þe lyms fulfille,
And þus sal he do namly, to al þa
Þat sal be save and til blis ga.
For þair bodys sal be semely and bright
With avenand lymes til alle mens sight.
Bot God sal amend on nane wise
Defautes of þe lyms of synful bodys,

The bodies of the sinful shall be foul and ugly to look upon.

For þair bodys sal alle unsemely be,
And foul, and ugly[1], opon to se.
Alle þat er gude þan and rightwyse,
Þat sal be save, sal first upryse,
And up in-to þe ayre be ravyste,
Againe þe comyng of Ihesu Criste,
To kepe him when he doun sal come,
Als domesman for to sitte in dome.
Þe mast parfite men sal Criste first kepe
And alle cum with hym in his felawshepe,

[1] The MS. has 'ungly'.

And with him ay be in body and saule,
Als þe apostel says, Saynt Paule:
Quoniam Christus Dominus in iussa et voce arcangeli,
et in tuba dei, descendet de celo, et mortui
qui in Christo mortui sunt resurgent primi.
Deinde nos qui vivimus, qui relinquimur, simul
rapiemur cum illis in nubibus
obviam Christo in aere, sic semper
cum Domino erimus.

The words of St. Paul.

He says "our Lord sal come doun fra heven,
In Goddis byddyng, and archaungel steven,
And in þe son of Goddes awen beme,
Alle þe world þan for to deme.
And þai þat er dede in Crist þan,
Sal first uprise, ilka man;
And sythen we, on þe sam manere,
Þat now lyves and er left here,
Sal þan with þam in cloudes be ravyste
Up in-to þe ayre for to mete Criste,
And swa with our Lorde ay sal be,
Fra þat tyme forward," þus says he.

The dead shall first arise and be ravished into the air to meet Christ,

Bot we synful þat sal rise þat tyde
Bynethe on þe erthe sal Crist abyde
In drede and sorow charged with synne,
For þai may nour-whare away wynne.
Þam war lever be depe in helle þan,
Þan com byfor þat domesman.
Þai wald fayne fle, if þai myght,
Or hide þam fra þat domesman sight
Under erthe, or ourwhar elles,
Als Saynt Johan, in þe apocalips, telles:
Reges terre et principes, et tribuni, et
divites et fortes, et omnis
servus et liber, absconderunt se in
speluncis et in petris moncium, et
dicent montibus et petris, 'Cadite
super nos', et collibus 'abscondite
nos, a facie sedentis super tronum
et ab ira agni.'

but the wicked shall remain on the earth.

5072 He says "kynges of þe lande and princes sere,
And cheftayns þat er under þam here,
And riche men of divers cuntré,
And strenthy men, and bond and fre,
5076 In caves þai wald þan hyde ilkan
And in cragges, and in roche of stan;
And sal say til montayns and roches þus;
'Fal opon us now and hyde us,
5080 Fra þe face of hym þat syttes in throne
And fra þe wrethe of þe lamb', þus tels Saynt Iohan.
Many maner of men sal haf dred þan,
To com byfor þat dreful domesman,
5084 Namely, synful men with-outen hope,
And yhit says þus þe haly man, Iope[1]:
Domine quando veneris iudicare terram,
ubi me abscondam a vultu ire tue, quia
5088 *peccavi nimis [in vita mea]?*
"Loverd", he says, "when þou sal come
To deme þe erthe and sytte in dome,
Whar sal I fra þi wreth hyd me
5092 For-why I haf synd ogaynes þe
Ful gretely in my life here?".
And yhit says Iob on þis manere:
Quis michi hoc tribuat
5096 *ut in inferno protegas me,*
et abscondas me donec
pertranseat furor tuus?
"Loverd, wha may gyf to me", says he,
5100 "Þat þou in helle may hyd me
And cover me at þe dredful day,
Unto þi wrethe be passed oway,"
Þan es it na wondre, als I sayde are,
5104 If þe synful men haf drede and care,
Þat sal dampned be and peryst
For to cum in þe syght of Ihesu Crist,
Þat til þam swa wrethful sal seme þan,
5108 When Job þus says þe halyman.

The wicked shall be in great dread.

The words of Job.

The wrath of Christ.

[1] Job (MS. Harl. 4196).

Christ shall come as Doomsman, with a multitude of angels.

Our Lord Crist, thurgh his grete myght,
Sal þan com doun fra heven bright,
Als domesman to sit in dome,
And with him grete multitude sal come
Of angels, and of archangels,
And of al other halghes, als þe buk teles;
Ecce Dominus veniet et
omnes sancti eius cum eo.
"Lo! our Lord sal com til þe dome
And alle his halghes sal with him come."
And sodanly he sal hym þan shewe,
Als says þe godspeller Saynt Mathewe:
"*Sicut fulgur exiit ab oriente,*
et paret in occidente, ita erit
adventus filii hominis, subitus,
choruschans, et terribilis."
"Als þe levenyng out gas in short tyde
Fra þe est, and shewes it in þe west syde,

He shall come as the lightning;

Right swa þe commyng of man son sal be,
Sodayne and bright and dreful to se.
He sal com doun, nathyng sal him lett,
Even onence[1] þe mount of Olyvet,
Whar he, in manhed, stey[2] up even
Fra his disciples, til þe fader in heven;
And in swilk fourme als he stey up þan,
He sal com doun to deme ilk man,
Gude and ille, bathe yong and alde,

And in the form of man.

Als þe angels til his disciples talde:
Hic Ihesus qui assumptus est a nobis
in celum, sic veniet et quemadmodum
vidistis eum euntem
in celum.
Þai sayd "Ihesu Crist þat here es uptane
Fra yhow, til heven, with flessch and bane,
Swa sal he com at þe world ende,
Als yhe saw hym up in-til heven wende;
In þat fourme of man he sal cum þan,
And sitte in dome als domesman.

[1] ageyns (MS. Y.). [2] stied (MS. Y.).

When Criste es common doun to deme,
In fourme of man, als he sal seme,

Christ shall judge all men in the vale of Jehoshaphat,

In a place he sal his dome halde,
Þat þe vale of Iosaphat es calde,
Whare alle men sal to-gyder mete,
Als Crist says, thurgh Ioel þe prophete:
Congregabo omnes gentes, et
adducam eas in valle Iosaphat.
He says "alle men I sal to-gyder calle,
And in vale of Iosaphat lede þam alle,"
And yhit mare to þat he says þus,
Als he thurgh þe prophete shewes us:
Consurgent et ascendent
omnes gentes in valle
Iosephat, quia ibi sedebo
ut iudicem omnes gentes.
He says "al men sal ryse to þe dome,
And in þe vale of Iosaphat come;"
"For þar," he says, "I sal sitte namly,
To deme alle men als þai er worthy."

which is in the middle of the earth.

Þat vale, þe vale of þe erthe men calles,
For imyd þe erthe, with-outen, it falles;
Iosaphat es þus mykel at say,
Als stede of dome, at þe last day.
Crist sal noght fully þan doun come
On þe erthe for to sitte in dome,
Bot up in þe ayre he sal sitte,
On a whyte cloude, als says haly wrytte:
Ecce apparebit dominus super
nubem candidam!
"Lo! our Lorde sal shew hym þan

Christ shall sit upon a white cloud.

On a whyte cloude, and sitte als domesman."
Even aboven þat vale namly,
Whare al men sal se his body.
Bot þe skilles why he sal þare sitte
Men may fynde here þat wille þam witte;
For þe vale of Iosaphat es sette
Bytwene þe mount of Olyvet

And Ierusalem, on þe other syde,
Þat standes imyddes þe world so wyde;
And þar es þe mount of calvery,
And þe sepulcre of Crist fast þarby.
And in þat cuntré standes Bethleem,
Noght ful ferre fra Ierusalem;
Þar-for Crist sal sytte þar þat day,
Onence þe myddes of erth þus for to say.

Christ shall sit opposite the middle of the earth, and say:

"Lo! here als yhe may alle now se
Þe vale of Iosaphat under me
Whare byred was my moder Mary
Of wham flesshe and blode for yhow tok I."

"Here is the vale of Jehosaphat where my mother Mary was buried; and here is Bethlehem where I was born."

He may say "lo! here, als yhe se now,
Bethleem whare I was born for yhow,
And in clotes lapped and layd was
In a cribbe, bytwen an ox and an asse."
He may say "lo here yhe may se stande
Ierusalem, þat es nere hande
Whare I had for yhow many buffet,
And with sharp skourges sare was bette,
And fra whethen þe crosse for yhow I bare,
Þat on my shulder was layd þare."

"Here is Jerusalem where I was beaten &c."

He may say also "lo! here þarby,
Als yhe may se, þe mount of calvery
Whar I was hanged upon þe rode,
Bytwen twa thefes for yhour gode;
Whare my payn for yhow was mast
And whare I swelt and yhelded þe gast."

"Here is Calvary where I was crucified."

He may say yhit þus alswa;
"Lo! here þe sepulcre a lytil þar-fra,
Whar I was layde for yhow als dede,
When I was beryd in þat stede."

"Here is the sepulchre where my body was laid.'

He may say alswa, als here es sett,
"Lo! here þe mount of Olivett,
Whar aungels appered in mens lykenes,
When I stey til [h]even þar blis ay es,
And tald yhow how my commyng shuld be
Tyl þe dome, als yhe may now se."

"Here is mount Olivet where angels appeared when I ascended to heaven."

Now haf yhe herd þe skylles why,
He sal sit oboven þat vale namly,
Þat men þe vale of Iosaphat calles
Þe whilk imyndes[1] þe world falles.

Another reason why Christ is to come down to the vale of Jehoshaphat.

Alswa another skille may þis be
Why he sal doun com in þat countré
For þar was his first commyng doun,
Anly for mans salvacioun,
When he first flessch and blod tok
Of þe mayden Mari, als says [þe] bok.
Þus sal he com doun at sitte þare,
To deme al þe world, als I saide are,

Christ shall appear very austere to the wicked, but very pleasing to the righteous.

Crist ful awsterne þan sal be
Agayn synful me[n] þat him sal se;
And dredful and hydus, als says þe boke,
He sal be to þam, when þai on hym loke,
And ful delitable unto þe sight
Of ryghtwyse men þat lyffed here ryght.
Bot alle þe parsons of þe Trinité
And þe godhed sal noght þan shewed be
To ille and gude, þat sal appere þan,
Bot Crist allane in fourme of man,
Goddes son þat þan sal deme us
And þarfor Saynt Johan says þus:
*"Omne iudicium dedit filio, ut honorifi-
cent filium, sicut honorificant patrem."*

All judgment is given to the Son of God.

"God has gyfen til his son," says he,
"Alle þe dome þat gyven sal be,
Þat men honour þe son ryght,
Als þai honour þe fadir ful of myght."
Þe gude men sal se hym in manhed þan,
With þe godhed, als God and man,
Þe whilk he sal noght fra þam hyde;
For þai sal se hym þan glorifide,
And þat sal be a blisful syght,
Swa fair he sal seme til þam, and bright.

[1] in myddes (MS. Harl. 4196).

þe ille men in manhed sal hym se.
Anly als he henged on þe rode tre,
Alle bla and blòdy als he þan was,
When he deyhed for mans trespas.
þat sight til þam sal be payne and drede,
For þai sal noght se of his godhede;
And for þe godhede es ful of blisse,
þarfor þe sight of it þai sal misse.
Bot in his manhed anly, als I say,
He sal shew hym til þam þat day,
For in fourme of man he sal þan seme
And in his manhede he sal þam deme.
He sal þan at his doun commyng,
þe taken of þe croys wyth hym bring,
On whilk he boght us fra elle pyn[1];
For he wald noght man saul tyn;
þat taken of þe crose alle men sal se,
Bot ful dilitable it sal be
Til rightwys men, and seme fule bright;
And dredful til synful mans syght.
þis taken of þe cros sal be shewed þan,
Als þe buk says, and be hyd fra na man:
Hoc signum crucis erit in celo, cum
dominus ad iudicandum venerit.
"þis taken of þe cros in heven sal seme
When our loverd sal com to deme."
þat es at say aboven in þe ayre,
þat til gude men sal sem bright and fayre.
þis taken, als I trowe, sal noght be
þe sam cros, ne þe sam tre,
On whilk God was nayled fot and hande.
Bot a taken of þat cros semande.
Yhit som trowes, and swa may wel be,
þat þe taken of þe spere men sal þan se
þat staynged[2] Crist until þe hert rote,
And of þe nayles þat hym thurgh hand and fote

The wicked shall see Christ as he appeared on the cross.

Christ shall bring with him the token of the cross.

The sign of the cross shall appear in the heavens.

[1] Hell pyne (MS. Harl. 4196).
[2] stanged (MS. Harl. 4196).

Til þe hard rode tre fast fested;
And of þe croun of thornes þat was thrested
On his heved fast, þat þe blode out rane,
When þe thornes hym prikked til þe harnpane
And of þe scourges alswa þat brast his hyde[1],
Þat þe blode ran doun, on ilk syde.
Alle þer takens sal þan be shewed
Byfor alle men, bathe lerd and lewed;

The wicked shall see these signs to their confusion.

Bot þe synful, þat dampned sal be,
To þair shenshepe þan sal þam se.
Crist sal shew þan his woundes wyde,
In heved, and fote and in his syde,
Þat fressche sal sem and alle bledand
Til þe synful, þat bifor hym sal stand.
He sal shew, to þair confusioun,
Alle þe signes of his passioun,
And þe enchesoun and þe manere
Of his ded þat he tholed here,
And alle þis sal he do þos openly,
To reprove þe synful men þar-by
And þat sal be þair shenschip þan,
For Saynt Austyn says þus, þe halyman:
Fortasse, in corpore suo, dominus cicatrices serva-
vit ut in iudico hostibus exprobaret,
ut convincens eos dicat: Ecce homo
quem crucifixistis; Ecce Deus et homo
quem credere noluistis: Videte vulnera
que infixistis; agnoscite latus
quod pupigistis propter vos
apertum est et intrare noluistis.

They shall see the scars of our Lord's wounds.

He says, "our Lord Goddes son almyghty
Parantere has keped, in his body,
Þe erres[2] of his wondes sere,
Þat he tholed for mans syn here,
For to shew þam til his enmys,
Whan he sal sytte in dome als iustys

[1] Also the skourges that his flesshe to-tere (MS. Addit 11305).
[2] Þe *sore* of his woundes swiþe clere (MS. Y.).

To reprove þam at þe last day,
And to atteyn þam, and þos say;
"Lo! here, þe man in flesshe and blode
Þe whilk yhe hynged on þe rode;
Lo! her God and man, þat man wroght,
In wham trow wald yhe noght;
Byhalde þe wondes þat yhe styked,
Sese here þe syd þat yhe priked,
Þe whilk for yhow was open ay,
And yhe wald entre be[1] ne way."
A how mikel shenshep sal be
To þe synful þat alle þis sal here and se!
Þe whilk til hym dos here na gude agayne,
Þat for þam tholed swa mykel payne;
And yhit noght þas þat dus na gud anly,
But other þat er swa ful of felony,
Þat ay dos yvel ogayn gude,
And ofte dos Godes son on rode
In þat, þat in þam es thurgh syn,
Of whilk þai wille never here blyn.
What may þai answer þan and say,
How may þai þam excuse þat day?
In nathyng may þai be excused þan,
Swa rightwys sal be þe domesman;
For þat day, als þe buke wythenes,[2]
Sal noght be shewed but ryghtwysnes,
Wyth gret reddour til synful namly,
Þat sal be demed, als þa her worthy.
Þai may defende þam be na ways
For Johan, wyth þe gilden mouth, þos says:
Non erit tunc locus defensionis,
ubi videbunt Christum exhibentem,
testimonia insigniaque sue passionis.
He sais "na sted of defens þar sal be
War þai sal Crist þan openly se
Gyfhand wytnes, and takens certayn,
Of his passioun and of his payn.

Behold him whom ye hanged on the cross and whose side ye pierced.

So righteous shall be the judge, that none shall be able to excuse themselves.

[1] *bi* (MS. Harl. 4196).   [2] witnes (MS. Harl. 4196).

On doomsday, angels and men, all shall tremble before the judge.

Alle sal haf gret drede þat day,
Bath gude and ille, als we here clerks say.
Þar sal be nouther aungel na[1] man
Þat þai ne sal tremble for drede þan;
Alle-if þai wat þat þai sal be safe,
Yhit sal þai þat day dre[2] hafe
Noght for þam-self, for þai er giltles,
Bot for þe gret reddure of ryghtwisnes,
And for þe gret austerité,
Þat Crist sal shew þat day to se,
Agayn þe synful men namly,
Þat sal be dampned, wyth-outen mercy.
When rightwys men þat sal be saf,
And aungels swa mykel dred haf
What dred and dole aght synful haf þan?
Þarfor þos says þe halyman:
Si columpne celi contremiscent et
pavent adventum Christi,
et angeli pacis amare flebunt,
peccatores autem quid facient!

If the righteous stand in awe of Christ's coming, what ought the sinful to fear?

He says "if þe pylers of heven bright,
Þat er haly men þat has liffed right,
Sal dred Cristes commyng and manhede,
And þe aungels alswa sal þan haf drede,
And yhit gret ful bitterly þar-to,
What sal þe synful men þan do,
Þat sal be dampned, als I sayd are?"
And says þe haly man þus mare:
Si iustus vix salvabitur, impius
et peccator ubi parebunt?
"If þe rightwys man" yhit says he,
"Sal unnethes þan saved be,
Þe synful and þe wykked man
Whyderward sal þai wend þan?"
Ryghtwysmen, als þe buk telles,
Sal be saf þan and nan elles.
Our Loverd in manhed sal þan sitt
Oboune[3] þe synful, als says haly writ,

[1] ne, [2] dred, [3] Oboven (MS. Harl. 4196).

Austerne and wrahte [1] wyth a fel chere,
Wyth þam to threp þat has lyfed ille here.

The severity of the Judge.

Helle bynethen þat es wyde and depe,
Sal þan be open þam to kepe,
Þe erthe þat þai sal on stand sal scake,
Thurgh þair syn, and tremble and whake [2],

The quaking of the earth.

Swa þat unnethes it sal þam bere,
Swa mykel þair syn þe erth sal dere.
Þe world obout þam sal be brinnande,
Þe devels on ilk syde þam sal stande,

The burning of the world.

Gret sorow sal be omang þam þar;
Þe heven oboven sal strike þam sar,
With thundirs dyntes and levenyngs togyder;
Þai wald þan fle and wate never whider;

Thunder and lightning shall strike the wicked.

Þai sal be umset swa on ilka side,
Þat þai may nouthir fle ne þam hide.
Many accusers þar sal be þan,
To accuse þam byfor þat domesman;
For I fynd written, als yhe sal here,
Fiften maneres of accusours sere,
Þat sal accuse in þat dredeful day
Þe synful men, þat es to say,

Fifteen accusers shall appear against the wicked:

Conscience þat es called Ynwitt,
And þair awen syns, and hali writt,
Gods creatures þat we ken,
Devels and aungels and haythen men,
And martirs þat has feled tourments sere,
And othir þat wranges has tholed here.
Mens sons and doghters unchastyede,
Pover men þat þair nede myght noght hyde,
Suggettes, and benefices receyved here.
Þe tourmentes of Cristes passioun sere;
And God hym-self and alle þe trinité,
Alle þere ogayne þe synful sal be.

1. Conscience, 2. Sin, 3. Holy Writ, 4. Creation, 5. Devils, 6. Angels, 7. The Heathen, 8. Martyrs, 9. Sons and daughters, 10. The Poor, 11. Subjects, 12. Benefits received, 13. Christ's passion, 14. God, 15. The Trinity.

First sal þair awen conscience,
Accuse þam þan in Cristes presence,

[1] wrathe (MS. Harl. 4196).

[2] qwake (MS. Harl. 4196).

Openly and noght in priveté;
For na thyng þan sal hidde be,
All things shall be revealed.
Alle thyng sal be shewed þar oppenly;
For Danyel says þus in his prophecy:
"Sedit iudicium et libri aperti sunt."
"Þe dome sattand þe bokes er oppen wyde";
And þus sal be sene þat tyde.
Þe bokes er conscience and noght elles,
Als þe glose þar-on þus telles:
Consciencie omnibus revelabuntur.
I. Conscience.
"Conscience", it says, "of ilka thyng
Sal be shewed til alle mens knawyng."
II. The sins of the wicked shall betray them.
Þair syns alswa, bathe mare and les,
Sal þam accuse, als þe boke bers wittnes.
For þair syns sal ay witth þam last,
Als þai war bunden obout þair nekes fast,
Þe whilk þam sal accuse þat day;
Agayn wham þai sal noght kun say;
And als stolne thyng wreghes a thefe funden,
When it es obout his neke fast bounden,
Right swa þair syns sal wreghe þam þar,
Als þai bunden obout þair nekes war,
And þan sal þair syns say þus;
Til ilka synful man "þou wroght us,
And we er þin with-outen dout,
And þou has lang borne us obout."
III. Holy writ.
Alswa accuse sal haly writt,
Namly þas men þat knawes it,
Or þe poyntes has herde þat falls þar-to,
And wald noght aftir haly writt do.
IV. Creation.
Yhit sal Godes creatures sere,
Accuse þam on diverse manere,
Als þe son and þe mone and þe sterns,
And þe elementes þa[t] us governs;
And alle þe werld sal be þan redy,
To accuse þe synful men oppenly;
For alle creatoures hate þam sal,
When he es wrathe þat es maker of alle.

V. Devils shall accuse the wicked, just as one thief does another.

Alswa devels sal accuse þam þar
Of alle þair syns, bathe les and mar.
And of þa syns þat þai sal out-say,
Til whilk þai egged þam, bathe nyght and day,
And of þas þai sal þam þar accuse,
Als a thefe his felaghe of theft duse,
Þat hym accuses of þe same thyng
Þat he with hym did thurgh his eggyng;
Þe devels at þe dome sal be redy,
Þat to tempte men here ay er bysy;
And þai write alle syns, bathe les and mar,
Of whylk þai may accuse þam þar,
And alle syns þai sal reherce þan,
And þar-for þus says Iob, þe halyman:
Scribis Domine contra me amaritudines,
id est, permittis scribi contra me peccata amara.
"Loverd, þou suffers here", says he,
"Be writen bitter syns ogaynes me."

VI. Angels shall say that the wicked would not follow their counsels.

Aungeles alswa, als we here clerkes say,
Sal accuse þe synful men at þat day,
For God þat til þam þair sauls touke,
For to kepe here als says þe buke,
Sal aske of þam, at his comyng,
Acount to yhelde of þair kepyng;
Þan sal þe aungels answere þar-to,
And say þus, "our rede þai wald noght do
Bot agayne our wille foly þai wald use",
Þus sal aungels þe synful accuse.

VII. The heathen shall accuse the false christian.

Alswa haythen men, als says þe buke,
Þat never baptem ne right trouthe tuke,
Als Iewes and Sarzyns and Paens,
Þat wate noght what Criestes law bymens,
Sal þan accuse als men sal se,
Þe fals cristen þat dampned sal be,
For þe haythen men at þat grete assys
Sal þan be halden als men rightwys,
To regard of þe fals cristen men
Þat wald noght kepe þe comandmentes ten.

Bot spendes þair fyve wittes in vayne,
Þarfor þai sal have mykel mare payne,
In þe pitte of helle þat þam sal mar griefe
Þan þe haithen men of mysbylyefe.

VIII. The Saints and Martyrs shall accuse the sinful of cruelty.

Þe halghes alswa sal accuse alle þa,
Þat sal be dampned and to helle ga;
And namly martirs, Godes awen knyghtes,
Þai sal accuse þe synful wyghtes,
Als þe tirauntes þat þam pyned and sloghe,
And othir þat þam til tourmentes droghe,
Of wham vengeance til God þai cry,
Als þe appocalips þus shewes þar-by:
Usquequo Domine sanctus et verus, non vindicas
sanguinem nostrum de hiis qui habitant in terra.
Þat es "haly Loverd, sothefast and gude,
How lange sal be ar þow venge our blude
Of our enemys þat in erthe duelles."
On þis manere þe appocalips telles;

They shall cry to God for vengeance.

Sen þai to God ay vengance cry,
Of þam þat of þair blude er gilty,
Howe suld þai þan in þe tyme of wreke
Be stille and noght ogayne þam speke?
Alswa alle þas þat has tholed here
Fals[h]edes and wrangs on sere manere,
Sal þat day accuse þam sone,
Þat þam has here gret wranges done.

IX. Sons and daughters shall accuse their parents.

Yhit sons and doghters þat unchastyd war
Sal accuse þa[i]r fadirs and modirs þar,
For-þi þat þai war rekles and slawe
To chasty þam and hald þam in awe,
And to teche þam gude thewes,
And þarfor þe wys man þus in buke shewes
De patre impio conquerentur filii, quoniam
propter ipsum sunt in opprobrium.
"Þe sons sal pleyne þam þan", says he,
"Of þe ille fader and agayn hym be,
For thurgh defaute of hym er þai
In grete reprove", þat es to say,

In defaut of his disciplyne,
Parchaunce, be dampned til helle pyne,
And þe fader alswa be with þam spilte,
For he es þe cause of þair gilte.
Yhit þe pover sal þam ple[y]ne thurgh right,
Of þe riche men in Godes syght,
And accuse þam þan ful grevosly,
For þai had of þam na mercy,
For to helpe þam here in þair nede,
Nouthir to clathe þam ne to fede,
Bot lete silver and gold on þam rust,
Þe whilk þai had in hurde uptrust;
And þar-of til pure wald noght gyve,
When þai sawe þam at meschyve,
Þar-for þe ruste of þat moweld moné
Agayne þam þan sal wittnes be.
And wormes and moghes on þe same manere,
Þat in þair clathes has bred here,
Þe whilk þai had here over mesur,
And of þam wald noght parte *til* þe pur,
Sal þat day be in wittenes broght,
For þe pure þat þai helped noght.
Alswa þa þat sugettes war til man,
Sal accuse þair soveraynes þan,
And[1] þam has greved thurgh *maystré* and myght
And of other wald do þam *na* right.
Þe benefices þat God did þam here,
Sal þam accuse on sere manere,
For agayne þam sal Crist allege sone,
And shewe þam what he had þam done,
And reherce his benefices, mare and les,
To reprove þam of þair unkyndenes.
Yhit þe tourmentes of Cristes passioun,
Þat he tholed for mans salvacioun,
Sal þam accuse at þat gret dome,
For-why þus says Saynt Ierome:
Crux contra te perorabit, Christus
per vulnera sua, contra te allegabit,

X. The Poor shall make complaints against the rich.

XI. Subjects shall accuse their rulers.

XII. The gifts that God has given man shall make accusation against the wicked.

XIII. Christ's sufferings shall bear witness against the sinful.

[1] Þat?

cicatrices contra te loquentur,
clavi de te conquerentur.

The testimony of the cross.

He says "þe croyce on whilk he dieghed for man
Sal stratly pray ogayne þe þan,
And Crist, thurgh his wondes wide,
Ogayne þe sal allege þat tyde;
Þe erres of his wondes sal speke
Og[a]yne þe and of þe aske wreke;
Þe nayles þat in his hend and fete stak,
On þe sal pleyne and grét playnt mak."

XIV. God and XV. the Trinity shall accuse the unrighteous.

At þe last, God hym-self, mast of myght,
And þe trinité sal accuse þam right,
For þai wrethed God in þair legge pousté,
And alle þe parsons of þe trinité,
Bathe þe fadir and þe son and þe haly gast.
Þar-for þat accusyng sal be mast,
Bot þe secunde parson þan alle sale deme,
Þat es Crist Godes son, þat þan man sal seme.
Alle þat sal com byfor Crist þat day,
Sal strayt acounte yhelde, ar þai passe away,
Of alle þair lif howe þai here lyved,
Þan sal be sene what þai God gryeved

All accusations shall be made openly before saints and angels; wicked men and devils.

And byfor alle þe werld shewed sal be,
Oppenly and noght in privité;
And byfor halghes and aungels bright,
And byfor devels horribel til mans sight,
And byfor alle wykked men alswa,
Þat sal be dampned til endles wa.
For alle sal be þan þare, gude and ille,
To deme and be demed als rightwysnes wille;
For Crist, þat rightwyse domesman,
Sal calle alle men byfor hym þan,
Als þe prophet David bers witnes,
In psauter whare þus writen es:
Advocavit celum desursum et terram,
discernere populum suum.
He says "he sal bifor hym calle
Þe heven fra aboven and þe erthe alle,

For to deme right his folk þat day."
And þis vers es þus mykel at say,
He sal calle þan heven byfor hym tit,
Þat es to say, haly men and parfit,
Þat with hym in dome þan sal sitt,
And wyth hym deme, als says haly writt;
Bot þe erthe es noght elles to telle,
Bot wykked men and devels of helle,
Þe whilk he sal calle at his wille,
For to chede[1] out þe gude fra þe ille.
Þan sal ilka man þarof þair lyfyng
Be sette until and[2] hard rekkenyng,
For men sal þan strayte acount yhelde
Of alle þair tyme of yhouthe and elde;
Noght anly of ane or twa yhere,
Bot alle þe tyme þat þai lyfed here,
And specyaly of ilka moment,
Of alle þe tyme þat God þam lent.
A moment of tyme es nan othir thyng,
Bot a short space als of a eghe twynklyng.
Na moment sal be unrekend þan,
Als Saynt Bernard says, þe halyman:
Sicut non peribit capillus de capite,
ita non erit momentum de toto
tempore de quo sane
non conqueratur.
He says "als nan hare of alle þe hed
Sal perisse þat tyme in na sted,
Right swa sal be na moment,
Of alle þe tyme þat God had[3] sent,
Of whilk sal be made na pleynyng."
In þe tyme of þat last rekkenyng,
Alswa þai sal yhelde acount certayne,
Of ilk idel worde, spoken in vayne,
Þat es to say, þat war fruytles,
Als haly writt bers wittnes:

Heaven and earth shall come before the judge.

Each man will be called to a hard reckoning.

Account must be given of every moment of our life.

[1] chese (MS. Harl. 4196). [2] ane (MS. Harl. 4196).
[3] has (MS. Harl. 4196).

De omni verbo ociosi in die iudicii
reddenda est racio.
Þe buke says shortly on þis manere:
Every idle word and thought will be judged.
"Of ilkan idel word and vayne here,
Reson sal be yholden right
At þe day of dome, in Goddes sight;"
And noght anely of idel wordes sayd,
Bot of ilk idel thoght þat God noght payd,
For excuse þam may þai noght
Nouther of idel worde ne of thoght,
Þat þai spak or thoght aftir þai had witt,
Of whilk þai war never here qwitt;
Wharfor our Loverd God alle-myghty,
Spekes þus thurgh þe prophet Ysay:
Ego cogitaciones eorum venio ut congregem
cum gentibus ad iudicandum sicut iudico gentes.
The words of Isaiah.
He says "I com to gadir with men
Þe thoghtes of þam þat I ken,
For to deme þam alle, mar and les,
Als I sal men deme, thurgh rightwysnes."
Many aght be dredand þar-for,
And yhit sais þus Saynt Gregor:
Ergo sic Deus vias cuiuscunque considerat
ut nec minutissime cogitaciones, que
apud vos usu valuerunt, in iudicio
indiscusse remaneant.
St. Bernard on the doom.
He says "God", þat alle wysdom kan,
"Swa byhaldes þe wayes of ilk man
Þat þe lest thoghtes þat thurgh use had yhe
In þe dome sal noght undiscussed be."
And noght anely of idel word and thoght,
Bot of alle idel werk þai ever men wroght;
Þai sal alswa yhit acount yhelde
Noght anly of gret dedes of elde,
Bot of smale dedes of þair yhouthe,
Fra þe tyme þat þai any witt couthe,
Þat þai had wroght, bathe nyghtes and days,
And þarfor Salamon þus says:

Letare iuvenis in adolescencia tua, et in
bono sit cor tuum in diebus iuventutis tue,
et ambula in viis cordis tui et in tuitu
oculorum tuorum; Et scito quod pro
omnibus hiis te adducet
dominus in iudicium.
He says "þou yhung man be glad and blithe, The words of Solomon.
In þi yhouthede þat passes swithe,
And þat þi hert in gude be stedfast,
Whilles þe days of þi youthe sal last
And in þe ways of þe herht ga
And in þe syght of þin eghen twa;
And wytt þou for alle þis of yhouthede,
Our Loverd sal þe into þe dome lede;"
Whar resons sal be yholden sere;
And þarfor says Iob on þis manere:
Et consumere ne vis peccatis adolescencie mee.
"Loverd wil þou waste me to noght
Thurgh þe syns þat I haf wroght,"
Alswa men sal þan yhelde acount sone,
Noght anly of þat þat þai wrang had done
Witandly thurgh þair knawyng,
Bot alswa of þat þat þai did thurgh erryng, Sin committed through ignorance will be judged.
Of whilk þai sal noght be excused þan,
Als in buk þus says þe wyse man:
Pro omni errato, sine bonum sine malum
sit, adducetur homo in iudicio.
He says "for ilka thyng þat erred es
Be it gude or ille, mar or les,
Man, at þe last day, sal be ledde
To þe dome þat es mast dredde;"
And þarfor David, als þe psauter shewes us,
Was ful dredand, þat says þus:
Et ignorancias meas me memineris.
"Loverd" he says, "ne mene þou noght
Of my freyle unknawynges of thoght."
Yhit sal þai yhelde acunt withdrede,
Noght anly of ilk apert ille dede,

Many good deeds will appear as sinful.

Bot alswa of ilkan ille dede privé,
Þat semed by syght þat gude suld be;
For some dede þat ille es, sems gud here,
For Saynt Gregor says on þis manere:
Interdum sordet in oculis iudicis quod
fulget in oculis auditoris.
He says "some tyme es foule in þe domes man sight
Þat in eghe of þe herer shynes bright."
Bot at þe dome sal þat discused be,
Als in þe psalme men may written se:
Cum accipero tempus,
Ego iusticias iudicabo.
God says þis wordes thurgh þe prophet David
And many othir þat accordes þar-with,

The doom shall be given through righteousnes.

He says "when I haf tyme receyved right
I sal deme rightwysnes, thurgh myght."
Alswa yhit men byhoves nedly þan,
Yhelde acount byfor þe domes man,
Noght anely of werkes þat þai had wroght,
Bot alswa of dedes þat þai did noght,
And of werkes of mercy and of almus
Þat þai noght did, for þe godspelle shewes þus:

Of works not done.

Esurivi et non dedistis michi manducare,
sitivi et non dedidistis michi bibere.
Þis es, als yhe sal aftirward here,
How God sal say on þis manere:
"I hungerd, and yhe me noght fedde,
I thrested, and yhe me na drynk bedde."
For þis þai sal be aresoned straytly,
And for other werkes noght done of mercy.
And noght anely for þa werkes noght don,
Bot for þe gude þat þar-of myght haf commen son.

Men shall give account of the souls entrusted to them.

Men byhoves alswa acount yhelde
Of þair saules, þat þam byhoved welde,
And haf in kepyng whille þai myght lif,
Of whilk þai sal þan answer gyf.
Now if a kyng of a riche kyngryke
Þat had a doghter, þat war hym like

Of bewté and of face and body,
Þe whilk he luved specialy
And eghtild to mak hir qwene of worshepe, *The king and his 'reeve'.*
And bytaght hir til his ryfe to kepe,
If he þar aftir keped hir mys,
Me thynk it war na dout of þis
Þat ne þe kyng wald haf rekkenyng,
And acount and answer of þat kepyng.
For it semes þat þe kyng had grete encheson
To sette hym for þat kepyng to reson,
And þe mare rekkesly[1] þat he hir yhemed
Þe mare grevosly hym aght be demed.
What suld þe kyng of heven do þan,
Of a man or of a woman,
Til wham he has bytaght to kepe here,
His doghtir þat es hym leve and dere, *The soul is God's daughter.*
Þat es man saul his awen liknes,
Whilles it fra dedly syn keped es,
Þe whilk he eghteld to coroun qwene
In heven þar ioy sal ay be sene?
Whaswa es rekles and kepes it ille,
He sal be aresoned, and þat es skille,
Of þe kepyng of it þat he tuke;
Þarfor þe wyse man says þus in his buke:
Custodi solicite
animam tuam.
Þat es on Ynglis in þis manere,
He says "kepe þi saul bysily here".
Bot he es sely þat may sikerly say
In þe tyme of þe dede at his last day
'I yhelde my saul in þis dede stour
Til þe Loverd þat es my saveour.'
Men sal yhit yhelde acount stray[t]ly *Men shall answer for the custody of the body.*
Noght of þair saules with-in anely
Bot alswa of þair bodys with-oute
Þat þai had to kepe, and bare aboute
Of whilk þai sal yhelde rekkenyng,
Sen þai had þar-of þe kepyng.

[1] reklesly (MS. Harl. 4196).

A man's body is as a castle.

Ilka mans body may be cald,
Als a castelle here for to hald,
Þat til man es gyfen of God to kepe
For his profit and Goddes worshepe.
Þe enemys ofte assales it hard
And þarfor says Saynt Bernard:
Bonum castrum custodit
qui corpus suum custodit.
"A gude castelle" he says, "kepes he
"Þat his body kepes in honesté."
Man sal yhelde acount alswa,
At þe dome, ar þai þeþen ga,
Þat stratly of þam sal be tane;
Noght anely of þe saules by þam ane,

Soul and body conjointly must be accounted for.

Ne anely of þair bodys þar-by,
Bot of bathe togidir ioyntly,
Þat es to say, ilkan sal þan
Yhelde acount of alle hale a man,
For a man properly may noght be cald,
Bot-if þe body and saul togidir hald
Þe saule be itself man es nane,
Ne þe body with-out saule by it ane.
Bot man may be called on twyn manere,
Whilles þai bathe er knyt togyder here.
For þes clerkes þat gret clergy can

Inner and outer man.

Calles man bathe Inner man and utter man.
Inner man onence þe saule anely
And utter man onence þe body.
Bot þe body and saule bytwene þam twa,
Makes bot a man and na ma,
Þarfor men sal yhelde acount ioyntly
Of bathe togyder, þe saule and þe body;
And forþi þat God, aftir his stature,
Made man mast digne and noble creature
Þarfor if man be til God frawarde
And unkynde and of hym tak na rewarde,
Þat ilk dignité of man namely,
Sal, at þe dome, yhelde hym gylty.

Yhit sal men yhelde acount [noght] anely
Of þair self, bot of other many,
Þat es to say, of ilka neghebur,
Þat men fals to help and to socur.
For God til ilk man commandes right
To helpe his neghebur after his myght.
And þas, þat may helpe and wille noght,
Sal þan til ful strayt acount be broght.
Alswa fadirs and modirs, at þat day,
Sal yhelde acount, þat es to say,
Of sons and doghtirs þat þai forthe broght,
Þe whilk þai here chastied noght.
And loverds alswa of þair meigné
Þe whilk þai lete uniustifyed be
And maysters of þair disciples alswa,
Þat þai lete be unthewed, and untaght ga,
And chastid þam noght, ne þam wald lere,
Forþi says Salamon on þis manere:
Virga discipline fugabit stulticiam
in corde pueri colligatam.
"Þe wande", he says, "of disciplyne smert,
Sal chace foly out of þe childes hert."
Þarfor maysters som tyme uses þe wand
Þat has childer to lere undir þair hand.
Prelats of ordir and of dignyté
Sal acount yhelde in sere degré
Of þair suggets undir þair powere,
How þai þam reweld in þis lyf here,
And answer of þam þat lyfed noght wele,
For þus says þe prophet Ezechiele:
Ecce! ego requiram gregem
meam de manu pastoris.
God says þus thurgh þe prophete:
"Lo! I sal aske my flok of shepe
Of þe hird þat had þam undir his hand;"
Of þis word aght prelates be dredand.
Men sal alswa yhelde rekkenynges sere
Of al gudes þat God has gefen þam here,

Men must give an account of their neighbours,

Fathers and Mothers of their children,

Lords of their households,

Masters of their disciples,

Priests of their subjects,

Men of gifts received.

Gifts of nature, grace and fortune.

Als of gudes of kynde and gudes of graces,
And gudes of hap þat men purchases.

I. Gifts of nature.

Þe gudes of kynd er bodily strenthe,
And semely shappe of brede and lenthe
And delyvernes and bewté of body;
Swilk gudes of kynd here has many.

II. Gifts of grace.

Gudes of grace may þir be,
Mynde, and witte, and sutilté,
And fair shewyng of speche sutille,
And knawyng bathe of gude and ille,
Vertus of grete devocioun
And luf of lyf of contemplacioun.

III. Gifts of fortune.

Gudes of hap er þir to gesce,
Als honours, power, and ryche[s].
Of alle þir gudes men byhoves
Yhelde acounte, als þe buke pruves,
And answer straytly of þam alle.
I drede many in arrirage[1] mon falle,
And til perpetuele prison gang,
For þai despended þa gudes wrang,
For-whi God has gyfen here nathyng,
Of whilk he wille noght haf rekkennyng.
Som sal yhit, als I sayd ar,
Yhelde acount ful straytly þar
Of þe gudes þat þai wald noght bede
Til other þat of þam had nede,
For alle er we als a body here,
For þe apostel says on þis manere:
Omnes enim unum
corpus sumus.

We are all as limbs of one body.

He says "we er alle als a body",
Þat has diverse lyms many.
And als a lym of a body here
Es redy, aftir it has powere,
To serve alle þe other, mar and les,
Of þat office þat gyven it es,

[1] rerage (MS. Harl. 4196).

Right swa ilk man þat here lyfes,
Of alle þat God thurgh grace him gyfes,
Suld other serve, þat þar-of has nede,
Als he wille answere at þe day of drede.

Of mutual help.

Ful many men lyfes here of þa
Þat er halden for to do swa,
Als he þat gret and myghty es,
Es halden to defende þam þat er les;

The strong should assist the weak.

And þe ryche þat mykel rychesces has,
To gyf þam þat here in povert gas;

The rich should give to the poor.

And men of laghe alswa to travayle
And to counsaile þam þat askes counsayle;
And leches alswa, if þai wyse ware,
To hele þam þat er seke and sare;
And maysters of þair science to ken,
Namly, þam þat er unlered men;
And precheours Goddes worde to preche,
And þe way of lyf other to teche.
Þus es ilk man halden with gude entent,
To help other of þat God has þam lent

Each man is bound to help his neighbour.

Frely for Goddes luf, and for noght elles,
Wharfor Saynt Petre þe apostel þus telles:
Unusquisque, sicut accipit graciam, in alterutrum illam administrare debet.
He says "ilk man þat grace has here
Als he resayves grace, on þe saue manere
Suld he it ministre and frely bede
Til ilkan other þat þai[1] of has nede"

"Give as ye have received."

And þus es ilk man halden to do,
For in þe godspelle yhit says God mar þarto:
Quod gratis accepistis,
gratis date.
He says "þat þat yhe haf of grace fre
And frely resayved, frely gyf yhe."
Þus sal men þan yhelde resons sere
Of alle þair lyf, als writen es here,
Þat es of alle tymes spended in vayne,
And of ilka moment of tyme certayne;

We shall have to yield an account of every moment of our lives,

[1] Þar?

Of every idle word and thought,

And of ilkan Idel word and thoght,
And of ilkan ydel dede þat þai wroght,
Outher in elde or in þair yhouthe,
Aftir þe tyme þat þai witt first couthe,
And of dedes þat þai thurgh erryng did;
And noght anely of open werkes bot of hid,
And noght anely of werkes wroght, bot unwroght
Als of werkes of mercy þat done war noght;

of soul and body,

And of þair awen saules þai sal reken þar,
And of þair bodys þat þam obout bar;
And noght anly of ayther by þam-self þan,
Bot of bathe togyder als of a man;
And yhit noght anely of þam-self alle,

and of our neighbours.

Bot of þair neghburs answer þai salle;

Fathers, mothers,

And fadirs and modirs sal rekken þat tyde,
Of þair sons and þair doghtirs unchastide;
And loverdes alswa of þair men namly,
Þe whilk þai wald noght iustify;

Teachers,

And maysters of þair disciples alswa,
Þe whilk þai lete untaght in folis ga;

Prelates and priests,

And prelates and prestes of ilka suggette,
Þat þai wald noght in right rewel sette;

all will have to yield a strict account of those under them.

And alle other þat wrang and in ille entent
Þe gudes spended þat God had þam lent,
And of alle wrang haldyngs of gudes sere,
Of whilk þai parted noght til other here
Þat of þam had nede, als þai myght se;
Of alle þir thynges men sal aresoned be.
At þe day of dome, als God has ordaynd,
Whar nathyng sal be hid ne laynd,
Of alle þir, men sal yhelde acount strayt,
Sal nathyng þan be þar to layt.

Happy is that man who may give a good reckoning.

Ful sely es þat man or womman,
Þat a gude rekkenyng may yhelde þan,
Swa þat he may pas qwyte and fre
Of alle thyng, þat may rekend be.
And swa sely may be alle þas,
Þat fra hethen in charité gas;

For he þat has here gude endyng,
Sal pas wele þar, with light rekkenyng.
At þe day of dome, als byfor es talde,
Alle men sal be bathe yhung and alde,

Young and old shall be judged.

And gude and ille, alle sal com þider.
Swa mykel folk com never togyder,
Ne never was sene sythen þe werld bygan,
Als sal be sene byfor Crist þan,
Þat sal be demed aftir þai haf wroght.
Bot som sal deme and sum noght,
For som sal deme with þe domes-man,
Þat thurgh dome sal noght be demed þan.

Some shall 'deme' with the doomsman,

Som sal be demed þan ryghtwysly,
Þat sal deme on na party;
Bot many other þar sal seme,
Þat sal nouther be demed ne deme.
Þa þat sal deme and noght demed be,
Sal be parfit men with God privé.
Of þa þat demed sal be and dem sal noght,
Sal some til blisse be demed and broght;

Others shall 'be demed' to bliss;

And sum sal be demed to helle to wende,
Whar pyn sal be with-outen ende.
Bot alle þat trowed noght als trow we,
Sal nouther deme ne demed be;
Bot for þai wald noght til our trouthe come,
Þa sal wende til helle with-outen dome.

Many shall go to hell without being judged.

First þas þat with Crist sal deme þat day
And noght be demed, er namly þai
Þat here forsuke þe werldes solace,
And folowed rightly Cristes trace,
Als his apostels and other ma,
Þat for his luf tholed angre and wa;
Þa sal deme with Crist and nan elles,
For-whi in þe godspelle þus he telles:
Vos, qui secuti estis me, sedebitis
super sedes duodecim, iudicantes duodecim
tribus Israel.
He says "yhe þat folowes me here lyfand,

Sal sitt opon twelf setes demand
Þe twelf nacions of Israel,"
Þat es, þas þat God sese here als lele.

Men of charity.

Som sal noght deme, bot demed be
Til blis, als men of grete charité
Þat blethely wirk wald þe werkes of mercy,
And keped þam here fra syn dedly.

False christians shall 'be demed' to hell.

Som sal noght deme, bot be demed
Til helle, and fra God be flemed,
Als þas þat er fals cristen men,
Þat keped noght þe comandmentes ten,
And wald noght here forsake þair syn,
Bot whils þai lyfyed ay dwelle þar-in.
Som sal noght be demed þat day
Þat sal wende to helle and dwelle þar ay,

Pagans and Jews go straight to hell without judgment.

Als paens and sarazyns þat had na law,
And Iewes þat never wald Crist knaw,
Þarfor þai sal ga til payne endeles,
With-outen dome, for þus writen es:
Qui sine lege peccant,
absque lege peribunt.
"Þas þat with-outen lawe uses syn
With-outen law sal perysshe þar-in."
And þar-for at þe day of dome namly,
Ilk man sal haf as he es worthy.
A ful hard day men sal þat day se,
When alle thyng sal þus discussed be.
Þat day, sal na man be excused
Of nathyng þat he wrang here used,
Þat sounes in ille on any manere,
Of whilk he was never delyverd here.[1]

There is no mercy for the wicked; none shall plead for them.

Þe synful sal þare na mercy have,
For nathyng may þam þan save;
For-why þai sal þan na help gett
Of sergeaunt, ne auturne, ne avoket,
Ne of nan other for þam to plede,
Ne þam to counsayle ne to rede,

[1] Þe whiche sowneþ to ille in eny manere dede.
Of þe whiche he hade in thouȝt no manere drede (MS. Y.).

Ne na halghe sal for þam pray.
Þis may be cald a ful harde day,
Forwhi þan, als þe buke bers witnes,
Sal noght be shewed bot rightwysnes,
And grete reddure, with-outen mercy,
Until alle synful men namely.

The day of doom is a day of righteous judgment;

Þa þat of þair syn here wald noght stynt;
Þai sal þat day for ever be tynt
Fra God, with-outen any recoverere,
And delyverd be until þe devels powere.
Ful wa sal synful men be þat day,
And til helle pyne be put for ay,
And þarfor men may calle þat day,
Þe grete day of delyveraunce,
Þe day of wreke and of vengeaunce,
Þe day of wrethe and of wrechednes,

To the wicked it is the day of wrath.

Þe day of bale and of bitternes,
Þe day of pleynyng and accusyng,
Þe day of answer and of strait rekkenyng,
Þe day of iugements and of Iuwys,
Þe day of angre and of angwys,
Þe day of drede and of tremblyng,
Þe day of gretyng and goulyng,
Þe day of crying and of duleful dyn,
Þe day of sorow þat never sal blyn,
Þe day of flaying and of af[r]ay,
Þe day of departyng fra God away,
Þe day of merryng and of myrk[n]es,
Þe day þat es last and þat mast es,
Þe dai when Crist sal make ende of alle;
Þus may nan discryve þat day and calle.
Our loverd þat alle thyng can se and witt
At þe dredeful day of dome sal sitt,
Als kyng and rightwyse domesman,
In dome to deme alle þe werld þan,
Opon þe setil of his mageste.
Þat day sal alle men byfor hym be,

Christ shall sit that day upon his throne as king and judge.

Bathe gude and ille, mare and les;
þan sal noght be done bot rightwysnes.

The final doom.

He sal deme al men of ilka degré,
Til ioy or payne þat demed sal be,
And[1] rightwyse domes-man and suthefast
And gyf a fynal dome at þe last.
Bot how he sal deme I sal shewe,
Als telles þe godspelle of Mathewe;
Hys angels þan, aftir his wille,

he good shall be separated from the bad.

Sal first departe þe gude fra þe ille,
Als þe hird þe shepe dus fra þe gayte,
þat falles to be putt til pastur strayt.
By þe shepe understand we may
þe gude men þat sal be saved þat day.
By þe gayte understand we may
þe ille men, þat þan dampned sal be.
þe gude sal be sette on his right hand,
And þe ille on his lefte syde sal stand;
þan sal our loverd say þus þat tyde
Til þam þat standes on his right syde:
Venite, benedicti patris mei,
possidete paratum nobis regnum
a constitucione mundi.

The words of Christ to those on his right hand.

He sal say þan, "commes now til me,
My fadir blissed childer fre,
And weldes þe kyngdom þat til yhow es dight
Fra first þat þe werld was ordaynd right."
For I hungerd and yhe me fedde,
I thrested and at drynk yhe me bedde;
Of herber grete nede I had,
Yhe herberd me with hert glad,
Naked I was, als yhe myght se,
Yhe gaf me clathes and clad me;
Seke I was and in ful wayke state,
Yhe wisit me, bathe arly and late;
In prisoun when I was halden stille,
Til me yhe come with ful gude wille.

[1] *Als?*

Þan sal þe rightwys men þat day,
Til our loverd answer þus and say;
'Loverd when saw we þe hungry,

The question of the righteous.

And to gyf þe mete war we redy;
And when myght we þe thresty se,
And gaf þe drynk with hert fre;
When saw we þe nede of herber have,
And to herber þe vouched save;
When saw we þe naked and we þe cled,
And when saw we þe seke and in prison sted,
And visited þe with gude wille,
And comforted þe, als was skille?'
Our loverd sal þan þam answer þus,
And say, als þe godspelle shewes us:
'Suthly I say yhou, swa yhe wroght,

The reply of Our Lord.

Þat ilka tyme when yhe did oght
Until ane of þe lest þat yhe myght se
Of my brether, yhe did til me.'
Þan sal our loverd til alle þas say,
Þat þan on his lefte syde sal stand þat day,
And spek til þam with an austerne chere,
Þir wordes þat er hydus to here:
Discedite a me maledicti, in ignem
eternum, qui preparatus est diabolo
et angelis eius.
"Yhe weryed wyghtes wende fra my sight,

Christ reproaches those on his left hand with their want of love towards him.

Until þe endeles fire þat es dight
Til þe devel and til his aungels."
And þan sal he say þus, als þe buke tels,
'I hungred and had defaute of mete,
And yhe wald noght gyfe me at ete;
I thrested, and of drynk had nede,
And yhe wald na drynk me bede;
I wanted herbor, þat I oft soght,
And alle þat tyme yhe herberd me noght;
Naked with-outen clathes I was,
And with-outen clathes yhe let me pas;

Seke I was, and bedred lay,
And yhe visite me nouther nyght ne day;
In prison I was, als wele wyst yhe,
And yhe wald na tyme com til me.'
þan sal þai answere, als men sal here,
Til our loverd, and say on þis manere:

The inquiry of the wicked.

'Loverd when saw we þe haf hunger or thrist
Or of any herber haf grete brist;
Or naked, or seke, or in prison be,
And we na thyng did ne mynystred to þe?'
þan sal our loverd answer ogayne
And say til þam þir wordes certayne:

The answer given to them by Christ.

'Suthly I say yhou, als falles þar-to,
Alle tyme þat yhe wald noght do
Til ane of lest þat myne er kydde,
Als lang til me yhe noght didde.'
þus sal our loverd reherce openly
Til rightwys men, þe werkes of mercy,
For to make þam openly kyd,
Til grete worshepe of þam þat þam dyd;
And shew til þe synful, als falles þar-to,
þair unkyndenes, þat wyld noght do
þe werkes of mercy for his luf,
Til þair grete shenshepe and repruve.

When Christ has said these things, the wicked shall go along with the devils into hell.

When he has þus sayde and made ende,
þe synful with þe devels sal wende
Until helle fire, þat never sal slake.
A ful hidus cry þan sal þai make,
And say 'allas! þat we ever war wroght.
In manskynd; whyne war we noght!
Whyne had God made us swa,
þat us thurt never haf feled wele ne wa!
Now sal we bryn in þe fire of helle,
And with-outen ende þar-in duelle.'
Helle þan þam sal swelghe als-tite
With-outen any lenger respyte;
And alle þe fire þat þan sal be sene,
And alle þe corrupcions þat ever has bene,

And þe filthe and alle þe stynk
Of alle þe werld þan sal synk
Doun with þam in-til þe pitte of helle,
To eke þair sorow þat þar sal duelle.
Bot þe ryghtwys men, als þe buke bers wytnes
Sal wende til blisse, whar lyfe es endeles,
With our loverd and hys aungels ilkane
Shynand brighter þan ever son shane.
Now have yhe herd, als es contende
In þis fift part, how þe werld sal ende,
And how Crist, at his last commyng,
Sal in dome sitte and discusse alle thyng.
Here may a man read þat has tome,
A large proces of þe day of dome,
Þat a lang tyme aftir I haf redde
Suld contene by skille, ar alle war spedde;
Bot ye sal understand and witte,
Als men may se in haly writte,
Þat thurgh þe wysedom and þe vertu,
And þe myght of our Lord Ihesu,
Alle þe processe þat sal be þat day,
Of whilk any clerk can speke or say,
Sal þan swa shortely be sped and sone,
Þat alle sal be in a moment done.
A moment es als of a tyme bygynnyng,
Als short als an eghe twynkelyng.
A grete wondir may þis be kyd,
Omang alle wondirs þat ever God dyd,
Þat in swa short tyme at his commyng,
He mught deme and discusse al thyng;
Bot of þis suld nane muse, lered ne lewed,
For als grete wordirs[1] has God shewed;
Als grete a wonder es when he wroght,
With a short worde, alle þe world of noght,
And of þis þe prophete bers wittnes,
Þat says þus, als it wryten es:

The righteo shall wend endless blis

All shall be done in the twinkling of an eye.

[1] wondirs (MS. Harl. 1964).

Quia ipse dixit et facta sunt,
ipse mandavit et creata sunt.

God spake and all was done.

"God sayde," says he, "and alle was done
He bad and alle was made sone."
Þus in a short tyme alle thyng made he,
Mare wondir þan þis mught never be,
Þan may he als shortly make endyng
Of alle thyng, als he made bygynnyng.
For swa witty and myghty es he
Þat na-thyng til hym impossibel may be.
Þe processe of þat day þat I haf talde,
Al þe men of þe world, bathe yhung and alde,
Sal se and undirstand it alle,
In als short tyme als it sal falle.
Now haf yhe herd me speke and rede
Of þe wondir þat þan sal be and drede.
Bot alle þogh yhe haf herd me rede and say
Of þe reddure, þat sal be done þat day
Untille alle synful men namely,
Þat sal be dampned with-outen mercy,
Als men may in þis part wryten se,
Na man þarfor suld in dispayre be;
For alle þat has mercy here sal be save,
And alle þat here askes mercy sal it have,
Yf þai it sekes whilles þai lyf bodily,
And trewely trayste in Goddys mercy,
And amende þam and þair syn forsake,
Byfor þe tyme ar þe dede þam take,
And do mercy here and charité,
Þan gette þai mercy and saved sal be.
Bot if þe dede byfor haf þam tane,
Ar þai haf mercy, þan gette þai nane,
Bot reddure of rightwysnes anely,
For þan sal be shewed na mercy.
Here may ilk man, if he wille,
Haf mercy þat dus þat falles þar-tille;
Þoghe he had done never swa mykel syn,
If he amended hym, he myght it wyn;

None should despair, for all may obtain mercy.

The mercy of God reaches over all.

For þe mercy of God es swa mykel here,
And reches over alle, bathe fer and nere,
Þat alle þe syn þat a man may do,
It myght sleken, and mare þar-to,
And þar-for says Saynt Austyn þus,
A gude worde þat may comfort us:
Sicut scintilla ignis in medio maris,
ita omnis impietas viri ad miseriam dei.
"Als a litel spark of fire," says he,
"In mydward þe mykel se,
Right swa alle a mans wykkednes
Un-to þe mercy of God es."
Here may men se how mykel es mercy,
To fordo alle syn and foly.

However great a man's sin, there is forgiveness for it.

For-why if a man had done here
Als mykel and als many syns sere,
Als al þe men of þe werld has done,
Alle myght his mercy fordo sone;
And if possibel whare, als es noght,
Þat ilk man als mykel syn had wroght,
Als alle þe men þat in þe werld ever was,
Yhit mught his mercy alle þair syn pas.
Þan semes it wele, als men may se,
Þat of his mercy here [t]he[re] is grete plenté,
For his mercy spredes on ilka syde
Thurgh alle þe werld, þat es brade and wyde,
And sheues it be many ways,
And þarfor þe prophete David says:
Misericordia Domini plena
est terra.

The earth is full of mercy.

"Þe erthe", he says, "es ful of mercy."
Þan may men it fynde here plenteuously;
And he þat has mercy, ar he hethen wende,
At þe grete dome sal fynde Criste his frende,
Whar rightwysnes anely sal be haunted,
And na mercy þan be graunted.
After þe grete dome alle þe werld brade
Sal seme þan als it war new made.

After the doom the earth shall be purified.

6348 Þe erthe sal be þan even and hale,
And smethe and clere als cristale;
Þe ayre obout sal shyne ful bright,
Þan sal ay be day and never nyght,
6352 For þe elementes alle sal þan clene be
Of alle corrumpciouns þat we here se;
Þan sal alle þe werld, in alle partys,
Seme als it war a paradys,

The stars shall shine brighter than the sun does at present.

6356 Þe planetes and þe sternes ilkane,
Sal shyne brighter þan ever þai shane.
Þe son sal be, als som clerkes demes,
Seven sythe[1] brighter þan it now semes;
6360 For it sal be als bright als it first was,
Byfor ar Adam did trespas.
Þe mone sal be als bright and clere,
Als þe son es now þat shynes here;

The sun shall stand in the east,

6364 Þe son sal þan in þe este stande,
With-outen removyng, ay shynande,

And the moon opposite to it in the west.

And þe mone ogayne it in þe weste,
And na mare sal travayle bot ay reste,
6368 Als þai war sette at þe bigynnyng,
When God made þam and alle thyng;
Þai war þan, als men may trow,
Mykel brighter þan þai er now.

The moving heavens shall cease to perform their usual course.

6372 Þe movand heve[n]s with-outen dout,
Sal þan ceese o turnyng obout,
And na mare obout in course wende,
For of alle thyng þan sal be made ende.
6376 Þe movand hevens now obout gas,
And þe son and þe mone þair course mas;
And þe othir planetes ilkane,
Moves als þai þair course haf tane;
6380 And alle þe elementes kyndely duse
Þat þat es nedeful til man use.
Þus ordaynd God þam to serve man,
Bot of alle swylk servise þai sal ceese þan.
6384 For alle men aftir domesday
Sal be war þai sal duelle for ay,

[1] sythes (MS. Harl. 4196).

Þe gude in blis, in rest and peese,
Þe ille in payne þat never sal ceese.
What nede war þat þa creatures þan,
Shewed swilk servyse mare for man.
Na qwik creature sal þan be lyfand,
Thurgh out þe werld in na land,
Ne nathyng sal growe þan, gresse ne tre,
Ne cragges ne roches sal nan þan be,
Ne dale, ne hille, ne mountayne;
Bot alle erthe sal be þan even and playne,
And be made als clere and fayre and clene,
Als any cristal þat here es sene;
For it sal be purged and fyned with-oute,
Als alle other elementes sal be oboute,
And na mare be travayled o[1] na side,
Ne with na charge mare occupide.
Now haf yhe herd me byfor rede
Of þe day of dome þat many may drede,
And of þe wondirful takens many,
Þat salle falle byfor þat day namly,
And how þe werld þat we now se,
Aftir þe dome als new made sal be,
Als here es contened, wha-swa wille luke,
In þe fifte part of þis buke;
Here on now wille I na langer stande,
Bot ga til þe sext part neghest folowande,
Þat specialy spekes, als writen es,
Of þe paynes of helle þat er endeles,
Þat[2] alle men, þat here lyfe byhoves lede,
Aght specialy mast to drede;
For þa paynes er swa fel and hard,
Als yhe sal here be red aftirward,
Þat ilk man may ugge, bathe yhunge and alde,
Þat heres þam be reherced and talde.

Nothing shall live or grow upon the earth.

The sixth part speaks of the pains of hell.

Her begynnes þe sext party of þis boke
þat spekes of þe paynes of Helle.[3]

[1] on [2] Bot (MS. Harl. 4196).
[3] This heading is absent from MSS. Galba E IX, Harl. 4196).

Many speak of hell, but few know what the wicked suffer there.

Many men here spekes of helle,
Bot of þe paynes þar fune can telle,
Bot wha-swa here mught wit andk[n]aw wele
What paynes þe synful þar sal fele,
Þai suld in grete ferdlayk be broght,
Ay when þai on þa paynes thoght;
For þe mynde of þam myght men feer,
Swa bitter and swa horribel þai er;
Bot forþi þat many knawes noght right,
Whatkyn paynes in helle er dight,
With-outen ende for synful men,
Þarfor I sal shewe yhow, als I can,
Aparty of þa paynes sere,
Als yhe may sonê aftirward here.

Where hell is.

Bot first I wille shew whare es helle,
Als I haf herd som grete clerkes telle,
And sythen wille I shew yhow mare,
And speke of þe paynes þat er þare.
Som clerkes says, als þe buke bers witnes,

Hell is in the middle of the earth.

Þat helle even in myddes þe erthe es;
For alle erthe by skille may likend be
Til a rounde appel of a tre,
Þat even in myddes has a colke,
And swa it may be tille an egge yholke;
For als a dalk es even Imydward
Þe yholke of þe egge, when it es hard,

The earth is in the middle of the heavens

Ryght swa es helle pitte, als clerkes telles,
Ymyddes þe erthe and nourwhar elles.
And als þe yholk ymyddes þe egge lys,
And þe white obout on þe same wys,
Right swa es þe erthe, with-outen dout.
Ymyddes þe hevens þat gas obout.
Þus may men se by an egge hard dight,
How heven and erthe and helle standes right.
Ful hydus and myrke helle es kyd,
For-why it es with-in þe erthe hyd,
Þider þe synful sal be dryven,
Als tyte als þe last dome es gyven.

With alle þe devels ay þar to duelle,
Þat now er in þe ayre and in helle,
Þar sal þai alle be stoped togider;
Wa sal þam be þat sal wende þider,
For þar es swa mykel sorow and bale,
And swa many paynes with-outen tale,
Þat alle þe clerkes þat ever had wytt,
Þat ever was, or þat lyfes yhitt,
Couth noght telle ne shew thurgh lare,
How mykel sorow and payne er þare.
And if it thurgh kynd myght be swa,
Þat an hundreth thousand men or ma,
Had an hundreth thousand tunges of stele,
And ilk tung mught speke wysely and wele
And ilka tung of ilka man,
Had bygunnen when þe werld bygan,
To spek of helle, and swa suld speke ay
Whils þe werld suld last til domes day,
Yhit mught þai noght þe sorow telle,
Þat to synful es ordaynd in helle;
For-why na witt of man may ymagyn
What paynes þar er ordaynd for syn.
Bot men may fynd, wha-swa wil loke,
Som maner of paynes wryten in boke,
Omang all other paynes þat er in helle,
Als men has herd wyse clerkes telle;
Bot what man es swa wyse and wytty
Þat couthe telle þa paynes proprely,
Bot it war he þat had bene þare,
And sene þa paynes bath les and mare?
Bot he þat þar commes for certayne,
May noght lightly turne agayne;
He most duelle þar and never oway com,
For þe buke says þus of wysdom:
Non est agnitus, qui reversus
est ab inferis.
Þat es on Ynglisse "men knawes nane,
Þat turned fra helle þat þider was gane."

The pains of hell cannot be numbered.

The 'wit' of man is unable to imagin what the pains of hell are like.

None return from hell.

For alle þat er þar most duelle for ay,
Þai may never be broght oway,
Bot-if war thurgh miracle anely,
And thurgh specyal grace of God almyghty,
Thurgh whilk som, þat in helle has bene,
And horrible paynes þar has sene
Has þene broght oway fra alle þat stryf,
And bene turned ogayne fra ded til lyf;
Als Lazar was Mary brother Maudalayne,
Þat saw and herd þare many a payne,

Lazarus went to hell and remained there four days.

Þat tyme namely when he was ded,
For his saul þan was at þat sted,
Four dayes, als God vouched save,
And swa lang his body lay here in grave;
And at þe last God raysed hym ryght
Fra ded til lyf thurgh his myght;
Bot þat þat he saw he noght forgatt,
And sone þare-after als he satt
With Crist at þe meete in Martha hows,

He told a little of what he had seen there,

He talde a party of þa paynes hydus;
Bot yhit durst he noght al telle,
For drede of Crist, þat he saw in helle,

But though he lived fifteen years after, he never laughed nor made merry.

Yhit lyfed he after fyften yhere,
Bot he lughe[1] never, ne made blythe chere,
For drede of dede þat he most efte dreghe,
And of þe paynes þat he saw with eghe.
For how bitter þe dede es nan may witt,
Bot he anely þat has feled itt,
And what paynes in helle er, nane wil wene
Bot he anely þat has þam sene.

The two sons of Simeon went to hell and at the crucifixion rose again.

Alswa twa of Symeon sons ryght,
Þe whilk Caryn and Lentyn hight,
When þa first war dede and hethen went,
Þai saw in helle many a tourment,
And sithen when Crist dighed on þe rode,
Þai rase fra ded and obout yhode,
And tald how Crist, byfor þat he ras,
Til helle come and tuke out þat his was,

[1] loghe (MS. Harl. 4196).

And mykel couthe þai þan telle
Of þe paynes þat þai saw in helle.
Bot þai had no leve als I wene
To telle alle þat þai þar had sene;
Wharfor þai lyfed here ay in penaunce,
And never aftir made blithe countinance,
Of wham es writen in a pistel þus,
Þat Pilat sent til Tyberius,
Þat þan emparour of Rome was,
For to certifie hym of þis cas.
And yhit many other þat war dede,
Has bene sumtyme at þat stede,
And sene þar many hydus payne,
And thurgh miracle turned til lyf agayne;
Bot omang alle þat þar has bene sene,
I fynde wryten paynes fourtene,
Thurgh whilk þe synful sal be pyned ay,
In body and saul aftir domesday;
Þe whilk er als general paynes of helle,
And whilk þas er I sal yhow telle.
Þe first es fire swa hate to reken,
Þat na maner of thyng may it sleken.
Þe secunde es calde als says som,
Þat na hete of fire may overcom.
Þe thred alswa es filthe and stynk
Þat es stranger þan any hert may thynk.
Þe ferthe es hunger sharpe and strang.
Þe fift es brynnand threst omang.
Þe sext es swa mykel myrknes,
Þat it may be graped, swa thik it es.
Þe seve[n]d es þe horribel sight
Of þe devels þat þar er hydusly dight.
Þe eghtend payne es vermyn grete,
Þat þe synful men sal gnaw and frete.
Þe neghend es dyngyng of devels hand,
With melles of yren hate glowand.
Þe tend payne es gnawyng with-in
Of conscience þat bites als vermyn.

Those who visited hell, had no permission to disclose all its secrets.

There are fourteen general pains which the wicked shall suffer in hell.

1. Heat, 2. Cold, 3. Filth and Stink, 4. Hunger, 5. Thirst, 6. Darkness, 7. 'Sight' of devils, 8. Vermin, 9. Beating by devils, 10. Gnawing of conscience,

11. Scalding tears,

Þe ellevend es hate teres of gretyng,
Þat þe synful sal scalden in þe dounfallyng.

12. Shame and disgrace,

Þe twelfte es shame and shenshepe of syn
Þat þai sal haf þat never sal blyn.

13. Bonds of fire,

Þe threttend es bandes of fire brinnand,
Þat þai sal be bunden with fote and hand.

14. Despair.

Þe fourtend payne despayre es cald,
Þat þe synful sal ay in hert hald.
Alle þir er generale paynes in helle;
Bot þar er other ma þan tung may telle,
Or hert may thynk or eer may here,
Of special paynes þat er sere,
Þe whilk many, aftir þai er worthy,
Sal thole ever-mare in saule and body;
Bot of alle þa paynes can I noght say,
For na man þam reken ne specyfy may,
Bot yhit wille I speke som-what mare
Of þe general paynes þat I shewed are,
And with som autorities þam bynd,
Als men may in sere bukes writen fynd.

I. The first pain is unquenchable fire.

Þe first als I tald es þe fire hate,
Þat na thyng may sleken ne abate;
Whare þe synful men sal bryn thurgh hete
Of whilk God spekes þus thurgh þe prophete:
Ignis succensus est in furore
meo, et ardebit usque ad in-
ferni novissima, id est, usque
in eternum.
"Fyre es kyndeld in my wreth", says he,
"And sal bryn until ende of helle sal be,
Þat es ever-mare, als God vouches save,
For helle sal never-mare ende have."
Þat fire es swa hate, and ay brynnes,

All the water on earth would not be sufficient to lessen the heat of hell fire.

Þat if alle þe waters þat standes or rynnes
On erthe, and alle þe sese with-oute,
Þat encloses alle þe erthe oboute,
Suld ryn in-til þat fire swa hate,
Yhit myght it noght it sleken ne abate,

Na mare þan a drope of water shire
If alle Rome brend, mught sleken þat fire.
For þe fire of helle þat es endeles,
Es hatter þan fire here es,
Right als þe fire þat es brinnand here,
Es hatter and of mare powere,
Þan a purtrayd fire on a waghe,
Þat es paynted outher heghe or laghe,
With a rede coloure til mens sight,
Þat nouther brynnes ne gyfes light,
Ne on othir manere avales ne ders.
Of þir twa fires I fynde writen twa vers.
Quam focus est mundi picto fervencior igne,
Tam focus inferni superat fervenicia mundi.
"Als þe fire of þe werld hatter es
Þan a fire paynted, be it mare or les,
Rightswa þe fire of helle passes thurgh hete,
Alle þe fires of þe werld, smale and grete,
And for-þi þat þe synful brynned ay here,
In þe fire of fole yhernyngs sere,
It es right þat þai brynne þare
In þat hate fire for ever-mare.
"Est locus indignis ubi non extinguitur ignis,
Non qui torquetur, nec qui torquet, morietur."
Þe secunde payne es grete calde,
Þat þe synful sal fele, als I ar talde;
Þat cald sal be swa strang and kene,
Þat if þe mast roche þat man has sene,
Of þe mast mountayne in any land,
War al attanes in fire brynnand,
And even Imyddes þat cald war,
It suld frese and turne al in-til yse þar;
And for-þi þat þai, omang other vice,
Brynned ay here in þe calde of malice,
And ay was dased in charité,
Þarfor it es right þat þai be
In þat strang calde ever-mare lastand,
Whar þai sal frese, bathe fote and hand.

The fire of hell is endless.

The wicked on earth lived in burning lusts, therefore shall they burn in hell for ever.

II. The second pain is intense cold.

A burning mountain would freeze if cast into this cold.

The devils shall alternately torment the wicked by heat and cold.

Þe devels sal tak þam fra þat fire,
And cast þam, with ful grete ire,
In-til þat cald to eke þair payne,
And efte þam cast in þe fire ogayne;
Þus sal þai cast þam to and fra,
And ever-mare þai sal fare swa.
Of þis þe haly man bers wittenes
Iob þat says þus, als writen es:
Ab aquis nivium transibunt
ad calorem nimium.
"Fra waters of snawes þe synful sal wende
Til þe over mykel hete þat has nan ende."
And Saynt Austyn says on þis manere,
In a buke, als es writen here.
Dicuntur namque, mali candere
exterius calore ut ferum in for-
nace, et interius frigore ut
glacies in yeme.

The sinful shall be burning without through heat, and frozen within through cold.

"Þe wikked sal outwith be glowand
Thurgh hete, als men in fire brynnand,
And with-in thurgh calde sharpe and kene,
Als yse þat es in wynter sene,"
Þus sal þai ay be in calde and hete;
Þis tourment es ful strang and grete.

III. The third pain is stink and filth,

Þe thred payne es, als men heres clerkes telle,
Þe grete stynk and filthe þat es in helle;
Of þis Saynt Ierom, þe haly man,
Says þus, als I here shewe yhow can:
Ibi est ignis inextinguibilis,
et fetor intollerabilis.
"Þe fire es þar of swa grete pousté,
Þat it may never mar slekend be,

So great is this pain that it passes man's imagination.

And swylk filthe and stynk es in þat ugly hole,
Þat nan erthely man mught it thole;"
For na man in erthe may ymagyn
Swa mykel filthe, als sal be þar-in,
Whar-for þar sal be mare stynk
Þan tung may telle or hert thynk.

Þe whilk stynk, with filthe and fen,
Sal be strang payne til synful men,
And yhit þe fire þat bryn þam sal,
Sal gyfe a st[r]ang stynk with-alle,
For it sal be fulle of brunstane and pyk,
And of other thyng þat es wyk;

The fire in hell shall give forth a strong stink, through the brimstone and pitch that is there.

And for þe synful delyted þam here namly,
In þe filthe and stynk of lechery,
It es right þat þai be ay omang
Þe stynk and filthe in helle swa strang.
Þe ferthe payne es, als I haf herd say,
Þe strang hunger þat þar sal last ay,

IV. The fourth pain is hunger.

Þe whi[l]k þe synful in helle sal fele,
Ever-mare als þir clerkes knawes wele.
Þe strenthe of hungre sal þam swa chace
Þat þair awen flesshe þai sal of-race;

The sinful shall tear off their own flesh.

And for hungre þai sal yherne it ete,
For þai sal gett nan other meete;

For hunger they shall be mad.

For hungre þai sal be als brayne-wode,
Bot þe dede þar sal be þair fode,
Als says þe prophet in a stede:
'Þai sal be fedde with þe dede:'
Mors depascet
eos.
Þis es on Inglys þus to rede:
"Þe dede þam sal dolefuly fede."

Death shall be their food.

For als he þat has here hungre grete,
Thurgh kynde langes mast aftir mete,
Right swa þe synful þat sal duelle þare,
Yhit sal lange aftir þe ded wel mare
Þat þai mast hated and drede here,
Bot dighe may þai noght on na manere,

They shall desire to die, but in vain.

Of þis Saynt Ion bers wittnes,
Als in þe apocalipse writen es:
Disiderabunt mori, et mors
fugiet ab eis.
"Yherne þai sal to dighe fra þair wa,
And þe ded sal ay fle þam fra;"

The wicked shall be tormented by hunger because they would not, while on earth, give to the poor.

And forþy þat þai wald gyf na mete
Til þe poer, þat here hunger had grete,
Ne of þam had nouther reuthe ne mercy,
Bot used ay outrage and glotony,
It es right þat þai haf þis payne
Grete hungre in helle ay þar ogayne.

V. The fifth pain is great thirst.

Þe fifte payne es, als sal befalle,
Grete threst þat þai sal haf with-alle.
Swa mykel in helle sal be þair threst,
Þat þair hertes sal nere clewe[1] and brest;

A flame of fire shall be the drink of the sinful.

Bot þe flaume of fire þai sal drynk,
Menged with brunstan þat foul sal stynk,
And with smoke of fyre and wyndes blast,
And with other stormes þat ay sal last,
Þat alle togider þan sal mete;
And þarfor says David þe prophete:
Ignis et sulphur et spiritus
Procellarum pars calicis eorum.
He says þus, als we writen fynde,

Fire, brimstone, storms with wind shall be part of their drink, along with smoke and stench.

"Fire and brunstan and stormes with wynde,
A part sal be þar of þair drynk,"
And þat sal be menged with smoke and stynk;
Yhit sal þai drynk, ogayne þair wille,
Another manere of drynk þat es ille,
Þat sal be bitter and venemus,
And be cald þair wyne, for þe prophet says þus:
Fel draconum vinum eorum, et venenum
aspidum insanabile.

Gall of dragons, and venom of snakes, shall be their wine.

"Galle of draguns þair wyne sal be,
And wenym of snakes þar-with," says he,
"Þat may noght be heled wele,"
Swa violent it es to fele.
Þir wordes, aftir þe lettre, er hard to here,
Bot men may þam take on othir manere.
Þai sal swa brynnand threst thole,
Þat þair hertes sal bryn with-in als a cole,

[1] clefe (MS. Harl. 4196).

For na licour sal þai fynd to fele,
Þat þair threst mught sleke and þair hertes kele;
Þai sal for threst þe hevedes souke
Of þe nedders þat on þam sal rouke,
Als a childe þat sittes in þe moder lappe,
And when it list, soukes hir pappe;
For I fynd þis word in haly writt,
Als Iob says þat witnesses it:
Caput aspidum
sugent.
"Þe heved of nedders þat on þam sal fest"
He says, "þai sal souke þan for threst."
Strang payne of threst þan haf þai
When þai sal souke for therst[1] swilk venym ay.

The wicked for thirst shall suck the heads of adders.

And for-þi þat þai wald never blethely
Gyf til poer at drynk þat war thresty,
To sleken þair threst, ne on þam thynk,
Ne nouther gyf þam mete ne drynk,
And on þair-selven na drynk wald spare
Na day, til þai drunken ware,
It es þan right þat þat þai in helle fele
Brynnand threst þat never sal kele;
Þat sal þai haf when þai com þider,
And sharp hungre alswa bath to-gydre,
Þat never sal cesse, als I sayde ar;
For þir twa paynes with othir er endel[e]s þar,
Of þis Saynt Ierom bers wittnes,
Þat says þus, als writen es:
In inferno erit fames infinita,
et sitis infinita.

They shall suffer in this way because they would not give drink to the poor.

"In helle sal be whar never es rest
Endel[e]s hungre and endeles threst."
Inferni pene sunt hec, vermes, tenebreque
flamma, chorus demonum, fetor, frigusque fa-
mes, sitis, horror.

This pain is endless.

Þe sext payne es over mykel myrknes,
Þat in helle sal be ay endeles;

VI. The sixth pain is darkness.

[1] threst (MS. Harl. 4196).

This darkness is so thick that it may be felt.

Þat swa thik es þat men mught it grape,
Fra whilk þe synful sal never eschape.
For na hert may thynk ne tung telle,
Swa mykel mirkenes als es in helle,
Of whilk Iob spekes, als þe buk shewes wele,
And says, þe synful sal grape and fele
Myrkenes, als mykel at mydday
Als at mydnyght, þat sal last ay:
Palpabunt tenebras in meridie,
sicut in media nocte.

In hell there is no day, but ever night.

"In helle es never day bot ever nyght;
Þar brynnes ay fire, bot it gyf[es] na light."

The wicked shall see pains and torments by means of the sparks which the fire shall scatter.

Bot yhit þe synful sal ay se
Alle þe sorowe þat þar sal be,
And ilka payne and ilka tourment,
Thurgh sparkes of fire þat obout sal sprent.
Bot þat sight sal be til þam þare,
Na confort, bot sorowe and kare.
Þus to eke þair paynes, þai sal haf sight,
With-outen any comfort þar of light;
And for-þi þat helle es ay lightles,
It es cald þe land of myrkenes,
Þat es depe and myrke and hydus,
Þarfor says Iob, þe haly man, þus:
Ut non revertar ad terram
tenebrosam.
He says; "Loverd þat I noght turne away
Til þe myrke land", whare sorow es ay,
Whare wonyng es ay hydus and ille,
Als Iob says þat þus spekes mar þar-tille:
Ubi nullus ordo, sed sempiternus
horror inhabitans.

Hell is a land of horror, where the wicked are tormented, because they loved darkness rather than light.

"Þar nan ordre wonand es," says he,
"Bot uglynes þat ever mare sal be."
And forþi þat þe synful in þair lyf here,
Lufed ay myrknes of syns sere,
And wald noght turne þam when þai myght,
Fra þat myrknes til Goddes light,

It es right þat þai duelle þare,
In þat hidus myrknes ever-mare,
And never-mare aftir light se;
A strang payne til þam þat sal be.

VII. The seventh pain is the 'sight of devils'.

Þe sevend payne es of þe fourtene
Þe sight of devels þat sal be sene
Omang þe synful þat sal be in helle,
In whas company þai sal ay duelle.
Þat sight sal be swa hidus to se,
Þat alle þe men of cristianté
Couthe noght, thurgh witt, ymagyn right,
Ne descryve swa hydus a sight,
Als þai þan sal se in helle ever-mare,
Of ugly devels þat sal be þare,

There are more 'ugly' devils in hell than any man can reckon or tell.

For þan sal be ma devels in helle,
Þan any tung can reken or telle;
And ilkan sal mare grysely seme
Þan any man can ymagyn and deme:
For swa hardy es na man, ne swa balde
In þis werld, nouther yhung ne alde,
If he myght right consayve in mynde,
How grysely a devel es in his kynde,
Þat durst for alle gude of mydlerde
A devel se here, swa suld he be aferde;

The sight of a devil would cause the hardiest man to become mad for fear.

For þe hardyest man in flesshe and bane
Þat here lyfes, yf he sawe ane
Of þa devels in þair awen lyknes,
Suld wax wode for ferde and be wittles.
For-why na witt of man may endure
To se a devel in his propre figure.
How sal þai fare þan þat ay sal þam se,
And ay in company with þam be?

The sinful shall ever look upon devils.

Þe synful sal ever-mare on þam luke
For þus we fynde wryten in boke:
In inferno videbunt eos, facie ad faciem,
quorum opera in terris dilexerunt.
"In helle þai sal þam se, face to face,
Whas werkes þai lufed and folowed þe trace,

This sight shall cause much crying and sorrow.

Whilles þai war here in erthe lyfand;"
And with þat syght, als I understand,
Þai sal duleful crying and sorow here,
For. Saynt Austyn says on þis manere:
Demones igne scintillante
videbunt, et miserabilem
clamorem flencium et la-
mentancium audient.

The wicked shall see the devils through the sparks of fire that shall fly about.

"Þai sal se þar devels with eghe,
Thurgh sparkes þat of þe fire sal fleghe,
And here þar-with on ilka party,
Þe wreched synful grete and cry."
And þe sorow and dule þat þai sal make,
Sal never-mar þar cees ne slake;
And forþi þat þat here hated to se,
And to here þat þat gude suld be,
And þarfor it es reson and ryght,
Þat þai ay se þat grysely syght,
And þat þat[1] heryng haf of duleful dyn,
To eke þair payn for þair sin.

VIII. The eighth pain is 'horrible venemous vermin' that shall, moving to and fro, gnaw and suck the sinful.

Þe aghtend payne, als þe buke says us,
Es þe horribel vermyn venemus.
Þe whilk sal on þe synful rouke,
And ever-mare þam gnaw and souke,
Als ugly draguns, and nedders kene;
And tades swa hydus was never here sene
And othir vermyn ful of venym,
And wode bestes grysely and grym,
Þat with tethe sal with þam ay gnaw and byte,
On alle þair lyms, whar þai had delite
Synful werkes here for to wirk,
Agayne þe law of God and of haly kyrk.

Thus shall they suffer because they thought sin sweet.

Þus for þai did ay ogayns Goddes lawe,
Vermyn and wode bestes sal þam ay gnawe,
For þair syn þat þam thoght here swete,
Þarfor God says þus thurgh þe prophete:
Dentes bestiarum immittam in eos, cum furo-
re trahencium in terra atque serpencium.

[1] þai?

"I sal send in þe synful", says he,
"Þe tethe of bestes þat felle sal be
With wodenes of þam in-til erthe drawand,
And of nedders þam fast gnawand."
Þus sal wode bestes and vermyn gnaw þam ay
And never-mare pas fra þam oway;
And þat payne þe synful byhoves ay dreghe,
For-why þair vermyn sal never dieghe,
Bot ever-mare lyfand with þam duelle,
Þarfor God says þus in þe godspelle:
Vermis eorum non morietur,
et ignis eorum non extinguetur.
"Þair vermyn salle never deghe," says he,
"Ne þair fyre salle never slekend be;"
And to þat says þus Saynt Austyne,
Þat spekes here of þat vermyne:
Vermes infernales sunt immortales qui, ut pis-
ces in aqua, ita vivunt in flamma.
He says, "vermyn of helle salle ay lyfe,
And never deghe þe synfulle to gryefe,
The whilk salle lyfe in þe flawme of fyre,
Als fyssches lyfes in water schyre."
Þat vermyn on þam salle ay crepe,
In þam fest þair clokes full depe;[1]
Þai salle umlapp þam alle oboute,
And gnaw on ilka lym and souke;
With vermyn þai salle alle coverd be,
Swa þat na lym of þam salle be fre,
And swa þai salle be ay gnawand
On þair lyms, whether þai lyg or stand;
Vermyn in helle salle be þair clethyng
And vermyn salle þare be þair beddyng.
Na clathes þai salle have to gang in,
Ne na beddes to lyg in bot vermyn,
Wharfor I fynd wryten þare I have red,
How þe prophete discryved swilk a bed
To þe kyng Nabogodonosor,
And sayd þus to mak him ferd þarfor:

Wild beasts and vermin shall remain with the wicked for ever.

Their vermin shall never die.

The vermin shall live in the flame of fire, as fishes do in clear water.

Vermin shall be the clothing of the wicked.

[1] And in þaim feste þair *clowes* ful depe (MS. Harl. 6923).

Subter te sternetur tinea, et
operimentum tuum vermes.
He says "of wormes þi bed salle be
Þat salle be strewed thyk under þe,
And þi covertoure on þe sene
Salle be vermyn fulle felle and kene."
Swilk beddes er ordaynd in helle
Ffor synfulle men þat þar salle dwelle.
Þus salle þai be pyned for þair syn,
Ever-mare with fyre and vermyn,
And with many other payns ma;
Ffor God vouches safe þat it be swa,
Ffor þus fynd we wryten in haly wrytt,
In a boke of þe Bibelle þat hate Iudyth:
Dabit dominus ignem et vermes
in carnes eorum, ut urantur
et senciant, usque in sem-
piternum.
It says "fyre and vermyn þat ay salle lyfe,
Our lord tylle þe flesch of synfulle salle gyfe,
Swa þat þai salle bryn ever-mare,
And ay fele of vermyn bytyng sare."
Þis payne es mare to fele and se,
Þan alle þe paynes þat may be
In þis werld here, mare and les,
Als þe boke openly bers witnes,
Þus salle vermyn in helle be gret payne,
Bot yhit may men say here ogayne,
Ffor men may in som boke wryten se,
Þat after þe gret dome þat last salle be,
Na quyk creature salle lyf þan,
Bot anely aungelle, develle and man,
'How suld in helle þan or ourwhare elles,
Any vermyn lyf als men telles,
Or any other best þat moght dere?'
To þis may men gyf answere
On þis manere, wha-swa kan;
Þe vermyn þat salle be þan,

Worms shall be the bed of the sinful.

Such beds are prepared for those that dwell in hell.

This pain surpasses all earthly pain.

How may vermin live in hell since no living thing shall live after the doom?

Als I understand, noght elles es
Bot devels in vermyn lyknes, The devils take the likeness of vermin.
Þat salle byte and knaw þe synfulle þare,
To eke þair payne and mak it mare.
Þus salle þe devels gnaw þam with-out,
In lyknes of vermyn alle obout.
And þair conscience als vermyn,
Salle gnaw þam over-alle with-in,
And þat gnawyng salle be fulle hard,
Of whilk I salle speke sone *afterward.*
Þat vermyn in helle salle be mare *grysely*
Þan vermyn here es, *and mare myghty.*
By vermyn here *þan þat greves sare,*
Men aght to drede þe *vermyn þare;*
And forþi þat þe synfulle was here *namely,*
Ay fulle of hateredyn and of envy,
And wald noght amend þam of þat syn,
Bot lete it gnaw þam ay with-in,
It es ryght and skylle thurgh Godes lawe,
Þat þe vermyn in helle ay þam gnawe.
Þe neghend payne es to understand, IX. The ninth pain is beating by 'devils with glowing hamers.'
Dyngyng of devels with hamers glowand;
Ffor þe devels þe synfulle salle ay bete
With glowand hamers huge and grete
And als smyths strykes on þe yren fast,
Swa þat it brekes and brestes at þe last,
Right swa þe devels salle ay dyng The devils shall strike the sinful without ceasing.
On þe synfulle, with-outen styntyng;
And with hamers gyf swa gret dyntes,
Þat alle to powdre moght stryke hard flyntes;
Ffor harden dyntes gaf never engyne,
Þan þai salle gyf, als says Saint Austyne:
Sicut machina bellita percutit
muros opidi, ita demones ym-
mo asperius et crudelius, corpora malorum
et animas flagellabunt, post iudicium.
He says "als men may se ane engyne cast, As a warlike machine strikes the walls of a city,
And at þe walles of a castelle stryke fast

With a stane þat es huge and hevy,
Swa salle devels stryke þase[1] mare felly
Þe ille bodyse and saules þat salle dwelle,
After þe last gret dome in helle."

So shall devils strike the souls and bodies of the wicked.

Þus salle þai dyng on þam ever-mare,
With gret glowand hamers, and nane spare.
And þis payne tylle þam salle be endles,
Als þe bok here-ol bers witnes;
Ffor þai salle have power ay and leve,
Þe synfull men to dyng and greve,
Als in a boke es schewed tylle us,
Þat Saynt Austyne made, þare he says þus:
Parata iudicia blasphemtoribus, et percu-
cientibus malleis stultorum corpora.
"Þe domes salle þan be redy
Tille þe sklaunderers of God alle myghty,
And tylle þase þat salle be ay smytand
Þe bodyse of synfulle with melles in hand."
And forþi þat þai wald noght take
Haly disciplyne here, for Godes sake,
Þarfor þe devels salle stryk þam þare,
With hevy melles ay, and nane spare.

The sinful shall thus suffer for neglecting 'holy discipline.'

Þe tend payne es þe gnawyng with-in
Of þair conscience þat never salle blyn;
Ffor with-in þam salle þe worme of conscience frete
Als with-outen salle do vermyn grete,
And swa salle þai ever-mare, with-outen dout,
Be gnawen and byten with-in and with-out.
Ffulle mykelle sorow salle þan be in helle
Omang þe synfulle þat þare salle dwelle;

X. The tenth pain is gnawing of conscience.

Ffor þai salle ever þus cry and say,
'Allas! Allas! and walaway!
Whi ne wald we never are trow,
What payne and sorow here es now.'
Þan salle þai pleyne þam of þair wickednes,
And say þus, als in boke wryten es:
Quid nobis profuit superbia, quid divicia-
rum iactancia, omnia transierunt velud um-

The wicked shall ever make lamentation.

[1] þuse?

bra, et tanquam nuncius percurrens, et tanquam
navis procedens in fluctuantem aquam, et tan-
quam avis transvolans in aere, cuius itineris non
est invenire vestigium.

"What avayld us pryde", þai salle say,
"What rosyng of ryches or of ryche aray?
Alle þat pomp als we se now,
Es passed oway als a schadow,
And als messanger bifore rynand,
And als schypp þat gase in water flowand,
And als foghel fleghand in þe ayre als wynd,
Of whase gate men may na trace fynd."

They shall say: 'What availed us all our pride, boast of riches and rich array, which like a shadow has passed away?'

Þus salle alle þair pomp oway pas,
And be als thyng þat never was,
Þan salle þam thynk when alle es oway,
Alle þair lyfe here bot als ane howr of a day,
Þof þai never so lang had lyfed here,
Þai may say on þis manere:
'Right now born we war in þe world to be,
Ryght now in alle our delytes lyfed we,
Ryght now we deghed and passed oway
Now er we in helle and swa salle be ay,'
Þan salle þai knaw how ille þai haf lyfed,
When þe worme of conscience þam has greved,
Þat with-in salle þam ay gnaw and byte
Ffor þai in vanyté had here delyte,
And for-þi þat conscience styrd þam noght,
To forsake þair folyes þat þai wroght,
Bot folowed ay here þair flesschly wille;
Þarfor it es gud, ryght, and skylle,
Þat þe worme of conscience with-in,
Ever-mare in helle þam gnaw for þair syn.

The gnawing of conscience shall remind them of their vanity

Þe ellevend payne es teres of gretyng
Of þe synfulle þat, with-outen styntyng,
Sal grete ever-mare, als says þe boke;
Ffor-whi what for sorow, and what thurgh smoke
And what thurgh cald, and what thurgh hete
Þat þai salle thole, þai salle ay grete,

XI. The eleventh pain is, scalding tears.

Tears shall ever more run from the eyes of the wicked.

And þus teres fra þair eghen salle ryn
Ever-mare and never salle blyn.
Swa mykelle water als salle falle þan,
Ffra a mans eghe may gesce na man;
Ffor-whi þai salle ay be gretand,
And þair teres salle be ay flowand,
And fra þair eghen ryn swa fast,
And þair gretyng swa lang salle last,

In all the world is not so much water seen as shall fall from their eyes.

Þat in alle þe world here, als I wene,
Es noght swa mykelle water sene,
Als fra þair eghen salle falle þare;
Ffor þai salle be gretand ever-mare.
Wharfor Saint Austyn says þus,
Whase wordes er auctentyke tylle us:
In inferno plures effundentur lacrime
quam sunt in mari gutte.

More tears are shed in hell than there are drops in the sea.

"In helle," he says, "out-yhetted salle be,
Ma teres þan dropes er in þe se,"
Þe synfulle salle þare þus ever-mare grete,
And þair [teres] salle be of swa gret hete,
Þat þe water þat þan salle doun-ryn,
Ffra þair eghen, salle þam schald and bryn,

This water shall be hotter than molten lead or boiling brass.

Ffor it salle be hatter þan ever was
Molten led or welland bras,
Als I have herd gret clerkes telle,
Þat has descryved þe payns of helle;
And for-þi þat þai had here ay lykyng
In þair syn and never forthynkyng,
Ne sorow þarfore, for þam thoght it swete,
Þarfor þai salle in helle ay grete,
And with þair teres be schalded sare,
To eke þair paynes, als I sayd are.

XII. The twelfth pain is disgrace.

Þe twelfte payne es schame and schenshepe,
Þat þe synfulle salle have in helle swa depe,
Of ilka syn þat ever þai dyd;
Ffor-whi þare salle be knawen and kyd
Alle þair syns of thoght, or word and werk,
Als says Saint Austyne þe gret clerk:

Omnia in omnibus patebunt, et se abscondere non valebunt.

"Alle þair syns in þam salle shewed be
And þai may nouther þan þam hyde ne fle."
Þai salle have mare schame of þair syn þare,
And þair schendschepe salle be mare,
Þan ever had any man here in thoght
Ffor any velany þat ever he wroght,
And þat schame with þam salle last ay,
And never salle pas fra þam oway;
Þai may say þus þat þare þan dwelles,
Als þe prophete in þe psauter telles;

The disgrace of the wicked in hell.

Tota die verecundia mea contra me est, et confusio faciei mee cooperuit me.

Þat es, "my schamefulnes," says he,
Alle day es ogayns me,
And þe schenschepe of my face
Salle cover me, in ilka place."
Þai salle swa schame ay of þair syn,
Þat þam salle thynk als þai suld bryn,
Ffor þe gret schame þat þai salle have þare,
Þat never salle cese, bot last ever-mare;
Wharfor if na payne war in helle,
Bot þat schame anely, þat I of telle,
It suld be tylle þam þare mare payne,
Þan any man couth here ordayne;
And forþi þat þai here in þair lyfe,
Durst never for schame of syn þam schryve,
Bot with-outen schame to syn was bald,
It es ryght þat þai have, als I tald,
Schame in helle for þair syn,
Of whilk þai wald here never blyn.

For shame shall they burn,

And be through it in more pain than is possible here.

Þe threttende payne es, als clerkes wate,
Þe bandes of fyre brynand fulle hate,
With whilk þe synfulle salle be bonden,
Als in som boke wryten es fonden;
And þa bandes of fyre salle never slake.
Ffor þai wald never þair syn forsake,

XIII. The thirteenth pain is bonds of fire with which the sinful shall be bound.

The sinful in hell shall be bound with burning chains.

Þai salle be with þa bandes brynand,
In helle hard bonden, both fote and hand,
And straytely streyned ilka lym,
Thurgh þe devels þat er ugly and grym.
Þair wonyng in helle salle be endeles,
Omang stynk and fylth in gret myrknes,
Whare ever es nyght and never day,
Als men may here gret clerkes say.
Þan salle þai fele, when þai þare come,
Godes vengeance thurgh ryghtwise dome,
Ffor þair syn þat him here myspays,
Wharfor God þus in þe gosspelle says:
Ligatis manibus et pedibus, mittite
in tenebras exteriores.
"Lat bynd þair hend and þair fete fast,
And in-to þe utter myrknes þam cast,"
Þat es in þe deppest pytt of helle,
Whare mare sorow es þan tong may telle.

Their heads shall be turned downward and their feet upward,

Þare salle þair hevedes be turned dounward,
And þair fete upward bonden hard,
And þair bodyse be streyned bi fete and hed,
With brynand bandes glowand red;
Þai salle be pyned on þis manere,
With other paynes many and sere,
Als a gret clerk says openly,
In a boke þat he made thurgh study,
Of sere questyons of divinité,
Þat es cald 'Flos Sciencie'
Þat es on Ynglys 'þe flour of konyng'
Whare wryten es many privé thyng;
In þat boke þus he telles,
How þai salle hyng þat þar þan dwelles:
Capita, inquit, eorum erunt ad-invicem deorsum versa,
pedes sursum erecti, et undique penis distenti.
He says "in þe grond of helle dongeoune

And in strong pains they shall be strained and racked.

"Þe hevedes of synfulle salle be turned doune,
And þe fete upward fast knytted
And in strang payns be streyned and tytted."

And for-þi, þat þai war here ay redy
To syn, with sere lyms of þair body,
Þarfor þai salle be bonden þare
Be divers lyms, als I sayd are,
With brynand bandes hate glowand,
Þat ever mare salle be lastand;
And for-þi þat þai wald noght God knaw,
Na kepe þe ordre here of his law,
Bot turned þam ay fro God-ward,
And on þe world þair hertes sett hard,
And swa mysturned here þair lyfyng
In-tylle vanyté and flesschly lykyng,
Þarfor it es ryght and resoune,
Þat þai be turned up-swa-doune,
And streyned in helle and bonden fast,
With bandes of fire þat ay salle last.

The sinful shall be bound for ever with burning bonds.

Þe fourtende payne es despayre to telle,
In whilk þe synfulle salle ay dwelle,
With-outen hope of mercy þan,
Ffor Salamon says þus, þe wise man:
Omnes qui ingrediuntur ad infernum non revertentur, nec apprehendent semitas vite.
He says "alle þase þat tylle helle wendes,
And in despayre salle be omang fendes,
Salle never after turne ogayne,
Ne tak þe ways of lyfe certayne."
For when þai er dampned thurgh iugement,
And with body and saule tille helle er sent,
Þai salle never after, with-outen dout,
Have hope, ne thynk to com out,
Bot ever-mare dwelle with-outen hope,
Ffor þus says þe haly man Job:
Quia in inferno nulla est redempcio.
"Ffor in hell", he says, "es na redempcyoune"
Thurgh na help of frende; for na devocyone
Of prayer, ne almusdede, ne messe,
May þam help, ne þair payn mak les.

XIV. The fourteenth pain is despair.

There is no redemption for those in hell.

A strang payn salle þis be in helle,
Ever-mare þus in despayre to dwelle,
With-outen hope of recouverere.
þis passes alle þe payns of þis lyfe here,
Ffor here has na man payn swa strang,
þat he ne has som tyme hope omang,
Outher of remedy þat men may kast,
Or þat it salle end and noght ay last;
Elles suld þe hert, thurgh sorow and care,
Over-tyte fayle, warn som hope ware;
Ffor in sorow here hope comfortes best.
And men says, warn hope ware it suld brest.
Bot in helle na hope may falle in thoght,
And þair hertes brest may noght;
Ffor þai er ordaynd to lyf ay þare,
Swa þat þai may be pyned ever-mare.
Bot þe lyfe of þam in þat stede
Es wers and bytterer þan þe dede.
Bot better it war to be fully slayne,
þan over-lang lyfe in strang payne;
Bot þe synfulle salle ay þare in payne be,
And na ded may þam sla bot ay þam fle,
Als þe boke openly schewes us,
Whare we may fynd wryten þus:
Mors fugiet ab eis.
"þe ded", þat here es strang and hard
"Salle ay þan fle fra þam-ward,"
þe payns of þe ded þai salle ay dreghe,
Bot þai salle never-mare fully deghe;
þai salle ay lyf in sorow and stryfe,
Bot þair lyf salle seme mare ded þan lyfe;
þair lyfe in mydward þe ded salle stand,
Ffor þai salle lyfe ever-mare deghand,
And deghe ever-mare lyfand with-alle,
Als men dose þat we se in swowne falle;
And for-þi, þat þai here mykelle lufed syn,
And thurgh over-mykelle hope ay lyfed þar-in,

No hope in the hearts of those in hell.

Death is better than continual pain.

The wicked who are in hell, shall desire to die, but death shall flee from them.

And to leve þair syn had never wille,
þarfor it es gud, ryght and skylle,
þat þai be ay for þair foly,
In helle with-outen hope of mercy.
Now have I schewed yhow, als I couth telle,
þe fourtene generalle payns in helle;
Bot yhit es over þase a payne generalle,
þat of alle other es mast principalle,
þat es tharnyng for ever of the syght namly,
Of our Lord God alle-myghty.

The greatest pain in hell is the great yearning for the sight of God.

Ffor whilk syght þat þai for ever have tynt,
þai salle have sorow þat never salle stynt;
And þe sorow þat þarfor salle falle
Salle be mast payne to þam of alle,
For als þe syght of God in heven, es
Mast ioy of alle other, mare and les,
Right swa þe tharnyng for ever of þat syght,
Es þe mast payne in helle dyght;
Ffor alle þe payns þat in helle may be,
Suld noght þam dere if þai moght him se.
Yhit salle þare be sere payns many ma
Als þe boke says, and mare sorow and wa
þan alle þe men of erth, ald and yhong,
Moght thynk with hert or telle with tong,

The pains of hell cannot be reckoned.

þat þe synful men þat salle wende
Tille helle salle have with-outen ende,
þe whilk payns and sorow salle never cees;
Ffor þare salle never be rest ne pees,
Bot travail and stryfe with sorow and care,
Fulle wa salle þam be þat salle dwelle þare;
þai sall thynk on nathyng elles,
Bot on þair payns, als som clerkes telles,
And on þair syn þat þai here wroght,

In hell the wicked shall never be at peace.

Swa salle payns and sorow troble þair thoght;
Ffor þare salle be þan herd and sene,
Alkyn sorow and trey and tene.
þare salle be wantyng of alkyn thyng,
In whilk moght be any lykyng,

And defaut of alle thyng þat gud moght be,
And of alle þat ille es gret plenté.

In hell shall be 'doleful din.'

In helle salle be þan fulle dolefulle dyn,
Omang þe synfulle þat salle dwelle þar-in,
Þat ever-mare salle þus cry and say:
"Allas, allas and walaway!
Þat ever we war of wemmen borne,
Ffor we er fra God for ever lorne?"
Þan salle þai grete and goule and with teth gnayste
Ffor of help ne mercy þar þam noght trayste.[1]

Devils shall roar and yell about the wicked;

Þe devels obout þam þan in helle,
On þam salle ever-mare rare and yhelle;
Swa hydus noyse þai salle þan make,
Þat alle þe world it moght do qwake,
And alle þe men lyfand þat herd it,
To ga wode for ferd and tyne þair witt.
Þe devils ay omang on þam salle stryke,
And þe synfulle þare-with ay cry and skryke;
Þare salle be þan mare noyse and dyn,
Þan alle þe men of erth couth ymagyn;
Ffor þare salle be swilk rareyng and ruschyng
And raumpyng of devels and dyngyng and dusching
And skrykyng of synfulle, als I said are,
Þat þe noyse salle be swa hydus þare,
Omang devels and þase þat salle com þider,
Ryght als heven and erth strake togyder.
Ane hydus thing es it to telle
Of þe noyse þat salle þan be in helle;

Full of ire they shall stuff the wicked in the fire.

Þe devels, þat ay salle be fulle of ire,
Salle stopp þe synfulle ay in þe fyre,
Swa þat þai salle glowe ay als fyre brandes
And ay when þai may weld þair hands,[2]
Ffor sorow þai salle þam hard wryng;
And walaway þai salle ay syng.
In helle salle be þan swa gret thrang,
Þat nane may remow for other ne gang.

[1] Þai salle gret and with teth gnayste,
For mercy þar þaim nane traiste (MS. Harl. 6923).

[2] MS. Harl. 6923 reads *styr* for weld.

On na syde, backward ne forward
Ffor þai salle be pressed togyder swa harde,
Als þai war stopped togyder in ane oven,
Ffulle of fyre bineth and oboven;
Bot never-þe-les helle yhit es swa depe,
And swa wyde and large, þat it moght kepe
Alle þe creatures, les and mare,
Of alle þe world if myster ware.
Ilka synfulle salle þare on other prese,
And nane of þam salle other eese,
Bot ever fyght togyder and stryfe,
Als þai war wode men of þis lyfe,
And ilk ane scratte other in þe face,
And þair awen flessch of-ryve and race,
Swa þat ilk ane wald him self fayn sla,
If he moght, swa salle him be wa,
Bot þare-to salle þai haf na myght,
Ffor þe ded salle never mar on þam lyght.
Ffulle fayn þai wald þan ded be,
Bot þe ded salle ay fra þam fle;
After þe ded þai salle yherne ilk ane,
Als in þe apocalypse schewes Saint Iohan:
Desiderabunt mori, et
mors fugit ab eis.
"Þai sall yherne", he says, "to deghe ay,
And þe ded salle fle fra þam oway;"
Omang þam salle ay be debate,
Ilk ane of þam salle other hate.
Þai salle be fulle of hateredyn þan;
Ilk ane salle other wery and ban,
And say "cursed kaytif and wa worth þe,
And weryed mot þou ever be,
And weryed mot þai be ever-mare,
Þat þe gat and þat þe bare,
And þe tyme þat þou was born alswa,
Ffor þi payne es tylle me sorow and wa;
It pynes me and greves me sare,
Als mykelle als myne awen payn or mare,

The wicked shall be pressed as into an oven, full of fire beneath and above it, nevertheless hell is large enough to hold all the wicked.

The damned shall scratch each others faces.

They shall be full of hatred and shall curse their fellows.

Ffor my payne it ekes, and mase mare grevus."
Ilk ane tylle other þan salle say þus.
Those in hell shall curse each other;
Þus ilk mans payne salle other dere,
And nane of þam salle other forbere;
Nouther son, ne doghter, ne syster, ne brother
Ffader ne moder, ne yhit nane other;
Ffor ilk ane salle other hate dedly,
And ilk ane gryn on other and cry.
Ilk ane salle gnaw þair awen tonges in sonder,
And ilk ane salle þare on other wonder.
Þus in helle salle þai far ay,
They shall slander God;
And þar-with sklaundre God and say:
"Whar-to made God us tylle his lyknes,
And lates us now dwell þare sorow ay es;
Bot it semes þat God made us in vayne,
When we er þus putted tille endles payne,
Or he us made for noght els to dwelle
In erth, bot to be fyre brandes in helle."
And curse the day of their birth.
Þai salle wery þe tyme þat þai war wroght,
And say "allas whine war we noght."
Þus salle þai sklaundre God omang,
Swa hard þair payns salle be, and swa strang;
Þai salle ilk ane on other stare and gryn,
Als wode men dose here, and makes gret dyn;
An hydus thing to here it ware,
Wha-swa couth telle þe payns þare,
Als properly als þai salle þare be.
Bot þat couth noght alle þe men of cristianté.
Ne alle þe clerkes þat ever had witt,
The pains of hell are innumerable.
Sen þe world bigan, ne þat lyfes yhit
Couth never telle, bi clergy, ne arte
Of þa payns of helle þe thowsand parte.
Ffor þe noumbre of payns þat þare griefes
Passes þe mens witt þat here liefes,
Or þat ever lyfed in any degré,
And þat may men bi skylle þus se;
Ffor ilka syn þat þe synfulle has wroght,
Whar it never swa lytelle venyalle thoght,

þai salle have certayne payne þare,
After þat þe syn es les or mare.
Wha couth þan telle, war he never swa wyse,
Alle þe syns and alle þe folyse,
Both dedly and alswa venyale,
And leve nane untald, gret ne smale,
þe whilk a man has here fallen in,
Ffra þe tyme þat he first bigan to syn,
Both in thoght, in word and dede?
Alswa say nane es þat tyme couth rede.[1]
And for ilka thing done here in vayne,
In helle es ordaynd certayne payne
Tille synfulle men þat salle dwelle þare.
þan bihoves þam, als I sayd are,
Ffor ilka syn þat þai dyd here,
Have certayne payne singulere;
And for ilka manere of syn and foly,
Be pyned in helle specyaly.
And als oft-sythe als þai here newed þair syn
Als oft-syth þair payn salle new þare bigyn;
þarfor swa many payns tylle þam salle falle,
þat na witt may comprehende þam alle;
Ffor na syn þat þai ever here dyd,
Dedly ne veniele, salle be hyd,
Bot alle openly sene and nan be laynd,
Ffor whilk salle be þare sere payns ordaynd;
Wha moght þan alle þe payns telle,
þat þe synfulle men salle have in helle?
Ffor-whi if a man fra hethen pass oway
In a dedly syn, at his last day,
Ffor ilka venyel syn, þat ever dyd he,
He salle þan diversly pyned be;
And als oft renoueld[2] salle be ilk payne,
Als he turned new tylle ilk syn ogayne.
And þe lest payne þare es mare to se,
þan alle þe payns of þis world may be,

There is a pain for every sin;

And for every thing done here in vain.

So many pains shall there be in hell that no wisdom may comprehend them all.

The least pain of hell is greater than all the pains of this world.

[1] Als wha say na man couth thaim rede (MS. Harl. 6923).
[2] renewed?

The sorrow of this world is but joy compared with the pains of hell.

Ffor alle þe payns of þis world here,
Þat ever was sene fer or nere,
Als to þe lest payne þare moght noght be tald,
Bot als a bathe of water, nouther hate ne cald[1]
Ffor alle þe sorow of þis world, ilka dele,
War noght bot als solace and ioy to fele,
Als to regard of þe lest payne,
Þat es in helle; þis es certayne,
Ilk synfulle salle haf syght þare
Of alle þe payns, both les and mare,
Þat alle þe synfulle men salle dreghe.
Þan salle ilk ane se þare with eghe
Men and wymmen, many a thousand,
On ilk syde obout, in sere payns dwelland;

The sight of another's pain shall be a source of suffering to the damned.

And þat syght, þat ilk ane salle þare se
Of ilka payne, tylle þam payne salle be;
Ffor alle þe payns þat salle falle tylle ilk man
Salle be sorow tylle alle þat sese þam þan.
Þus salle ilk ane dreghe mare payn in helle,
Þan hert moght ever think or tong telle;
What of payns þat to þam-self salle be dyght,
And what of payns þat þai salle have of syght.
Ffor alle þe payns, þat þare salle be knawen,
Salle greve ilk man als mykelle als his awen;
Swilk payns to here, als men may here rede,
Aght to mak ilk man of helle have drede;

If a man understood what were the sufferings of those in hell, he would hate all folly.

For I trow þat here es no man lyfand,
Swa hard-herted, þat wald understand
And trow what payns in helle er wroght,
Þat he ne suld have gret dred in thoght,
Þe whilk suld mak him hate alle foly,
Wharfor he war swylk payns worthy.
Bot alle þase þat wille þair syn forsake,
Whils þai lyfe here, ar þe ded þam take,
And of alle thing have forthynkyng
Þat þai have done ogayns Godes bydyng,

[1] Als a leuke bath nouther hate ne calde (MS. Harl. 6923).

And turn þam tylle God fra þair syn,
And ask his mercy and trayst þar-in,
And be lufand un-tylle him and bowsom,
In þa payns of helle salle never com,
Bot tylle þe blys of heven mon þai wende,
And have þare þair lykyng with-outen ende.
Here have I spoken of þe payns of helle,
Als yhe have herd me openly telle,
And of þe sext part of þis boke made ende.
Now wille I tylle þe sevend part wende,
Þat es þe last part of alle;
Þe whilk spekes als I shew yhow salle,
Specialy of þe ioyes in heven,
Þat er mare þan any tong may neven.
Bot fyrst I wille schew yhow whare heven es,
Als clerkes says and þe boke bers witnes;
And efter þat I salle schew yhow mare,
And telle yhow of sere ioyes þat er þare.

Those who turn to God here, shall never feel the pains of hell.

Here bygyns þe sevend part of þis boke Þat es of þe ioyes of heven.

Many þe blys of heven covaytes,
Bot fone þe ryght way þider laytes;
And som thurgh syn er made so blynd,
Þat þe right way þider þai kan noght fynd,
Som wald be þare, with-outen dout,
Bot þai wille noght travaille þare obout;
Bot whasa wille tak þe way þider-ward,
Behoves in gud werkes travaille hard;
Ffor tylle þe kyngdom of heven may no man com
Bot he ga bi þe way of wisdom;
Þe way of wysdom es mekenes
And other virtuse, mare and les.
And þat way es cald a gastly way,
Bi whilk men suld here travaille ay,
Þat es þe way þat ledes men even
Untylle þe hegh kyngdom of heven.
Bi other way may nane, bot he fleghe,

Many desire the the bliss of heaven but few seek the right way.

Man may only reach heaven by the way of wisdom.

Heaven is the highest place that God has made.

Pass up tylle heven it es swa heghe;
Ffor it es þe heghest place þat God wroght,
And þe first, when he made alle thing of noght.
Na man may gesce swa lang space,
Als es fro hethen untylle þat hegh place;
Ffor bitwene us and þat heghe heven
Es alle þe firmament to neven,
Þe[1] clerkes bi skylle hevens calles,
Þe whilk er ay moveand als falles.
Þus er oboven us hevens sere,
Bot alle er þa noght olyke clere;
Ffor þe heghest heven es wele bryghter
Þan þe other hevens þat er lagher;
Ffor þe heghest has swa mykelle bryghtnes,
And swa fayre and swa delytable es,
Þat alle þe men of erth couth noght
Swa mykelle ymagyn, ne think in thoght.

God has made several heavens.

Sere hevens God ordaynd for sere thyng,
Bot þe heghest God made for our wonyng.
Þese hevens er oboven us heghe,
Als clerkes says, þat er wise and sleghe;

1. The starry heaven.

Ane es, þat we þe sterned heven calle,
Þare þe planetes and þe sternes er alle,
Þat men may se here, on nyght, schyne;

2. The crystalline or watery heaven.

Ane other es, þat clerkes calles cristallyne,
Þat next oboven þe sterned heven es,
And es mare þan þat of wydenes;
Som clerkes it calles on þis manere;
Þe water heven, þat es als clere
Als cristalle, þat hoves oboven þare,
Ryght als water þat frosen ware;
Þus telles Berthelemewe in þe boke
Of propertes of sere thinges to loke:

These two heavens revolve round the earth, which is very small.

Þir twa hevens ay obout-rynnes,
Both day and nyght, and never blynnes;
Þe erth, þat þa hevens obout-gase,
Es bot als a poynt Imyddes a compase;

[1] Þat?

Hell in the middle of the earth, is the lowest place.

Swa lytelle it es semand with-out
To regard of þa hevens obout;
And Imyddes þe erth es ordaynd helle,
Þare þe synfulle, þat salle be dampned salle dwelle
Als men may before rede and se,
And lawer þan helle may na place be;
Þus both þe hevens obout-gase ay
And never salle ceese untylle domesday;
Ffor clerkes says þat knawes and sese,
Of þir twa hevens þe propertese,
Þat if þai moved noght, alle suld perysscb,
Both man and beste, foghel and fyssch
And alle þat under þam may be,
Þat lyves and growes, both gresse and tre,
All suld be smored[1] with-outen dout,
Warne þa hevens ay moved obout;
Ffor if þai stode never swa schort while stylle,
Alle þat on erth es suld perysch and spylle;
Þus telles gret clerkes of clergy,
Þat has bene lered in astronemy
And knawes þe constellacyouns
And þe heven þat þe erth envirouns.

The starry and the watery heavens revolve continually, should they stop all things would be destroyed.

Of þair moveyng þan have yhe no wonder,
Ffor it norysschl[es] alle þat es þare-under,
In wate and drye, in hate and cald,
Ay whils þai move, als I bifore tald,
Þir hevens obout-gase alle erthly thynges
And þam norysches and forth-brynges,
Ffor als clerkes says þat to þam tentes
Þai tempre þe streng[t]he of alle þe elementes
Ay als þai move whils þai obout-ga.

The motion of these heavens nourishes all things.

Bot þe thred heven es oboven þa twa,
Swa wonderly heghe and swa ferre
Þat nathyng may be heghere;
Yhit som clerkes ma hevens nevens,
And says þat þare er other seven hevens,

3. The third heaven is above the others.

[1] Al schulde be spilt wyth-outen doute (MS. 22283).

Þat semes lawer, als men may se,
Þan þe twa hevens falles to be,

Some say that the planets are heavens and are seven in number: 1. Moon, 2. Mercury, 3. Venus, 4. Sun, 5. Mars, 6. Jupiter, 7. Saturn.

Ffor-whi þe clerkes þe planetes alle
Bi certayne skylle hevens þai calle.
And seven planetes er oboven us;
Ffyrst þe Mone and Mercury and Venus,
Sythen þe Son and þan Mars and Iubiter,
And Saturnus oboven þan þat es hegher.
Ilk ane þair course obout ay mase
In þair cercles, als God ordaynd hase;
Þai styk noght fast, als smale sternes dose,
Ilk ane his course mase thurgh use;
Ilka planete falles for to be
Hegher þan other in ordre and degré;

The Moon is the lowest, Saturn is the highest planet.

Þe Mone, þe fyrst and lawest, es sene,
And Saturnus þe heghest es, als I wene;
Oboven us er alle þe planetes seven,
And þe cercle of ilk ane es called ane heven
Þat er wonderly bryght and fayre;

The air may be called a heaven.

Yhit ane other heven es called þe ayre
Þat es lagher, þar þe foghles has flyght,
And þat heven es mast nere our syght
Bot it es noght swa clere ne clene
Als þe other hevens oboven er sene:
Alle þe cercles of þe planetes alle
Þat we here clerkes þus hevens calle,
Er bryght and clere, als þe bokes schewes us
And ilk planete es ferrer þan other fra us;

The distance of the earth from the moon is 500 winters, so says Rabbi Moses.

Ffra þe erth untylle þe cercle of þe mone, es
Þe way of fyve hundreth wynter, and na les,
Þat es als mykelle space at say,
Als a man moght ga, in playne way,
In fyve hundreth yhere fully,
If he moght lyfe swa lang in body,
Als a gret philosiphir þat hyght
Rabby Moyses telles ryght
Þat thurgh witt mykelle couth se;
And over þat alle, swa says he,

Each circle of a planet contains the 'way of 500 years'.

Þat ilka cercle þat es sene
Of ilka planete, may contene,
Als men may fynd wryten here,
Þe way of fyve hundreth yhere
Als es gesced in brede and thyknes,
Swa mykelle and thyk ilk ane es,
Þat es at say, als mykelle space here
Als a man moght ga in fyve hundreth yhere.
Þof þat travaille him suld noght gryfe
If he here swa lang moght lyfe;
And fra þe poynt of þe erthe tille Saturnus
Þe heghest planete may be gesced þus,
Þe way of seven thowsand yhere
And thre hundreth, als es wryten here,
Þat es at say, als es here contende,
Als mykelle space als a man moght wende
In seven thowsand yhere, and[1] playn way gang
And th[r]e hundreth, if he suld lyf swa lang;
Swa þat ilk yhere be acounted halely
Of thre hundreth days and fourty,
And þat þe way of ilka day
Be fully of fourty myle of way,
And þat ilka myle fully contene
A thowsand pases or cubites sene.
Raby Moyses says alle þis,
Þat er noght alle my wordes bot his;
Bot whether alle þis be soth or noght,
God wate, þat alle thyng has wroght,
Ffor he made alle thyng thurgh myght and sleght
In certain noumbre and mesure and weght;
Bot swa sutelle and wise may na man be,
Þat þat mesuryng knawes swa wele als he;
Ffor na thyng þat may be, mare or les,
Or þat ever was, tylle him unknawen es;
Himself fra erth, upward met þat way,
When he stey tylle heven on halghe Thursday,
Þat wate he best thurgh wytt and sleght,
What space þat way contened of heght.

Saturn, the highest planet, is distant from the earth 7300 years;

Each year consists of 340 days

A days journey is 40 miles, and each mile contains 1000 cubits.

Christ measured this distance when he ascended to heaven on Holy Thursday.

[1] in?

Bi alle þe hevens had he gane,
And passed alle þe sternes ilk ane,
And up tylle þe heghest heven he went,
And alle þis way he passed in a moment,
In þe heghest part of þe sterned heven.

Above the planets are the stars,

Oboven alle þe planetes seven,
Standes swa many sternes smale,
Þat na man may þam telle bi tale,
Þat standes fast þare, als þe buke pruves,
And er led obout with þe heven þat moves,

Like nails in a wheel they go about with the heavens.

Als nayles er in a whele with-out,
Þat with þe whele er turned obout;
Bot þe planetes er noght led swa,
Ffor in þair cercles obout þai ga.
Þe sternes semes smale, als we deme,

The stars appear small to us, but they are not really so.

Bot swa smale er þai noght als þai seme,
Ffor þai er schewed fra us swa fer,
Þat we may noght se how mykelle þai er;
Bot þe lest sterne þare þat we on-luke.
Es mare þan erth, als says þe boke;
Ffor clerkes says, if alle erth in fyre ware,
And possibel war þat a man war þare,
Him suld thynk, þof it bryned bryght,
Les þan þe lest sterne þat schynes on nyght,
Þan aght þat heven gret space contene,
Þare swa many sternes may be sene.
Alle þir hevens here sene may be,

The highest heaven no one can see.

Bot þe alther-heghest heven may na man se.
Tille þat heven couth clerk thurgh arte,
Þe space gesce bi ane hundreth thowsand part

It is so high that a stone of a hundred men's lifting would take 1000 years before reaching the earth.

Ffor it es swa heghe, als Sydrak says,
Þat if a stane þat war of pays,
Of ane hundreth mens lyftyng,
Might falle fro þeþen, it suld be in fallyng
A thowsand yhere and na les,
Ar it come at þe erth, swa heghe it es;
Bot aungels þat fro heven er sent,
May com doune tylle erth in a moment,

And up ogayne tylle heven may flegh,
In þe space of a twynkellyng of ane eghe.
And swa may a saule þat es clene and lyght,
Com þider fro hethen in als schort a flyght,
Thurgh þe myght of God and thurgh noght elles
And swa has done many þat þare dwelles;
þis may be halden a gret ferly,
Omang alle þe wonders of God alle-myghty,
þat ane aungelle may pass swa many myle,
Ffra heven tylle hyder, in swa schort awhyle.
And a saule thurgh Godes myght and grace,
May fro hethen com þider in swa short space.

The souls of the righteous may pass from earth to heaven in the twinkling of an eye.

This heven es þe alther-heghest place of alle,
Hegher es na thyng þat may bifalle,
þe whilk alle thyng contenes of dignyté,
And in nathyng contende may be,
It contenes over-alle, on ilk party,
Bath bodily thyng and gastly,
And als helle es lawest place þat may falle,
Swa es þis heven alther-heghest place of alle;
And als sorow es ay in þe lawest place,
Swa es ay in þe heghest, ioy and solace.
And als tylle þe lawest place, drawes us syn,
Swa tylle þe heghest may vertues us wyn.

Heaven is the highest place of all.

Sorrow is in hell, but joy in heaven.

þis heven es cald heven empiry
þat es at say heven þat es fyry,
Ffor it semes alle als fyre of gret myght,
þat brynnes noght bot schynes bryght.
þis heven falles noght obout to ga,
Ne moves noght als dose þe other twa,
Bot standes ay stylle, for it es þe best,
And þe most worthi place of pees and rest
þat God has ordaynd for þair wonyng,
þat gyfes þam here tylle ryghtwise lyfyng.
þis heven es cald Godes awen se,
Ffor þar syttes þe haly trinité,
And alle þe orders of aungels,
And alle þe blyssfulle spirites þat in heven dwels,

The highest heaven does not move as the other heavens do.

It is called God's own seat.

And þe saules of gud men and clene,
Þat in þis world ryghtwyse has bene.
And at þe dredfulle day of dome,
When alle men salle bifor God come,
Þan salle alle the ryghtwyse men wend þider,
In body and saule both togyder,

There shall be more joy in heaven than heart may think or tongue tell.

Þe whilk anely þan salle be save,
And fulle blys in body and saule have.
Þan salle mare ioy be in heven,
Þan hert may thynk or tong kan neven,
Or ere may here or any eghe se,
Þe whilk þai salle have, þat save salle be;
Þan passes þat ioy alle mens witt,
Als es fonden wryten in haly wrytt.
Quod oculus non vidit, nec
auris audivit, nec in cor ho-
minis ascendit, quod preparavit
Deus diligentibus se.
"Eghe moght never se, ne ere here,
Ne in-tylle mans hert com þe ioyes sere
Þat God has ordaynd þare and dyght,
Tylle alle þat here lufes him ryght."
Ffor swa mykelle ioy þare salle be,
Þat alle þe men of Cristianté,
If ilk ane war parfyte in clergy
In divinité and in astronomy,

None, though ever so learned can tell a thousand part of the joys of heaven.

In gemettry and gramer, and arte,
Couth noght gese bi þe thowsand parte,
Ne think in hert ne with tong neven,
Þe ioyes þat þan salle be in heven.
Ffor swa wyse here was never man yhit,
Ne swa sleghe, ne swa sotelle of wytt,
Had he never swa mykelle understandyng,
Bot God anely þat knawes alle thyng,
Þat couth telle a poynt or ymagyn
Of þe ioyes in heven þat never salle blyn,
Als proprely als þai er þare to say,
Bot als þe boke þam schewes, swa we may.

All*e* manere of ioyes er in þat stede. — All kinds of joy are in heaven:
Þare es ay lyfe with-outen dede; — Everlasting life,
Þare es yhowthe ay with-outen elde,
Þare es alkyn welth ay to welde.
Þare es rest ay, with-outen travayle; — Rest,
Þare es all*e* gudes þat never sal fayle; — Goods,
Þare es pese ay, with-outen stryfe; — Peace,
Þare es all*e* manere of lykyng of lyfe; — Pleasure,
Þare es, with-outen myrknes, lyght; — Light,
Þare es ay day and never nyght; — Day and never night,
Þare es ay somer full*e* bryght to se, — Bright summer and never winter,
And never mare wynter in þat contré:
Þare es alkyn druryes and rychesce, — Riches,
And mare nobillay þan any man may gesce; — Nobility,
Þare es mare worsche[pe] and honoure, — Honour,
Þan ever had kyng here or emparoure;
Þare es alkyn power and myght — Power,
And endeles wonyng sykerly dyght; — Security,
Þare es alkyn delyces and eese, — Delights,
And syker peysilbilnes[1] and pese;
Þare es peysebell*e* ioy ay lastand, — Joy,
And ioyfull*e* selynes ay lykand; — Happiness,
Þare es sely endeles beyng,
And endeles blysfulhede in all*e* thyng;
Þare es ay blysfull*e* certaynté,
And certayne dwellyng ay fre;
Þare es laykyng and myrthes sere; — Play and mirth,
Þare es laghyng and lufly chere; — Laughter,
Þare es melody and aungels sang; — Melody and song,
And lovyng and thankyng ay omang; — Praise,
Þare es all*e* frendschepe þat may be, — Friendship,
And parfyte luf and charyté; — Love,
Þare es acorde ay and anehede, — Unity,
And yheldyng of mede for ilk gud dede; — Rewards,
Þare es lowtyng and reverence, — Reverence,
And boghsomnes and obedience; — Obedience,
Þare es all*e* vertuse with-outen vyce, — Virtues,

[1] *peysibilnes?*

þare es plenté of dayntes and delice;
þare es alle þat lykes and may avayle,
And nathyng þat greves or may fayle;
þare es alle þat gud es at wille,
And na thyng þat may be ille.

Wisdom,

þare es alle wisdom with-outen foly,
And honesté with-outen vilany;

Beauty.

þare es bryghtnes and bewté
Of alle thing þat men salle þare se.
Alle þir ioyes er þare generalle,

The greatest joy in heaven is the sight of God's face.

Bot þe mast soverayne ioy of alle
Es þe syght of Godes bryght face,
þat passes alle other ioyes and solace;
Ffor swa mykelle may na ioy be,
Als es þe syght of þe trinité,
þat es þe Fader, and Son, and Haly gaste.
þe syght of whilk salle be ioy maste;
Ffor-whi swa mykelle ioy and blys
Na ioy may be als es þis.[1]
Ffor alle þat þan salle se him ryght,
May knaw alle thing thurgh þat syght,
þat ever was, and es, and salle be,
Als men may afterward rede and se.
Here have I shewed on a general manere
þe ioyes of heven, many and sere.

Of the special 'blisses' and their contraries.

Bot now will I specialy shew yhow mare
Of seven maners of blysses þare,
And of seven schenschepes in helle alle-swa,
þat er even contrary tylle þa,
And whilk blysses falles specyaly
Tylle þe saule, and whilk tylle þe body,
Of þas þat God in heven salle se;
And whilk schendschepes salle appropried be
Tylle þe bodyse of þase, þat salle ga
Tylle helle, and whilk tille þe saules alle-swa.
I spak bifore of sere ioyes generaly,
Bot now will I here sere blysses specify,

[1] Forwhi þar may be ioy ne blis,
Swa mekyl to fele als is þis. (MS. Harl. 2394.)

And þair contraryes þat er hard,
Als yhe salle here be red afterward.
Saint Anselme says, þe haly man,
Als I here schew yhow kan,
Þat omang alle þe ioyes of heven,
Salle be sene specialle blysses seven,
Þat þe bodyse salle have þat salle be save,
And other seven þat þe saules salle have
In þe kyngdome of heven alle to-gyder,
After þe dome, when þai com þider;

The souls and bodies of the righteous have seven special blessings.

Bot tylle þe synfulle bodyse þare ogàyne
Þat salle be dampned tylle helle payne,
Seven specialle schendschepes salle falle
And other seven tylle þe saules with-alle
In helle to-gyder lastand ever-mare,
Wa es þam þat salle dwelle þare.

The wicked, on the contrary, are tormented in soul and body by seven pains.

Heres now, ar I pass ferrer,
Whilk þa specyalle blysses er,
Þat er appropried tylle þa bodyse
And tylle þe saules of men ryghtwyse,
And þair contraryes, þat I schendschepes calle
Þat tylle þe synfulle bodyse and saules salle falle.

The 'blisses' of the body and their cóntraries.

Þe fyrst blys es bryghtnes cald
Þat þe saved bodyse salle ay hald;

I. Brightness is the first bliss.

Ffor be þair bodyse never swa dym here,
In heven þai salle be fayre and clere
And mare schyneand and mare bryght,
Þan ever þe son was tylle mans syght;

The bodies of the righteous shall shine brighter than the sun.

Swa fayre a syght bifore was never sene,
Als salle be þan, ne swa clene,
When ilka body þat salle be save,
Swa mykelle bryghtnes þare salle have;
Ffor if a man had eghen swa bryght,
And if swa moght be, swa mykelle syght,
Als had alle þe creatures lyfand,
Yhit moght he noght, als I understand,
Ogayne swa mykelle bryghtnes loke,
Als a body salle have, þus says þe boke.

The bodies of the damned shall be dark and hideous.

Bot þe dampned bodyse þare ogayne
Salle be foule and stynkand als carayne;
And fulle myrk and dym salle þai be
And fulle hydus and wlatsom to se;
Ffor swa foul a syght saw never man
Als þe dampned bodyse salle be þan,
Þat with þe saules salle dwelle in helle depe,
Þis salle to þam be payne and schendschepe.

II. The second bliss is swiftness.

Þe secunde blys after es swyftnes,
Þat ilk body salle have þat ryghtwise es;

The bodies of those saved shall fly whither they please.

Ffor in les while þan a man may wynke,
Þai salle mow fleghe whider þai wille thynke
With body and saule togyder thurgh flyght,
Ffra heven tylle erth and ogayne ryght,
And fra þe ta syde of þe world wyde,
If þai wyld, tylle þe tother syde;
And whider-swa þai þair thoght wille sett
Nathyng þam salle ogayne-stand ne lett.
Þis may þai do with-outen travayle,

This swiftness shall never fail.

And þis swyftnes salle never fayle;
Ffor als þe lyght of þe son, thurgh strenthe,
May fleghe fra þe est tylle þe west on lenthe,
Ryght swa þai may whyder þai wille, fleghe
In a schort twynkellyng of ane eghe.
Ffor þai salle be als swift þan
Als any thoght es here of man.

The bodies of the sinful shall be heavily laden with sin.

Bot þe synfulle bodyse salle ever-mare
On a contrary manere fare;
Þai salle be swa hevy charged with syn,
Both with-outen and with-in,
Þat þai salle have no myght to stand,
Ne unnethes to styr fote ne hand,
Ne yhit nane other lym of body,
Þair syn salle weghe on þam swa hevy.

III. The third bliss is strength and might.

Þe thred blys es strenthe and myght
Þat þe ryghtwise bodyse salle have thurgh ryght,
Ffor thof þai feble here and wayke ware,
Swa mykelle myght þai salle have þare,

And swa mykelle strenthe ay lastand,
Þat na thyng salle mow ogayne þam stand;
Swa þat þai salle mow remowe at þair wille,
Ilka mountayne and ilka hille,
Þat ever was in þe world sene;
And if þai wild, alle þe erth bidene,
With-outen any ogayne-standyng,
Or any lettyng of any-thyng;
And in þat dede have no mare swynk,
Þan a man has here to loke or wynk.

The righteous shall remove at will mountains and hills.

Bot þe synfulle bodyse, þat dampned salle be,
Salle be swa wayke and swa feble to se,
Þat þai salle unnethes mow stand,
Ne myght have anes to lyft þair hand
To wype þe teres fra þair eghen oway,
And þat waykenes salle last with þam ay.

The bodies of the sinful shall be weak and feeble.

Þe ferth blys alle-swa es fredome
Þat þe saved bodyse salle have þat salle come
Tylle heven, whare alkyn ioyes er,
To do what þai wille with-outen daunger;
Ffor-whi þai salle never fele na thyng
Bot þat at salle be at þair lykyng;
And na thing salle þam warn ne lett,
To do þair wille whare-swa it es sett;
Ffor alle thing tylle þam salle be boghand,
And na thing salle ogayne þam stand,
Ne ogayns þam na thing be sett,
Þair wille ne þair purpose to lett,
Nowther men, ne stele, ne stane, ne tre,
Ne noght elles, swa fre salle þai be;
Þai salle mow passe ay whare þai wille
And alle þair lykyng þan ful-fylle.
Þis fredom and þis fraunches
Salle be appropried tylle þe saved bodyse
With þe saules of þam þat God salle chese,
And þis fredom þai salle never lese.

IV. The fourth bliss is freedom.

The righteous shall ever do what they please;

Bot on contrary manere ogayne þat blys,
Þe dampned bodyse salle fredom mys;

The wicked shall be treated as slaves.

Ffor þai sall*e* be stresced in hell*e* als thrall*e*,
And all*e* þat may greve thole with-all*e*;
Þai sall*e* be chaced ogayne þair will*e*
Tyll*e* all*e* manere of thing þat es ill*e*;
Þus sall*e* þai in hell*e* in thraldom be,
Ffra whilk þai may never mare fle.

V. The fifth bliss is Health.

Þe fyft blys, als clerkes wate wele,
Es hele þat þe saved bodyse sall*e* fele,
With-outen seknes or grevaunce,
Or angre, or payne, or penaunce;
Ffor Ivel ne payne sall*e* never þam greve,
Bot in hele and lykyng þai sall*e* ay leve,
In heven with ioy on ilka syde,
Ffor þare sall*e* þai be glorifyde.

The damned shall be tormented by disease.

Bot þe dampned bodyse, on other-wyse,
Sall*e* have strang yvels and angwyse,
Als saules has þat in purgatory dwels
Ffor certayne tyme, als þe boke tels.
Bot swa lang lastes no sekenes þare.
Als in hell*e*, for þat lastes ever-mare;
Ffor purgatory, als wryten es,
Has ende, and hell*e* es endeles.

VI. The sixth bliss is perfect joy.

Þe sext blys es þe gret delyte,
Þat þe saved bodyse sall*e* have swa parfyte
Þat no man lyfand kan ne may,
Swa mykell*e* yhern here, nyght ne day;
Ffor here moght never man far swa wele,
With swa mykell*e* delyte als þai sall*e* fele
In all*e* þair wittes, ne swa mykell*e* ioy have,
Als God on þam sall*e* þan vouche save.
Þai sall*e* have swa mykell*e* ioy þare,
Þat nane of þam sall*e* desyre mare;
Ffor als þe iren þat es glowand,
Thurgh strenthe and hete brynand,
Semes better to be fyre-bryght,
Þan iren, als tyll*e* any mans syght,
Right swa þa þat in heven sall*e* won
Sall*e* seme bryghter þan fyre, and schyne als son

The righteous shall be filled full of joy.

And be fulle-fyld ay in þat place
Of þe luf of God and of his grace,
And of alle delyces and ioy and blys,
Þe whilk þai salle never-mare mys;
And als men here oft has sene
Þat a vesselle dypped alle bidene
In water, or in other lycour thyn,
Be þe vesselle never swa wyde wyth-in,
Has water bath with-in and with-out,
Binethen, oboven, and alle about,
And na mare water with-in may hald,
Ne nane other thing þat lycoure es cald,
Right swa þe ryghtwise salle have ioy, mare
Þan þai may think or yhern þare;

They shall be unable to desire more joy.

Bot þe dampned bodyse ogayn-ward
Salle in helle fele payns strang and hard;
Ffor þai salle bryn in fyre, ilk ane,
Þat salle be menged with bronstane
Ffulle hate brynand, and with pyk,
And with other thing þat es wyk,
Omang vermyn þat salle þam byte,
And devels þat ay salle þam smyte,
With other payns strang and felle,
Ma þan hert may thynk or tong telle.

The damned shall be tormented by fire and vermin &c.

Þe sevend blys es endeles lyfe,
Þat þe saved salle have, with-outen stryfe,
Ever-mare in heven swa heghe;
Ffor þai salle ay lyf and never deghe,
And with God alle-myghty þare ay won,
Þat es sothfast Fader, and sothfast Son,
And þe Haly Gast in Trinité;
And in þat lyfe his face þai salle ay se.

VII. The seventh bliss is everlasting life.

Now if a man moght lyf here,
In þis world a thowsand yhere,
Yhit suld his lyfe be broght tylle ende,
And fra þis world bihoved him wende.
Yhit suld him thynk, and he toke kepe,
His lyfe noght bot als a dreme in slepe,

Life on this earth is but a dream compared with that in heaven.

Þan suld þe lenthe of alle his lyfedays,
Seme bot als a day, als þe prophet says:
Quoniam mille anni ante oculos tuos, tanquam
dies hesterna que preteriit.
He says þus: "Lord! a thowsand yhere
Bi-for þine eghen, þat alle thyng sese here,
At þe last, es noght bot als yhister-day,
Þat was awhile and es passed oway."
Þus when þis lyfe tylle ende es broght,
Alle þe tyme of it semes als noght;
Þan es a day mare in heven swa clere,
Þan here er many thowsand yhere;
And many thowsand yheres here es les,

A day in heaven is more than a thousand years on earth.

Þan þare a day, als þe boke bers witnes.
Þan salle þe lyf be als lang þare,
Als þat day lastes, and þat es ever-mare;
Ffor þare es ay day and never nyght,
Þarfor þe prophet says þus ryght:
Melior est dies una in atriis
tuis super milia.
He says: "Loverd! better es a day lastand
In þi halles þan a thowsand;"
Þat es, better es in heven a day,
Þan a thowsand here þat passes oway;
Ffor alle þe days þat here may falle,
Passes oway, and þis lyf with-alle,
And in a day in heven salle be contende
Þe tyme þat never salle have ende;
Þan salle þat day, als þe boke us leres,
Pass many hundreth thowsand yheres.
And als in helle salle be nyght,
Als day salle be in heven bryght;

In heaven is ever day and in hell night without end.

Ffor als men in heven salle ay day se,
Ryght swa salle nyght ay in helle be.
Þus salle day in heven be contende,
And nyght in helle, with-outen ende;
Bot se we noght how schort a day es here
To regard of a hundreth yhere?

Yhit es a hundreth yhere les
To regard of þe tyme þat es endeles;
Ffor Saint Austyn telles in a sarmon,
Þat a day here may be a porcyon,
Of ane hundreth yhere, als men may se,
Alle-if þat porcyon fulle lytylle be,
Bot þe space of ane hundreth yhere es
Na porcyon of endelesnes;
Ffor if a thowsand yhere þat es mare
Of endlesnes a porcyon ware, Eternity.
After a thowsand thowsand yheres to kast,
Endlesnes suld sese þan at þe last,
And þat wille noght þe reson of endelesnes
Suffer þat it be schorter þan it es;
Ffor if endlesnes any end moght hald,
Þan war it endlesnes unproperly cald.
Bot in þat endlesnes es contende
Alle þe tyme þat may have nane ende;
And lyfe in heven salle als lang be
Als men salle tyme þare with-outen ende se,
Þan semes it wele, als I sayd are,
Þat lyfe salle be þare ever-mare
Wharfor ilk man with hert stedfast,
Suld seke þat lyfe þat ay salle last,
Þe whilk ilk man may lyghtly wyn,
Þat here lyfes wele and wille fle syn,
And leve noght þat lyf þat lastes ay
Ffor þis lyfe here þat passes oway;
Ffor þat lyfe es syker, and swa es noght þis. Heavenly life is secure and full of joy.
Þat lyfe es swa fulle of ioy and blys
Þat a man salle thynk þare a hundreth yhere,
In þat lyfe, schorter þan a day here.
Tylle þat ioyfulle lyf may alle men com
Þat meke of hert er here, and bowsom.
Þus salle endles lyfe appropryed be,
Tylle þe saved bodyse þat ay God salle se.
Bot þe dampned þat tylle helle salle wende, The sinful in hell shall live in death.
Salle have ded þare with-outen ende,

And þat ded salle ay new þam gryefe.
In þat ded þai salle ay lyefe,
And swa be pyned, in þair wyttes fyve,
Þat þair lyfe salle seme mare ded þan lyve.
Þai salle seme, whether þai lyg or stand,
Als men in transyng, ay deghand;
Þai salle ay deghand lyf, and lyfand dyghe,
And ever-mare payns of ded þus dryghe,
And þare-with be tourmented, ay omang,
With other bytter payns and strang;
Þar-for þe lyfe in helle may be cald
Life in hell is the second death.
Þe secund ded, and swa may we it hald.
Þan may þai say, þat salle lyf þare,
Allas! þat ever moder þam bare.
Here have I tald, als yhe moght here,
Of seven manere of blysses sere,
Þat þe saved bodyse salle have thurgh ryght
With þe saules in heven bryght,
And of þe seven schendschepes alle-swa
Þat es even contrary tylle þa,
Þe whilk þe bodyse in helle salle have ay,
Þat salle be dampned at domesday.
The special spiritual blessings and their contraries.
Bot I wille schew yhow yhit with-alle,
Seven manere of blysses, þat salle falle
Tylle þe saules namely with þe bodyse,
Of alle þe men þat er gude and ryghtwise,
Þat salle be saved at þat tyde,
And in heven be gloryfyde;
And yhit seven schendschepes wille I neven,
Þat er even contrary tylle þa seven,
Þe whilk salle falle, with-outen ende,
Tylle þa saules of þe synfulle þat salle wende,
With þe bodyse, untylle helle pytt,
Als es fonden in haly wrytt.
I. Wisdom, Knowledge of the Holy Trinity.
Þe fyrst blys þat þe saules salle have
Of ryghtwise men, þat salle be save
Es wisdom; for þai salle knaw and se
Alle þat was, and es, and yhit salle be.

Þai salle have knawyng of God fully,
And of þe myght of þe Fader alle-myghty,
Þai salle knaw þe wytt of þe son and taste,
And þe gudenes of þe Haly-gaste:
Þus salle þair knawyng parfyte be,
In alle þe haly trinité.
Þai salle knaw alle thing and wytt,
Þat God has done and salle do yhit,
In heven, in helle and in erth aywhare,
Þus wise þai salle be ever-mare.
Ffor þai salle have swa mykelle grace,
When þai se God, face to face,
Þat nathyng, þat God ever dyd, Nothing shall be hid from the righteous.
Salle be layned fra þam ne hyd,
Þat es to say, of þat God vouches save,
Þat any creature knawyng may have;
Ffor Saint Austyn þat mykelle couth of clergy,
Says in a sarmon þat he made openly,
Þat, in þe syght of God þat þai salle se,
Thre manere of knawyng tylle þam salle be.
Ffor þai salle se him þare both God and man, They shall see all things in God, as in a mirror.
And þam-self þai salle se in him þan,
And alle men and alle thing, les and mare.
Þai salle se, and knaw in þat syght þare,
Als we may thre thynges se here
In a myroure of glas, þat es clere;
Ane es þe myrour þat byfor us es,
Ane other es our awene face and lyknes,
And þe thred we may þar-in se yhit,
Þat es alle thyng þat es onence it;
Right swa men salle se God als he es,
In þe myroure of his bryghtnes,
Als properly als possible may be,
Tylle any creature him to se.
Þai salle se þam-self in him so bryght,
And alle men to-gyder, at a syght,
And alle other thyng þai salle knawe,
And se over-alle, both hegh and lawe.

Alle men þan salle se þat þare salle dwelle,
Alle þe creatures in heven and helle.

They shall learn all the secrets of God;

Þare salle be schewed þan tylle þam, apertly,
Sere privetese of God alle-myghty,
Þat na man here moght knaw ne wytt
Thurgh clergy, ne thurgh haly-wrytt;

How he is invisible, unchangeable and everlasting.

Þat es, how God invysible es,
And unchaungeable, and endles;
And how he was bifor alle thing,
And with-outen any bygynnyng;
And how, and whi, he salle be
With-outen ende, þai salle þan se;
Alle thyng þat now es fra þam hyd,
Salle þan tylle þam be knawen and kyd.

The righteous shall see the reason and cause of all things;

Þai salle þan se þare, openly,
Of alle thynges þe skylle and þe cause whi;
Als whi ane es chosen here and taken,
And ane other left and forsaken;

Why one is chosen and another left;

Whi ane es uptane tylle a kyngdom,
And ane other es putted in-tylle thraldom;
And whi som childer er ded and lorn
In þair moder wambe, ar þai be born;
Þai salle knaw, with-outen drede,

Why some die in their childhood and others live to extreme old age;

Skylle whi som deghes in þair barnhede,
And som after when þai mast strenthe weld;
And whi som lyfes tylle þair mast eld;
Þai salle yhit sertaine skylle se þan
Whi som er born in fayre schap of man,
And som in uncomly stature,

Why some are rich, and some poor.

And whi som er ryche here, and som pore,
And whi som childer geten in hordom,
Er baptized, and has cristendom,
And som þat er in lele wedlayk born,
Ar þai be cristened, er ded and lorn;
And whi som bi[g]ynnes to be stedfast
To lyfe wele, and endes ille at þe last;
And whi som has here ille bigynnyng,
And, at þe last, mase a gud endyng.

Of þir thynges, and of other many,
Þe skylles salle be knawen þan openly,
In þe boke of lyfe þat open salle be, *The 'book of life' shall be open to them*
Þe whilk es þe syght of þe trinité.
Þus salle alle men, þat in heven þan dwelles,
Knaw and witt, als Saint Austyn telles,
And in þe bryghtnes of God openly se
Alle thing þat ever was, or yhit salle be,
And alle þe soth of ilk thyng, and skylle,
Als fer-forth als God vouches safe, and wille.
Þare salle ilk man als wele knaw other, *The righteous shall know each other as a man knows his sister or brother.*
Als a man here knawes hys syster or brother,
And wyt of what contré þai ware,
And wha þam gatt, and wha þam bare.
Ilk ane salle knaw þan other thoght
And alle þe dedes þat þai ever wroght;
Þus wyse salle þai be þat salle come
Tylle þe kyngdom of heven, after þe dome.
Þai salle be Godes sons, and tille him lyke, *They shall be God's sons.*
And be made his heyres of hevenryke,
And be alle als Godes of gret myght,
Als þe prophet, in þe psauter, says ryght:
Ego dixi: 'Dii estis et
filii excelsi omnes.'
He says: "I sayd, 'yhe er Godes alle
And Godes sons men salle yhow calle'."
Wharfor it semes, þat when þai com
Tylle heven, þai salle be fulle of wysdom
And fulle of myght, lastand ever-mare,
When þai salle alle be als Godes þare.
Bot now may þou ask me and lere
A questyon, and say on þis manere:
'Salle þai oght think þat salle be safe, *Shall the righteous think of their sins?*
On þe syns of whilk þai þam schrafe
Here in þair lyfe, and made þam clene,
And of þam assoyled has bene?'
Saint Anselme answers to þis,
And says þat þou þat salle have heven blys,

Salle love God and thank him þare
Of alle gudes, both les and mare,
Þat he has done tylle þe here,
And tylle alle other, on þe same manere,
Þe whilk, at þe day of dome, salle be safe,
And with þe endles blys salle have.
Gret gud he dose þe, whils þou lyfes,
When he þi syns þe here forgyves;
How moght þou þan, with hert fre,
Thank God of þat þat he has forgyven þe,
Alle þe syns þat þou has wroght,
If þou moght thynk on nane in thoght?

The remembrance of sin shall not grieve the righteous.

Bot þou salle þis understand wele,
Þat na mare grevance salle þou fele,
Ne na mare payne have, ne myslykyng,
When þou has of þi syns meneyng,
Þan he has, þat som tyme had in stryfe

Like a wound perfectly healed it shall be forgotten.

A sare wound, with swerd or knyfe,
Þat parfytely es haled and wele,
Of whilk he may na mare sare[1] fele;
And als þou now has na schame of þe dede
Þat þou dyd in þi barnhede,
Or þat þou dyd in þi dronkennes,
Of whilk tylle þe now na schame es.
Na mare schame salle þou þan have in thoght,
Of þe syns þat þou here has wroght,
Of whilk þou ert here schryven parfytely,
And þat God has forgyfen here, thurgh mercy

Peter now has no shame for his denial of Christ.

And na mare þan Petre now has schame
Of þat, þat he forsoke our Lord bi name;
Or Mary Maudelayne now has of hir syn
Þat scho som tyme delyted hir in.
Na mare schame salle men þan have
Of þair syn here done, þat salle be save.
Bot for-þi þat God þat boght us fre,
Wyld thurgh his mercy and his peté,

[1] The MS. has 'sale'.

And couth, thurgh his awen wytt clere,
And myght wele, thurgh his awen powere,
Swa gret syns þam frely forgyve
And þe woundes hale[1], þat war gryfe,
Whare-thurgh þai had deserved wele
Þe pyne of helle ever-mare to fele,
Þarfor þai salle luf him þe mare,
And þe mare him love and thank þare,
And als wele for other mens trispas
And other mens syn þat he heled has,
Als for þair awen þat þai wroght here,
Þarfor says David, on þis manere:

But because of the great redemption wroght for them, the righteous shall praise and thank God for his goodness.

Misericordias Domini
ineternum cantabo.

The redeemed shall sing of the mercy of God.

He says: "I salle þe mercyes syng
Of our Loverd, ay with-outen cesyng."
And swa salle alle syng, with-outen ende,
Þat tylle þe blys of heven salle wende;
And swa moght þai on nane wise syng,
Warn þai had of þair syns meneyng,
Þat þai had done here bodily
And God forgaf thurgh his mercy;
Þus salle þe saule be fulle of wysdom þare,
And alle thing knaw and se, als I sayd are.
Bot þe saules þat with þe bodyse salle synk
In-tylle helle, salle on na gud thynk,
Ne have witt, ne knaw, ne fele
Na dede þat ever was done wele,
Bot on þair payns salle be alle þair thoght
And on þair syns þat þai had wroght;
Ffor þai salle on nathyng have meneyng,
Bot anely on þair awen wicked lyfyng,
And on þair sorow, with-outen ende,
And on þair wrechednes þat salle þam schende
Þe whilk þai salle, ay, bifor þam se,
And þat syght tylle þam schendschepe salle be.

The remorse of those in hell.

[1] The MS has 'have'.

II. The second spiritual bliss is friendship.

Þe secund blys þat þe saule salle fele,
With þe bodyse, als þir clerkes wate wele,
Salle be frendschepe and parfyte love,
Þat es mare þan ever man moght here prove;
Ffor ilk ane salle mare luf other þan,
Þan ever lufed here any man,
And als parfytely and als lang
Als he salle luf him-self omang.
And þat luf salle be fested swa fast,
Þat it salle never fayle, bot ay last;
Ffor als ilka lym of a body
Lufes alle þe other lyms kyndely,
And yhernes, ay, gretly þair hele,
Swa parfyte þat luf salle be and lele;

All in heaven shall be of one will.

Ffor þai salle alle be of ane assent
And of a wille and of ane entent;
Ffor þai salle be þan alle als a body
In sere lyms, and als a saule anely;
And God þair heved salle be þare,
Þat salle þam luf als mykelle or mare,
Als dose þe heved of þe body þat loves
Þe lyms kyndely þat on it moves.
Þat clere luf and þat alliance
Salle never-mare fayle, thurgh na distance,
Ne thurgh stryfe, þat man may make;
Þat band of luff salle never slake.
Bot even þe contrary salle men se,
Omang þe saules þat dampned salle be;

The damned shall be full of hatred and wrath.

Ffor þai salle be fulle of felony,
Of hatred, of wreth and of envy;
Swa þat ilk ane wald with other fyght,
And strangelle other, if þai myght.
Þus salle þai hate and stryfe ilk ane,
Ffor peese salle be omang þam nane,
Ne rest, ne eese, ne worschepe,
Bot travayle, and pyne, and schendschepe.
Bot God alle-myghty, and alle-swa alle his
Þat with him salle dwelle in heven blis,

Sall*e* þam in sorow and pyne se
And of þam þai sall*e* have na peté,
Bot hate þam als Godes enmyse.
And þat hatredyn sall*e* þan be ryghtwyse;
Ffor þe fader, þat þan salle be save,
Na peté of þe son þare sall*e* have,
Þat sall*e* be dampned tyll*e* helle payne;
Ne þe son, þat sall*e* be saved þare ogayne,
Sall*e* have na reuthe, ne na pyté,
Of þe fader þat dampned sall*e* be;
Ne þe moder, on þe same manere,
Of þe doghter þat scho lufed here;
Ne þe doghter of þe moder na mare;
Ne þe brother of þe syster þare;
Ne þe syster of þe brother.
Nane of þam sall*e* have reuthe of other;
Ne nane other, þat sall*e* be saved þan,
Sall*e* have reuthe ne peté of dampned man.
Bot when þe ryghtwyse þe synfull*e* sall*e* se
Pyned in hell*e*, glad þai sall*e* be,
Ffor twa skyls, and ioyfull*e* and fayne;
Ane es, for-þi þat þai er skaped þat payne,
Ane other es for-þi þat Godes vengeance
Es ryghtwise, and his ordinance.
Þis proves þe prophete, als þe boke schewes us,
Þare he says in þe psauter þus:
Letabitur iustus, cum
viderit vindictam.
He says þat "ilka ryghtwyse man
Full*e* glad and blyth sall*e* be þan,
When þai Godes vengeance se
On þe synfull*e*, þat þan dampned sall*e* be.
Þe thred blys, als men may in boke rede,
Es veray acord and anehede,
Þat þe saules sall*e* have in heven to-gyder,
With þe bodyse, when þai com þider;
Ffor ilk ane sall*e* folow others will*e*,
And ilk ane othe[r]s lykyng fullfyll*e*;

The redeemed shall feel no pity for those in hell.

No pity is shown to those in hell.

III. The third spiritual bliss is unity and concord.

And als þine ane eghe folows ryght.
Þe tother, þare it settes þe syght,
And nouther may turne, hyder ne þider,
Bot þai both ay turne to-gyder,
Right swa salle God acord with alle his,
And ilk ane with other in that blys;
And to what thyng þe saule has talent,
To þat þe body salle, ay, assent;
And what-swa God þan wille be done
To þat þai salle assent alle-sone;
And what thyng swa þai þan wille,
Þat salle God als-tyte fulle-fylle.
Þis acorde and anehede sall never ceese,
Bot ever-mare last with rest and peese.
Alle salle þai be alle ane in company,
And als a saule and a body.

The damned shall fight and curse one another.

Bot þe dampned þare ogayne salle stryve,
Ilkane with other, for þair wicked lyve;
Ffor ilk ane salle hate other þan,
And ilk ane salle wery other and ban;
Ilk ane salle yherne with other to fyght,
And ilk ane wald sla other if þai myght;

The body shall hate the soul, and the soul the body.

Þe body salle hate þe saule bi skylle,
Ffor þe saule here thoght ay þe ille;
Þe saule salle ay hate þe body,
Ffor þe body wroght þe foly;
And for-þi þat þe saule fyrst syn thoght
And þe body it afterward wroght,
And wyld noght leve, ne stand þare ogayne,
Untylle þe ded þe body had slayne.
Þar-fore bath to-gyder salle dwelle,
With-outen ende, in þe pyne of helle.

IV. The fourth spiritual bliss is power.

Þe ferth blys, omang þe tother alle,
Þat to þe saules, with þe bodyse, salle falle,
Þe whilk salle be saved, es powere;
Ffor þai salle þare have both fer and nere,
Swa mykelle power and maistry
And lordschip, and be swa myghty

þat alle thyng þan salle be done
8492 At þair wille, hastily and sone;
And what-swa þai wille think in thoght,
Alle salle be at þair wille þare wroght;
Ffor alle thing salle be tylle [þam] boghand,
8496 And nathyng salle ogayne þam stand;
Ffor God salle fulle-fylle alle þair lykyng,
And folow þair wille in alle thing.
þus salle þai haf þare gret powere,
8500 And heghnes, for þair awen gret lawnes here,
þat þai had in þair lyfe days,
And þarfor God, in þe gosspelle says:
Qui se humiliat
8504 *exaltabitur.*
He says: "Wha-swa here lawes him ryght
He salle be heghed, in heven bryght."
Bot þe dampned þare ogayne halely,
8508 Salle want alkyn power and maistry,
And þare-with þat salle tharne alle thing,
Of whilk men moght have lykyng.

Those in hell shall lack all power and be in great dread and fear.

þai salle ay be in gret dred and awe,
8512 And under fote ay be halden lawe.
þai salle have nathyng at þair wille,
Bot alle thing þat salle lyke þam ille.
Mykelle sorow þam salle þan bityde,
8516 Ffor þair heghenes here, and þair pryde,
Als þe bok says þat beres wytnes,
And als in þe same gosspelle wryten es:
Qui se exaltat hu-
8520 *miliabitur.*
þat es, "wha-swa heghe here wille him bere
He salle be lawed" and putted in daungere,
þat es in gret daunger of fendes,
8524 In pyne of helle, þat never endes.
þe fyft blys þat salle falle alswa,
To þe saules, þat with þe bodyse salle ga
Tylle heven-ryke, es honoure and worschepe,
8528 Of whilk God him-self salle tak kepe;

V. The fifth spiritual bliss is honour.

The redeemed shall be crowned as kings and emperours.

Ffor þai salle have þare sere honours,
And be corouned, als kynges and emparours.
And sytt in setyls schynand bryght,
With alkyn nobelay, rychely dyght;
With bryghtnes of lyght þai salle be cled,
And gret reverence þam salle be bed,
And be honourd als Godes frendes dere,
Ffor þe worschepe þat þai dyd him here,
In gud werkes, þat tylle him war swete,
Þarfor þus says David, þe prophete:
Omnis honorati sunt
amici tui Deus.
"Þi frendes, Loverd, þat honourd þe
Es mykelle honourd, and swa ay salle be."

The damned shall be reviled and despised.

Bot þe dampned, þat with syn er fyled,
Þare ogayne salle be revyled,
And despysed, and ay schent with-alle,
And stresced ogayne þair wille als thralle,
And pyned with gretter paynes sere,
Þan ever was sene in þis world here;
Þai salle [thole] alle thyng þat schendschepe es
With payn and sorow þat es endles,
Omang hete and cald, vermyn and stynk,
And alkyn fylth þat hert may think;
And alle þe sorow þai þat salle fele,
Salle be endles, als þai salle knaw wele.

VI. The sixth spiritual bliss is security.

Þe sext blys þat to the saules of ryghtwise
Salle be appropryed þan with þe bodyse,
In þe kyngdom of heven, es sykernes,
To dwelle ay þare whare alkyn ioy es,
Ffor þai salle be þare syker and certayne
To have endeles ioy, and never-mare payne,
And to won ay þare, with-outen dout,
And with-outen lettyng, and putting out,
And with-outen alle manere of drede;
Ffor of nathyng þare þai salle have nede,
Þai salle noght far, als men fares here
Þat lyfes ay in dred and were;

Ffor here, both kyng and emparoure
Has dred to tyne þair honoure;
And ilka ryche man has dred alle-swa
His gudes and ryches to for-ga;
And ilk man, þat here fares wele,
Has ay dred angers to fele.

The righteous shall have no fear of losing their happiness.

Bot þai þat salle com tylle heven blys,
Salle never have dred þat ioy to mys;
Ffor þai salle be syker Inoghe þare,
Þat þair ioy salle last ever-mare.
Bot þe dampned men þare ogayne,
Salle ay be dredand in þair payne,

The wicked in hell shall be in continual dread.

Þat þair payns suld eked be,
And be made mare grevous to se,
Ffor þe devels sal, ay, on þam gang
To and fra, over-thewrt and endlang;
And omang þam ay ymagyne,
How þai may eke þair sorow and pyne;
And þe mare payne þat þai tille synfulle salle seke
Þe mare þai þair awen payne salle eke.
And, if þai do swa, it es na ferly,
Ffor þai er ay fulle of Ire and envy.
Þe devels salle ay opon þam gang,
And ay on þam stamp with þair feth omang

Devils shall stamp upon them.

And threst þam doune, in fyre and smoke,
And þarfor says Iob þus in a boke:
Vadent et venient super
eos demones horribiles.
He says, "grysely devels salle gang and com
On þe synfulle þat tylle God war unbowsom."
Þus dredand salle þai ay be þare,
Þat þair payne suld be ay mare and mare;
Ffor þai salle be certayne þare þai dwelle,
Þat þai salle never com out of helle.
Þe sevend blys es ioy parfyte,
Þat þe saules salle have, with gret delyte,

VII. The seventh spiritual bliss is perfect joy.

With þe bodyse þat saved salle be,

And won in heven, whare þai salle ay God se
Ffor-whi ilk ane þare salle þat tyde,
In body and saule be gloryfyde,
And fulle ioy and blys have with-alle,
With alle manere of delyces þat may falle.
Ilk ane with other salle be knawen,
And fele other mens ioy als þair awen;
And mare ioy and blys moght never be,
Þan ilk ane salle þare-on other se.
Þai salle se, in heven-ryke swa wyde,
Many sere ioyes, on ilka syde;
Ffor þare salle be mare sere ioyes þan,
Þan ever couth noumbre erthly man;
Of whilk syght þai salle mare ioy have,
Þan any man moght yhern or crave.

The happiness of the redeemed shall be perfect.

Ilk ane salle be payed swa wele
Of his part of ioy þat he salle fele,
Þe whilk he salle parfytely have þare,
Þat he salle willen yhern no mare;
Þare salle ilk ane many thowsandes se
In sere ioyes, als him-self salle be.
And þe syght of ilka ioy þan,
Salle be swa delytable tille ilka man,
Þat þe ioy of a syght þare salle pas
Alle þe ioyes þat ever in erth was;
And alle þat tylle heven salle be tane
Salle þare þan se þa ioyes ilk ane.

The sight of joy shall be itself a source of happiness to those who are saved.

And þe syght of ilka ioy þare, salle be
Ioy tylle ilka man þat it salle se,
Þan salle ilk man have ma ioyes in heven,
Þan hert may thynk, or tong kan neven;
Þai salle have ioy, with-in and with-out,
Oboven, benethe, and alle obout.
Oboven þam, þai salle have ioyfully
Of þe syght of God alle-myghty,
Binethe þam, of þe sternes and planetes sere,
And þe world þat þan salle be bryght and clere;

Oboven þam, of heven þat þai bryght salle se,
And of other creatures þat fair salle be,
With-in þam, of þe glorifying of man,
8644 Of þe body and saule to-gyder þan;
With-outen þam, of þe blysfulle companyse
Of aungels, and of men ryghtwise.
Þai salle have ioy in alle þair wittes,
8648 In heven with God þare he syttes;
Ffirst þai salle se with þair eghen bryght
Many a fayre blyssfulle syght;
Þai salle þair God apertly se,
8652 And alle þe thre parsons in trinité,
Þe Fader, and Son, and Haly-gaste,
Þat sight salle be þair ioy maste.
Ffor als he es, þai salle him se þan,
8656 Sothfast God, and sothfast man;
Thurgh whilk syght þai salle knaw,
And se alle thing both heghe and law
And se alle þe werkes þat ever God wroght;
8660 And ilk mans dede, and ilk mans thoght,
And alle þat salle in helle be þan,
Ilka develle and ilka man,
And alle payns þat salle be þare,
8664 Þai salle se, both les and mare;
And alle erth, and þe hevens obout,
And alle þat es, with-in and with-out;
Alle salle þai se, thurgh myght and grace,
8668 In þe bryghtnes of Godes face,
Of whilk þai salle ever-mare have syght,
Þat þe mast ioy es in heven bryght.
And for þai salle ay þus God bihald,
8672 Þai salle knaw alle thyng, þat þai knaw wald.
In þis lyfe here men sese him noght,
Bot anely thurgh ryght trowth in thoght,
Als thurgh a myroure be lyknes,
8676 Bot þare salle men se him als he es.
Here men him sese gastly, thurgh grace,
Bot þare salle men se him, face tylle face.

They shall have joy in all their senses.

The sight of the Trinity shall be the greatest joy

In the brightness of God's face the redeemed shall see and know all things.

And þat syght þare salle alle men have,
With-outen ende, þat salle be save.

They shall see the virgin Mary.

Þai salle alle-swa se þare, apertly,
His blysfulle Moder Saint Mary
Þat next syttes God in heven bryght,
Oboven alle aungels, als es ryght;
Ffor he chese hir tylle his moder dere,
And of hir toke flessch and blode here,
And vouched safe to souke hir brest,
Þarfor it es ryght scho sytt him nest.
Scho es swa fayre þare scho syttes,
Þat hir fayrnes passes all mens wittes;
A gret ioy þat may be cald,
Hir fairnes anely to behald.
Þai salle se þare, als þe boke telles,
Alle þe neghen orders of aungels,

The beauty of the angels.

Þat er swa fayre on to loke,
And swa bryght, als says þe boke,
Þat alle fayrnes of þis lyfe here,
Þat ever was sene, fer or nere,
Þat any man myght ordayne defautles,
War noght a poynt to þat fairnes,
Þat þai salle se þar of þat syght
Of þe ordres of þe aungels bryght.
Þai salle se þam fulle pleysand þan,
And servisabylle tylle God and man;
And ilk ane ordre, in þair degré
Salle do þat þat mast lykand salle be,
Bath tylle God and tylle man ryght;
A gret ioy salle be þare of þat syght,

The angels shall shine brighter than the sun.

Ffor ilk ane aungelle bi him-ane
Salle clerer schyne þan ever son schane;
Þat syght men may a gret ioy calle,
To se þe aungels swa bryght alle,
Þat in heven salle be sene to-gyder;
Þat syght salle alle se þat salle com þider.
Swa fayre a syght, als þat salle seme,
Couth never na wytt here ymagyn ne deme.

The redeemed shall see patriarchs, prophets, apostols, evangelists and other righteous men.

Þai salle se in heven alle-swa
Patriarches, and prophetes and other ma,
And apostels and evangelistes,
Þat folowd nane other lyf bot cristes.
Þai salle se Innocentes many ane,
Of whilk som was, in Goddes name slane,
And other martyrs and confessours,
And haly heremytes and doctours,
Þat haly wryt wald teche and ken;
And many other haly men,
Lered and lewed, þat lyfed wele here,
Both religiouse and seculere.

The righteous in heaven shall see holy virgins.

Þai salle se haly virgyns þare
Þat here lufed God, ay mare and mare,
And keped þam chast, for Godes sake,
Of whilk sōm wald þe ded for his luf take.
Þai salle se þare in ioy and blys,
Other þat God salle chese for his,
Als wedded men þat lyfed wele here,
And other many of states sere.
A fayr syght salle be þan to se,
Of alle þe fayr folk þat þare salle be,
Þat bryghter salle schyne þan ever schane son,
Þis syght salle alle se þat þare salle won.

They shall be honoured as kings and emperors.

Þai salle alle-swa apertly se
Ilk ane be worscheped in his degré,
With gret nobelay, and have sere honours,
And alle be als kynges and emparours,
Coround with ryche corouns of blys,
A fulle delytabelle syght salle be þis.
Þai salle se þare þe gret medes,
Þat men salle have þare, for þair gud dedes,
After ilk ane of þam has lyfed here;
And þas er swa mykelle, and many, and sere,

The rewards of those who are saved, shall last for ever.

Þat never ende salle þai have bot last ay,
Þat na man, thurgh wytt, mesure may,
Ne þam reken, ne telle þam kan,
Swa many medes þai salle have þan.

þair medes salle be swa precyouse,
And swa delitable, and plenteuouse,
þat na man lyfand, als þe boke says,
Couth ne myght þam gesce ne prays.
Bot þa medes salle lyke þam als wele,
þat þam secse, als þam þat salle þam fele.

They shall see heaven brighter than the sun.

þai salle se heven fulle large and wyde,
And round and even, on ilka syde,
And bryghter schynand þan ever schane son;
Wele salle þam be þat þare salle won.
A delitable syght þat salle be
Tylle þam þat salle dwelle in þat contré.
þat contré swa fayre es on to loke,
And swa bryght and brade, als says þe boke,

This world is a dunghill compared with heaven.

þat alle þis world, þare we won yhit
War noght bot als a myddyng-pytt
To regard of þat contré swa brade,
þat God swa mykelle and fayr has made.
þat contré es halden swa large a land,
þat with-in þe space of þat myght stand
Many a thowsand of werldes sere,
þof ilk world war als large als þis here;
And þat land es cald soveraynly
þe kyngdom of God alle-myghty,
þe whilk es made als a ceté,
Whare men salle many wonynge-stedes se,
þare alle þe haly men salle dwelle,
þarfor says Crist þus in þe gospelle:
Multi mansiones sunt,
in domo patris mei.

Many dwelling places are in heaven.

He says "wonyng-stedes er many
In þe hows of my fader God alle-myghty."
Our Loverd, his fader hous calles
His kyngdom, þat tille alle his falles,
þe whilk es as a cité bryght,
With alkyn ryches dubbed and dyght,
Als says Saint Iohan, Godes derlyng dere,
In þe apocalyps, on þis manere:

Vidi sanctam civitatem Ierusalem novam descendentem
de celo, paratam sicut sponsam viro suo ornatam.

The words of St. John on the holy city.

"I saw," he says, "þe haly cete
Of Ierusalem, all*e* new to se,
Comand doun fra heven bryght,
Of God all*e*-myghty rychely dyght,
Als bryde, made fayre tyll*e* hir brydegome;"
þus says Saint Iohan he saw come.
þis cete es for to understand,
Haly kyrk þat here es fyghtand
Ogayne þe devell*e* and his myght,
þat it assayles, both day and nyght;
Bot þat fyght sall*e* noght last ay,
It sall*e* last no langer þan tyll*e* domesday.

The church militant.

þan sall*e* haly kyrk, of fyghtyng cees,
And be with God, in rest and pees;
Ffor it es bryde, and God es brydegome;
þan sall*e* þai both to-gyder come,
And in heven won ay to-gyder;
And all*e* þair childer sall*e* þan com þider.
þat to þam has bene bowsom and trewe;
And þat bi-takens þe cete newe;
Ffor þan sall*e* haly kyrk þat tyde,
In heven be new gloryfyde,
And won ay þare with God all*e*-myghty,
In ioy, and myrthe, and melody.
Bot yhit haly kyrk, þat es Godes bryde,
Bihoves be fyghtand, yhit here to abyde

Christ is the bridegroom of the church.

þe comyng of Crist þat es hir brydegome,
þat ay es myghty for to over-come,
Ffor haly kyrk fyghtes for Godes ryght;
And God overcomes thurgh his myght.
On twa-wise may haly kyrk be tane,
And, at þe last, sall*e* bath be in ane;
On a manere es cald haly kyrk fyghtand,
On ane other es haly kyrk over-comand.
þir clerkes says als þe boke beres witnes,
þat haly kyrk, þat here fyghtand es,

Es noght els, bot a gaderyng
Of alle cristen men of lele lyfyng.

The church triumphant.

Haly kyrk over-comand es alle-swa
God with alle þe company of þa
Þat dwelles with him, in his blys,
Þe whilk he has hyght tylle alle his.
Under haly kyrk, þat here fyghtand es,
Er alle gud cristen men, mare and les.
Under haly kyrk þat es over-comand,
Er alle haly men in heven wonand.
Bot haly kyrk þat here fyghtes fast,
After þe day of dome at þe last,
In þe bryght cetè in heven salle won
Ever-mare, with hir spowse Godes Son;
Ffor þan salle þe noumbre fulle-fyld be
Of alle haly men in þat cetè,
Thurgh haly kyrk þat es Godes spowse;
And þat cetè Crist calles his Faders howse,
Ffor þare salle alle men þat er ryghtwise and haly,
Ever-mare dwelle in aungels company;
And ilk ane salle have a blysfulle wonyng,
And ioy parfyte, with-outen endyng.

No one knows how the city of heaven is made.

Þis cetè of heven þat es wyde and brade,
Na man wate properly how it es made,
Ne can, thurgh wrytt, ymagyn in thoght,
Of whatkyn matere it es wroght,
It es noght made of lyme ne stane,
Ne of tre; for of swilk matere has it nane,
Als þir erthly cetese er made of here,
Þat er made of corruptybelle matere;
Ffor na thyng falles to be in þat cetè,
Þat corruptybelle or fayland may be.
Bot þe matere þare-of, als I trow,
Es of alle thing þat es of gret vertow.

It is not made with hands.

Þis cetè was never made with hand,
Bot thurgh þe myght and witt of God alle-weldand
Þis cetè contenes alle heven-ryke
Bot nane wate properly to what it es lyke;

We fynd wryten, þat it es fayre and bryght,
Bot na man kan deseryve it ryght;
Ffor swa wyse clerk was never of lyve,
Þat þe fairnes of it couth properly descryve,
Bot alle-if I kan noght descryve þat stede,
Yhit wille I ymagyn, on myne awen hede,
Ffor to gyf it a descripcion;
Ffor I have þare-to, gret affeccyon;

Hampole says that although he cannot describe heaven, yet he will give an imaginary description out of his 'own head'.

And gret comforth and solace it es to me
To thynk and spek of þat fayr ceté;
Þat travaille may greve me nathyng,
Ffor þare-in have I gret lykyng.
Ogayne ryght trowth nathing I do,
If I lyken þe ceté þat me langes to,
Þe whilk men may lyken on som party,
Bath to bodily thing and gastly.

Heaven may be likened both to 'bodily and spiritual things.'

And for-þi þat alle thing þat es clere and bryght
Es mast lykand here tylle bodily syght,
Þarfor I wille it lyken tille bodily thing.
Þat es fayre to syght with gastly understandyng.
Þe bryght ceté of heven es large and brade,
Of whilk may na comparyson be made
Tille na ceté þat on erth may stand,
Ffor it was never made with mans hand.
Bot yhit, als I ymagyn in my thoght,
I lyken it tylle a ceté þat war wroght
Of gold, of precyouse stanes sere,
Opon a mote[1], sett of berylle clere,

Heaven may be likened to a city of precious stones, set upon a mountain;

With walles, and wardes, and turrettes,
And entré, and yhates, and garettes;
And alle þe walles war made, of þat ceté,
Of precyouse stanes and ryche perré;
And alle þe turrettes, of cristalle schene,
And þe wardes enamyld, and overgylt clene,
And þe yhates of charbucles suld falle,
And þe garettes aboven of rubys and curalle;

The walls of which are formed of precious stones and of pearl;

[1] MS. Lands. 348 reads 'mount'.

And at þat cete had lanes and stretes wyde,
And fayr bygyngs on ilka syde,
Alle schynand als gold bryght burnyst
And with alkyn ryches replenyst;

And the streets paved with precious stones;

And þat alle þe stretes of þe ceté and þe lanes
War even paved with precyouse stanes;
And þat þe brede and lenthe of þat ceté
War mare þan here es of any cuntré;
And þat alle manere of melody
Of musyk and of mynstralsy,
Þat moght be schewed with mowthe or hand,
War continuely þare-in sownand,
And þat ilk day, on sere manere suld falle,
Swa þat na man moght irk with-alle.

And each lane and street full of sweet savours;

And þat ilka lane and ilka strete,
Of þis ceté war fulle of savours swete,
Of spycery and of alle other thyng,
Of whilk any swete savoure moght spryng;
And þat þar war plenté of mete and drynk,
And of alle other delyces þat man may thynk;

And each citizen endowed with as much beauty as Absalom;

And þat ilka citesayne þat wonned þare,
Had als mykelle bewté or mare,
Als Absolon, þat swa fayre was,
Whase bewté moght bi skylle pas
Þe bewté of alle manere of men erthly,
Swa clene he was in lym and body;

As strong as Sampson;

And þare-with als mykelle strenthe had omang
Als Sampson had, þat was so strang,
Þat a thowsand men armed clene
He over-come and felled doune alle bi-dene;

As swift as Asahel;

And þat ilkane war als swyft to pas
And to ryn, als Assahelle of fote was,
And swa swyft was to ryn and ga,
Þat thurgh rase wald turne bath buk and ra;
And þat ilkane had þare-with als mykelle lykyng
And als mykelle þair wille in alle thing,

As wise as Solomon;

Als Salamon had, þat als God vowched save
Þat had alle thyng þat he wald have;

And þat ilkane þar-with, had als mykelle fredome
Als August had þat was emparour of Rome, As free as Augustus;
Tylle whame alle landes of þe world obout
Served, and tille him war underlout;
And þat ilkane had with-alle als continuele hele
Als Moyses had þat was swa lele, As healthy as Moses;
Þat God wald never with yvelle dere him,
Bot anely þat he made his eghen dym;
And þat þare-with, if possible ware,
Ilkane moght als lang be lyfand þare,
Als Matussale namely dyd here, As old as Methusaleh;
Þat lyfed nere a thowsand yhere;
And þat ilk ane moght als mykelle wisdom weld,
Als Salamon had, þat men swa wise held,
Þat thurgh his wisdom had knawyng
Of alle thing and understanding;
And þat ilk ane þare-with lufed als wele or mare,
And als gud frende ay tylle other ware,
Als David tylle Ionathas was kyd, As friendly as David and Jonathan were;
Wham he lufed als he his awen saule dyd;
And þat ilk ane with þat honourd ware
Of alle þe other þat wond þare,
Als Ioseph was of þe Egypciens ryght, As honoured as was Joseph by the Egyptians;
Wham þai lowted als loverd of gret myght;
And þare-with þat ilk ane war in alle thing
Als mykelle als was Alexander the gret kyng As great as Alexander;
Þat conquerd Affryk, Europe and Asy,
Þat contened alle þe world halely;
And þat ilkane acorded with other in anehede,
Als Lisyas with Sampson dyd in dede, As closely united as Lysias and Samson;
Of whilk nouther wald nathing do,
Bot als ayther of þam assented þare-to;
And with alle þis, þat ilkane als syker ware
Of þair dwellyng, to won lang þare,
Als Ennoc and Hely, on þe same wyse, As secure as Enoch and Elijah;
Þat er syker of þair dwellyng in paradyse,
Ffra þe tyme þat þai war þider ravyst,
And salle be untylle þe comyng of Anticrist;

And as joyful as one escaped from the gallows.

And over alle þis, þat ilkane als mykelle joy had
Als he suld have þat war lad
Tylle þe galows, and sodainly in þe gate
War tane and putted tille a kynges state;
And, þare-with, þan[1] tylle ilk ane suld falle
Alle þe ioyes þai moght have alle.
He þat alle þes had, als bifore wryten es,
Suld pass alle þe world in worthines:
What man, thurgh witt, couth telle ioy mare
In þis world to weld, þan alle þis ware?
Ffor wha-swa had alle þese, withouten dout,
Had here ioy inoghe, both with-in and without
With alkyn delyces þat he moght have here,
Specialy in alle his wittes sere,
Þat es to say, in syght and hereyng,
And in smellyng, tastyng and feleyng;
Bot yhit alle þir blysses þat yhe herd me neven
War als noght, als to regard to þe blys of heven;
Ffor als mykelle difference, or mare, suld be
Bitwene heven and swilk a cetė,
Als es bitwene a kynges palays
And a swynsty þat es lytelle to prays,

No comparison may be made between the city of heaven and an earthly city made of gold and pearl.

And na mare comparyson may be made
Bitwene þe cité of heven, wyde and brade,
And swilk a ceté made of gold and perré,
Þan bitwene alle þe world and a faulde may be;
Alle-swa alle ryches þat may here be sene
War noght bot als muk þat es unclene,
To regard of þe precyouse rychesce
Of þe ceté of heven þat na man may gesce.
And alle þe melodyse of þe world sere,
War noght bot als sorow to here,
To regard of þe blyssfulle melody
Þat in þe ceté of heven es ay redy.
And alle swete savours þat men may fele,
Of alkyn thing þat here savours wele,
War noght bot als stynk to regard of þat flayre
Þat es in þe ceté of heven swa fayre;

[1] þat?

And alle þe worschepe þat here may be,
War noght bot als schendschepe to se,
To regard of þe gret worschepe
Of whilk men salle in heven tak kepe.
Alle þe fairnes þat Absolon had in syght,
The beauty of Absolom would be reckoned ugliness in heaven;
War noght bot laythede[1] in heven bryght.
Alle þe strenthe of Sampson þat was pereles,
War noght tald þare bot wayknes.
Alle þe delyces þat had Salomon þe kyng,
War noght in heven bot myslykyng.
Alle þe swyftnes of Assahel þat had he,
The swiftness of Asahel would be but sloth;
War noght þare bot slawnes to se.
Alle þe fredom þat August had whilom,
The freedom of Augustus but slavery;
War noght tald þare bot thraldom.
Alle þe hele þat here had Moyses
War noght tald þare bot als seknes.
Alle þe eld þat Matussale had here,
War les þare þan þe lest day of þe yhere.
Alle þe wisdom þat Salomon had redy
The wisdom of Salomon but folly;
War noght tald þare bot als foly.
Alle þe luf þat David Ionathas lufed,
The love of David and Jonathan but hatred;
War noght þare bot als hatereden proved.
Alle þe honoure þat þe Egypciens Ioseph dyd,
War noght in heven bot schendschip kyd.
Alle þe myght þat Alexander had aywhare,
The might of Alexander but weakness;
War noght tald bot wayknes þare.
Alle þe acord þat Lisyas had in his lyfe
The unity of Lysias and Sampson but strife;
With Sampson, war þar bot als strife.
Alle þe sykernes þat had Ennoc and Ely
The security of Enoch and Elijah but insecurity.
Of þair dwellyng in paradyse, namly,
War noght bot als unsykernes
Of wonyng in heven þat es endles.
Þus may I lyken, als I ymagyn,
Þe cetè of heven and þe blys þare-in,
Tylle a cetè of gold and of precyouse stanes sere
Bot þe cetè of heven es mare bryght and clere,

[1] MS. Lansd. 348 reads 'filþe'.

And es sett on swa heghe a hylle,
Þat na synfulle man may wyn þar-tylle;

The hill upon which Heaven is set, signifies holy meditation.

Þe whilk hylle I lyken tylle berylle clene,
Þat es clerer þan any þat here es sene;
Þat hille es noght els bi understandyng,
Bot haly thoght and brynand yhernyng,
Þat haly men had here to þat stede,
Whils þai lyfed, bi-for þair dede;
Ffor God wille þat þai als heghe up-pas,
Als þair thoght and yhernyng upward was.
Yhit I lyken, als I ymagyn in thoght,

The walls of Heaven made of precious stones signify good works.

Þe walles of heven tylle walles þat war wroght
Of alle manere of precyouse stanes sere,
Cymented with gold fulle bryght and clere;
And swa bryght gold ne swa clene,
Was never nane in þis world sene,
Ne swa ryche stanes, ne swa precyouse,
Als obout heven er, ne swa vertuouse.
Þe precyouse stanes, gastly may be

The gold denotes charity.

Gud werkes, and þe gold charyté,
Þat obout þase in heven salle schine clere,
Þat dose gud werkes in charyté here.
Þe turrettes of heven, gret and smalle,
I lyken tylle turrettes of clere crystalle;
Bot þe turrettes of heven er mare clere shynand

The towers signify the honours of the righteous.

Þan ever was cristalle in any land.
Þa turrettes, gastly, sere honours may be,
Þat gud men, in heven, salle fele and se.
Þe wardes of þe cetè of heven bryght

The 'wards' of silver and gold denote strength, power and might.

I lyken tylle wardes þat war stalworthly dyght
And clenly wroght and craftily tayled
Of clene sylver and gold and enamayld.
Bot þa wardes of þe cetè of heven,
Er mare crafty and strang þam any kan neven,
Bot gastly to speke, þa wardes swa dyght,
May be tald strenthe, and power, and myght,
Þat þas salle have þat in heven salle dwelle,
Als yhe moght here me bifore telle.

þe yhates I lyken of heven swa brade,
Tylle yhates þat war of charbukelle stanes made
Bot swa clere charbukelle was never sene,
Als þa yhates of heven er ne swa clene;

The gates betoken meekness

Bot þa yhates, gastly to speke, er mekenes
And fredom of ryght fayth and bowsomnes,
þat gyfes way and entré tylle men boghsom,
Intylle þe ceté of heven for to com.
þe garettes oboven þe yhates bryght
Of þe ceté of heven, I lyken þus ryght,
Tylle þe garettes of a ceté of gold,
þat wroght war, als I before told,
Of fyne curalle and rych rubys,

The watch-towers wrought of coral and rubies, and ornamented with fine gold wire denote lordship and dignity.

And of other stanes of gret prys,
With fyne gold wyre alle obout frett,
And bryght besandes burnyst omang sett.
þe garettes of heven, gastly, may be
Heghe state, and lordschip, and dignité;
Ffor alle þat salle won in þat ceté þare,
Salle bere heghe state þare-in ever-mare.
þe lanes alle-swa and þe stretes alle,
þat in þe ceté of heven may falle,
And þe wonyng-stedes þat er þar-in,
I lyken here, after I ymagyn,
Tylle þe lanes and stretes, less and mare,
Of þe ceté of gold þat I spak of are,
With þe bygynges on ilk syde standand,
þat of fyne gold war made, bryght schynand;
Bot in na ceté þat men may neven,
Er stedes and lanes swa bryght als in heven;

In no city are there such bright places as in heaven.

Ne swa bryght wonyng-stedes als er þar-in,
Can na man, thurgh wytt, ymagyn,
þe whilk salle schyne, with-in and with-out,
And on ilka syde alle obout,
Whare alle ryghtwyse men salle won at ees,
In ioyfulle quyete, and rest, and pese;
And þarfor haly kyrk, þat oft prays
Ffor þe saules in purgatory, þus says:

Tuam Deus deposcimus pietatem, ut eis tribue-
re digneris lucidas et quietas mansiones.
"Loverd God, we ask þi peté,
þat þou vouche safe, als we pray þe,
To gyf þam wonyng stedes bryght
And restfulle", þat nede has of rest and lyght.
Na bodily eghe moght never here se
A poynt of swilk bryghtnes, als in heven salle be.
Ilka lane in heven and ilka strete
Most schyne bryght, bi skylle, for þar salle mete
Aungels and men bryghter schynand,
þan ever schane þe son in any land;

The bodies of each man in heaven shall shine as bright as the sun.

Ffor þe body of ilk man salle schyne so bryght
þat tylle alle a contré, ane moght gyf lyght;
And ilka hare þare, on þair hede,
And on þair body, on ilka stede,
Salle be als bryght als es þe son,
þat we may se here whare we won,
Fulle bryght schynand oboven us,
And þarfor says þe boke þus:
Fulgebunt iusti sicut sol.
"þe ryghtwis men salle schyne als þe son,"
In heven whare þai salle ever-mare won.
Now sen a ryghtwis man salle schyne als bright
Als þe son dose, þan mon he gyf lyght
Als fer als þe son dose and ferrer,
Fforwhi he salle þan be wele bryghter.
And yhit salle alle þat gret bryghtnes,
þat ryghtwis men salle have þare be les
þan þe bryghtnes of God alle-myghty,
Als salle be knawen þare openly,
Ryght als þe sternes here, whare we won,
Semes als to þe bryghtnes of þe son;
Ffor we salle be þare als sternes in bryghtnes,
And God bryghtest als son of ryghtwisnes.

The lanes and streets in heaven are longer than those of any country on earth.

Ilka lane and strete þat in heven may be,
Es lenger þan here es any contré,

Ffor þe roume and þe space þat ès contende
In þe cete of heven has nane ende.
Þa stretes and lanes, gastly to telle,
Er alle haly men þat þare salle dwelle;
And þair wonyngstedes may be þe medes,
Þat þai salle have for þair gud dedes.
In þat cete salle be mare rychesce
Þan alle þe men of þe world may gesce;
Bot þase ryches gastly to understand,
Er sere blysses and delyces ay lastand,
Þe whilk alle þas, þat tylle heven salle wende,
Salle fele and se þare with-outen ende.
Þe pament of heven may lykened be,
Tille a pament of precyouse stanes and perré;
Bot þe pament of heven salle schyne mar clere
Þan ever schane gold or precyouse stanes here;
And þat pament es sett swa fast,
Þat it salle never fayle bot ay last,
In whilk may na crevyce be sene,
It es swa hale, and even, and clene.
Þis pament of heven als of perré,
Gastly to understand may be
Parfyte luf and lyfe endeles,
With pese, and rest and sykernes,
Þat alle salle have þat salle won þare,
And þis pament salle last ever-mare.
Þus may a man þat kan and wille,
Alle þe cete of heven lyken bi skylle,
Tylle bodily thing þat es fayre and bryght,
And mast delytabelle here to syght,
And to precyouse stanes of vertow,
And to sylver and gold and thing of valow,
Þat men may here bodily se,
Bot swilk thinges may nane in heven be.
Of verray ryches, gret plenté es þare,
Þat er a hundreth thowsand-fald mare
Þan alle þe ryches of þe world here,
Þat ever was sene, fer or nere,

The streets and lanes of heaven denote holy men who shall dwell for ever in heaven.

The pavement of heaven denotes perfect love and endless life.

The riches of heaven surpass all earthly wealth.

Þat fayles and passes oway;
Bot þe rychesce of heven salle last ay,
9208 Þat er alle thing, als God vouches save.
Þat men in heven yhernes to have.

Above the city of heaven shall bright beams only be seen.

Oboven þe ceté of heven salle noght be sene.
Bot bright bemes anly, als I wene,
9212 Þat sal schyne fra Goddes awen face,
And sprede obout and over þat place.
His bright face sal alle þas se,
Þat sal duelle in þat blisful cité;
9216 And þat syght es þe mast ioy of heven,
Als men mught here me byfor neven.
And alle-if þat cité be large and wyde,
Men salle hym se, until þe ferrest syde.
9220 And als wele þas þat sal be fra hym fer,
Als þas þat sal þar til hym be nerrer;
For als men of fer landes may haf sight
Of þe son, þat we se here schyne bright,
9224 And als þe same son þat shynes byyhond þe se
Shewes it here, and in ilka cuntré
Alle þe day, aftir þe ryght course es,
Bot when cloudes fra us hydes hir[1] brightnes;
9228 Right swa þe face of God alle-myghty,

All shall see the face of God, as plainly as they see the sun on earth.

Sal be shewed in heven appertely,
Tille alle þe men þat þider sal wende,
Þogh som suld duelle at þe ferrest ende.
9232 Bot ilk man, als he lufes God here,
Sal won þar, som fer and som nere,
For som lufes God here mar þan sum,
And som lufes hym les þat til heven sal com
9236 Alle þas þat God here lufes best,
When þai com þar sal be hym nerrest,
And þe nerrer þat þai sal hym be,
Þe verreylyer þai sal hym se;
9240 And þe mare verraly þai se his face,
Þe mare sal be þair ioy and solace.

[1] MS. Harl. 4196 reads 'his'.

Bot þa þat here lufs hym les,
Þai sal won þar, aftir þair luf es;
Bot ilk man sal se hym in his degré,
In what syde of heven swa he sal be.
Here haf yhe herd of many fayre sight,
Þat ay salle be sene in heven bright;
Ful glade and ioyful alle þas may be,
Þat swilk fayre sightes, ay, þar sal se,
And of mykel ioy may þai ay telle
Þat in þat cité of heven sal ay duelle.
Alswa ilkan sal haf in þair heryng,
Grete ioy in heven and grete lykyng,
For þai sal here þar aungel sang,
And þe haly men sal ay syng omang,

The righteous shall have great joy in their hearing.

With delitabel voyces and clere;
And, with þat, þai sal ay here
Alle other manere of melody,
Of þe delytable noys of mynstralsy,

They shall hear all kinds of sweet music.

And of alkyn swet tones of musyke,
Þat til any mans hert mught like;
And of alkyn noyse þat swete mught be,
Ilkan sal here in þat cité,
With-outen instrumentes ryngand,
And with-outen movyng of mouth or hand,
And with-outen any travayle,
And þat sal never mar cese ne fayle.
Swilk melody, als þar sal be þan,
In þis werld herd never nan erthely man,
For swa swete sal be þat noyse and shille
And swa delitabel and swa sutille,
Þat alle þe melody of þis werld here,
Þat ever has bene herd, fer and nere,
War noght bot als sorowe and care
Als to þe lest poynt of melody þare.
Omang þam alswa sal be swete savour,
Swa swete com never of herbe ne flour,
When þai war in seson mast,
Or war mast of vertu for to tast;

Among them all shall be sweet savours, sweeter than those springing from any herb or flower.

Ne of spicery mught never spryng,
Ne yhit of nan othir thyng,
Þat thurgh vertu of kynde suld savour wele
Swa swete savour als þai sal fele;

No one can tell how sweet each one shall smell to another.

For na hert may thynk, ne tung telle,
How swete sal ilkan til other smelle;
Þat savour sal be ful plenteuouse,
And swa swete and swa delicious,
Þat alkyn spicery þat men may fele,
And of alle othir thyng þat here savours wele,
War noght bot als thyng þat stynked sour,
Als to regarde of þat delycious savour.
Þan sal þat savour þat es swa swete,
Be ioy til þam, ay when þai samen mete,

Each one shall sing with angels and thank God for his mercy.

Alswa ilkan þat sal won þar,
Sal syng with angels, als I sayd ar,
In swilk tones þat sal be swete to here,
With ful delitabel voyces and clere;
Bot þai sal love God ay in þair sang,
And thank hym of his mercy ay omang;
And ilkan of þat blisful company
Sal speke with othir þar ful swetely,
With laghyng and with lufly sembland,
And say "weles us þat here er wonnand",
And thank God omang þat þam gun wysse
Til mekenes, þat þam led til þat blysse
With anger þat þai had in þair lyf days,
Þan may þai say þus als David says:
Letati sumus pro diebus quibus
nos humiliasti, annis quibus
vidimus mala.
"Loverd ful glad for þe days er we,
In whilk þou made us lawe to be,
In þe yheres in whilk we saw illes."
Þus may þai syng and say for sere skilles.
Þan sal þair sang and þair spekyng,
Be til þam gret ioy and lykyng;

Alswa þai sal fele worshepes grete,
For ilkan sal be sette in a ryche sete,
And, als kynges and qwenes corouned be
With corouns dight with ryche perré,
And with stanes of vertu, precyouse to prays,
Als David til God thus spekes and says:

Each one shall be crowned as kings and queens.

Posuisti Domine super caput eius
coronam de lapide precioso.
"Loverd on hys heved þou sette ryght,
A coroune of preciouse stanes dight;"
Bot swa fayre coroune was never sene
In þis world, on kynges heved ne qwene.
Þis coroune es þe coroune of blys,
And þe stane es ioy þat þai sal never mys.

The crown of precious stones set upon the heads of the righteous denotes their great bliss and joy.

Þis worshepe þat þai sal fele, sal pas
Alle þe worshepes þat ever here was,
Of whilk þai sal þar mar ioy have,
Þan any man can yherne or crave.
Þus sal þai have in þair wittes fyfe
Parfite ioy with endeles lyfe,
In þe heghe blisful cité of heven,
Whar sere ioyes er ma þan tung can neven;
For þai sal many hundreth thowsand se
Of men and wemen in þat cité,
Þat many sere ioyes þar sal haf,
Als þai er worthy and God vouches saf.

There shall be seen in heaven hundreds and thousands of men and women.

And alle þe ioyes þat þai alle sal se,
Sal be ioyes til ilka man þat þar sal be,
With-outen his awen ioyes, les and mare,
Þat til hym-self sal be appropried þare;
For þe sight of ilk ioy þat þai sal se þan,
Sal be ioy þar til ilka man;
For other mens ioyes tham sal like als wele,
Als þai sal þair awen þat þai sal fele;
Þan sal a man haf ma ioyes in heven
Þan any tung couthe telle or neven;
For ilk man sal haf special ioy and mede,
For ilk gude thoght and ilk gude dede,

Each good deed shall receive a separate reward

Þat he ever thoght or wroght open or privé.
Þan may never þair ioys noumbred be,
Þat ilk man in heven when þai com þider
Sal in body and saule haf alle togider,
And never mare of na ioy fele irkyng,
For þai sal ay be new als at þe bigynning,
Of whilk þe leste ioy þar to fele and se,
Sal be mar þan alle þe ioyes of the werld may be

The righteous in heaven shall never be tired of praising God.

Þai sal be fed þar and cled wele,
With ioy of sight þat þai sal fele,
Þai sal wirk þar nan othir thyng,
Bot love ay God with-outen irkyng,
Als a versifiour says in a verse þarby,
Þe whilk es made in metre þus schortly:
Visio sit victus, opus est
laus, lumen amictus.

They shall be fed with the sight of God.

"With þe sight of God þai sal be fed,
And with brightnes of light þai sal be cled,
And þair werk sal be ay lovyng,"
In whilk þai sal haf gret likyng.
Bot þair mast ioy in heven sal be

The sight of the Trinity shall be their greatest joy.

Þe blisful sight of þe trinité,
Þe whilk þai sal se ever-mar;
And þat ioy sal pas alle othir þar,
For ay whilles þai þat sight sal se,
Of alle ioyes þai sal fulfilled be;
And if þai suld þat syght mysse,
Þai myght noght þan haf parfite blis.
For if a man war pyned in helle,
With ma payns þan tung may telle,
And he of Goddes face mught se oght,
Alle his payns suld þan gryefe hym noght.
Now haf I redde here how men sal hafe
Parfite ioy in heven þat sal be safe;

The damned shall have great sorow and pain for ever.

Bot þe dampned men þar ogayne
Sal haf ful sorowe and parfite payne,
With-outen ende for þair wikked lyfe,
For þai sal in alle þair wittes fyve,

Be turmented on sere manere,
With grysely payns, many and sere,
Þat es to say, in syght and heryng,
In smellyng, tastyng, and felyng.
First þai sal in helle about þam se
Mare sorow þan ever in þis werld mught be,
And þe sorow þat þai sal se þar,
Sal be strang payne til þam ever-mare.
Þair wonyng in helle, als says þe buke,
The misery of the damned.
Þai sal se ful of fire and of smoke,
And ful grysely, and myrk, and dym,
And about þam devels ful grym,
Þat with sere payns sal payne þam ay,
Als men mught here me byfor say:
And alle-þogh þai in helle want light,
Yhit sal þai of alle payns haf sight,
Thurgh þe sparkes of fyr þar, als says Saynt Austyn
Noght til þair comfort bot til þair pyne;
Yhit mare sorow þam sal bytyde,
Þai sal here in helle, on ilka syde,
There shall be great noise in hell;
Ful hydus noyse and duleful dyn
Of devels and of synful men þar-yn:
Þai sal here devels þar, rare ful hydusly,
And þe synful men goule and cry;
Þai sal þar, in smellyng, fele mare stynk, *And foul stench;*
Þan hert may here ymagyn or thynk,
Of brynnand brunstan and of pyk,
And of alkyn othir thyng þat es wyk.
Þat stynk, als yhe sal understand wele,
Sal be strang payne til þam to fele;
Al-swa þai sal ilkan other wery,
And myssay and sclaundre God allemyghty,
Þai sal ay stryfe and be at debate,
And cursing and strife.
And ilkan other sal despice and hate.
Omang þam sal never be pees,
Bot hatreden and stryfe þat never sal cees.
Þair throtes sal ay be filled omang,
The throats of the wicked shall be filled with
Of alle thyng þat es bitter and strang,

flame and smoke mixed with brimstone and pitch.

Of lowe and reke with stormes melled,
Of pyk and brunstane togyder welled,
Of molten bras and lede with-alle,
And of other welland metalle:
Þis sal be strang payne til þam to last,
Omang alle othir paynes, lest and mast,
With stryf þat sal be omang þam þan,
When ilkan sal other wery and ban;

There shall be great cold and heat in hell;

Al-swa þai sal fele, als I byfor talde,
Outrageus hete and outrageouse calde,
For now þai sal frese in yse, and now in fire bryn
And be gnawen with-outen and with-in;
Within, als yhe sal understand,
With wormes of conscience ay bytaud;

Dragons, adders, toads, and other vermin;

With-outen, with dragons felle and kene,
Swa hidus was never here nane sene,
With neddirs and tades and othir vermyn,

Beasts of prey as wolves, lions and bears shall gnaw the sinful.

And with many hydus bestes of ravyn,
Als wode wolfes, lyons and beres felle,
Þat sal noght be elles, bot devels of helle,
In liknes of hydus bestes and vermyne,
Þat sal þam gnaw without, to eke þair pyne,
Als in þe sext part of þis boke es wryten.
Þus sal þe synful be gnawen and byten
With outen, thurgh hydus bestes and vermyn,
And thurgh þe worme of conscience with-in.

Devils shall smite them with glowing hammers.

Þe devels alswa sal stryke þam felly,
With glowand hamers, ful huge and hevy,
Þat sal seme of iren and stele;
Þir payns þai sal with alle other fele.
Þus sal þai ever-mare be pyned þar,
In alle þair fife wittes, als I said ar,
With sere payns als es gode skille,
For þai here used þair wittes ille.

These pains shall torment the soul as well as body.

Alle þir payns þat yhe herd me telle,
And many ma þat salle be in helle,
Þai sal thole ay þar þat sal wende þider,
In body and saule alle to-gider.

þus sal þai ever mar contynuely
Haf parfite payne þar, with-outen mercy,
Fra whilk payne and sorow God us shilde,
Thurgh prayer of hys moder mylde,
And þe right way of lyf us wysse,
Whar-thurgh we may com til heven blysse. Amen.
Now es þe last part of þis buke sped,
And alle þe maters þar-in haf I red,
þat contenes, als yhe mught here,
Bathe general and special ioyes sere,
þat alle þas þat til heven sal come,
Sal haf aftir þe day of dome;
And sere schendshepes of helle alswa,
þat er even contrary til þa,
þe whilk, þas þat sal til helle wende,
Sal haf þar, with-outen ende.

The matters of this book are now brought to an end.

Whar-for wha-swa of þis wil take hede,
May be stird til luf and drede;
Til drede, thurgh mynde of þe hydusnes
Of payne and sorow þat in helle es;
Til luf, thurgh mynd of ioyes and blisse sere
þat God hetes til alle þat lufes hym here.

Those who have read these things and will take heed, may be 'stirred to love and dread'.

Bot þe drede es noght medeful to prufe,
þat accordes noght halely with þat lufe;
For if drede stand by itself anely,
Na mede of God it es worthy,
þarfor drede suld be lufes brother,
And ayther of þam stand with other,
For wha-swa lufes God on ryght manere
He has grete drede to wrethe hym here;
þan lufes he his bydynges to fulfille,
And dredes to do oght ogayne his wille,
Delites to be with God ay,
And dredes to be put fra hym oway.

Fear without love is not worthy of reward.

For men suld noght drede God anly for payne
Bot men suld drede to tyn þe ioy soverayne,
þat es, þe syght of God of heven,
þe whilk yhe herd me byfor neven;

Love and fear must go together

Þat[1] es þat luf ay with þat drede,
And þat dred of God es worthy mede,
For þogh we suld never helle se,
Ne [for] syn suld never punyst be,
In purgatory ne in helle,
Ne in þis werld whar we duelle,

We should love God for himself.

Yhit suld we luf God for hym-self ryght,
And drede to tyne hys luf and of him þe syght,
For, sikerly I dar wele say þis,
Þat wha-swa wyst what ioy and blys
Of þe syght of God in heven war,
And als proprely had sene it als es þar,
He had lever thole here þis payne,
Ilk day anes, alle qwik[2] to be flayne,
Ar he þe syght of his face suld tyne,
Þat in heven so bright sal shyne.
Many sere ioys ma þar sal falle,
Bot þat sight es mast principalle ioy of alle;
For þat ioyful sight sal contene
Alle other ioyes þat sal þar be sene,
Of whilk ioys, þe lest sal pas
Alle þe ioy þat ever here was.

Earthly joys are passing vanity.

For ioy here es noght bot passand vanité,
Bot þe ioyes þat er þar ever-mar sal be,
Til whilk ioyes þat has nan ende,
God us bring when we hethen wende. Amen.
Now haf I here als I first undir-toke,
Fulfilled þe seven partes of þis boke,

The contents of the 'Pricke of Conscience'.

Þat er titeld byfor to have in mynde.
Þe first es of þe wrechednes of mans kynde;
Þe secunde es of þe werldes condicions sere,
And of þe unstabelnes of þe werld here;
Þe thred es of þe ded þat es bodily;
Þe ferthe alswa es of purgatory;
Þe fift es of domesday, þe last day of alle,
And of þe takens þat byfor sal falle;

[1] Þau (MS. Harl. 4196.)
[2] The MS. reads 'qwilk'.

þe sext es of þe paynes of helle to neven;
And þe sevend part es of þe ioyes of heven.
In þir seven er sere materes drawen
Of sere bukes, of whilk som er unknawen,
Namly til lewed men of England,
þat can noght bot Inglise undirstand;
þarfor þis tretice drawe I wald
In Inglise tung þat may be cald
Prik of Conscience als men may fele,
For if a man it rede and understande wele,
And þe materes þar-in til hert wil take,
It may his conscience tendre make,
And til right way of rewel bryng it bilyfe,
And his hert til drede and mekenes dryfe,

It is called the 'Prick of Conscience', because if a man read and understand well the matters therein, it will make his conscience tender and stir him to dread and mekness.

And til luf and yhernyng of heven blis,
And to amende alle þat he has done mys.
For þe undirstandyng of þir maters seven,
þat men may in þis buke se and neven,
May make a man knawe and halde in mynde,
What he es here of his awen kynde,
And what he sal be, if he avyse hym wele,
And whar he es, for to knaw and fele.
Yhit may he se when he it redes
What he es worthy for his dedes,
Whether he es worthy ioy or payne
þis tretice may make hym be certayne,
For þar-in may he many thynges se,
þat has bene, and es, and þat sal be;
þus may þis tretice, with þe sentence,
Pryk and stirre a mans conscience,
And til mekenes and luf and drede it dryfe,
For to bring hym til ryght way of lyfe.

It will bring him into the right way of life.

Of alle þeis I haf sere maters soght,
And in seven partes I haf þam broght,
Als es contende in þis tretice here,
þat I haf drawen out of bukes sere,
Aftir I had in þam understandyng,
Alle-if I be of symple kunnyng.

The author desires to be excused for faulty rhymes.

Bot I pray yhou alle, par charité,
Þat þis tretice wil here or se
Yhe haf me excused at þis tyme,
If yhe fynde defaut in þe ryme,
For I rek noght, þogh þe ryme be rude,
If þe maters þar-of be gude.
And if any man þat es clerk,
Can fynde any errour in þis werk,

He desires that if any man find an error, he will correct it.

I pray hym he do me þat favour,
Þat he wille amende þat errour;
For if men may here any errour se,
Or if any defaut in þis tretice be,
I make here a protestacion,
Þat I wil stand til þe correccion
Of ilka rightwyse lered man,
Þat my defaut here correcte can.
Þis tretice specialy drawen es
For to stirre lewed men til mekenes,
And to make þam luf God and drede;
Ffor wha-swa wil it here or rede,
I hope he sal be stirred þar-by.

The man that reads this book, and is not 'stirred' thereby, must be either foolish or wicked.

Yf he trow þat God es alle-myghty,
And he sal it here or se,
And may noght þar-by stirred be,
It semes þat he es wittles,
Or over mykel hardend in wikkednes.
Bot alle þas þat redes it, loud or stille,
Or heres it be red with gode wille,
God graunt þam grace þat þai may
Be stird þar-by til ryghtwyse way,
Þat es, tille þe way of gude lyfyng,
And at þe last be broght til gude endyng.
And yhe þat has herd þis tretice red
Þat now es broght til ende and sped,
For þe luf of our Loverd Ihesu,

Pray specially for the compiler of this book.

Pray for hym specialy þat it dru,
Þat if he lyf, God safe hym harmles,
And mayntene hys lyf in alle gudenes,

And if he be ded, als falles kyndely,
God of his saule haf mercy,
And bryng it til þat blisful place
Whar endeles ioy es and solace,
Til whilk place he us alle bryng;
Þat for us vouched safe on rode to hyng. Amen.

Explicit tractus qui dicitur, Stimulus Consciencie.

Here endes þe tretice þat es called Pryk of Conscience.

NOTES.

Page 1. l. 5 *spede*, prosper. 8 *endyng*, death. 9 *ar*, ever. 17 *beyng*, existence, 25 *sythyn*, afterwards.

Page 2. l. 48 *skylle*, cause, reason. 49 *dom*, dumb. 50 *bughsom*, buxom obedient. 51 *lof*, praise. 56 *at*, that.

Page 3. l. 71 *herth*, earth. 74 *digne*, worthy. 76 *wytte*, *skille* and *mynde*, sense, reason and memory. 82 *felle*, skin. 96 *mon (=mun)*, shall.

Page 4. l. 107 *hight*, promised. 115 *kydde*, showed. 121 *love*, praise. 122 *unkynd*, lit. unnatural and hence ungrateful. 129 *wake (=wayke)*, weak.

Page 5. l. 139 *lyggus*, lies. 162 *unkunnand*, ignorant. 156 *can*, knows 166 *unskylwys*, without reason. 169 *unkunnyng*, ignorance.

Page 6. l. 183 *trofles*, idle stories, uninstructive fables. 182 *And til*, evidently an error for *un-til*. 187 *kun*, learn by rote, pret *kund*. 196 *unknawyng*, ignorance. 208 *tyttest*, soonest.

Page 7. l. 226 *lytherness*, wickedness. 230 *mynd*, to put in mind. 237 *lettyng*, hindrance. 242 *mase*, makes. 250 *thoght*, an error for *yhouthe*.

Page 8. l. 253 *þer (=þir)*, these. 272 And to all that might be pleasure to him. 283 *pays*, pleases.

Page 9. l. 306 *þat þam thynk hard*, that to them seems hard. 320-321 MS. Y. has the following reading:

"He saiþ 'in his wordes trowed þey,
And alowed his preysyng as þei couþ sey'."

loved = *alowed* = praised, *lovyng* = *preysyng* = praise.

Page 10. l. 326 *quert*, joy. 336 *drawen*, composed. 354 *to rede*, to be read.

Page 11. l. 368 *to luk*, to be seen. 381 *tuk kepe*, took notice.

Page 12. l. 421 *shortly*, briefly. 424 *ertou*, art thou.

Page 13. l. 443, 444 *geten*, conceived. 455 *caytefte*, wretchedness. 459 *glet*, slime. *loper*, coagulated. 471 *alstite*, immediately.

Page 14. l. 475 *ligge*, lie. 477 *gowl*, howl, yowl. 496 *gretyng*, weeping. 503 *sembland*, appearance.

Page 15. l. 509 *pure*, poor. 520 *rym* (=*reme*), membrane. 535 *fulfild*, filled with.

Page 16. l. 566 *fen*, mud, dirt, filth. 575 *eghen*, eyes.

Page 17. l. 593 *wantes*, is lacking. This verb is here used impersonally with the dative. 594 *laykyng*, sport, play.

Page 18. l. 613 *brethe*, vapour. 614 *hard ne nesshe*, hard nor soft. 628 *myddyng*, dunghill. 645 *graythely*, carefully.

Page 19. l. 684 *tas*, toes.

Page 20. l. 689 *wyght*, brave. 691 *angers and yvels*, pains and diseases. 698 *mescheefes*, misfortunes. 701 MS. Y. reads:

"Steches gowtes and other maladys."

707 *welks*, fades, lit. becomes white. 712-15 MS. Y. reads:

"Man he saiþ as a flour bright
Furst comeþ forþe to þe sight,
And sone es broken and passeþ awey
As a *schalde webbe* in somers day."

Page 21. l. 725 *floresshe*, should be *flouresshes*. 729 *neghen*, nine. 731 *bycom*, became. 741 *yhere*, years. 756 *held*=*eld*, old age. 757 *hele*, health. *weld*, govern.

Page 22. l. 762 *fon* (pl. of few) =*fone*, see l. 764, 765. 773 *rouncles*, MS. Y. reads: *ryveleth*, wrinkles. 774 *His mynde es short*, His memory is not retentive. 775 *hand*=*and*, breath. 776 *wax*, should be *waxes*. 777 *gas*, goes. 780 *for-worthes*, comes to nothing. 781 *moutes*, moults, falls off. 786 *lyghtly*, easily. 788 *souches*, suspects, is suspicious. 789 *trowyng*, opinion, belief. 791 *sembland*, appearance.

Page 23. l. 797 *lakes*, censures, blames. 798 *granand*, groaning. 799 *angerd*, troubled, disturbed. 812 *sleghe*, crafty, wise. 816 *frount*, forehead. 817 *heldes*, bends, bows. 822 *pouce*, pulse. *styringes*, movements. In Wicliffe's Apology we have 'His *steringes*' "voluntatis suae *motus*."

Page 24. l. 856 *what-kyn*, what kind of. 860 *ugly*, horrible. 863 *to-gnaw*, gnaw away.

Page 26. l. 917 *uglynes*, horror. 939 *aght*, ought.

Page 27. l. 949 *fikel*, treacherous, deceptive. 961 '*world of world*', eternity. 966 *hight*, called.

Page 28. l. 996 *sternes*, stars.

Page 29. l. 1027 *bisens*, examples.

Page 30. l. 1060 *wayn*, vain. 1064 *tharlles*=*thralles*, slaves. 1074 *ken*, know. 1090 *fraistes*, tries.

Page 31. l. 1106, 1108 *tane*, the one, the first. 1127 *yhernyng*, lust, desire.

Page 33. l. 1181 *sleghtes*, crafts, contrivances. *qwayntyse*, cunning. 1183 *tilles*, leads. 1186 *waytes*, watches. 1189 *taries*, mocks, deludes. 1197 *fantome*, vanity. It sometimes signifies a lie;

"This is no *fantum*, ne no fabulle,
ȝe wote wele of the Rowuntabulle."

The Avowynge of King Arther &c., Robson's Met. Rom. ii, p. 57.

Page 34. l. 1205 *bymene*, to be explained. 1207 *whyn*, O that! 1208 *neghe*, approach, come near. 1217 *ken*, keen. 1224 *wawes*, waves. 1228 *wolwes*, wolves. 1229 *worow men bylyve*, strangle men quickly, see Glossary. 1230 *rogg* = *rugg* = tear, rend.

Page 35. l. 1239 *pases*, paths, narrow passages. 1250 *umset*, surrounded. 1260 *be taken* = *be-taken*, to betoken. 1268 *flay*, to terrify, frighten.

Page 36. l. 1272 *oftesythes*, oft times. 1277 *sho*, she. *lates*, lets. 1279 *wa to wele*, woe to weal. 1281 *þir*, these.

Page 37. l. 1319 *drove*, disturbs, afflicts. 1322 *tokenyng* = *takenyng*, token, sign. 1334 *happy*, fortunate, see l. 1339. 1338 *þa*, those.

Page 38. l. 1368 *syker*, sure, certain. 1374 *gestes*, guests. 1375 *hethen*, hence.

Page 39. l. 1385 *commelyng*, a foreigner, used to translate *advena*. 1390 *swythe*, quickly. 1393 *lele*, loyal. 1397 *war* = *ware*, cautious, careful. 1400 *dede*, death, see l. 1402. 1403 *over-lightly*, very easily. 1413 *variand*, varying, see l. 1426. 1415 *vedirs*, weathers, see l. 1424.

Page 40. l. 1432 *wate*, knows. 1443 *douiland*, evidently an error for *domland*, Sc. *drumly*, N. E. *dromland*, dark, cloudy.

Page 41. l. 1452 *Now er men wele, now er men wa*, Now are men happy, now are men sorrowful. 1453 *faa*, foe. 1456 *pyn*, pain. 1459 *orlitel* = *over-litel*, *mesur*, moderation. 1460 *bigg*, well furnished. 1463 *fande*, try. 1464 *smert*, *smart*, quick. 1468 *were*, war. 1470 *saghtel*, reconciliation, concord. 1478-79 The correct reading seems to be:

"Þarfor þe world þat clerkes sees þus helde,
Es als mykel to say als þe *werldes* elde."

Page 42. l. 1487 *to mette*, to measure, *mete*. 1492 *haterel*, top of the head, the poll. 1502 *elde*, age. 1520 *havyng*, behaviour.

Page 43. l. 1522 *costage*, expense. 1525 *hauntes*, practises. 1528 *wrynchand*, twisting.

> "And, if som smithfeild Ruffian take up som strange going: some new mowing with the mouth: some *wrinchyng* with the shoulder, som new disguised garment, or desperate hat—whatsoever it cost—gotten must it be and used with the first; or els the grace of it is stale and gone." The Scholemaster by R. Ascham, p. 44. Ed. Major 1863.

1539 *hypand als a ka*, limping as a cow. 1540 *new gett*, new fashion. 1543 *gang*, walk. 1548 *hasty myschewes*, sudden misfortunes. 1551 *wreth*, to make angry, irritate. 1557 *fyndynges*, inventions.

Page 44. l. 1561 *controves*, contrives.

Page 45. l. 1599 *unbowsome* = *unbuxom*, disobedient. 1616 *þam sall be wa*, to them shall be woe.

Page 46. l. 1651 *clomsed*; *cursed* is perhaps too strong a rendering, if the word is derived from O.E. *clomsen, clumsen.* The literal meaning would seem to be 'benumbed' and hence 'stubborn', 'blockish'.

Page 47. l. 1680, 1681 *dede*, death. 1682 *redes*, explains. 1686 *kyndely*, natural. 1687 *twynyng*, separation. 1688 *full*, very. 1704 *onence*, against.

Page 48. l. 1709 *twyn*, separate. 1718 *gayn-turnyng*, returning. 1732 *wild*, desired, pret of *wille* or *willen*, to desire. The pret of wille as an auxiliary verb = *wald.*

Page 49. l. 1750 *a dede brayde*, a death assault, pain. 1776 *mynde*, remembrance. 1777 *thurgh kynde*, naturally. 1781 *swet*, pret of *swete*, to sweat.

Page 50. l. 1788 *skulkes*, hides. 1810 *overalle*, everywhere. 1817 *tast*, experience.

Page 51. l. 1820 *stoure*, conflict. 1849 *samen*, to be together. 1852 *A* = *ane*, one.

Page 52. l. 1881 *reward*, regard. 1883 *thewes*, manners. 1890 *dede hand*, death's hand.

Page 53. l. 1907 *fested*, fastened. 1913 *occupyde*, filled. 1915 *at a titte*, with a sudden jerk, with a tug. 1917 Each vein and each sinew and member.

Page 54. l. 1938 *unsleghe*, unwise, foolish. 1944 *wayte (= wate)*, knows 1946 *forluke*, foresee.

Page 55. l. 1970 *wake*, watch. 1971 *dedys*, death's. 2000 *yhate*, gate.

Page 56. l. 2011 *chalanges*, claims. 2025 *felled*, felt. 2027 and 2036 *tynes*, loses. 2044 *drighe*, suffer.

Page 58. l. 2088 *myndles*, forgetful. 2101 *thraws*, throes. 2102 *quathes* = *wathes*, evils, dangers.

Page 60. l. 2163 *laghe*, law. 2167 *Thar*, need. 2172 The sense would seem to require that we should read: 'he þat *can* this lif despyse' instead of '*he þat þis lif despyse*'.

Page 61. l. 2196 *swippes*, passes quickly. 2206 *alle-if*, although. 2210 *aparty*, partly. 2216 *redde*, told.

2217 'Why þe dede es swa gretely drede' should be?
'Why the dede es swa gretely to drede'.

2224 *fare*, go. 2226 *grymly*, savagely. *gryn*, to open the mouth wide. *blere*, put out the tongue. 2224-27 MS. Y. reads:

"Ffor as wode lyons þey schul fare,
To raumpe on hem and grenne and stare,
And grymly on hem grone and hare tonges blere,
And with hidous lokes hem sore afere."

2231 *ferdnes*, fear.

Page 62. l. 2249 *drogh*, drew. 2257 *flit*, depart. 2264 *ta* = *tane*, the first. 2265 see l 2011.

Page 63. l. 2309 *sleght*, wisdom, craft.

Page 64. l. 2320 *saghe*, saw. 2342 *warne*, unless.

Page 65. l. 2353 *kynd*, natural. 2368 *war-so* = *whar-swa*, where-so.

Page 66. l. 2391 *grete mude; 'eger mode'* is a better reading; *mude, mode* = *mood*, mind. Cf. phrases '*milde mode*', '*evil mode*', 'mengid in *mode*', i. e. 'confused in mind'. 2416 *halely*, wholly.

Page 67. l. 2446 *þe* should be *þi*? 2449 *to see*, to be seen. 2453 *fele*, many. 2460 *aresoned*, called to account.

Page 68. l. 2466 *unsyker*, uncertain. 2467 *alowed*, praised. 2469 *sikerly*, securely.

Page 69. l. 2510 *awe*, ought. 2511 *yhelde*, reward. 2516 *what=wate*, knows.

Page 70. l. 2552 *deres*, injures, harms. 2562 *myspays*, displeases.

Page 72. l. 2623 *strik, strek*, straight, direct.

Page 73. l. 2666 *whate=wate*, knows. 2682 *spedde*, finished. 2685 *neghest*, next.

Page 74. l. 2722 *hentes*, receives, takes.

Page 75. l. 2750 ',For þai sal haf *[in]* a day þare."

Page 76. l. 2791 *crysom*, an error for *uncrysom*. *Chrisome* signifies properly the white cloth which is set by the minister of baptism upon the head of a child newly anointed with *chrism* after his baptism: now it is vulgarly taken for the white cloth put about or upon a child newly christened, in token of his baptism, wherewith the women used to shroud the child if dying within the month; otherwise it is usually brought to church at the day of Purification. *Chrisoms* in the bills of mortality are such children as die within the mouth of birth, because during that time they used to wear the chrisom cloth; and in some parts of England, a calf killed before it is a month old is called a chrisom-calf.—Blount in Halliwell p. 249.

Page 78. l. 2864 *nedly*, of necessity.

Page 80. l. 2915 *ferdelayk*, fear. 2933 *mot*, must. 2947 *acouped=acoulped*, accused. *felony*, crime.

Page 81. l. 2953 *qwyte*, free.

Page 82. l. 2991 *Als*, also. *grege*, increase. 2993 *sleuthe*, sloth. *potagre*, disease in the feet. 2995 *kylles*, ulcers. *felouns and apostyms*, whitlows and imposthumes. 2999 *swynacy*, quinsey. 3001 *meselry*, leprosy. 3008 *Thynk we*, let us think.

Page 83. l. 3037 *be it ane*, by itself.

Page 85. l. 3126 *was hoven*, was raised, see Glossary.

Page 86. l. 3148 *caffe*, chaff.

Page 87. l. 3173 *styther*, stronger. 3175 *loud or stille*, openly or secretly, publicly or privately. 3183 The sense requires *than* before *byhoves*. 3189 *sadde*, solid. 3192 *mene* = *mean*, moderate.

Page 88. l. 3213 *haf* for *has* or *hafes*? 3214 *hend and fete*, hands and feet. 3239 *are*, before. *wyn*, go.

Page 89. l. 3248 *defaut*, want. 3256 *dungen*, smitten, beaten.

Page 90. l. 3287 *For sum here þat als tite aftir þair dede*, sal wend strykly til heven blis. The word *þat* should be omitted or we must read: "For sum *er* here þat &c, &c." 3288 *strykly*, straight, direct 3289 *mys*, wrong. 3292 *boght*, redeemed. 3298 *stonde*, time.

Page 91. l. 3323 *smertly*, quickly, *smartly*. 3325 *fere*, frighten. 3331 *For it es nan &c.* = "For *there* is none &c. 3338 *Whar* = *war*, were.

Page 92. l. 3362 *hede*, head, chief. 3363 *hatreden*, hatred. 3367 *forsweryng*, perjury. 3370 *omang*, at intervals.

Page 93. l. 3400 *rede*, tell. 3402 *housil*, the Sacrament. 3404-9 MS. Y. has the following reading:

"General schrift þat may eche day be made
And benyson of bischop þat makeþ þe soul glade
And namly in þe ende of þe holy masse,
Ffor hit es grete mede boþe to more and lasse,
And knockyng on þe brest and knelyng in þe grounde,
And þe last anoyntyng on þe dethus stounde.

3408 *Knokyng of* þe *brest &c.* i. e. confession. 3413 *alans*, at once.

Page 94. l. 3434 *o[f]*, *o* is correct and very common in the 'Cursor Mundi'. 3447 *myster*, need.

Page 95. l. 3468 *sary*, sorrowful. 3473 *debate*, contest, strife. 3478 *ianglyng*, idle talk, idle stories. 3484, 85 *bann*, *ban*, curse. 3487 *na* should be *nane*. 3491 *ma*, more.

Page 96. l. 3507 *Ryse he*, let him rise. 3510 *forthynkyng*, repentance. 3514 *wolwarde*, wretched, plagued. 3515 *hardnes*, severity, affliction. 3519 *fayntise*, deceit. 3522 *unkyndnes*, ingratitude. 3534 *fande*, tempt, try. 4535 *sande*, message, messenger.

Page 97. l. 3546 *heke* = *eke*, increase. 3555 *theches*, teaches. Cf. *feth* = *fet*, *wythenes* = *wytenes &c.*

Page 98. l. 3589 *messyng*, mass. 3594 *twyn*, two. 3608 *byhyng*, ransom. 3610 *assethe*, amends, satisfaction. 3611 *Als*, also.

Page 99. l. 3624 *frende*, friends.

Page 100. l. 3678 *For alle be it onence* þe *doer dede*, i. e. 'For although it be against the *doers deed*.

Page 103. l. 3781 þ*at*, what.

Page 104. l. 3827 *thechyng*, teaching. 3835 *spers*, locks, fastens.

Page 105. l. 3844 *playn*, full. 3870 *lagher*, lower.

Page 106. l. 3877 *underloutes*, subjects.

Page 107. l. 3915 *large*, free, liberal. 3923 þ*ar-for*, i. e. for that (purpose). 3934 *gesce*, to be reckoned.

Page 108. l. 3951 *hat*, called.

Page 109. l. 3986 *aghtynd*, eighth. 3988 *neghend*, ninth. 3996 *pousté*, power.

Page 110. l. 4025 *Says us*, tell us. 4026 *world endyng*, world's ending. 4028 *lukes* þ*at yhow desayve na man*, i. e. 'see that na man deceive you'. 4036 *erthedyns*, earthquakes. 4053 *trowage*, homage, fealty.

Page 112. l. 4119, 25 *heghe*, to exalt. 4130 *lyvyng*, life.

Page 113. l. 4153 to 4215. The following lines on Antichrist are from the 'Cursor Mundi' fol. 124. (Cott. MS. Vesp. A. iii.)

Nu sal yee her, i wil you rede
Hu þat anticrist sal brede,

Nathyng sal I fene yow neu
Bot þat I find in bokes treu.
Þir clerkes telles þat or wise
Þat he o Iuus king sal rise.
And o þe kind, man clepes dane,
Þat prophet mas o þus his nam.
Dane he sais 'neder in strete,
Waitand hors to stang[1] in fete,
To do þe rider falle bi þe wai,
Þat als mikel es for to sai
By þe wai als nedder sal he sitt,
Þat all þaa men þat he mai witt,
Ridand in þe reule o right,
He sal þam smeit and dun þam light.
He sal þam give ful attre[2] dint,
Ute of þair trouth þam for to stint.
O fader and moder he sal be born,
Als other men es him biforn,
Bituix a man and a womman,
And noght of a maiden allan,
Als it es foli tald[3] o sum
Noght tuix a biscop and a nun,
Bot of bismer[4] brem[5] and bald,
And *geten* of a glotun scald,
Þat þar mai be na fuler tuin.[6]
He sal be geten al in sin.
Geten in sin and born in plight,
Over alle he sal be maledight.
In his *geting*[7] þe feind of helle,
Sal crepe in his moder to duelle;
Maister of errur and of pride,
Þar-in he sal his birth abide
Þof he be in prisun bunden,
Als it in hali writt es funden,
Þat Sent Gregor self has wroght,
Þarfor he sais, he lies noght
Þe kind o strenght þat he had ar
Þof þan his might be *laten* mare,
Þat his might es noght sal yee knaun;
Ur laverd has don it als for his aun.
Ffor if he moght, al wald he quelle
Ffor-þi he bunden has þat felle.[8]

[1] *stang* = *sting*, pierce. [2] poisonous. [3] reckoned. [4] a wicked one. [5] lustful. [6] combination. [7] conception. [8] wicked one.

He sal be losed þan o band
And mikel wa sal werc in land;
Þis es he þat sorful dring[9]
We rede of in bok o sceuing;[10]
An angel he sais isagh lendand
Wit a mikel cheigne in hand,
And bar þe kai o þe mikel pitt
Als sais Sant Iohn in hali writt.
To þe dragon suith he wan,
Þat men calles devel and sathan,
And in þat pitt him *sperd* fast
For to be laisd at þe last
To quils a thusand yeir at þe last;
Quen þat thusand yeir war past,
To walk his forth fra þat quile
And mani man for to bigile
Right sua þe devil sal descend
In anticrist moder lend,[11]
To fille þat caitif ful unclene
And umbelai hir al bidene,
Al in his weild[12] hir to receive,
And do hir þoru a man conceve,
Þat al þat birth þat þar es born
Be wick and fals and felun lorn,
Fforþi his nam es cald wit right
Sun o tinsel[13] þat maledight,
For al þat he may wirc þar-to
Al manskind he sal fordo.
Of his *geting* i tald yow ar,
Of his birth I telle you quar;
Ffor als þat crist him-selven chese
Be born in bethleem for ur ese,
His maidenhede for to bring in place,
Þat he tok for us wit his grace
Right sua sal þe feind him þis,
Chese him stede o birth iwise.
Þat best es titeld til his stalle,
Quar es þe rote of ivels alle,
Þar left o godd men makes sin in,
Þat es, tun o babilon wit-in;
Þis tun was quilum chefe o pers
O mani other alsua divers,
A tun o selcuth mikel pride,
Hefd o maumentri þat tide,

[9] chieftain. [10] 'book of revelations'. [11] loins. [12] power. [13] perdition'

Bethsaida and Corazaim
Þir tua cites sal foster him.
Ur laverd snaips[14] þir tua tuns,
And þus he sais in his sermuns:
'Corozaim ai bo ye waa,
And sua be ye Beth[s]aida,
And Capharnaum ai wa ye be!
Þe sinful sun sal regne in þe;
Þof þou þe rais up until heven
To helle depe sal þou be driven.'
Norys him sal enchaunters,
O nigramanci and o jugulors,
Of alle maner o craftes ille;
Of alle falshed þai sal him fille,
Þe wicked gastes his wiers[15]
Him foluand in al his afers.

Page 114. l. 4180 *upstegher*, one who goes up, from *stegh*, to ascend. MS. Y. reads *upstirt*. 4202 *weried*, cursed.

Page 115. l. 4210 *nuryst*, nurtured. 4213 *tregettour*, a magician. It sometimes signifies a cheat. Cf. O. E. *treget*, a trick. 4220 *se*, seat. 4228 *fals trowth*, false belief.

Page 116. l. 4248 *welk*, walked. 4257 *A* = *ane*, one. 4258 *thurgh fals miracles shewyng*, i. e. through the manifestation of false miracles. 4268 *suthfastnes*, truth.

Page 117. l. 4306 *stey*, ascend. 4316 *chace*, drive.

Page 118. l. 4339 *ourwar*, anywhere. 4349 *trace*, path, track, and hence example.

Page 119. l. 4359 *ferre*, far. 4368 *chymné*, fireplace.

"Damesele loke ther be
A ffuyre in the chymené
Ffagattus of fyre tre
That fetchyd was ȝare."

Sir Degrevant in Thornton Romances p. 234, Ed. Halliwell.

Page 120. l. 4400 *felaghshepe*, fellowship.

Page 122. l. 4477 *werray*, to make war on.

Page 123. l. 4541 *ful wrathe*, very wroth.

Page 124. l. 4558 *wathe*, torment. 4576 *fra þan*, from that time.

Page 128. l. 4700 *gun telle* = *gan telle*, did tell. 4703 *ken*, see. 4727 *brethe*, vapour.

Page 130. l. 4772, 74 *romyng*, *romiyng*, roaring. 4782 *byggyns* = *byggyngs*, buildings. 4786 *An*, an error for *And*. 4794 *to neven*, to be named.

Page 132. l. 4850 *bygged*, built. 4851 *yhed*, went. 4853 *brunstane*, brimstone.

[14] = *snubs*, curses. [15] protectors.

Page 133. l. 4891 *rayke obout*, spread about. 4906 *dasednes*, coldness. 4907 *wirkyng*, operation.

Page 135. l. 4961 *bemes*, trumpets. 4975 *movyng*, movement. 4979 to 5020. The following lines upon the resurrection of the body are from the 'Cursor Mundi' fol. 126.

Sant Paule us sais on þis-kin wise,
Þat littel and mikel, ald and yhing,
Alle at þat mikel uprising,
Sal be of eld as þai suld here
Haf deied in eild o thritte yere,
Þat eild þat crist had at his ded,
Quen he us broght al fra ur fed;[1]
And if þat ani her livand
Was wemmed[2] or on fote or on hand,
Als we se chances oft bitide,
On muth or nese or elles-quar,
Or bote upon his bodi bar,
Cripel, croked or turnd o baft,
Or limes ma gain[3] kindli craft,
Thoru ma or less o lim haf last,
At þis uprising þat sal be last,
Alle þaa þat Godd has chosin til his
Ffor to be broght into his blis,
Quatsum þai in þis liif has bene,
It sal na wem[4] o þam be sene,
Ne naking thing bot alle fairhede,
Als we in hali scripture rede;
Alle sal have right limes þar,
Þai aght to haf ne less ne mar,
Bot take tent quat I sai to þe;
O fair stature quat it sal be,
And o þair eild, o þam i mele,[5]
Þat Crist tas for his aun lele,
Þaas other sal ha fairhed nan,
For al welth sal þam be wan,[6]
O þaim it es to telle na tale,
Þat brued wituten bote es bale.
Þe childer þat es abortives,
Þaa þat er born olives,[7]
Sal rise in thritte winter eild,
To litel bote to þaim or beild,[8]
Ffor þaa war noght baptist iwiss,
Ne sal þai haf na part o bliss,

[1] enemy. [2] deformed. [3] against. [4] blemish, spot. [5] talk. [6] wanting. absent. [7] alive. [8] protection, safety.

Þir mikel maisters sais þat þai
Mai sauved be on nankin wai,
Þai sal haf nother wel ne wa
Bot in merckenes forever and a.
Þe men þat thoru þair aun gilt,
Wit hefding draght or hanging spilt
Thoru þaïr sin and þair feluni,
Wit hundes eten þe mast parti,
Mani wenes þat er unwise,
Þat þat flexs hale suld never rise,
And þat to wene es bot sotthede;[9]
Nu i sal þe sum resun rede,
Ute of alle skil it es and right
Ffor to mistru in goddes might.
Qnat man mai wiit, quat man mai lere.
Quat man may se, quat ere may here,
Quat man in erth mai thinc in thoght
Hu al þis werld ur laverd wroght,
Heven and erth al in þair haldes,
Þat mighti godd þat alle waldes?[10]
Qua can sai me hu of a sede,
He dos an hundret for to brede?
Thoru his mighti wille dos þat king
Ute of þe herd tre to spring
Ffirst þe lef and siþen þe flur,
And þan þe frut wit his savur,
Ilkin frut in his sesun;
Agh we þar-in seke resun
Hu he dos ilkin thing to nait,[11]
Certes þat war bot surfait,
Þe mar man suinc him þar abute,
Ffra spede[12] ferrer he sal be ute.
A sample sal i sceu yow þar-bi
Þat i fand o Sant Gregori,
Þar he was in a stede sumquar,
An crafti clerc and wis o lare,
And[13] asked him a questiun
Of a wolf and a leon,
And of þe thrid þat was a man,
Quar-of þe tale þus bigan.
A man welk thoru a woddes wai,
Þar ner þe stret a wolf him lai;
Þis wolf it was unmesur [of] mete,
Al þis mans flexs þar he ete,

[9] folly. [10] rules, wields. [11] prosper. [12] success. [13] also.

Als-suith he sua had don,
An hungre leon mete he son,
Up and dun his prai sekand;
Quen he nan oþer best þar fand,
Þis wolf he feld ant ete him al
Ne left he noither gret ne smalle;
Þe leon efter deied in hii,
Ded þar gun his coroigne lii,
And þar was roten al to noght,
Quar-in sal þis man be soght?
For i mai tru on nakin wise,
Þat þis man mai to liif uprise,
Sin nan es als i wene þat can
Tuin[14] þat erth þat com o man,
Ffra þat erth þat es bredd o best.
Sant Gregor gaf ansuer honest,
And o þat man þat was in were,
Þe soth he scend him al clere,
And provide him wit quik resun
Þat at þis resurrectioun,
Wit alle his limes, hale and fere,[15]
Sal [he] cume befor þe demstere;
Ffor þof his bodi al war brint,
And blaun overal [and] þe puder tint
Yett mai godd gedir it alagain,
And neu him at his wille wit main
Alle þe flexs þat was o þe man
Sothfast sal be raised þan,
It sal be delt in littel weve,[16]
Þat was o best al sal bileve,[17]
Þat bath þe tane and þe toþer made
Wel bituix þam can he schade.[18]
Sua haali sal þai þan rise þare,
Þam sal noght want a hefd hare,
Ne noght a nail o fote ne hand;
Þof quether we sal understand
Þat nail and hare þat haf be scorn,
Bes noght al quar þai war beforn,
Bot als potter wit pottes dos,
Quen he his neu wessel fordos,
He castes al þan in a balle,
A better for to mak wit-alle;
O noght he lokes quilk was quilk,
Bot makes a nother of þat ilk,
Wel fairer þan þe first was wroght;
Right sua sal crist, ne dut þe noght.

[14] separate. [15] sound. [16] pieces. [17] remain. [18] distinguish.

He þat es laverd of erth and heven,
Mai o þat ilk selvin even,
Þat first was molten into lame[19]
Mak a wel fairer licam,[20]
And if þar-of was mar or les
To mesur, als his wille es.

Page 136. l. 5003 *peryste*, destroyed. 5020 *avenand*, comely.

Page 137. l. 5054 For *we* the sense requires þe.

Page 139. l. 5126 *levenyng*, lightning. 5131 *onence*, opposite.

Page 141. l. 5188 *fast*, near, close. 5199 *clotes*, *clouts*, clothes. 5202 *nere-hande*, nigh, near. 5212 *swelt*, died.

Page 143. l. 5261 *bla*, livid. 5266 *misse*, to lose. 5293 *staynged=stanged*, pierced.

Page 144. l. 5298 *harnpane*, brain pan. 5299 *brast his hyde*, burst his skin. 5311 *enchesoun*, reason. 5327 *erres*, scars.

Page 145. l. 5332 *atteyn*, accuse. 5357 *reddour*, *reddure*, severity, lit. dread, fear.

Page 147. l. 5407 *threp*, dispute with, talk severely. 5410 *scake*, shake. 6417 *sar*, sore. 5428 *Ynwitt*, conscience.

Page 148. l. 5460 *wreghes*, bewrays, discovers.

Page 149. l. 5483 *egged*, instigated. 5487 *eggyng*, instigation. 5503 *kepyng*, custody. 5511 *bymens*, signifies.

Page 150. l. 5522 *halghes* = *hallows*, saints. 5526 *sloghe*, slew. 5538 *wreke*, vengeance.

Page 151. l. 5567 *uptrust*, uptrussed, hoarded up. 5570 *moweld* mone, mouldy money. 5572 *moghes* or *mows*, moths. 5574 *over*, above.

Page 152. l. 5602 *stak*, pret of stik to pierce. 5606 *legge pousté*, sovereign power. 5609 *accusyng*, accusation.

Page 153. l. 5649 *lent*, given pret of *len*, *lene*, to give, grant.

Page 154. l. 5672 *yholden*, yielded.

Page 155. l. 5716 for þe the sense requires *þi*.

Page 156. l. 5771 *bedde*, offered.

Page 157. l. 5784 *eghtild*, *eghteld*, endeavoured, aimed at. 5785 *ryfe*, reeve. 5785 *bytaght*, entrusted.

Page 158. l. 5831 *þeþen*, thence.

Page 159. l. 5871 *uniustifyed*, wronged.

Page 160. l. 5908 *Gudes of hap &c.* = Riches of fortune are these to be reckoned. 5913 *arrirage*, arrears.

Page 161. l. 5944 *leches*, physicians. 5951 *lent*, given, pret of *len*, to grant. 5958 *bede*, give.

Page 162. l. 5978 *reken*, give an account of, see l. 5984. 5987 *iustify*, to do justice to. 5994 *haldyngs*, possessions. 5999 *laynd*, kept secret. 6001 *layt*, seek, look for. 6003 *rekkenyng*, account.

Page 163. l. 6022 *seme*, appear.

[19] loam, earth. [20] body.

Page 164. l. 6058 *dwelle* seems an error for *dwelled.* 6079 þat *sounes in ille* on any manere, cf. the following passage from Ascham: "Some siren shall sing him a song sweete in tune, but *sownding in the ende to his utter* destruction. The Scholmaster, p. 72, ed. Mayor 1863.

Page 165. l. 6087 *halghes*, saints. 6091 *reddure*, see line 5357. 6112 *flaying*, terror. 6114 *merryng*, louring. 6122 *setil*, seat, throne.

Page 166. l. 6133 *departe*, divide. 6135 *gayte*, goats.

Page 168. l. 6205 *brist*, need. 6210 *Suthly*, truly. 6212 *kydde*, known. 6227 *whyne*, O that! 6229 *thurt*, needed. 6232 *swelghe*, swallow.

Page 169. l. 6248 *tome*, leisure. 6250 *redde*, promised. 6251 *spedde*, finished.

Page 172. l. 6348 *hale*, whole. 6365 *removyng*, removal. 6373 *o*, of.

Page 173. l. 6418 *ugge*, fear, dread.

Page 174. l. 6424 *fune*, few. 6429 *mynde*, memory. *feer*, terrify. 6432 *dight*, prepared. 6445 *colke*, core. 6447 *dalk*, hollow.

Pape 175. l. 6463 *stoped*, stuffed. 6466 *tale*, reckoning, number. 6469 *lare*, learning.

Page 176. l. 6522 *lughe*, laughed. 6523 *efte*, again. *dreghe*, suffer. 6535 *yhode*, went.

Page 177. l. 6564 *threst*, thirst. 6566 *graped*, felt, handled. 6571 *dyngyng*, smiting.

Page 178. l. 6575 *greting*, weeping. 6603 *wreth*, wrath.

Page 179. l. 6613 *shire*, pure, clean. 6614 *brend*, burned. 6619 *waghe*, wall. 6632 *fole*, foul. 6647 *dased*, cold.

Page 181. l. 6693 *pyk*, pitch. 6694 *wyk*, bad, nasty. 6704 *of-race*, tear off.

Page 182. l. 6729 *reuthe*, pity. 6736 *clewe*, cleave. *brest*, burst. 6738 *menged*, mixed.

Page 183. l. 6762 *to fele*, too much. 6763 *kele*, cool. 6765 *rouke*, squat, nestle. 6772 *fest*, fasten.

Page 184. l. 6814 *sprent*, scatter, fly. 6832 *uglynes*, horror.

Page 185. l. 6860 *aferde*, frightened. 6874 *Whas*, whose.

Page 186. l. 6877 *duleful* = *doleful*, sorrowful. 6884 *fleghe*, fly. 6900 *tades*, toads. 6902 *grym*, savage.

Page 187. l. 6936 *clokes*, claws, clutches. 6937 *umlapp*, surround. Cf. umluke, umset, umthink &c. 6947 þ*are*, where. 6950 *ferd*, afraid.

Page 188. l. 6955 *covertoure*, covering.

Page 189. l. 7009 *neghend*, ninth. 7015 *dyng*, strike, beat. 7016 *styntyng*, cessation.

Page 191. l. 7070 *rosyng*, boast. 7075 *foghel*, fowl, bird. *fleghand*, flying.

Page 192. l. 7119 *out-yhetted*, poured out, shed. 7126 *welland*, boiling. 7130 *forthynkyng*, repentance.

Page 193. l. 7159 *schame*, to feel ashamed. 7169 *bald*, ready eager.

Page 194. l. 7193 *hend*, hands. 7194 *utter*; outer. 7216 *tytted*, pulled with violence.

Page 195. l. 7230 *up-swa-doune*, upsidedown.

Page 196. l. 7264 *Over-tite*, very soon. *warn*, unless.

Page 197. l. 7296 *tharnyng*, desire. Tharn sometimes signifies to want, stand in need of. 7302 *tynt*, lost. 7303 *stynt*, cease. 7327 *trey and tene*, sorrow and grief. 7328 *wantyng*, absence, lack.

Page 198. l. 7338 *gnayste*, gnash. 7341 *rare*, roar. 7347 *skryke*, shriek. 7351 *duschyng*, dashing. 7352 *skrykyng*, shrieking. 7355 *strake*, struck. 7355 *stopp*, stuff. 7361 *wend*, use. 7364 *thrang*, throng, pressure.

Page 199. l. *kepe*, hold. 7373 *myster*, need. 7378 *scratte*, scratch. 7392 *debate*, contest, strife. 7396 *wa worth þe*, woe be to the. Cf. 'wele worth þe while', 'wa worth þe day.'

Page 201. l. 7451 *tyme*, evidently an error for *þam*. 7460 *newed*, renewed. 7461 *new*, anew.

Page 203. l. 7535 *laytes*, seeks.

Page 204. l. 7579 *hoves*, hangs over.

Page 205. l. 7601 *smored*, smothered. 7615 *tentes*, attends, takes notice. 7619 *wonderly*, wonderfully.

Page 206. l. 7633 *styk*, stand, remain.

Page 207. l. 7665 *gesced*, reckoned, see l. 7642. 7687 *soth*, truth. 7692 *mesuryng*, measurement. 7695 *met*, measured. 7696 *stey*, ascended *halghe*, holy.

Page 208. l. 7730 *pays*, weight.

Page 210. l. 7802 *gese* (guess), tell.

Page 211. l. 7816 *alkyn*, all kind of, *to welde* to be possessed or be enjoyed. 7825 *druryes*, gallantry. 7826 *nobillay*, nobility. 7846 *yheldyng*, bestowal. 7847 *lowtyng*, obeisance. 7848 *boghsomnes*, buxomness = compliance.

Page 214. l. 7939 *ta* = *tane*, the one. 7940 *wyld*, desired. 7942 *ogaynestand ne lett*, oppose nor hinder. 7953 *charged*, loaded.

Page 215. l. 7964-5 *mow*, be able. *remowe*, remove. 7969 *ogayne-standyng*, opposition. 7985 *warn*, forbid, refuse. 7987 *boghand*, compliant obedient. 8000 *mys*, lose, be without.

Page 216. l. 8003 *chaced*, driven about.

Page 217. l. 8039 *fulle-fyld*, filled. 8061 *felle*, fierce. 8075 *toke kepe*, took notice.

Page 219. l. 8122 *endelesnes*, eternity.

Page 220. l. 8158 *transyng*, trance.

Page 221. l. 8193 *taste*, experience. 8199 *aywhare*, everywhere.

Page 222. l. 8252 *barnhede*, childhood. 8262 *lorn*, lost.

Page 223. l. 8268 *skylles*, reasons. causes. 8300 *schrafe*, shrove.

Page 224. l. 8305 *love*, praise. 8319 *myslykyng*, dislike. 8320 *meneyng*, remembrance. 8323 *haled*, healed, made whole.

Page 226. l. 8385 *fested*, fastened. 8389 *hele*, health. 8405 *felony*, wickedness.

Page 227. l. 8448 *veray*, true.

Page 228. l. 8462 *alle-sone*, immediately. 8481 *wyld*, desired.

Page 229. l. 8500 *heghnes*, exaltation. *lawnes*, humilty. 8505 *lawnes*, humility. 8506 *heyhed*, exalted. 8507 *halely*, wholly. 8514 *lyke*, pl ase.

Page 231. l. 8582 *To and fra*, *overthwert and endlang*, To and fro, across, and from head to heels; *overthwert* across, *endlang*, in length: 'from head to tail' our modern *along*. 8590 *feth*, feet. 8591 *threst*, thrust. 8506 *unbowsom*, disobedient.

Page 232. l. 8608 *delyces*, delights. 8628 *tane*, taken.

Page 233. l. 8656 *sothfast*, true. 8674 *anely*, only.

Page 234. l. 8688 *nest*, next. 8706 *lykand*, pleasing. 8709 *bi him-ane*, by himself. 8710 *schane*, shone.

Page 236. l. 8790 *dubbed*, decorated.

Page 237. l. 8827 *a* = *ane*, one.

Page 238. l. 8840 *wonand*, dwelling. 8851 *wonyng*, abode. 8857 *tre*, wood. 8866 *welland*, ruling, governing.

Page 239. l. 8882 *langes*, there longs. 8897 *wardes*, out works of a castle. 8898 *garettes*, watch towers. 8902 *overgylt*, gilded over. *enamyld*, interwoven, mixed.

Page 240. l. 8900 *perrė jewelry*, see note on *besandes*. 8906 *bygyngs*, buildings. 8911 *brede*, breadth. 8938 *rase*, journey, course, way. *Ra*, roe.

Page 241. l, 8946 *underlout*, subject. 8966 *lowted*, reverenced.

Page 242. l. 9002 *swynsty*, a pigsty. 9017 *flayre*, smell, flavour.

Page 243. l. 9024 *laythede*, ugliness. 9026 *wayknes*, weakness. 9028 *myslykyng*, unpleasantness. 9032 *tald*, reckoned. 9035 *eld*, old age. 9049 *unsykernes*, insecurity.

Page 244. l. 9060 *brynand*, burning. 9084 *stalworthly*, strongly. 9085 *tayled*, carved. 9094 *charbukelle*, carbuncle.

Page 245. l. 9107 *frett*, ornamented. 9108 *besandes*, besants. Bezants were gold coins so called from Byzantium or Constantinople where they were first coined. They seem however to have been used for ornaments.

> "Her belte was of blenket, with briddus ful bold,
> Beten with *besandus*, and bocult ful bene.
> Her fax in fyne *perrė* was frettut and fold."
>
> "The Anturs of Arther" Robson's Met. Romances p. 14.

Page 246. l. 9136 *restfulle*, peaceful. 9156 *fer*, far; *ferrer*, farther.

Page 247. l. 9170 *gastly*, spritually. 9181 *pament*, pavement.

Page 248. l. 9211 *wene*, suppose. 9218 *alle-if*, although. 9221 *nerrer*, nearer.

Page 249. l. 9254 *sang*, song. 9255 *omang*, at intervals. 7261 *like*, please. 9270 *shylle*, shrill.

Page 250. l. 9304 *wysse*, show direct. 9312 *skilles*, reasons. 9315 *lykyng*, pleasure.

Page 251. l. 9358 *irkyng*, weariness, see l. 9365.

Page 253. l. 9423 *myssay*, to revile. 9430 *lowe*, flame. *reke*, smoke. *melled*, mixed.

Page 254. l. 9439 *outrageus*, extraordinary. 9447 *bestes of ravyn*, beasts of prey.

Page 255. l. 9474 *sped*, finished. 9490 *medeful*, deserv ng of reward.

Page 257. l. 9580 *kunnyng*, knowledge.

INDEX.

* The numbers refer to the pages.

GLOSSARIAL INDEX.

*A, ever, see 'Ay'.
A, 1852, one.
Abate, 1672, 3108, 5011, to put down, lessen, put an end to, 6596, Fr. *abbattre.*
Abayste, 1430, depressed; pret of abaisse or abash, Fr. *esbahir; 'abaschyd* or aferde, territus' P.P.
Aboven, 612, 4120, above; A. S. *ufan, be-ufan. bufan*, Du. *boven.*
*Abortives,
Abrege, 4571, 4577, to shorten; abreged, 4575, Fr. *abrèger*, Lat. *abbreviare.*
Abyde, byde, 5055, to wait for, A. S. *bidan*, *abidan*, Goth. *beidan*, to expect, look out for.
Acorde, 1302, 4514, 1) *vb. intr.*, French *accorder*, to agree with. 2) *sb.* 8465.
Accorde, *vb. tr.*, 3473, to reconcile.
Accusation, 5699, 6195.
Accuse, 3985.
Accuser, accusours, 3984.
Accusyng, 6104, accusation.
Acount, *vb.*, 7675, 5422, 5425.
Acouped, 2947, pret. of acoulp, to accuse, from Lat. *culpa.*
Acunt, acount, 3986, 6000, account, Fr. *compter*, Lat. *computare*, to reckon.
Adversité, 4642.
Aferd, 2303, *aferde* or trobelid (P.P.).
Afered, 2943, frightened.
*Afers, affairs.
Affecyon, 8876.
Afforce, 2536, 4253, to exert, endeavour.
Afray, 6112, fright, affright, Fr. *effrayer*, to scare, affright, *effroi*, terror. *Fray*, to scare birds is still in use among bird-scarers.
Aftir, after, 47, 553, 6016, 1) after, 2) according to; A. S. *æft*, *æfter*, afterwards, again.
Agayn, agaynes, agayns, 168, 1252, 4011, 4062, 4268, against; A. S. *ongean*, *ongen*, *agen*, opposite, against; *gean*, against, opposite; *gain* occurs often in the Cursor Mundi in this sense.
Agaynward, 1279.
*Agh, ought, see 'Awe'.
Aght, 1831, ought, pret of aw or agh.
Aghtend, aghtynd, 3986, 6895, eighth, Germ. *acht.* Sc. *aucht*, O. Fris. *acht*, *achta*, eight.
Agrege, *aggreggyn*, aggravo (P. P.) p 82, see 'Grege', Fr. *aggrèger*, to aggravate, from Lat. *gravis.*
Aioynt, 3302, enjoined.
Al, alle, 2269, 1) *adj.* all, 2) 9520 *adv.*, quite, entirely; A. S. *eall.*
Al-if, alle-if, 3650, 3687, although.
Alan, 24, alone.
Ald, alde, 214, 794, 6418, old, A. S. *ald*, *eald.*
Aldir-foulest, 527, foulest of all.
Alkyn, 613, 3248, 4948, all kinds of.

Allane, 5244, alone.
Alle, see al.
Allebydonen or albodene, alle-bidene, 3215, 8040, 8934, see 'Bidene.
Allege, 3894, to allay; A. S. *alecgan*, to lay down, put down, suppress.
Allege, 5584, to alledge, Fr. *allèguer*, Lat. *allegare*.
Alle-if, 4107, see al-if.
Alliance, 8399.
Allowt, p. 33, to bow to, see 'Lowt'.
Almus, 3609, alms, Gr. ἐλεημοσύνη, compassionate, A. S. *ælmesse*, *ælmes*, alms.
Almusdede, 3660, 3708, almsdeed.
Alowed, 2467, praised; O.Fr. *louer*, to praise, Lat. *laudare*.
Als, 17, 2991, 2995, as, also; A.S. *eallswa*, Germ. *als*, O. Fris. *alsa*, *als*.
Alsone, 4624, at once, immediately.
Alstite, 3767, 6232, 6460, at once, immediately, as soon.
Alswa, 81, 3682, also.
Alswa = als wha, 7447.
Altherbest, 2195, the best of all.
Altherfeblest, 746, the weakest of all.
Alther-heghest, 7722.
Alwytty, 2, allwise.
Amend, 5021.
Amended, 3773, in phrase 'are amended'.
Amidward, in the midst, in the middle of.
An, ane, 259, 1768, 4085, one, A. S. *ân*; ph. bi it *ane*, by itself, 3037, 3109; by tham ane, 5833.
Ande, 3054, breath. O, N. *anda*.
And if, 8075.
Anes, once.
Anger, angre, 691, 2100, 6039, sorrow, trouble, grievance; Icel. *angr*, narrow, grief, pain; *pl.* angers, 3538.
Angred, *adj.*, 302. troubled.
'And mani seke men have þai broght
Þat *angerd* war with divers evils.
(MS. Harl. 4196 f. 99.)
Anguise, anguyse, angwys, angwyse, 2240, 3518, 3547, 6107, anguish, sorrow; Lat. *angustia*, a strait, O. Fr. *anguisse*, Fr. *angoisse*.
Anhede, 16, 8448, unity.
Anly, anely, 1338, 2345, 4901, only.
Aparty, 1804, 2700, 3579, partly.
Apayre, appayre, 69, to impair, injure; Lat. *pejor*, Fr. *pis*, *pire*, worse. 'To *appayre* to waxe worse' (Palsgrave). *Apperyn* or make worse, pejoro, deterio'. (P. P.)
Apayred, 3691.
Apayrand, 1475, becoming worse.
Apert, appert, 4234, 4490, 5743, open. Fr. *apert*.
Apertely, 4238, 8651, openly.
Apostyms, 2995. O.Fr. *apostume*, Gr. *apostêma*, an imposthume.
Appere, 5219, 5243, to appear, to be seen.
Appropried, 9346, appropriated.
Ar, 9, 10, ever.
Ar, are, 178, 407, 440, 1763, *adv.* before, formerly; A. S. *æra*, before, early, Goth. *air*.
Aray, 7070.
Arely, arly, 1433, 6158, early.
Arely, in the morning, *mane*, 723, 724. A.S. *ærlice*, mane.
Aresoned, 2460, 5997, 'called to account'. O. Fr. *aresoner*, to question. Lat. *ratiocinare*.
Arrirage (rerage), 5912, arrears.
Arte, 7723.
Asethe see assethe.
Askes, 424, 4886, ashes; A. S. *asca*, Icel. *aska*.
Askyng, 2288, *sb.*, a petition, prayer,

A.S. *ascian*, to ask, Icel. *æskia*. O.Fris. *askia*.
'Like in Laverd, and gif sal he þe askinges of þi hert to þe.'
(Ps. xxxv.)

Assale, 1037, 5824, 8804.

Assay, 1399, to try; Lat. *exigere*, to prove by examination. O.Fr. *assaier*, Fr. *essayer*, to try.

Assent, 1) *vb.*, 4386, 8460; 2) *sb.*, 8391.

Assethe, asethe, 3610, 3747. This word is the earlier form of our 'assets'. We find other O. Eng. forms such as *assyth*, *syth*, *sithe* &c. A. S. *sæd*, *sade*, satisfied, Germ. *satt*, full, Icel. *sætt*, *sætte*, reconciliation.

"And who so harmes any man in his nede,
Sal noȝt be safe, bot he make *asseth* at his power."
(Castle of Love p. 107.)

Assoyle, 3860, 3862, to acquit. Lat. *absolvere*, O.Fr. *absolver*, *assoiler*.

Assygned, 4189.

Assys, 5514, assize. O.Fr. *assire*, to sit, *assise*, a set rate, '*Cour d'assize*', a court to be held on a set day.

At, 1. *conj.* 56, 171, that. 2. *prep.* 4139, 6152, to (before the infin. mood); 5569, in; 7730 to. Icel. *at*, to.

Atans, attans, attanes, 4785, 6642, at once.

Atteyn, 5332, to accuse, convict. Fr. *attaindre*, O.Fr. *atteinder*, to reach to, convict, accuse &c.

And pharisenes, fulle mekil schrews,
Went for to wit of his thewes,
For to *atteyn* him in sum thing,
Þat þai might wrye him to þe king.
(MS. Harl. 4196 f. 164.)

*Attre, poison, A.S. *attor*.

Auctentyke, 7116.

Aungel, aungelle, 6188, angel.

Austerne, awsterne, 5235, 6181, austere, stern.

Austerité, 5376, severity.

Auter, 3685, altar.

Autorities, 6593.

Auturné, 6084. Mid Lat. *attornatus*, one taking the place or turn of another. O.Fr. *atorné*.

Avail, avale, 3587, 6623.

Avant, 4298, advance. Fr. *avancer*, to push forwards, from *avant*, before, Lat. *abante*.

Avantage, avauntage, 1012, advantage.

Avayle, 3884, Fr. *valoir*, Lat. *valere*, to be well, be able, be worth.

Avenand, 5020, = avenant, comely, elegant. O.Fr. *advenant*, *avenant*.

Avise, *vb.*, 4000, to take note, observe. O.Fr. *adviser*, *aviser*. It. *avisare*.

Avoket, 6084, advocate. Lat. *advocare*, to call, or summon one to a place.

Avyse see 'avise'.

Aw, awe, 2510, ought, pret aght. A.S. *agan*, pres. *áh* &c., pret *áhte*. Goth. *aigan*, *aihan*.

Awe, 1870, anger, originally dread, fear; phrase: 'for luf ne *awe*'. Dan. *ave*, A.S. *ege*, *oga*, fear, dread. Icel. *ægir*, terrible.

Awen, awin, 90, 447, own, see 'aw'. It is sometimes found under the form *aghen* in the Cursor Mundi.

Awkeward, 1541, wrongly, awry. Sc. *akword*, awkwardly, perversely, wrongly. A.S. *awoh*, awry.

Ay, 12, 1752, 1753, always. A.S. *áva*, *a*, all, ever. O.Fris. *a*. Grm. *je*, ever, always.

Ayther, 1274, 5979, either. A.S. *æghwæther*, *ægther*, each.

Aywhare, 8195, everywhere. A.S. *æghwær*, everywhere.

Bad, 6275, pret of bid.

Bald, 6855, 7169, bold, eager, ready, Germ. *bald*, quick.

Bale, 6103, 6465, misery, calamity, woe. O.Fris. *bale*. A.S. *bealu*, torment, destruction. Icel. *bōl*, calamity, misery.

Ban, 3484, 3485, to curse. Swed. *bann*, excommunication. *banna*, to chide, curse.

Band, bande, 3209, bonds. A.S. *band*.

Bane, 629, 4804, bone. A.S. *bân*. Germ: *bein*, the leg. Welsh *bôn*, a stem, stock.

Baptem, 5509, baptism.

Bar, 5979, pret of 'bere'.

Bare, 1460, naked, poor. Germ. *baar*, bare.

Baret, contest, dispute, contention. O.Fr. *barat*. Icel. *baratta*, strife.

Barn, a child. A.S. *bearn*.

Barnhede, 8428, childhood.

Batailles, bataylles, 1247, armies, hosts. Fr. *battre*, to beat, *bataille*, battle, band of armed men.

Bath, bathe, 117, 5981, both. Goth. *ba*, *baioths*, Icel. *bâdir*, A.S. *butu*, *batwa*.

Baum, 652, balm. Fr. *baume*, Lat. *balsamum*, Greek *βαλσαμον*, a fragrant gum.

Be, 3736, 5369, by.

Beauté, beuté, bewté, 692, 5782, beauty. Fr. *beauté* from *beau*, *bel*, Lat. *bellus*.

Bed, bedde, 6152, 8534, offered, see 'Bede'.

Beddyng, *sb.*, 6944, bed.

Bede, 5958, 6193, to offer, furnish pret bedde. A.S. *beodan*, Germ. *bieten*, to offer. 'Bid' has this sense in the modern phrases: 'to *bid* the banns', 'to *bid* for a thing', 'to *bid* against a person'.

A pover man come untille his ȝate
Lazar he was and fulle lothly
With many biles on his body,
And fast þan gan he calle and crave,
His fille of crums þare for to have,
And þare was none þat wald him bede,
Mete ne drink for alle his nede;
Bot hundes come and likked his wowndes,
And lethid þe werking in þa stowndes.
(MS. Harl. 4196 fol. 104.)

Bede, 3722, prayer. A.S. *bead*.

Bedene, see 'Bidene'.

Bedred, bedreden, *adj.*, 6198. A.S. *bedrida*, one who rides about in his bed.

*Beft, beaten.

Behald, 579, behold. A.S. *behealden*, to regard.

*Beild, protection, safety. O.Fris. *belda*, to establish.

Beme, 4677, 4961, trumpet. A.S. *beâm*, beme.

Than sal be herd the blast of *bem*
The demster sal com *to* dem.
(Met. Hom. p. xii.)

Beme, 3097, beam, ray.

Benefice, benefyce, 116, 119, 5436, good deed, kindness, benefit. Lat. *benefacere*, to do good to any one, *benefactum*, Fr. *bienfait*, a good deed, benefit. Lat. *beneficium*, a kindness.

Benysoun, 3405, a blessing. Fr. *benisson* from *bénir*, to bless.

Ber, bere, 585, to bear, pret *bar*, *bare*.

*Bere, noise. O.Fris. *bere*, noise, alarm.

Bery, 5216, to bury. A.S. *birgan*, *byrigan*, to bury.

Beryng, *sb.*, burial.
Best, beste, 166, 470, a beast.
Bette, 5204, beaten.
Betyde, 4812, to happen.
Beyng, *sb.*, 17, existence.
Bid, 3663, to command, order. A.S *bidan.*
Bidder, 3679, a petitioner.
Biddyng, *sb.*, 3658.
Bidene, 7968, of Dutch origin. "It is a compound of the particle *by* and the demonstrative pronoun. *by dien* = thereby, therefore, and hence, immediately." (Marsh.)
Bigg, 1460, rich, well furnished. Icel. *bolga*, a swelling. The adjective 'bigly' occurs with the same sense in MS. Harl. 4196.

And þir er wretin þat we may luke,
And teche þe folk how þai salle trow,
And baynly tille his biddinges bow,
And ever-more honore him and his,
And so cum to his *bigly* blis.
(fol. 90.)

Bigg, 4850, to build. A.S. *byggan*, Icel. *byggia.*
Bighing, *sb.*, 3608, redemption.
Bihove, 1396, behove. A.S. *behovian*, to be fit, right.
Bilyfe, 9555, quickly.
Biry, 4548, to bury.
Bisschope, 3804, bishop.
Bisen, 1027, example. A.S. *bisen.*

And of Child Iesus *bisen* take.
(Met. Hom. p. 110.)

We sometimes meet with *bisen* as a verb = to signify, denote. Scottish writers use the verb in the sense of 'to portend', and the adjective as equivalent to ominous, portending. *Bisen* has also the meaning of 'appearance' and hence 'well-*besene*', 'well-*beseene*' = of good appearance, as used by Chaucer and Spenser.

*Bismer, a wicked one. A.S. *bismère*, an imfamous person.
Bisy, bysy, 1233, 5489, busy. A.S. *biseg.*
Bitter, 1775, 1935, painful. Icel. *beitr*, *bitr*, sharp.
Bitterly, 2988, painfully, sharply.
Bla, 5261, livid. O.H.Germ. *blao*, *blaw*, blue. N.Fris. *bla*, *blö.* Icel. *blar.* Dan. *blaeuw*, blue, livid. A more modern form is *blo.*

"Bernard, I saw my dere son hang
Als he had bene a maister thef,
With sides *blo* als þai him dang,
Þat are war white and me ful lefe,
Alle with blude his cors was cled,
And with spiting fro hevid to hele."
(MS. Tiberius E. vii, f. 83.)

Bla in the sense of blue occurs in MS. Harl. 4196 fol. 82:

Þe blude brast out both *bla* and rede,
Wers was never none done to dede."

Blaw, 4677, to blow.
Blawen, 685, blown.
*Blenk, fault.
Blere, 2226, to mock. *Blerynge* wythe mowe makynge. Patento, valgio. (Pr. Pm.) The knave *bleareth* his tonge at me, *tirer la langue.* (Palsgrave.)—In Sion College MS. xviii, 6, among *sins of the mouth* are given the following:

Laghyng, grynnyng and vayn lykenyng,
Dispycus bro, *bleryng* and maws makyng.
(fol. 5.)

Blethly, blethely, 184, 6051, blithely. A.S. *blithe*, joyful, blithe.
Blin, blyn, 1746, 5350, to cease, stop, pret. *blan.*
Blisfulhede, 7832.

Blissed, 6148, blessed.

Blode, 5196, blood. Germ. *blut*, Dan. *bloed.*

Blody, 5261, bloody.

Blude, 5537, blood, see 'blode'.

Blyn, 6111, see 'Blin'.

Boghand, 8495, obedient, *imp. part.* of *bogh*, to bend.

Iesus satt on his moder kne
With a ful blith chere said he
Bogh þou til us suith þou tre
Unnethe had he said þe sune
Quen þe tre it *boghed* dune.

Boghsom, bousom, bowsom, bughsom, 50, 85, 201, buxom, obedient, dutiful. A.S. *bocsam*, *buhsom*, from *bugan*, to bend, submit. Fris. *bocgsum.*

Boght, 113, 5273, bought, redeemed.

Bok, boke, buk, buke, 39, 51, 206, book. A.S. *boc.*

Bonden, 3210, bound.

Borwe, 3259, to borrow; phrase 'beg ne borwe'. A.S. *borh*, a surety, pledge. Germ. *bürge*, surety, bail.

Bot, 1. *conj.*, 24, 35, but, 151, except 2. *adv.*, 5849, only.
Scottish writers use *bot*, *but*, in the sense of 'without', as '*bot* dout', '*bot* remede'. A.S. *butan*, *buta*, *bute*, without, except, besides.

*Bote, remedy. A.S. *bóte.*

Bot-if, 1569, 4061, unless.

Bourd, 1593, jest, play, sport. Fr. *bourde*, jest. Bret. *bourd*, deceit, trick, joke. Gael. *burd*, *burt*, mockery.

Bousom, bowsom, 85, see 'Boghsom'.

Bow, 303, to be obedient.

Bowes, 658, boughs, see 'Bughes'.

Brade, 71, 1484, broad. A.S. *brâd.* Germ. *breit.*

Braide, brayde, 1750, an assault, attack.

Brast, 5299, pret of brest, to burst.

Brayde, see 'Braide'.

Brayne-wode, 6707, mad.

Brede, 5573, to breed (as vermin).

Brede, *sb.*, 1488, 5899, breadth, see 'Brade'.

Brede, 3597, bread. A.S.
Icel. *braud.* Germ. *brot.*

Breke, 412, 2078, to scatter, drive away.

Breke, 4465, to break. O Fris. *breka.* Goth. *brikan.* Germ. *brechen.*

*Brem, fierce. A.S. *breme.*

Brend, 6617, burnt, *p.* of *brin.*

Brest, 679, breast. A.S. *breost.*

Brest, 1787, 7264, to burst, pret. *brast.* A.S. *berstan.* O.H.Germ. *brestan.*

Brethe, 613, 4727, vapour, steam. Scott. *broth.* Germ. *brodem*, *broden*, steam, vapour. A.S. *bræth*, odour, scent, breath.

Brether, 6178, plural of 'brother'.

Bridalles, 4842, wedding feasts. A.S. *bryd-eale*, the marriage feast.

Brin, brine, bryn, 3181, 3183, 3974, 4920, 4921, to burn. A.S. *byrnan.* Du. *brennen*, *bernen.*

Brist, 6205, need, want. '*Brest* or wantynge, of nede. Indigencia.' (P. P.)
Dan. *bröst*, default.

Brunstane, 4853, 6693, bronstane, 8056, brimstone, i. e. *burning* stone.

Bryn, 4994, see 'Brin'.

Brydegome, 8809, bridegroom.

Buffet, *sb.*, 5203, blow.

Bughes, 680, boughs. A.S. *bog*, *boh*, from *bugan*, to bend.

Bughsom, 50, 1973, see 'Boghsom'.

Buk, buke, 307, 336, see 'Boke'.

Buk, 8938, a buck. Welsh *bwch.*

Bunden, 3208, 3851, *p.p.* of bind.

Burnyst, 8907, burnished.

Buxom, see 'Boghsom'.
Bycom, 743, become, became. A.S. *becuman*, to attain to, arrive at, Germ. *bekommen*, to get obtain.
Byd, 2847, in ph. '*bid a bede*', i.e. offer a prayer.
Byde, 1980, to wait for.
Bydyng, *sb.*, 4708, abiding, awaiting.
Bydyng, byddyng, *sb.*, 3673, 4607, 5043, command.
Bye, 3615, 4399, to buy, to redeem, pret. *boght*. A.S. *bycgan, bóhte*.
Byfalle, falle, 2100, 4807, befall, happen.
Byfor, 46, 368, 523, before.
Bygan, 33, began.
Bygged, 4850, built, see 'Bigg'.
Byggyn[g], bygynge, *sb.*, 4782, 9119, a building.
Bygile, bygyle, 1264, 4031, to beguile.
Bygyn, 477, 2019, 4081, to begin. A.S. *aginnan, beginnan*. The abbreviated form *gan, gun, can* is often used as an auxiliary of the past tense of verbs as, '*gan* say = *did* say' &c.
Bygynnyng, *sb.*, 495, 3677, beginning.
Bygunnen, 6476, *p.p.* of *bygyn*.
Byhald, 625, 5337, behold.
Byhove, *vb.*, 3959, 5760, behove. A.S. *behofian*, to be fit.
Byhufe, 70, behoof. A.S. *behefe*. O.Fris. *behof, behuf*.
Byhynde, 1958, behind.
Byhyng, *sb.*, 3608, redemption.
Bylyve, 1229, quickly, suddenly.
Bymene, 1205, to explain (passive). 5511, to signify (active).
Bynethe, bynethen, 612, 5055, 5409, beneath, from A.S *neothan*, beneath. O.Fris. *binetha*. Germ. *nieder*, lower.
Byred, 5195, buried.
Bysily, 5809, busily.
Bysy, 185, 4253, busy.
Bysynes, 545, toil, trouble.
Bytaght, 5785, 5796, entrusted, pret. of *biteche*, to entrust. A.S. *betǽcan*.
Bytaken, 4378, betoken.
Bytwen, bytwene, 3668. A.S. *betwuh, betweoh*, by two, between.
Byyhonde, 4458, beyond. A.S. *begiondan*.

Caffe, 3148, chaff. A. S. *ceaf*. German *kaff*.
*Caitif, a wretch.
Cald, calde, 767, 4040, *adj.* and *sb.*, cold. A.S. *cáld*. Germ. *kalt*.
Can, kan, kun, 156, 175, 607, 4800, 1) to be able; 2) to know, pret. *cuth, couth*. A.S. *cunnan*. Goth. *kunnan*, to know. Sw. *kunna*, to be able.

Thou ert Laverd that worthy drihte
That al ophaldes wiht thi mihte;
Thou that al craftes *kann*,
Of erth and lam thou made man.
(Met. Hom. p. 2.)

Þat was na clerc sa crafti kend,
Bituixand þe werlds end,
Þat moght þe clerc wit clergé mat
Þat *cuth* þe bokes þat he wrat.
(Cursor Mundi fol. 48.)
(MS. Vesp. A. iii.)

Care, 7263, grief.
Carion, carayne, 572, 7926, corpse. Fr. *charogne*. Lat. *caro*.
Cast, 1918, 1976, order, reckon, invent, pret. *kest*, p. p. *kasten*; hence O. E. *cast*, a lot, an artifice.
Castel, 4783, castle.
Catelle, 3521, wealth. Fr. *chatel*, O. Fr. *chaptel*, a piece of property (moveable). Lat. *capitale*, whence *captale, catallum*.
Cay, 3838, key. A. S. *cæg*. Fris. *kay*.

Caysere, 882, emperour.
Caytefté, caytifté, 455, 551, wretchedness. From O. Fr. *chaitif*, *caitif*. Fr. *chêtif*, poor, wretched. Lat. *captivus*, captive.
Cees, ceese, 3564, 6373, to cease.
Ceesyng, *sb.*, 8356, cessation.
Certayne, 3562, 5969.
Certaynté,
Certifie, 6546.
Cesyng, 8356, cessation.
Chace, 4316. 5879, to drive about, follow. O. Fr. *chacier*, *chacher*. Fr. *chasser*.
Chalange, 2011, 2253, *a)* to claim, *b)* to accuse. Fr. *chalenger*. Lat. *calumniare*.

a) see King Lear i, 2:
Chalengyn or 'cleymyn' *vendico*. *Chalengyn*, or 'undyrtakyn', *reprehendo*, *deprehendo*. (P. P.)

For qua-sa hides godes gift,
God man *chalange* him of thift.
(Met. Hom. p. 3.)

Charbukelle, 9094, carbuncle.
Charge, *vb.*, 2947.
Charged, 5056, loaded. Fr. *charger*. Lat. *carricare*.
Charité, 3627, charity.
Chast, 3829, chaste. Lat. *castus*.
Chastité, 3828, chastity.
Chastied, 5068, pret. of *chasty*.
Chasty, 3549, 5547, to chastise. O. Fr. *chastoier*, *chastier*. Fr. *châtier*. Lat. *castigare*.
Chaunge, 4254, to change. Fr. *changer*.
*Chefe, chief.
Cheese, chese, 79, 1583, 2132, to choose, pret. *ches*. A. S. *ceosan*. Du. *kiesen*.
Cheftayn, 5073. O. Fr. *chevetaine*.
*Cheigne, chain.
Chere, 1636, 2233, 6181, face, countenance. O. Fr. *chiere*, Fr. *chère*, face, visage.
Chese, 2132, choose, see 'Cheese'.
Childer, childre, 5881, 6148, children.
Chymné, 6368, 4377, fire place. Fr. *cheminée*. Lat. *caminus*.
Circumcid, 4187, circumcised.
Citesayne, 8925.
Clathe, *a) vb.*, 3553, 5565, (pret. clad, cled), to clothe. *b) sb.*, 5573, 6156, a cloth, pl. clathes. A. S. *cláth*, Germ. *kleid*, Icel. *klædi*, a garment. In MS. Harl. 4196 a '*surkot*' is called a *clath*.
Cled, 6169, pret. of clathe.
Clene, 6352, purified, clean; 3801, 3828, chaste, pure; entirely.
Clenly, 9085, neatly.
Clensen, clense, 3705, 4913, to cleanse.
*Clepe, to call.
Clergy, *sb.*, 5844. learning. O. Fr. *clergie*, science. Mid Lat. *clericia*. Fr. *clergé*.
Clerk, clerke, 3831, 6257, one of the clergy, a learned man. O. Fr. *clerc*, *cler*. Lat. *clericus*.
Clethyng, *sb.*, 1533, 6943, clothing.
Clewe (clefe), 6736. A. S, *cleofan*, *clúfan*. Du. *klouen*, *kleuen*. Sc. *clew*, to cleave, separate.
Cloke, 6936, a claw. A. S. *clea*, *cleo*. Sc. *cluke*, *cleuk*, O. E. *cloy*, *clow*, *clew*, *cle*, *cliver*. Mod. E. *clutch*, the earlier form of which was *clouch*, stands in the same relation to *cloke*, as *pouch* does to *poke*, *pitch* to *pyk* &c.

Syche buffetez he hym̄ rechez,
With hys brode *klokes*,
Hys brest and his brathelle
Whas blodye alle over.
(Mort. Arth. p. 67.)

Clomsed, 1651, cursed. This meaning is given on the authority of MS. Addit. 22283. The word occurs again in MS. Harl. 4196

Corrupcion, corrupcioune, 4873, 4948.

Costage, 1522, expense, cost O.Fr. *couster*, *coster*, to cost; *costenge*, expense, from Lat. *constare*, to stand one in, cost.

Cotidiene, 2987. daily.

Counsaile, *sb.* and *vb.*, 3927, 5943, counsaille, counsaylle, counsel. O.Fr. *counsail.* Lat. *consilium.*

Countenance, 6245.

Countrefette, 4311, counterfeit.

Cours, 4318.

Couth, 321, 3787, could, 5703, knew, see 'Can'.

Covatous, covayteous, 740, 4431.

Covayte, 5734.

Covaytise, *sb.*, 1180, 2990. O.Fr. *coveteise.*

Cover, 811, to recover.

Covert, *sb.*, 1578, *adj.*, 4489, secret. O.Fr. *covert*, secret, from *covrir.* Lat. *coöperire.*

Coverture, 6955.

Crafte, 4215, art.

Craftily, 9088.

Crafty, 9085.

Cragges, 6393, cliffs; 'a *krag* of stone'. (MS. Harl. 4196 fol. 187.) Welsh *careg*, a stone. Gael. *creag*, a rock.

Creatoures, creatours, 4127, 5430, 5472, created things (animate and inanimate).

Cresten, 4397, christian.

Crestendome, 3128, baptism.

Crevyce, 9186.

Cribbe, 5200, crib. cratch. Du. *kribbe.*

Cristal, cristale, 6349, 6397.

Cristanté, 3925,

Cristen, 197, 3783, 4136, christian.

Cristendome, 4082, 4168, baptism.

Crop, croppe, 663, 1906, top, summit. A.S. *crop*, top. *Croppe* of an erbe or tree, *cima*, *coma*, *capillamentum.* Pr. Pm.

The *crop* was evening to the rote.
(MS. Vesp. A. iii, f. 65.)

Crose, croyce, croys, croyse, 5272, 5275, 5279, 5283, 5596. O.Fr. *crois.* Fr. *croix.* Lat. *crux.*

Croun, *a)* (of the head), 1492. *b)* 4087, 5296, a crown.

Crysom, 2791, an error for *uncrysom.* O.Fr. *cresme*, from χρισμα.

Crystalle, 9078.

Cunnyng, counyng, 2350, 7207, knowledge, science.

Curalle, 9105.

Curtasy, 1519, 1530. Fr. *courtoisie*, courtesy, civility—Cotgrave.

Custom, 4054, 4055.

Cymented, 9068.

Dale, 1044, 1046, abode, dwelling.

Dalk, 6447, a hollow. *Delk* a small cavity in the body or in the soil (Forby). *Dalke*, vallis. Pr. Pm. Icel. *dala*, a dint. Dan. *dal*, valley. "Moni cunne riwle beoð; auh tuo beoð among alle þet ich chulle speken of. Þe on riwleð þe heort, þe makeð hire efne ant smeðe, wiðute knotte ant *dolke* of woh, inwit ant of wreinde."
(Þe Ancren Riwle p. 1.)

Dam, 1273, dame.

Dampned, 3706.

Dang, pret. of *ding*, to hammer, strike, see 'Dyng'.

Þan decius thoght grete hethinge,
Þat laurence was noght for him rad
And to his turmentours he bad,
Þat þai suld tak kobille stanes,
And *ding* his teth out al at anes;
And when þai with þe stanes him *dang*,
He stode ay laghand þam omang.
(MS. Harl. 4196 fol. 170.)

Dased, 6647, cold, weak; '*dasyt* wightis.' It also = stupified.
(G. Douglas, vol. ii, p. 567.)

t

Desayve, 4028, 4235, to deceive.
Descryfe, descryve, 2305, 6848, to describe.
Despende, dispend, 125, 2435, 5915, to spend, use.
Despice, *vb.*, 9426.
Destroie, distroie, 4453, 4472.
Destrucion, destrucioun, 4049, 4063, 4067,
Destruye, 4074, 4076.
Desyre, 8032.
Dette, 3617, 3861, debt.
Devocyoun, 5906, 7252.
Deygh, digh, dighe, 1747, 1748, 1780, 2060, 3636, to die; 5262, 6533, pret. *dighed*, *deyhed*, *did* (1779), *dieghed* (1780, 5596).
Dignité, 3872, 4809, dignity.
Dight, 448, 6149, *a)* prepared, *b)* decked, 8532. A.S. *dihtan*, to set in order. Germ. *dichten*, contrive, invent.
Digne, 74, 5853, worthy. Lat. *dignus*.
Dilitable, 5276, delightful.
Disciple, 5908.
Disciplyne, 5556.
Discrive, discryve, 1901, 6117, to describe.
Discusse, 6247, to investigate.
Dispayre, 6293.
Dispend, 2435, to spend.
Dispise, 4252.
Dissencion, 4061.
Distance, 8400.
Divers, 4788.
Diversly, 7473.
Divised. 987, divided.
Do, 4290, cause.
Doble, 2259, double.
Doctur, 3827.
Doghter, 2130, 5434, daughter. A.S. *dohter*.
Dole, 5381, pain, grief. Sc. *dool*, pl. *doles*.

Unto blis [he] wille himself me fetche,
So þat no *doles* ne salle me dretche.
(MS. Harl. 4166, fol. 171.)

Dom, dome, 49, 4323. dumb. A.S. *dumb*. Icel. *dumbs*, *dumbi*, dumb, *dumma*, to be still.
Dom, dome, 264, 1859, 3990, 4476, 4714, doom. A.S. *dom*, judgment.
Domland, *adj.*, 1443, louring, cloudy. *Douiland*, is printed as the reading of the Cottonian MS., but *domland* which is the reading of two Manuscripts is no doubt the correct word. *Domland* is a participle of the verb *domel*, to be dark. Icel. *dumba*, darkness. Sw. *dimba*, a fog. Dan. *dum*, dim. obscure. Brockett's Glossary has the northern word *dromland*, cloudy, muddy. With the double forms *domland* and *dromland* compare *skill* and *shrill*.
Cf. Burn's use of *drumly* in the sense of muddy, turgid.
Don, doun, 673, 2065, down; *of dune*, deorsum—Lye.
Donlight, 4293, to descend.
Donward, 663, 816, downward.
Dote, 785, talk silly, rave. Dutch *doten*, *dutten*, delirare, desipere—Kilian. 'Maddyn or *dotyn*, desipio' Pr. Pm. Sc. *doit*, to be confused, to dote. Icel. *dotta*, to slumber.

And als he went another way,
He met a man [þat] was wonder old,
Croked and cumberd, koghand for cold,
Lame he was in lith and lim,
With nese dropand and eghen dym
His handes tremblid, his teth roted,
He spak so dym men demyd he *doted*.
(MS. Harl. 4196, fol. 201.)

Douiland, see 'Domland'.
Douncom, 4821, 5171, to descend.

Douncomyng, *sb.*, 5271, a descending.
Dounfal, 4620.
Dounfallyng, 6576.
Doungangyng, *sb.*, 4779, setting.
Dounlay, 4415, to lay down.
Dounryn, 7123.
Dout, 4330, doubt, fear.
Draw, 1291, 1. to entice; 1476, 4007, 2. to go to, to incline to; 3. compile, compose, pret. *drogh*, *droh*, *drow*. A.S. *dragan*.

1. For il felawes oft *drawes*
God men til ivel plaws.
(Met. Hom., p. 115.)
2. To dede I *drawe* als ye mai se
(Ibid. p. 30.)
3. Mi speche haf I mint to *drawe*,
Of cristes dedes and his saw.
(Ibid. p. 2.)

Drawen, 336, composed.

In other Inglis was it *drawin*,
And turned Ic have it til ur awin
Language of the northin lede,
Þat can nan other Inglis rede.
(Met. Hom. xxii.)

Dre, 5373, sorrow. Cf. Sc. *dree*; see 'Dreghe'.
Dred, drede, 3969, 5935, dread.
Dredful, dreful, 4977, 5129, dreadful, sorrowful.
Dreghe, drighe, 2235, 3540, 6523, Sc. *drie*, to suffer. A.S. *dreógan*.
Drery, 791, 1455, sorrowful. Germ. *traurig*. A.S. *dreorig*.

Whi mi saule *dreri* ertou?
(Ps. xii, 6.)

Drighe, 2044, 2754, to suffer.
Drighten, lord. A.S. *drihten*.
*Dring, chieftain. A.S. *dreng*.
Drogh, droghe, 2249, 4419, 8527, pret. of *draw*.
Drop, 775, to drip.
Drope, 3063, a drop. Du. *drop*, drup. Icel. *dropi*. A.S. *dropa*.
Drove, 1319, to afflict, trouble.

Loverd hou fele-folded are þai,
Þat *drove* me, to do me wa.
(Ps. iii, 2.)

Drovyng, *sb.*, tribulation. Du. *droef*, *droeve*, troubled, sad, *droeven*, to disturb, trouble. Goth. *drobjan*. Germ. *trüben*. Cf. O. E. *drupi*, troubled, sorrowful.
Droubelonde, p. 40, see 'Domland' Compare '*drobly*, *drubly*, turbulentus, turbidus (of drestys), feculentus.' P. P.
Drury, 7825, gallantry. O. Fr. *druerie*, *drurie*, friendship. O.H.Germ. *trût*, *drût*, dilectus—Burguy.
Dubbed, 8790, decorated, from *dub*, to adorn, ornament. Fr. *douber*, to rig or trim a ship. Prov. *adobar*, to arrange, prepare.

"A garment to him gert he mak,
Side and wide, and wonder blak;
He gert it *dub* fra top til to,
With swerel tailes ful blak also."
(MS. Cotton Galba E. ix, fol. 39.)

Dule, 6387, pain, grief.
Dulful, duleful, 1116, 6110, doleful. Phrase, '*duleful* dyn'.
Dungen, 3256, p. p. of *ding*, to hammer, strike.
Dunwarde, 816, 2869, downward.
Dur, 4135, 4548, to dare.
Duschyng, *sb.*, 7351, a blow, a smiting. Dan. *daske*, to slap. Icel. *dust*, a blow. The verb and noun '*dusch*' is frequently used by Scottish writers in the sense of to *dash*, smite, beat down.

The byrnand towr down rollys with
a rusche,
Quhill all the hevennys dyndlit of
the *dusch*.
(G. Douglas vol. ii, p. 551.)
And sa hard on helmes he *duschit*,

Throw fine force [he] thame al to
fruschit
(Buik of Alex. p. 386.)

Dwine, 703, to dwindle, fade. A.S. *dwinan*, to fade. Icel. *dvina*, to diminish.

Dygh, dyghe, 2054, 2670, to die.

Dym, 1166, dark. A.S. *dim*. Icel. *dimmr*, dark, *dimma*, darkness. 'dedes *dim*' = dark deeds.
(Met. Hom. p. 111.)

Dyn, 4787, noise. Icel. *dynia*, to resound; *duna*, to thunder.

Dyng, 7015, 7031, to strike, beat. Icel. *dengia*. Sw. *dänga*. A.S. *dencgan*.

Dyngyng, *sb.*, 6571, a beating.

Dynt, 5418, 7017, blow. A.S. *dynt*.

Dysy, 1771, dizzy. A.S. *dysig*, O.E. *dusi*, foolish. O.Fris *dusia*, to be dizzy.

Edwyte, *vb.*, see p. 4, note 1, to reproach. A.S. *edwitan*. O.E. *atwite*. E. *twit*.

Eer, ear.

Eese, *vb.*, 1469, to please. *sb.*, 1563, ease, pleasure.

Eesy, 1402, easy, pleasant. Fr. *aise*, convenience, leisure. A.S. *eath*, easy, gentle.

Eft, efter, 6523, 6654, after, afterwards, again. A.S. *æft*, *æftan*, *æfter*, *efter*, again, afterwards.

Egg, 5483, to incite, instigate. O.N. *eggia*, A.S. *eggian*, to sharpen, to instigate. *Egg*, an edge.

Eggyng, *sb.*, 5187, instigation.

Eghe, 2234, 6261, eye. A.S. *egh*, *eage*; Germ. *auge*; pl. eghen, 575.

Eght, 4784, eighth. A.S. *ehta*, *eatha*.

Eghtend, 6569, eighth.

Eghteld, eghtild, 5784, 5800, to endeavour, to aim at. Sc. *ettle*, A.S. *ehtian*, *ehtan*, to follow after, pursue. Icel. *ætla*, to intend. This word is sometimes written *attled*, *eyteld*, *aghteld*.

For ur lord had *aghteld* yete
A child to rais of his [Adam's]
oxspring,
Þat all suld oute o baret bring.
(Cott. MS. Vesp. A. iii, fol. 9.)

Aghtel also signifies 'to endow with'.

Quà herd ever spek o mare bliss,
Þan *aghteld* was Adam and his.
(Ibid. fol. 53.)

Eke, heke, 3256, 6239, to increase. Germ. *auch*, also. Goth. *aukan*, to increase; A.S. *ecan*.

Eld, elde, 742, 1513, 1883, 4983, age, old age. A.S. *eald*; Germ. *alt*, old.

Elementes, 6352.

Elle, 5273, hell.

Elles, els, 1281, 1754, 3816, 7420, else, otherwise. A.S. *elles*.

Ellevend, 4798, eleventh. A.S. *endleofan*, eleven.

Emparour, 4089.

Empiry, 7761.

Empyre, 4050.

Enamayld, 8902, interwoven.

Enchauntemente, 4286.

Encheson, enchesoun, 5311. 5790, reason. O.Fr. *acheson*, Lat. *occasio*.

Endeles, 6067.

Endelesnes, endlesnes, 8122, 8124, eternity.

Endeward, 4007, towards the end.

Ending, *sb.*, 3772, end, death, 4026, 4156. Goth. *andeis*; Sansc. *anta*, end, death.

And when to king Edward was tald
How þat Brus þat was so bald
Had brocht þe Cumyn till *endyng*
Out of his wit he went wele ner.
(Barbour p. 33.)

Endlang, 8582, from head to tail.

A. S. *andlang;* Germ. *entlang*, along.

Enioynt, 3900, 3906, enjoined.

Enmy, 1037, 5329, enemy. O. Fr. *enemi*, Lat. *inimicus*.

Enoyntyng, *sb.*, 3409, anointing. Fr. *oindre;* Lat. *ungere*, to anoint.

Ensample, ensaumple, 708, 4532, example. O. Fr. *ensample*, Lat. *exemplum*.

Entent, 3696, 5960, 5991, intention, will. O. Fr. *entent*, from Lat. *intendere*.

Ententyfly, 624, 2550, carefully.

Entre, *vb.*, 5340.

Entré, *sb.*, 8898.

Envy, 4169.

Er, 49, 331, 805 &c., are.

Erdly, 4955, earthly. Germ. *erde*, [earth.

Ere, 782, ear.

Err, *vb.*, in phrase 'es *erred*', 5733, 'is done wrong'.

Erres, 5327, 5600, scars. Dan. *ar*, O. N. *ör*.

Errour, 4266.

Erryng, *sb.*, 5728, 5974, error.

Erthedyn, 4036, 4790, earthquake, a compound of *erthe* = earth and *dyn*, din, noise.

Ertou, 424, art thou.

Es, 30, is.

Eschape, 2678, to escape. O. Fr. *eschaper*, Fr. *échaper*, to shift away, slip out of.

Ese, 595, pleasure.

But theder come bothe ȝong and olde,
Into the temple for to her,
Goddes servyse on thair maner,
And for to make thair offerand thar
Efter that thair *esse* war.
(Met. Hom. p. 74.)

Ete, 4848, ate.

Ette, ete, 4675, 6191, to eat, pret. ete. Goth. *itan;* Germ. *essen*.

Evaungelistte, 5004.

Excused, 6077.

Exposicion, 3856, 4716, exposition.

Expound, 4272.

Faa, 1453, foe, *pl.* faes, faas. A. S. *fah*, *fá*, enemy. *Fa* as an adjective = bad, dirty occurs in the description of the two women, who appeared before Solomon, each laying claim to the same child:

Þair clathes was sa gnede and *fa*
Þat þai moght nan part þam fra.
(Cursor Mundi, fol. 48.)

Fader, 1386, father. O. N. *fadir;* Germ. *vater*.

*Fairhede, beauty.

Fal, fall, 171, *a)* to appertain to, belong to; 228, 3992, *b)* to happen. O. N. *falla*, to fall.

Fald, 4637, 4640, fold (for sheep). A. S. *fald*.

Fald = fold, as in twafald &c. Germ. *falten*, to fold.

Falshede, 1176, falsehood.

Fand, pret. of find.

Fande, 1463, 3534, 2228, to tempt try. A. S. *fandian*.

Fandyng, 314, temptation. A. S. *fandung*.

Fantome, 1197, vanity, lie. Greek *φάντασμα*, an appearance, whence the Fr. *fantosme*, *fantome*, a spectre, fantom, 'a *fantime* or a fabel'.
(Cursor Mundi, fol. 134).

Mennes sones to-when of hert unmeke?
Whi love yhe *fantom* and lighinge speke?
(Psalm v, 3.)

Far = fare, 3638.

†Fare, *sb.*, suffering.

Fare, 1863, 1. to go, depart, pret.

fore and ferd; 270, 1343, 2. to behave, conduct oneself. A.Sax. *faran.*
Fas, 3883, foes, *pl.* of fa.
Fast, 4211, quickly.
Fayn of, *adj.*, 4552, glad of. A.S. *fægn*, joyful fain; *fahnian*, to rejoice. We meet with *fain* as a verb in Ps. ix, 3.
I sal *fayne* and glad in þe.
Fayntise, 3519, weariness, literally deceit from O.Fr. *feintise*, *faintise*, from *feindre*, *faindre.*
Fayre, 4315, 9249, beautiful, beautifully. O.N. *fagr*, bright.
Fayrnes, 249, beauty.
*Fed, fede, enemy. Du. *vied*, hatred. A.S. *fæhth*, enmity.
Feer, *vb.*, 6429, to frighten. A.S. *fær*, fear. Sw. *fara*, to fear.
Fel, 5406, fierce, see 'Felle'.
Fel, 6416, many. A.S. *fela.*
Felaghe, 5485, fellow, companion.
Felaghshepe, felawshepe, 4400, 5032, fellowship, company.
Feld, 1247, field.
Fele, 2453, many; phrase '*to fele*', 'too much'. Germ. *viel.*
Felle, fel, *adj.*, 1820, *a)* cruel; 1743, *b)* dreadful. Fr. *felle*, cruel, fierce; *felon*, cruel, rough; *felonie*, anger, cruelty, treason.
*Felle, *sb.*, a wretch.
†Felle, a hill.
Felle, 82, 739, 3077, 4967, skin. O.N. *fel*, Du. *vel*, skin.
Felly, 4449, cruelly.
Felony, 5346, wickedness, see 'Felle'.
Feloun, 2995, a whitlow.
Felouns, wretches, see 'Felle'.
Fen, 566, dirt, mud. O.N. *fen*, a morass. Goth. *fani*, mud.
Fende, 36, 1253, 4160, fiend, devil. Germ. *feind*, enemy. Goth. *fian*, to hate.
Fer, 1866, 2329, 3895, far; *comp.* ferrer. A.S. *feor*, O.H.G. *fer.*
Ferd, 6864, *sb.*, fear; *adj.*, 6950, afraid. A.S. *forht*, Germ. *furcht*, fear.
Ferdlayk, ferdelayk, 2915, 6427, fear, see 'Ferd'; formed from the *adj.* ferd, afraid. The termination -layk = -ness, as revelaic, hendlaic &c.
Ferdnes, 2231, 2321, fear, see 'Ferd'.
Þe erth tremblid and al to schoke,
And halows in heyyn for *ferdnes* quoke.
(MS. Harl. 4196. fol. 82.)
Fere, 2291, to frighten.
*Fere, sound. Dan. *för.* Icel. *foerr.*
Fereth, fourth.
†Feren, fiery.
Ferforth, 3814, far. Ferrer-forthe, 2329.
Ferly, 2211, 2955, wonder. A.S. *ferlic*, sudden.
Ferth, ferthe, fierthe, fereth, 356, 1246, 1828, 3983, 4260, 4770, fourth. A.S. *feother*, *feower*, four.
Ferre, 5190, far, see 'Fer'.
Fest, pret. of fast, to fasten.
Al his clathes fra him þai kest,
And tille a peler fast him *fest*,
And scourges kene þai ordand þare
To bete opon his body bare,
(MS. Harl. 4196, fol. 76.)
Fested, 1907, 1909, fastened, *p. p.* of fest.
Festend, 5295,
Feyn, 4233, to feign. Fr. *feindre.*
Feyned, *adj.*, 2556, feigned.
Fickle, 1088, deceptive, false.
Semi Saxon *fiken*, *fikeln*, to deceive. A.S. *ficcan*; Fris. *fischeln*, to flatter (see Gloss. to 'Seinte Marharete', ed. Cockayne).
With þar tunges *fikeli* þai dide 'linguis suis dolose agebant'.
(Ps. v. 11.)

For in his tyme, I hard well say
Þat *fykkil* þai war all tyme of fay.
(W. C. vol. ii, p. 130.)
He moved was
Be *fykkyl* fals suggestyowne.
(Ibid. p. 132.)

Fife, 2431, five. Du. *vyf*.
Fift, fifte, 3088. 3966, 4776, fifth.
Fiftend, 4812,
Filand, 2365, defiling.
Fild, 2341, fild.
File, fyle, 1198, 1210, 2348, to defile, pollute. Hence O. E. *fyle*, file, a wicked wretch.
Filed, 2559, defiled. A. S. *fylan*, to make foul or filthy.
Filthede, p. 13 note, see 'File'.
Final, 3990,
Fine, 4913, to refine, purify. O. N. *fina*, to polish, cleanse.
Flay, 1268, 2244, to terrify. Sc. *fley*. Icel. *Flæja*, to frighten, put to flight·

Thow art bot a fawntkyne,
Ne ferly me thynkys!
Thou wille be *flayede* for a flye
That on thy flesche lyghttes.
(Mort. Arth. p. 175.)
Thou wenes for to *flay* us,
Ffloke-mouthede schrewe.
(Ibid. p. 232.)

Flaying, *sb.*, 6112, fear.
Flayne, 9520, flayed.
Flayre, 9017, smell. Fr. *flairer*, to smell.
Flaume, flawme, 6737, flame. Lat. *flamma*. Fr. *flamme*.
Flegh, 4394, flee, pret. flegh and flogh. A.S. *fleon*, *flion*. Germ. *fliehen*.
Flemed, 2977. 6054, banished, from *flem*, to banish. A.S. *flyman*, to banish; *fleam*, exile, flight.
Fleygh, flew, pret. of flegh.
Flitte, *vb. intr.*, 2257, 1. to depart, 3762, 2. *vb. intr.*, to remove. Dan. *flytte*, to remove.

2. And for þe fute [i. e. of the cross]
þay made a pit
Ffor no man suld it þeþin *flit*.
(MS. Harl. fol. 82.)

Flode, 4706, flood. O.N. *flód*, Sw. *flod*, a flood. O.N. *flæda*, to inundate.
Flogh, flew, pret. of flegh.
Fode, 458, food. A. S. *foda*, *fode*. Goth. *fodjan*, to nourish. Eng. to *foster*.
Fole, 126, fool. Fr. *fol*, foolish.
Fole, 6632. foul.
Fole, 1537, foal. Germ. *fohlen*, Goth. *fuld*, a foal, filly. Phrase "tatird *fole*."
"Tatird as a *foylle*." (T.M. p. 4.)
Folk, 4637, 6013, people.
Fon, fone, 530, 762, 764, 2693, few. (Foner, 765, 3731, fewer.) A plural form of the A. S. *feawa*. O. H. G. *foho*. Goth. *favs*, pl. *favai*.
Fontstane, 3351, fontstone.
For, *conj.*, 1263, 1291, 2034, because. Goth. *faur*, Germ. *vor*, in front of. The *for* in forbard, fordo &c. = Germ. *ver*, forth, away, out.
Forbard, 957, excluded.
Fordo, 3395, 3504, 6323, to do away with, destroy.
Forga, 1842, to forego, to go without.
Forganger, 4152, foregoer.
Forgeten, 3909.
Forgyfnes, 3817, forgiveness.
Forluke, 1946, foresee.
Formefader, 483, forefather. A.S. *forme*, first. In the Cursor Mundi we find *formast* = first used as an adj. '*formast* fader', (fol. 54), Cf. *form*-kind, *form*-birth, *form*-days. (fol. 51.)
Forsake, 4406, 6057, deny.

Forsweryng, *sb.*, 3367, perjury.
Forth-bring, 4163, 5868.
Forther-mare, 2892.
Forthir, 440. A.S. *forth*, forward. Germ. *fort.*
Fortone, 1273, fortune.
*Forth, way, course. A.Sax. *fór.*
Forthy, 375, therefore, because = for that.
Forthynkyng, *sb.*, 3510, repentance.
Forþi, forþy, 189. 375, 1854, therefore, because.
Forwhi, forwhy, 1249, 6458, wherefore, therefor = for which.
Forworth, *vb.*, 780, to come to ruin, to fail. A.S. *forweorthan.*

For Laverd of rightwise wate þe wai
And gate of wicked *forworth* salai.
(Ps. 1, 6.)

Fot, fote, 467, 778, 1493, foot.
Fourme, 3982, form, figure.
Fourtend. 4808, fourteenth.
Fra, 114, 3713, from. O.N. *frá*, from. Phrases: 'to and *fra*', 471, 603; '*fra* than', from that time', 4071.
Fraist, frayst, 1090, 1358, to attempt, to try. O.N. *fresta*, to try.
Fraunches, 7995, freedom.
Fraward, frawarde, 87, 256, 5854, froward.
Frawardnes, 1173.
Frayst, 1358, see 'Fraist'.

For þo þat to dremys overmoche trastys,
To scorne hem þe fende þen *frastys.*
(Handlyng Synne p. 15,)

Froly, 5902, 5958, 5965.
Frend, 1116, 6342, friend; *pl.* frend.
Frendshepe, 1884, friendship.
Fresshe, 1254, eager, ready. A.S. *ferse.* Du. *versch*, *frisch.*
Freyle, 4582, 5740, frail. Fr. *frêle.*
Frete, 6570, to eat. A.S. *fretan.*
Frett, 9107, ornamented.
Fro, 1586, 7735, from.
Front, frount, 816, 4410, forehead. Lat. *frons*, *frontis.*
Fruytles, 5666, not producing fruit.
Fude, food, see 'Fode'.
Ful, fule, fulle, 520, 789, 4129, 5276, *a)* very; phrase '*ful* late'. 2611, 2612, *b)* entire, complete, phrase '*ful* joy', '*ful* sorrow'.
Fulfild, 535, filled with.
Fully, 476, 4570, completely.
Fulfill, 5016, to fill up, make complete.
Funden, 4608, *p. p.* of find.
Fune, 6424, few, see 'Fone'.
Funstane, see 'Fonstane'.
Fygur, 2320, form, shape.
Fyland, 2357, defiling.
Fyle, 2349, to defile.
Fyn, fyne, 3337, 3338, to refine, purify, see 'Fine'!
Fynal, 6129.
Fyndynges, 1557, inventions.
Fyne, 3337, see 'Fine'.
Fyned, 3201, 3202, 6398, refined, purified.
Fyre-brand, 7421.
Fyre-bryght, 5035.
Fyry, 7762, fiery.
Fyver, 2989, 3029, fever. Fr. *fièvre.* Lat, *febris.*

Ga, gang, 193, 4100, to go. 3d pers. sing. *gase.* O.N. *ganga*; N. *ganga*, *gaa*, to go on foot, walk.
Gader, gadir, 1342, 2221, 3728, to gather. Germ. *gattern.* Du. *gaderen.*
Gaderyng, *sb.*, 8831.
Gaf, gve.
Gain-turnyng, 1718, returning.
†Gammen, sport, play.
Gane, 3750, gone.

Granand, 798, groaning. A.S. *granian*. Du. *groonen*.

Grape, 6566, 6801, to feel, grasp. A.S. *grapian*; Goth. *greipan*; O.N. *greipa*, Sw. *grabba*, to seize, grasp.

Þan answerd to him Peter and Ion,
And said þarof es wonder none;
Forwhi þou trowed noght Thomas,
Þat oure lord Ihesus resin was,
Untille þou saw his blody side,
And *graped* within his wondes wide;
Of evil bileve has þou ay bene,
And þat es on þi selven sene,
Þarfore ertow ay us fro,
When any thing es for to do.
(MS. Harl. 4196, fol. 173.)

Graunt, 3827, to grant.

Graythely, 645, carefully, thoroughly. It also signifies preparedly, readily, from *graythe*, *greithe*, to make ready. O. N. *greiða*. A. S. *ge-read*, ready. Prov. E. *gradely*.

Grege, 2991, to increase.

Gres, gresse, 4864, 6392, grass. A.S. *gærs*, *græs*. Sc. *gersse*.

Gret, 5392, to weep, see 'Grete'.

Gret, grete, 69, 644, 903, 3721, great, *comp.* gretter.

Gretand, 502, crying.

Grete, 7099, to cry. A.S. *grætan*, to weep. We have also O. Eng. *grete* a tear, weeping, see Ps. c. 1-10.

Gretely, 1831, greatly.

Gretyng, *sb.*, 496, 1451, 6109, a cry.

Grevaunce, 3019.

Greve, 3608, grieve. Fr. *grever*, to oppress, disquiet. Lat. *gravis*, heavy.

Grevosly, grevusly, 4537, 5562, grievously.

†Grise, terrible.

Grisely, 1757, 2233, horrible, dreadful. A.S. *agrysan*, to terrify, *grislic*, grisly.

Grisse, 4781, grass.

Groche, 297, to murmur, grumble. '*Grutchyn*, *gruchyn*, murmuro'— (P.P.) Fr. *gruger*, to grieve, repine; *groucer*, *grouchier*, *groucher*, to murmur, reproach.

Þai *gruched* þus and war noght fain.
(MS. Harl. 4196, fol. 38.)

Grotchand, 3542, murmuring.

Grund, grond, 209, 7213, foundation, bottom. Goth. *grundus*, O.N. *grunnr*.

Grym, 2250, savage, fierce. Germ. *grimm*, fury, wrath. Du. *grim*, probably connected with the O.E. *gram*, *grame*, grome, angry. A.S. *grama*, *gram*; Germ. *gram*.

Grymly, 2226, fiercely.

Gryn, 2226, to grind the teeth, open the mouth wide. N. *grina*, to wry the mouth, curl the nose. Du. *grinnen*, to grin, snarl.

Then shalle helle gape and gryn.
(T. M. p. 53.)

Bihald sal sinful rightwis thenne,
And with his tethe on him sal he *grenne*.
(Ps. xxxvi, 12.)

Grysly, 1404, dreadful, see 'Grisely'.

Gryslynes, 2310, terribleness.

Gud, gude, 8, 80, good, see 'Gode'.

Gude, *pl.* gudes, 1244, riches, goods.

Gudnes, gudenes, 134, 3676, 4586, goodness.

Gun, 4700, pret. of *bigin*. It is frequently written *gan*, *can*, and is used as an auxiliary of the past tense as '*gan* say' = 'did say'.

Gys, gyse, 1533, 1546, guise, fashion (of dress). Fr. *guise*, mode, way, fashion.

†Ha, to have.
Haf, 58, to have.
Haithen, haythen, 5521, heathen. Germ. *heide*, a heathen. Goth. *haithno*, *haithi*, the open country. E. *heath*. Du. *heide*, *heyden*. E. *hoiden*, a clown, a pagan.
Hald, halde, 794, 1283, to estimate, 3836, hold.
Halden, 99, 1596, 4398, 5950, 5960, (*p.p.* of hald), held, bound. A.S. *healdan*, Germ. *halten*, to keep, observe, hold. Phrase 'is *halden* for to do', 5937.
*Haldes, *sb.*, holds, fastnesses.
Haldyng, 5994, possession.
Hale, *adj.*, 3933, 6348, whole.
Hale, *vb.*, 8323, 8344, to heal. A.S. *hal*, healthy, whole.
Halghe, 6087, a saint.
Halghe Thursday, holy Thursday.
Haligast, 3, Holyghost.
Halow, 3823, a saint, *pl.* halowes. from A.S. *halgian*, to keep holy, consecrate. E. *hallow*.
Haly, 977, 3690, 4233, holy.
Haly, halely, 2416, 3710, 4254, wholly, see 'Hale'.
Halynes, 4240, holiness.
Hand (= and), 775, breath. O.N. *anda*, breath.
Hap, happe, 1282, 5897, fortune. O.N. *happ*.

Salamon was in mekil wele
Umset bath wit *hap* and sele.
(MS. Vesp. A. iii, fol. 50.)

Happy, 1334, fortunate, lucky.
Hard, 806, 1785, *a)* severe, painful; 662, *b)* firm. Germ. *hart*. O.N. *hardr*. Phrases '*hard* haldand' = close fisted, 790; '*hard* day', 6075, '*hard*-herted'.
Hardnes, 3515, suffering, pain.

For right als brede here bodily,
Sustenes and strenkithes þe body,
Right so þe gift of strenkith mai make
Þe hert stalworthe, to undertake
And to thole *hardnes* here in body,
For þe luf of god almighty.
(MS. Tib. E. vii, fol. 12.)

Hare, 675, 5001, hair. Du. *haer*, Germ. *haar*.
Harn-pane, 5298, brain-pan. O.N. *hjarni*, A.S. *hærnes*.

And with a sownd smate Targus but remede,
Throu ather part or templis of his hede;
In the *harnpan* the schaft he has affixt,
Quhil blude and brane al togider mixt.
(G. Douglas, fol. ii, p. 551.)

Haste, *vb.*, 2885, to hasten. Sw. *hasta*, to hurry.
Hastily, 3725, quickly.
Hasty. 1548, sudden, unexpected.

Symon answerd and said nay,
I may noght bere it [the cross] this day,
And *hasty* thinges I have to do.
(MS. Harl. 4196 fol. 82.)

Hastyly, 4544, speedily.
Hat, hats, 3038, 3189, hot; *comp.* hatter = hotter, 3097.
Hat, hatte, 3951, called, named. It is sometimes written *hatten*. A.S. *hátan*, to vow, promise. Icel. *heita*, to name, to be named. Goth. *haitan*, to call, to command.

And he said Ic haf sped ful ille,
For nan of thaim wille do mi wille,
[Thar] wald nan of thaim mi lare liste,
Bot an that *hatte* Teocist.
(Met. Hom. p. 149.)

Haterel, 1492, the poll.
Hatreden, 3403, hatred. 'Wic

hatreden' i. e. 'wicked hatred'.
(Ps. xxiv, 19.)

-reden was a common termination in Northern literature; *lufreden*, love (M. H. p. 30); *felawreden*, fellowship (MS. Harl. 4196); *monraden*, *monreden*, homage (Syr. Gawayne, Romances Ed. Robson A. 505).

Haunt, 1079, 1525, 4382, 6344. to practise. Fr. *hanter*, to frequent, haunt.

Havyng, *sb.*, 1520. behaviour. Germ. *haben*, to behave. A.S. *habban*, to have.

He [Edgare] wes a man of fayre *havyng*,
And dyde in hys tyme bot leful thyng.
(W. C. p. 275.)

Hawen, 3877, own.

Hawtayne, 255, haughty. Fr. *hautain* from *haut*, O.Fr. *hault*, high.

Haythen, 5431, heathen.

Hed, heved, hede, 486, 3596, 5002, 5658.

Hede, 592, heed. A. S. *hedan*, to keep, guard, observe.

*Hefding, beheading.

Hegh, heghe, *vb.*, 1191, 4953, 8506, to exalt.

Hegh, heghe, *adj.*, 1872, 1887, 4953, 4763; *comp.* hegher, 962; *superl.* heghest (and hext), 993. A.S. *heah*, high.

Heghen, 4119, to exalt.

And he þat mekes himself with wille,
He salle be *heghind* als it es skille.
(MS. Harl. 4196, fol. 109.)

Heghnes, 8500, exaltation, pride.

Heght, 4760, height.

Heke (= eke), 3546, to increase.

Held, 817, to bend down, stoop.

Alle *helded* þai samen.
Omnes declinaverunt simul.
(Ps. xiii, 3.)

Þe men þat wyght and willy ware,
Said "to þi steven we stand
Whaso heved so *heldes* brede of an hare,
Hardily hag of his hand."
Þe hevedes halely gan *held*
And did him honoure alle.
(MS. Harl. 4196, fol. 207.)

Held (= eld), 756, old age.

Hele, 757, 1326, 2035, health.

Hend, 3214, 5602, *plural* of hand. O.N. *hendr*.

Hend þai haf, and noght sal þai
Grape with þam night ne dai.
(Ps. cxiii.)

Þai hent Joseph be *hend* and fete.
(MS. Vesp. A. iii, fol. 25.)

Thai wrang thair *hend* and wep ful sar.
(Met. Hom. p. xviii.)

Hende, 1764, 2693, 4005, end.

Hend, polished.

Henged, 5260, hanged. O.N. *hanga*, to hang, pret. *héck*.

Hent, *vb.*, 2722, to receive. Hent, *pret.* O.N. *henda*, to seize.

Herber, *sb.*, 448, 6153, lodging. Sc. *herbery*, to shelter, to house. *vb.*, 6154, to lodge. A.S. *heribyrigan*, to lodge; *beorgan*, to shelter.

Bot Godd sun he wald sua be gest,
In clene sted al most he rest,
A clene bowist he ches forþi,
For to mak in his *herbergeri*.
(MS. Vesp. A. iii, fol. 55.)

Here, 526, to hear.

Heremyte, 8724.

Hert, 255, 3547, heart.

Herth, 71, 409, 4861, earth. Goth. *hairto*.

Hete, 9490, to promise. A.S. *hátan*.

Hethen, 509, 3704, 6007, hence.

Heved, 675, 771, 4082, 5002, head.

Heven, 7756, heaven. A.S. *heofon.*
Hevenryke, 403, 1898, the kingdom of heaven.
Hever, 3932, ever.
Hevy, 4583, sorrowful.
Hew, 4889, hue. A.S. *heaw, hiew,* form, fashion, colour.
Hewed, 3713, hewn. A.S. *heawian.* Germ. *hauen.* We have also the Northumbrian *hag,* to cut chop. O.N. *höggva.*
Hey, 3044, high.
Heyghe, 4897, high; heyghest, 4896, highest.
Hider, hyder, 508, 1417, hither.
Hidos, hidus, 1744, hideous, frightful. O.Fr. *hide, hisde, hidour, hisdour,* dread; *hisdouse,* dreadful.
Hight, 1) 107, promised; 2) 966, 6530, called, named.
Hir, 582, her.
Hird, hirde, 6134, 4638, keeper = the *herd* in shep*herd.* Germ. *hirt,* a herdsman. O.N. *hird,* to keep guard.
Honest, 5892, honourable.
Honesté, 5829, honour.
Honour, *vb.*, 8535.
Hordom, 8259. A.S. *hórdom.* Icel. *hór,* adultery.
Horribel, 5619, 6430.
Hortel, 4787, hurtle. Du. *horten,* to dash against.
Housil, 3402, the sacrament. O.N. *hunsl, husl,* a sacrifice.
Hove, *vb.*, 3126, to hover, remain above, hang over. W. *hofian, hofio,* to hang over.
†Hove, cessation.
Hoven, *p.partic.* of *heave,* to raise, 'was *hoven*' = was presented (i. e. to the priest for baptism). It is a phrase that often occurs in reference to the baptismal rite. Macpherson and others givé it the meaning of 'baptised', but this is a secondary sense.

Þan at þe fyrst of þat cas
Þe Kyng of Brettane *howyn* was;
And all þe Barnage of his land
Þan baptyst wes
(W. C. p. 98.)

Syne *howyn* he wes, and cald
Henry. (W. C. p. 309.)

Or ȝyf a man have *hove* a chylde,
God hyt forbede and shylde,
Þat þat chylde shulde any have
Of hys godfadrys, maydyn or knave.
(Handlyng Synne p. 55.)

Þe fyrst Sacrament ys holy bapteme
Hove of watyr, and noyted wyth creme.
(Ibid. p. 294.)

How-swa, howso.
Hufe, 4179, hoof. Dan. *hov,* Du. *hoef.*
Hundreth, 4524, hundred. O.Norse *hundrad.*
Hunger, 4035, famine, *pl.* hungers.
Hurde, 5567, treasure, hoard. A.S. *hord,* treasure. O.H.G. *hort.*
Hyde, 5299, skin (of the human body). O.N. *hud, hydi.* Germ. *haut,* Du. *huyd,* skin of a beast.

His clathes fra him sone þai tugged,
And alle his *hide* in sunder rugged.
(MS. Harl. 4196, fol. 82.)

Hydus, 4773, hideous.
Hydusly, 6568.
Hydusnes, 9487.
Hyng, 675, (pret. hang) to hang.
Hyngand, 1536, hanging.
Hynged, 5334, hanged.
Hypand, 1539, halting, hopping. O.N. *hipp,* saltus.

It [þe foule] *hipped* bifore him in þe gate,

Tille it come at þe abbay ȝate,
(MS. Harl. 4196, fol. 93.)
Hope came *hippynge* after,
That had so y-bosted
How he with Moyses maundement,
Hadde many men y-holpe.
(Piers Ploughman p. 351.)

Ianglyng, 3478, chattering. O.Fr. *jangler*, to chatter.
Sum men in kirk slomers and slapes,
Sum tentes to *iangillyng* and iapes.
(MS. Harl. 4196, fol. 185.)

Iaunys, 700, jaundice. Fr. *jaunisse* from *jaune*, yellow.

Ilk, ilka, ilkan, 53, 89, 137, 138, each.

Ill, ille, 80, 174, 660, evil, bad. O.N. *illr*.

Impossibel, 6281.

Imyd, imyddes, 5168, 5186, in the midst of.

Imydward, 6447.

In-als-mykelle, 1712, in as much.

Insight, 253, knowledge; generally explained by 'perception'.
For thou gaf man skil and *insiht*.
(M. H. p. 2.)
For bathe thir foules [doufes] haves crowding
Insted of sang, and stille murning,
And bitakenes that sinful man,
That schilwisnes and *insyt* can,
Suld of thir fules bisenes take.
(M. H. p. 159.)

Instrumentes (musical), 9264.

Invisile, 972, invisible.

Iointly, 8835.

Ioly, 589. joyful. Fr. *joli*, merry.

Ire, 8588.

Irk, *vb.*, to tire, get weary of 8918.

Irkyng, *sb.*, 9359, weariness. A.S. *eargh*, slothful.

†Ithen, frequent.

†Itheuli, frequently.

Iugement, 2802, 6106.

Iustify, 5987, to do justice to.
Ordayne thy selvene,
Bathe jureȝ and juggeȝ,
And justiceȝ of landes,
Luke thou *justyfye* them wele,
That injurye wyrkes.
(Mort. Arth. p. 56.)

Iustys, *sb.*, 5330, justice.

Iuwis, 6106, judgement.

Ivel, *sb.*, 8588, disease.

Ka, 1539, cow, *pl.* ky.

Kan, see 'Can'.

Kast, *vb.*, 7261, to devise.

Kay, cay, 3835, 3838, key, see 'Cay'.

Kaytif, 7396, wretch.

Kele, 8725, to cool.

Ken, 1074, 5215, 5946, to see, to teach, show. O.N. *kenna*, to perceive by sense, observe.

Kend, pret. of ken.

Kene, 1228, 4383, fierce, cruel, sharp. Germ. *kühn*, bold, daring. O.Sw. *kôn*, *kyn*, quick, prompt, daring.

Kepe, *a)* 5029, to guard, take care of; *b)* 7371, to hold, contain. A S. *cepan*, to observe.

Kepe, *sb.*, 381, 597, care, as in phr. 'tuk *kepe*'.

Kepyng, *sb.*, 4196, 5503, 5819, care, custody.

Kidde, 4342, pret. of kithe, to show, discover. A. S. *kýthan*.

Kirk, kyrk, 3684, church.

Knaw, 83, to know.

Knawen, 8609, known, acquainted with.

Knawyng, *sb.*, 45, 147, 4010, 5727. knowledge.

Knytted, 7215, knotted.

Kun, *vb. infin.*, 187, to learn. A.S. *cunnan*, to know, 5459.

Kydde, kid, 4342, (pret. of kithe or

kythe, to show, to discover)=shown, discovered, known.
Kylle, 2995, ulcer. Icel. *kýli.*
Kynd, *sb.*, 52, 1515, nature.
Kynd, *adj.*, 2535, natural.
Kyndel, 6603.
Kyndely, kyndly, 127, 1686, 3714, 6380, according to nature, naturally.
Kyngryke, 5780, kingdom.
Kynred, 4167, kindred.
Kyrke, 4472, church.
Lade, 3421, load. A. Sax. *hlad, hladan*, to load. O.N. *hladi*, a heap.
Lagh, laghe, law, 2163, 2267, 4144, 5942, law. O.N. *lag*, order, law; *leggia*, to lay down.
Lagh, 1092, to laugh (pret. *loghe.* Sc. *leuch.*) Germ. *lachen.*
Lagher, 3870, lower. Comp. of *laghe*, low. O.N. *lagr.* Swed. *lag.*
Laghter, 1451. laughter.
Laghyng, *sb.*, 7840, laughter.
Lake, *vb.*, 797, to censure, blame. Du. *læcken*, to be wanting, blame, accuse, from *lack*, *laecke*, want, fault, blame. Swed. *lak*, fault, vice. *Lake* is generally written *lakke.*

(see Piers Ploughman l. 2736.)

Lakkyn or blamyn vitupero culpo. (P. P.)

When he was went þe folk of Tours,
Harmed him behind his bac,
And fast omang þam gan him *lac.*
(MS. Harl. 4196, fol. 191.)

'Lame, loam, earth. A. S. *lám.*
Laue, *sb.*, 8905, pathway.
Lang, 632, long. O.N. *langr.*
Lang, *vb. impers.*, 8882, to long for.
Langer, 6410. longer.
Langly, 3188, for a long time.
Lapped, 523, 841, 5219, folded. Wiclif has *wlap*, to fold.
Lare, 6469, learning. A.S. *láre.*
Large, 4259, liberal.
Latoun, 4371, latten, brass, tinned iron. Fr. *laiton*, brass.
Latsom, 793, see 'Wlatsom'.
Latte, late, 1567, 1869, to let. Germ. *lassen*, to permit. A.S. *lætan.* O. N. *latr*, lazy, slow. In this sense it is connected with E. *late.*
Laude, 338, see 'Lewd'.
Laverd, 416, Lord. A.S. *hlaford.* O.N. *lavardr.*
Law, lawe, *adj.*, 862, 4764, low, meek, see 'Lagher'. *vb.*, 8505, to humble.
Lawed, 885, see 'Lewd'.
Lawed, 8522, humbled.
Lawnes, 8500, humility.
Layk, to play. A.S. *læcan*, to play; *lác*, play.

Unreufulli þai can him raipe
Fful snoberli him for to snaipe,
Þe folk þat was sa fade
O clai þai kest at him þe clote,
And *laiked* wit him siti-sote.
(Cursor Mundi fol. 135.)

Laykyng, *sb.*, 594, sport, pleasure.
Layn, 5999, to keep secret. O.N. *leyna.* Prov. E. *lane*, to hyde.
Laynd, 5999, pret. of 'Layn'.
Layt, *vb. tr.*, 6001, to seek. A.S. *wlitan.* Icel. *leita*; Sw. *leta*, to look for.

"It es no nede he sais to teche
A hale man for to have a leche
Bot þe man þat feles sekenes sare
Nedes to *layt* a leches lare.
(MS. Harl. 4196, fol. 181.)

Laythede, 9024, ugliness, foulness. A.S. *láth*, evil.
Leche, 5944, physician. A.S. *læce.*
Lede, *a)* 593, 5719, to lead, *b)* 2640, to bring. O.N. *leida.*
Ledyng, *sb.*, 4217, instigation.
Leef, 684, leaf.

Lef, 4100, leave, permission.

Lef, 192, to leave. O.N. *leifa*, to leave. A. Sax. *laf*, remainder, whence the Sc. *laf*, *lave*.

Lefe, 2978, beloved, dear. Comp. *lever*. A.S. *léof*. Du. *lief*, dear.

Legge, *adj.*, 5606, liege = supreme, sovereign. Fr. *lige*. Ph. '*legge* pousté'.

Bot, and I lif in *lege pousté*
Þar ded sall richt wele vengit be.
(Barbour, p. 108.)
For gif I leif in *liege pousté*
Thow sall of him weill vengit be.
(Buik of Alex. p. 190.)

Legge is not a very common form of the word; it is usually written *lege* or *liege*.

'*Liege* pousté (Buik of Al. p. 361).

Wold ȝe worþilych, lorde quoth Gawan to þe kyng,
Bid me boȝe fro þis benche and stonde by yow þere,
Þat I wyth oute vylanie myȝt voyde þis table,
And þat my *legge* lady lyked nat ille,
I wolde come to your counseyl, bifore your cort ryche.
(Syr Gawayn and þe Grene Knyȝt l. 346.)

Lele, 1393, 4253 loyal, faithful.

*Lend, loins. A.S. *lendenu*.

*Lendand, descending.

Lenger, 3932, 6233, longer.

Lent, 5993, pret. of *len*, to grant, give. A.S. *lænian*.

Adam, for þou has left mi lare,
And broken þe bode þat I bad are,
And mare wroght efter þi wife,
Þan efter me þat *lent* þe life,
Unto þi body sal I send
Sexty wowndes and ten to lend,
Right fra þi hevid unto þi hele,
Eghen and eres and ilka dele
And alle þi lims on ilka side
Witht sorows sal be ocupide.
(MS. Harl. 4196, fol. 77.)

Lenthe, 5899, length, see 'Lang'. Ph. 'on *lenthe*' = along.

Ler, lere, 155, 1525, 4663, 5874, to teach, learn. A. S. *læran*. Sw. *læra*. Germ. *lehren*.

Lerd, lered, *adj.* and *sb.*, 117, 4197, 4414, learned, taught, the clergy, as distinguished from the laity. Ph. '*lered* and lewed', 6266.

Leryng, *sb.*, 170, learning.

Lese, 2915, to lose. A.S. *lesan*.

Lesson, 3857.

Lest, leste, 165, 469, 2322, 6177, least.

Lesyng, *sb.*, 4274, lie. A.S. *leasian*, to lie; *leas*, empty, false.

Lete, 1556, 5989, to let.

†Leth, loosening.

Lett, 238, 3921, 5130, to hinder. A.S. *latián*. Goth. *latjan*, *galatjan*, to delay. Prov. German *letzen*, to retard, impede, hinder.

Lettre. 6759.

Lettyng, *sb.*, 237, 1996, 4900, hindrance.

Leuke, 7481 (note), warm. A.S. *wlac*, tepid. Dunbar has *luikhartit*. '*Lewke*, not fully hote, tepidus. *Lewkenesse*, tepor.' (P. P.)

Léve, *adj.*, 5797, dear, see 'Lefe'.

Leve, 6539, leave.

Levenyng, *sb.*, 5126, lightning. It occurs also under the form *levin*, N. *ljon*, *ljun*, lightning.

Lever, 5058, rather, comp. of *leve*.

Lewed, *adj.*, 117, 4414, 5302. ignorant, lewd. Ph. 'lered and *lewed*'. A.S. *læwd*, *læwde*, laicus; *leod*, the people, the laity. '*Lewde*, not letteryd, illiteratus; —unknowynge in what so hyt be, inscius, ignarus.' (P. P.)

Libard, 1228, leopard.
Licour. 6763, liquor.
Life, 530, to live.
Life-days, 4981.
Ligg, ligge, 475, 3507, 4546, 4553, to lie; p. part. *liggen*, *lygyn*. A.S. *lecgan*. O.N. *leggia*, to lay; *liggia*, to lie.
Light, *adj.*, *a)* 688, full of levity, fickle. *b)* 3346, joyful.
Lightles. 6819, dark.
Lightly, 786, 1320, 4460, easily. *Lightlyer*, 4241.
Lightnes, 308, levity.
Like. 7851, to please. N. *lika*, to be to one's taste.
Likand, 7834, pleasing.
Likyng, 292, pleasure.
List, liste, *vb. impers.*, 795, 2012, 6767, please, desire. A.S. *lystan*, to have pleasure in. O.N. *lyst*, pleasure. Germ. *lust*.
Lith, 1917, limb, member.

I schall the bette every *leth*,
Hede and body, wythout greth, [i. e. quarter]
Yf thou make more pressyng.
(Sir Cleges 292)

A.S. *lith;* Germ. *glied*, a joint, bodily member. N. *lidr*.
'*Lythe* fro *lythe*, or lym fro lym membratem.' (P. P.)
Lither, 1059, wicked. A.S. *lyther* from *lithe*, slow.
Lof, 51, to praise, see 'Love'.
Lof, *sb.*, 1843, love, see 'Love'.
Lokand, 3016, hurting.
Loke, 5271, to look, see.
Loper, 459, coagulated, clotted, thick. Prov Dan. *lubber*, anything coagulated. O. N. *laupa*, to run, congeal. O.H. Germ. *leberen*, to coagulate. Harl. MS. 4196 reads *lopyrd*.

And of his mouth, a petuus thing to se,
The *lopprit* blude in ded thraw voydis he.
(G. Douglas vol. ii, p. 621.)

Lorn, lorne, 547, 4165, lost; *p. p.* of *lese*, to lose. A.S. *lesan*. Germ. *verlieren*, to loose, 7337.
†Lou, a pit.
Loud, 3782, loudly, openly, publicly as in phrase '*loud* and stille', 3782. Germ. *laut*, sound. O.N. *hliod*.
Louse, lowse, 1792, 2182, 3841, 3852, 3853, to loose. Goth. *laus*, loose, empty; *lausjan*, to loose.
Love, 321, to praise. Du. *loven*, to praise. Dan. *lov*, praise. Icel. *lofa*, to praise. Germ. *loben*.

Of mouth of childer and soukand
Made þou *lof* in ilka land.
(Ps viii, 3.)

Loverd, 1384, 3669, lord.
Lovyng, 321, 2129, 3789, praise.

Hafe mercy of me Laverd and se
Mi mekenesse of my faes þat be
Þat upheves me fra yhates of dede,
Þat I schewe forth to sprede,
Þine *loveynges* everilk-one,
In yhates of doghtres Syon.
(Ps. ix, 14, 15.)

Low, 9431, flame. O.N. *logi*. Dan. *lue*, *love*. A.S. *læg*, *lig*. O.E. *loge*, *leie*.

And brint in þair sinagog fire ful bright
Þe *lowe* it swath sinful dounright.
(Ps. cv.)

Lowt, 8966, to reverence.
Lowting, *sb.*, 7847, obeisance. A.S. *hlútan*, to bow, stoop. O.N. *lúta*, to stoop.

'He sagh þaim knele þis calf abute,
Als Godd him selven love and *lute*.
(Cott. MS Vesp. A. iii, fol. 37.)

Luf. lufe, 1) *sb.*, 69, 142, love. 2) *vb.*, 594, 1844.

Lughe (or loghe), 6524, pret. of *lagh*, to laugh.
Þe felons *logh* him til hething.
(Cott. MS. Vesp. A. iii, fol. 87.)
Lufly, 690, lovely.
Luke, 1) 205, 4028, 4726, to see. 2) 368, to be seen.
Lusty, 4231, full of lust.
Lycherous, 4231.
Lychery, 4902.
Lycour, 6763.
Lyfand, 2319, living.
Lyfe, 37, 82, 1869, to live.
Lyfte, 1444, sky, air. This word also appears as *luft* or *loft*. O.N. *lopt*, air, sky. A.S. *lyft*.
And als he loked up til heven
Open he saw the *liftes* seven.
(MS. Tib. Vesp. A. iii, fol. 71.)
Lyftyng, *sb.*, 7731, support.
Lyfyng, lyvyng, *sb.*, 4130, 5642, 7227, life.
Lyg, 6942, to lie.
Lyght, to come on, 7383, pret. *laght*.
Lygyn, 3202, lain, p. part. of *lygg*.
Lyggys, lies.
Lyghtles, 4729, dark.
Lyghtly, 3393, 3482, easily or soon. '*Lyghtely* or sone *leviter*. *Lyghtly* or esyly faciliter.' (P. P.)
Lyke, 1119, to please, see 'Like'.
Lyknes, 73, likeness.
Lykng, 183, 272, 7984, pleasure, lust. '*Lykynge* or luste (lyste s.) delectacio'. (P. P.)
Lym, 1912, 3641, 3630, limb. A.S. *lim*.
Lyse, 651, lice.
Lyst, 1636, to please, see 'List'.
Lyther (=luther), 3454, bad, wicked.
Lythernes, 226. wickedness. Germ. *liederlich*, loose, disorderly. Cf. '*Lyder* or wyly (*liþire* or wily k.) cautus'. (P. P.) Ignave, lazy, *lither*. Desidieux, idle, lazie, *lither*, slouthfull (Cotg).

Ma. 3997, more. A.S. *ma*, *mara*, greater, more.
Majesté, 4713.
Malice, 4186, 6646.
Maliciouse, 4169.
Manace, *sb.*, 4350, menace. Fr. *menace*. Latin *minæ*, *minacia*, threats.
Manhed, 5132, manhood.
Mar, maie, 323, 380, 1) more. 2) greater; superl. *mast*, greatest. 1047. A.S. *mara*.
Marterdom, 3825, 4380.
Martir, *sb.*, 3825, 4384; *vb.*, 4374.
Martird, 4374.
Mas, mase, 242, 255, makes.
Mast, 4090, greatest; superl. of *ma*.
Mayntene, 1) 1108, to serve. 2) 4091, to maintain, keep. Fr. *maintenir*. Lat. *manutenere*.
Mayster, 5946, 5880, teacher.
Maystré, 5580, mastery.
Mede, 96, 3545, meed, reward. A S, *méd*. Goth. *mithe*, hire.
Medeful, 9491, miritorious.
Meignè, 5870, meiny, family, household. Fr. *mesnie*. O. Fr. *maignée*, *menie*.
Meke, 1) *adj.*, 395, meek. 2) *vb.*, 172, to cause, to be meek, to humble.
Melled, 9431, mixed. Fr. *mêler*.
Melles, 6572, hammers. Fr. *mail*. Lat. *malleus*.
Melody, 9011.
Men, mene (=mean), 3187, 3194, middle. Fr. *moyen*. Lat. *medius*.
Mencion, 3940.
†Mene, to mention.
Mene, *vb.*, 5740, to remember. Goth. *meinan*, to think, intend. O.N. *munna*, to remember. Germ. *meinen*.

Meneyng, *sb.*, 8320, remembrance.
Menged, 6738, 6748, mixed, the pret. of *meng*, to mix, to *ming*-le. Germ. *mengen*; Du. *mengen*, to mix. *Meng* and *ming*, to mix, occur very frequently in O.E.

The busy bee her honey now she *mings*.
(Surrey, p. 40. Ed. Bell.)

For askes als it ware brede I ete,
And I *mengid* mi drinke with grete.
(Ps. ci, 6.)

Mengyng, *sb.*, 4704, mixtura, commixtura (P. P.)
Merk, 4402, mark. A.S. *mearc*; O.N. *merka*, to mark.
Merryng, *sb.*, 6114, louring. Du. *moeren*, to make thick, muddy.
Meschyve, 5569, misfortune, sorrow. Fr. *meschief*, *meschef*.

He [Dives] luked up and saw fulle sune,
Þe lazar set in goddes kne,
And unto hevyn þus cried he,
Ffador Abraham mend my *mischefe*.
(MS. Harl. 4196, fol. 105.)

Meselry, 3001, leprosy, from *mesel*, a leper. O.Fr. *mesel*.
Mes, 3688, mass. Fr. *messe*, the sacrifice; *pl.* messes, 3605, the mass.
Messanger, 2021.
O.Fr. *messatge*, a message, from Lat. *missus*, sent.
Messe, 3722, mass.
Messyng, *sb.*, 3589, mass.
Mesur, 1459, 5574, moderation. Fr. *mesure*. Lat. *mensura*.

For foul he was out of *mesur*.
(Y. & G., p. 11.)

Mesure, 7690, measure.
Mesuryng, 7692, measurement.
Mete, mette, 1487, to measure, pret. *met*. O.E. *mett*, a measure. Germ. *messen*. Goth. *mitan*.
Met, 7695 (pret. of *mete*), measured.
Meyne, 4628, see 'Meigné'.
Midward, 435, middle.
Mikel, 924, great. O.N. *mikill*, great.
Ministre, 5958.
Miracle, 6550.
Mirk, dark, see 'Myrk'.
Mirkenes, 6802, darkness, see 'Myrknes'.
†Misfar, misfortune.
Misse, 5266, to lose.
Mister, myster, 3477, need, necessity. Lat. *ministerium*. Span. *menestre*.
*Mistru = mistrow.
Mistyly, 4364, 'mysty or prevey to mannys wytte, *misticus*.' (P. P.)
Mispay, 7189, displease.
Miswroght, 1993, miswrought.
Moder, 447, 463, mother. O.N. *modir*.
Moghes (mowes), 5572, moths, maggots. A.Sax.* *mogthe*. We may compare this with O.E. *mawk*, a maggot N. *makk*; Sw. *mâsk*, a grub, worm.
Moght, 571, might.
Mon, man, 96, 7518, shall. O.N. man, mun.
Moné, 5570, money.
Mon, mone, 992, 4702, the moon. O.N. *mana*. Germ. *mond*.
Moneth, 4988, month.
Montayn, mountayne, 5078, 6394.
Morn, 2668, morrow. Germ. *morgen*. O.N. *morgun*.
Most, 3878, must.
Mot, 4207, may, must, pret. most, 7397. 7398.
Mount, 4896, mountain; *pl.* mountes, 4458.
Moute, 781, to fall off, moult Du, *muiten*. Pl. D. *muten*.
Moveyng, movyng, *sb.*, 4956, 7609, movement, motion.
Mow, 7965, to be able.

Moweld, 5570, mouldy. Dan. *mulne*, to become mouldy, *mul*, mould.
Mude = mood, 2391, anger. It is generally written *mode*.
Mught, 282, 2285, 4241, might.
Multiply, 3727.
Murnyng, *sb.*, 1846, mourning. O.H. Germ. *mornen*, to grieve.
Muse, 6266. Fr. *muser*.
Myddes, 2938, 4220, midst.
Myddyng, *sb.*, 628, a dunghill. Dan. *mödding*, a dunghill. O.N. *moddyngia*. A. S. *midding*. 'A *myddynge* sterquilinum.' (P. P.)

Syne sweirnes at the secound bidding,
Come lyke a sow out of a *midding*
Ful slep was hes grunyie.
Dunbar (Ed. Laing) The deadly Sins.

Myddyng-pytt, 8770.
Mydlerd = middle earth, 2302, 6850, the earth.
Myrour, myroure, 8216, 8217.
Mydward, 553, 4909, 6319, in the middle of.
Myghtes, 1673, powers.
Myghtfulnes, 752.
Mykel, mykelle, 237, 439, 926, great.
Mynde, 1) *sb.*, 59, 167, 2050, memory, recollection; 2) *vb.*, 230, to remember, to call, to mind. O.N. *minna*.
Myndles, 2088, forgetful.
Mynstralsy, 9259.
Mynystre, 6207.
Myrk, 456, dark. O. Norse *myrkr*, darknes.
Myrknes, 194, 6114.
Myry, 904, merry.
Mys, 1) *sb.*, 109, wrong. 2) *adv.*, 3770, ill, wrongly. 3) *vb.*, 5266, to lose. O.N. *missa*, to lose. Du. *missen*, to fail, miss.
Mysbylyefe, *sb.*, 5521, unbelief.
Mysdoer, 4151.
Myslykyng, *sb.*, 9028, dislike.
Myslyvyng, 3773, wrong living.
Myspay, 1120, 7189, to displease.
Myspray, 1993, to pray wrongly.
Myssay, 9424.
Myster, 7373, need.
Mysturn, 1617, 7227,
Myswroght, 1993,

Na, 472, 6201, no. A. S. *na*.
Nacion, 4358.
*Nait, to prosper. A.S. *neotan*, to enjoy, use.
Namly, 171, 3738, especially, chiefly.
Nan, nane, 19, 57, none.
Nathing, 44, nothing.
Nedder, 870, adder. A.S. *nedder*. Goth. *nadrs*, Icel. *nadr*.
Ne, 465, 466, not, nor.
Nedly, 2864, 3318, 5760, of necessity, needs. A.S. *nead*. Germ. *noth*, need, want.
Neghe, 1) *adj.*, near, nigh. 2) *vb.*, 1208, to approach, come near. A.S. *neah*, *near*, nearer, *nehst*, next
Neghebur, neghbur, 5983, neighbour. A. S. *neah-bur*. German *nachbar*.
Neghen, 729, nine. A.S. *nigon*.
Neghend, 3988, 4790, 6571, ninth.
Neghest, 2920, 6411, next.
Negremancien, 4212, necromancer.
Nek, neke, 677, 5457, neck. A.S. *hnecca*. Du. *nak*, *nek*, *nik*.
Nere, 1866, near.
Nerehande, 5202, nigh. It also = nearly.

Þan lifed he lang in wedowhede,
Unto eld so gan he pas,
Þat al his hare *nerehand* white was.
(Cott MS. Galba E. ix, fol. 33.)

Nese, 626, nose. A.S. *næse*. Germ. *nase*.
Neshe, nesshe, 614, 3110, 4949, soft. Phrase 'hard and *nesshe*'. A.S. *hnesc*, tender, soft Germ. *nass*, wet.
Nest, 676, next, see 'Neghe'.
Neven, 969, 4794, to name. O N. *nafn*, a name.
Never-þe-latter, 3650.
New, *adv*., 7475, anew.
New, 7460, to renew.
New-made, 6407.
Nites, 651. nits.
Nobelay, 8532.
Noght, 1) 61, 131, not; 2) 46, 2073, nought. A.S. *naht*, *nauht*, *noht*.
Norysshes. 7610, nourishes.
Nother, nouther, nowther, 167, 465, 940, 1842, 6023, neither.
Noumbre, 7432, number.
Nourwhare, 5057, nowhere. *Nohwar*, *nouhwar* (Ancren Riwle).
Noyse, 4705, 9259, sound. French *noise*, rumbling stir.
Nurist, nuryst, 4198, nourished, nurtured. Fr. *nourrir*. Latin *nutrire*.
Nuyes, *sb*., 3538. It. *noiare*, to trouble.
Nuye, *vb*., 1234, 4395, to annoy, to trouble. Fr. *nuire*.
Nygromancy, 4286.
Nyghtes and days, *advs*., 4286, 5704.

O, 6401, of. O.N. *af*.
Obedience,
Oboune (oboven), 5405, above.
Obout, 1905, 4051, 4326, about.
Obout-ga, 7593, 7613, revolve round.
Obout-rynn, 7583, run about.
Oboven, 849, 2875, 4123, above.
Occupide, 1913, 6401, filled with.
Of, 1867, 1874, over, upon.
Offer (the host) 3597.
Offeryng, *sb*., 3700.
Office, 3791.
Of-race, tear off, 6704, from *race*. Sc. *rase*. Germ. *reissen*. O. N. *rekja*, to undo.
Of-ryve, 7379, to pluck off.
Oftsythe, 7460.
Ogayn, 1) *prep*., 304, 4042, against. 2) *adv*., 391, 2271, 4034, 4140, again.
Ogaynes, 4144, against; 6366, opposite.
Ogayne-standyng, *sb*., 7969, opposition.
Ogayn-ward, 8053, on the other hand.
Oght, 10, 306, aught.
Olyke, 7560, alike.
Omang, 1) *adv*., 7424, at intervals. 2) *prep*., 2240, among.
Onence, 1355, 3678, against; 5131, 5192, opposite.
Onluke, 7717, to look on.
Or (= over), 1459, too.
Or (= are), 2067, before
Ordayn, 4654,
Order, ordre. *sb*., 3695, 7636.
Ordinance, 8438.
Orison, 3498, prayer. Fr. *oraison*.
Ourwhar, 6953, anywhere; 4339, ouhwhar (Ancren Riwle).
Out-broght, 3220.
Outga, 5126.
Outher, 1651, 3913, 4410, other. A.S. *outher*.
Outrage, *sb*.. 1) 1516, 1523, excess; 2) 5010, 5011, defect. Fr. *outrage*, excess, violence, from Lat. *ultra* beyond Fr. *outre*.
Outrageouse, 9440.
Outragiousté, 5010.
Outsay, 5482, to speak out.
Outtake, 2808, to take out.
Outwith, 6669.
Out-wyn, 4462.

Plede, *vb.*, 6085.
Plenté, 6333.
Plenteuus, plenteous, 4618.
Plenteously, 6341.
Pleynand, 799, complaining.
Pleyne, *vb. tr.*, 5552, 7061, complain against.
Pleynyng, *sb.*, 5662, 6105, complaint. Fr. *plaindre* from Latin *plangere*, to complain.
†Plight, danger.
Pomp, 7077.
Pople, 4245, people.
Por, poer, 6728, poor, see 'Pover'.
Porcyon, 8118.
Possibel, 6328.
Potagre (or Podagra), 3033, a disease on the feet and joints of the limbs.
Pouce, 822, pulse.
Pouder, poudre, 412, 427, 878, dust. Fr. *poudre.* Lat. *pulvis.*
Pousté, 3996, 5606. Lat. *potestas.* O.Fr. *poesté.*
Pover, 1872, 5435, poor. French *pauvre*, Lat. *pauper.*
Povert, 1638, 5941, poverty.
Power, 3748, 5884.
Poynt, 2311, particle, particular.
Poyntes, 5470.
Prayer, 3596.
Preche, 3815, 4265, 5948. French *prêcher*, Lat. *predicare.*
Prechours, precheours, 4264, 5948.
Prechyng, *sb.*, 4261.
Precious, 4432.
Precyouse, 9009.
Prelate, 5990.
Prese, 7367, to press.
Prest, 1222, 3548, 3598, 5990. O.Fr. *prestre.* Lat. *presbyter.* Greek *πρεσβυτερος.*
Pesumpcion, 4249.
Prike, 5338, to pierce.
Principalle, 7299.
Principaly, 3701.
Prisoun, 6159.
Prive, pryve, 110, to deprive.
Privé, privy, 1794, 1940, 4493, 6025, secret.
Prively, pryvely, 4482, 4486, secretly.
Priveté, 5617, secret.
Privetese, 2403, secrets.
Process, processe, 6249, 6256.
Propre, 6866.
Properly, 3632, 3816.
Propertes, 7582, properties.
Pryveté, privité, 3775, 4651, secret.
Pryvyng, 1813, deprivation.
Psauter, 284, psalter.
Punnys, punyssche, 4878, 4914, to punish.
Pur, 2498, 2499, pure.
Purchased, 3803.
Purches, 3919. Fr. *pourchasser.* O.Fr. *purchacier.*
Pure, 509, 3609, poor.
Pured, 2721, purified.
Purgatory, 3724.
Purged, 6398.
Pursue, 4450, persecute. Fr. *poursuivre.* Lat *persequi.*
Purtrayd, 6619, painted. O.Fr. *portraire.* Lat. *protrahere.*
Putt, putted, 4584, 6135, cast, put. Dan. *putte*, to put, put into. O.N. *potta.*
Pyk, 6693, pitch. Du. *pik.* Germ. *pech.* '*Pike* and terr'. Cursor Mundi fol. 66.
Pylers, 5388, pillars.
Pyn, pyne, 1) *sa.*, 1322, 2121, 2224, 6029, punishment; 2) *vb.*, 3959, to punish, to suffer pain. Germ. *pein*, trouble, pain, punishment. O.N. *pina*, to torment, punish. A.S. *pinan.*
Pyté, 3575, 4147, pity. Fr. *pitié.* Lat. *pietas.*

Qwake, 7343, quake, pret. *qwoke.*

Quathe = wathe, 2102, danger, harm. A. S. *wite.* Pl. D. *quat,* bad.

Quayntis, quayntyse, qwayntys, 1181, 1348, 4327, craft, device.

Qwene, 4461, queen.

Quert, 326, joy. Fr. *cœur, queor,* cf. '*hearty*', 'in good *heart*'.

Mi rightwis helpe fra Laverd in *quert*
That sauf makes right of hert.
(Ps. vii, 11.)

Questyon, 7205.

Quilk, qwilk, 1165, which.

Quyk, qwik, 3981, 6390, 6981, alive. A. S, *cwic.*

Quyken, qwyken, 1723, *vb. intr.,* to live.

Qwitt, quyte, qwitte, qwyte, *adj.,* 2953, 3617, 5679, blameless; phrase 'all *qwite*' = 'scot free', 6004 '*qwyte* and fre'.

Quyte, qwitte, *vb.,* 3920, to release, absolve. Lat. *quietus.* Fr. *quitte.*

Ra, 8938, roe. A. S. *rah.* Icel. *ra.* Germ. *reh.*

Harte, Hynde, Daa, *Ra.*
(Acts. Ja. I. 1424, c. 39)

Race, 7381, tear.

Rane, 5297, pret. of *Rin.*

Rare, 7341, to roar.

Rareyng, *sb.,* roaring.

Rase, 8938, course, journey. Sc. *Race, raiss.* A. S. *ræs.* Icel. *reisa,* iter facere—Jam.

Raump, *vb.,* 2225. Ital. *rampare,* to paw like a lion.

Raumpand, 2907.

Raumpyng, *sb.,* 7351.

Raunson, 3619. Fr. *rançon.*

Ravisshe, ravissche, 2909.

Ravyn, 9448, plunder, *rapine,* see 'Reve'. A. S. *reáf, reáfung,* spoil, plunder, robbery.

Ravyste, 4309, 5050, 5077, ravished.

Rayke, 1) to roam, wander, go abroad and hence, 2) to spread about, 4891. O.N. *reka;* Icel. *reika,* to ruin. *Rake* to walk, range or rove about. (Brockett.) It occurs also under the forms *roke, rokke.* This word does not occur in A. Saxon but appears in Laȝamon.

Bi this tal her may we se,
That wis and wair bihoves us be,
That Satenas ne ger us *rayk*
Fra rightwisnes to sinful laik.
(Met. Hom. 58.)

O. E. *rayk* = path, way, road.

Rayne-shours, 4317.

Receyved, 5436, received.

Reche, 554, 3814, 6311, to reach, extend; pret. *roght.* A S. *ræcan.*

Recoverere, recouverere, 2961, 6095, 7257, recovery.

Red, rede, 1) *sb.,* 2014, 4303, 5505, 6086, advice. 2) *vb.,* 1677, to advise, to tell, 3) to discuss (pret. *red, redde),* 3953, 6286, 6288. *Red,* 6947, told.

And wit him þai-plaid siti-sott,
And badd þat he suld *rede*
Quilk o þaim him gaf þe dint.
(Cott. MS. Vesp. A. iii, fol. 91.)

'*redel rede*', fol. 40 our modern phrase *read* a riddle.

——Bring a besant to of ryng
And ȝif it for þaire dreme *redeing*
Þai *rede* þe dremys þan als þam lykes.
(Cott. MS. Galba E. ix, fol. 37.)

Reddour, reddure, 6091, 6304. Sw. *radda,* to fear. O. E. *rad, red,* fear. A. S *hreth.*

Of dreidful *raddour* trymlyng for affray,
The troianys fled right fast, and brak away.
(G. Dougl. p. 577, vol. ii.)

Rede, 6621, red.
Redempcyoune, 7251.
Regard, in phrase 'to *regard* of', 7484, compared with.
Regne, 4032, 4200, to reign.
Regyon, 4080.
Reherce, 2386, 4748, rehearse.
Reke, 9585, to care.
Reke, 9431, smoke. Sc. *ruke*. A.S *rék*.

For waned als *reke* mi daies swa
And mi banes als krawkan dried þa.
(Ps. ci, 4)

Reken, 5978, to account for.
Rekken, 3100, 5985, 6003, 6009, to reckon; 6557, 6590, to tell. A.S. *reccan*.
Rekkenyng, rekennyng, *sb.*, 3986, an account.
Rekles, 5546, careless. A. Sax. *recce-leas*, from *récan*, to *reck* care for.
Reklesly, 5792, carelessly.
Reklesnes, 3907, 3909, carelessness.
Releas, *sb.*, 3565.
Relese, *vb.*, 3813.
Relesed, *pt.*, 3575.
Religion, 4522, 8728, belief.
Religiouse, 1888.
Reme, see 'Rym'. A. Sax. *reama*, *reoma*, a film, membrane, *rim*.
Remedy, 7261.
Remenand, 3897, 3910, remnant.
Remow (or remu), 7365, to remove.
Removyng, *sb.*, 6365, removal.
Repentance, 3905.
Reprove, 5314, reproof; 5555, 6221.
Resayve, 446, 5957.
Reson, resoune, 5966, 7225, reason.
Reson, 3676, account.
Respyte, 6233.
Restreyned, 3873.
Reuful, sorrowful.
Reuthe, 6729, pity, from the verb *rew*, A. S. *reówan*, to have mercy or pity.

But more and more ay cried he
And said Lord Ihesu *rew* on me.
(MS. Harl 419, fol. 41.)

Reve, reave, 251, 308, to rob (with violence), to plunder. A. Sax. *reáfian*. O Fris. *râva*.
Reverence, 7847.
Revyled, 8544.
Reward, 1880, 5855, regard. Ital. *guardare*. Fr. *regarder*, to look.
Rewel, *vb.*, 5885, to rule.
Rewel, *sb.*, 5991.
Rewme, 4033, realm. O.Fr. *reaume*.
Rightwis, rightwes, 135, 511, righteous.
Rightwisnes, rightwysnes, 3579, 3605, righteousness.
Roche, *sb.*, 5078, 6393, rock. Fr. *roche*. '*Rochen* stan' occurs in MS. Vesp. A. iii, fol. 57.
Rode = rood, 1780, cross.
Rode-tre, 5260.
Rogg, 1230, to tear in pieces Sc. *rug*. It is generally explained 'to shake', but this is only a secondary meaning of the word. Sw. *rycka*, raptare, trahere- Jam.

2. Tort. Do *rug* him.
3. Tort. Do dyng him.
(T. M. p. 28.)

So was he [Christ] *rugged*, raced and revyn
þe purper clath þat he in stode,
Was hardened all with his awin blode,
So þat it cleved on ilka side,
Fful fast both unto flessche and hide,
þai *rugged* it of with outen rest,
When it so to þe flessh was fest.
(MS. Harl. 4196, fols. 81 & 71.)

Romyng, romiyng, *sb.*, roaring, loud noise, 1) 4772, from *rome*. Sc. *rame*, to roar, growl; 2) 4774, from *romy*, to roar or growl. A.S.

hremian, to roar, *reomian*, *hreaman*. Sw. *raama*.

He [the bare] began to *romy* and rowte
And gapes and gones. (Robson's Met. Rom. p. 63, xii, 3.)

Rosyng, *sb.*, 7070. Sc. *rusyng*, boasting, from *ros*, to praise, boast. Sc. *ruse*. Swed. *rosa*, to praise. Icel. *hrosa*. Dan. *rose*.

And he þat sekes here to have *rose*
Þe dedees noght worth þat he dose.
(MS. Harl. 4196, fol. 58.)

Rot, rote, 664, 676. 5293, root.

Rote, 784, to rot. A.S. *rotian*.

Rouke, *vb. intr.*, 6765, 6897, to crouch, lie close.

Ruck, to squat (Ray). *Rook* is used by Shakespeare and Chaucer. O.N. *hruku*, to squat. Du. *hurken*, to crouch, 9168.

Rouncle, 773, to wrinkle. A.Sax. *wrinclian*. Swed. *ryncka*. Sc. *runkle*, *runkill*.

Rychesces, 5940.

Ryfe, 5785, reeve. A.S. *geréfa*.

Ryghtwysnes, 3179, righteousness.

Rym, 520, reme.

Rim, peritoneum or membrane enclosing the intestines.
(Brockett.)

Ryn, 471, 781, 4318, to run. A.S. *yrnan*.

Rysyng, 3976, resurrection.

Ryve, 888, 1230, *pret.* rafe, *p.part.* ryven, to split, to tear.

Sacrament, 3599.

Sadde, 3229, hard, thick, solid. A.S. *sæd*. '*Sad* trowth' = firm faith.
(MS. Harl. 4196, fol. 41.)

Saghe, 2320, saw.

Saghtel, *sb.*, 1470, peace, reconciliation. Cf. *vb. saght*. Sc. *saucht*, to reconcile, make peace with. In the Anturs of Arther (Rd. Robson) we have the verb *Saȝtun* and the noun *saȝtenyng*. In the Thornton Romances p. 252 we have the noun *sauȝthlynge* which is more common than *saghtel*. A.S. *sehtian*, *saethlian*. O.N. *sætta*, to reconcile; *sátt*, *sætt*, reconciliation. A.S. *saht*. Cf. Swed. *sakta*, to place. Eng. *settle*.

†Sake, fault.

Sal, salle, 41, shall.

Salde, 4849, (pret. of *selle*) sold.

Salle, see 'Sal'.

Sam, 12, 25, same.

Samen, 1849, together. O.N. *saman*.

Sande, 3535, message, a messanger. A.S. *sand*, a sending = the southern word *sonde*.

This bodword can the levedi tru,
To Godds *sand* sco can hir bu.
(MS. Vesp. A iii, fol. 61.)
Goddes sun and Godes *sande* [Christ]
Com to les mankind of bande.
(Met. Hom. p 8.)

Sang, 9254, song. A.S. *sang*.

Sar, sare, *a) adj.*, 1461, 1775, 3635, 6972, sore, sorrowful. *b) sb.*, 5945, a sore; ph. 'seke and *sare*'. *adv.*, 7402, sorely. A.S. *sár*.

Sarmon, 4535.

Sarowe, 3218, sorrow. A.S. *sorh*.

Sary, 3468, sorrowful. A.S. *sargian*, to be in pain &c.

Saufe, 2959, safe, saved.

Saul, saule, 129, soul. A.S. *saul*, *sáwl*, *sáwol*.

Save, *adj.*, 3776, saved.

Saveour, 4224.

Savour, 656, 9016, smell.

Sawen, 445, sown, *p.part.* of *saw*, the pret. of which is *seu*. A.S. *sáwan*, to sow, pret *seow*.

Say, 4025, to tell, relate.

Scake, 5410, to shake. A.S. *scacan.*
*Scald, a scold.
Scalden, schald, 6576, 7124, to scald.
*Schade, to distinguish.
Schame, 1) *sb.*, 7145; 2) *vb.*, 7159, to feel shame.
Schamefulnes, 7155, verecundia.
Schendschepe, 7146, disgrace, shame.
Schent, 845, A.S. *scendan*, injure.
Schrafe, 8300, pret. of *schrife.*
Schryve, 7168, to shrive.
Schrywen, 2631, shriven.
Schyre, 6934, see 'Shire'.
Science, 5946.
Sclaunder, 4252, slander.
*Scorn, shorn.
Scratte, 7378, to scratch.
Sculke, 1788, to hide. Sw. *skyla, skolka.* Dan. *skiule.* Du. *schulen*, to hide.

Bot ilkan *sculked* thaim awai.
(MS. Vesp. A. iii, 76.)

Se, 4220, seat.
Seculere, 1888,
Secunde, 3974, 6637.
Sees, 6373, to cease.
Sek, 566, sack. A.S. *sæc, sacc.*
Seke, 772, 5945, sick. A.S. *sec, seóc.*
Sekenes, 2024, 2026, sickness.
Sekful, 566, sackful.
Sekkes, 4530, sack-cloth
Selcouthe, 1518, wonderful. A S. *seld—cuð* = seldom known, rare.
Selden, 260, seldom. A.Sax. *seld, seldon.*
Selve, selven, 6780, self.
Sely, 5810, 6002, 6006, happy. A.S. *sælig.*
Selynes,
Semande, 5290, apparent.
Sembland, 791, appearance.
Seme, 6022, to appear, be seem.
Semely, 73, 5012, seemly. Icel. *sæma.* Germ. *ziemen*, to be fitting, to befit.
Sen, syn, 57, 2212, 5536, since. Sc. *syne.*
Septre, 4098, sceptre.
Sepulcre, 5188.
Sere, 48, 337, 5966, several, severally.
Sergeaunt, 6084.
Servage, 1157, bondage.
Servand, servaunte, 1082, 1083, 3668, 3672, servant.
Servisabylle, 8704.
Servise, servyse, 6383, service.
Sete, 6046, seat.
Setil, setyl, 6122, 8531, seat, throne.

He [David] wiste that Gode til
him havid suorn,
That ane suld of his sede be borne;
To site in *setlis* that was his.
(Met. Hom. p. xxi.)

Sette, 5991, 6140, to place; phrase '*sett* hard', 7226.
Sevend, 362, 3984, seventh.
Sext, sexte, 360, 3982, 4780, sixth.
Sexti, 4525, sixty.
Shane, 6243, pret. of *shine.*
Shap, shappe, 672, 1799, 4893, form, shape.
Shendshepe, shenshep, shenshepe, shenschip, 380, 1171, 3341, 5315, 6221, ruin, disgrace.
Shepe, 6134, sheep.
Shewyng, *sb.*, 5904, manifestation. A Sax. *sceawung.* The 'Bok of *sceuing*' is the name given to the 'Book of Revelations' in the Cursor Mundi.
Shille, 9270, shrill.
Shire, 6612, pure, clean = our modern word *sheer.* A.S. *scire.*
(Ps. xi, 7.)
Sho, scho, 583, 1277, she.
Short, *adj.*, 774, not retentive (as applied to the memory).
Short, 6269, brief.
Shortly, 4848, 6278, briefly.

Shote, 1906, shoot.
Shrife, 3508, to confess, to receive confession, shrive, pret. *shrafe.* A. S. *scrifan.*
Shryfte, 2647, confession, shrift.
Shuld, 3776, 5013, should.
Shulder, 5206, shoulder. A. Sax. *sculder.*
Siker, 8559, certain, sure. Germ. *sicher.* O. Fris *sikur.*
Sikerly, 2469, 5810, confidently, surely, securely.
Sikernes, 8557, security.
Singulary, singulerly, 4584, individually.
Singulere, 7453.
Skaped, 8436.
†Skathe, danger.
Skil, skill, skylle, 1) 50, 91, the reason as a faculty of the mind. 2) 48, 607, 3789, reason, cause. O. N. *skil.*
Sklaunder, sklaundre, 7042, slander.
Skomfit, 2269.
Skoul, 2225, to scowl.
Skrike, 7341, to shriek. O. Norse *skrikja.* O. Fris. *skria.*
Skrykyng. *sb.*, 7352, shrieking.
†Skurn, to shun. A. S *scunian.*
Sla, 4185, 7272, to slay, pret. *slogh.* O. Fris. *sla.* A. S. *slean*, pret. *sloh.*
Slaghter, slaughter. A. S. *slæge*, a slaying, 3367.
Slake, 6224, 6888, mitigate, lessen, quench, stop. The original meaning is to loosen, let loose, 7177, to slacken. A. Sax. *sleacian*, to slacken. Sw. *slocken*, to slake; *sloka*, to droop. O N. *slakr.* A. S. *sleac*, loose, slow.

At pasch of Iewes þe custom was,
Ane of prison to *slake*
Withouten dome to latt him pas
Ffor þat hegh fest sake.
(MS. Harl. 4196, fol. 209.)

Slaver, 784, to slobber, drivel.
Slaw, slawe, 188, 5546, slow A. S. *sláw.*
Slawly, 3192, slowly.
Sleghe, 7570, wise. O. N. *slaegr.* O. E. *sleeche.*
Sleght, 7685, 7639, wisdom, cleverness. Pl. *sleghtes*, 1181.

For I sal se thine hevenes hegh
And werkes of thine fingres *slegh.*
(Ps 8, 4.)
Mi mouth sal speke wisedome on heght,
And thoght [i. e. meditation] of mi hert *sleght.*
(Ps. xviii.)

Sleke, sleken, *vb*, 6313, 6558, 6763, 6778, 6882, to lessen, to mitigate, quench, cool, see 'Slake'.

It sal *slek* þaire thrist for ever.
(MS. Harl. 4196, fol. 51.)

From the Sw. *slocken* we have *slokken* in the same sense.

It wille not *slokken* ay þaire thrist.
(Ibid.)

Sleuthe, 3299, sloth. A. S. *slæwth.*
Sloghe, 5526, pret. of *sla*
Sloterd, 2367, bespattered. Cf. Prov. E. *slotter*, 1) *sb*, filth, nastiness, 2) *vb.*, to dirty, bespatter with mud. Sc. *slotter*, to pass time idly or *sluggishly.* *Sluttry*, drowsy. Prov. Germ. *schlottern*, to dable in wet; *schlott*, mud. Icel. *slodda*, to trudge through mud. Welsh *yslottian*, to paddle.
Slouh, slow, p. 15, slough, skin.
Slyghe, 2662, wise, clever.
Smale, 3420, 3977, 4992, small. A. S. *smale.*
Smert, *adj*, 1) 2940, 5878, severe, 2) 1464, quick; *vb.*, 1317, to smart, A. S. *smeortan*, to smart.
Smertly, 3323, quickly.
Smethe, 6349, smooth, A. S. *sméthe.*

Smored, 7601, destroyed, literally smothered. A. S. *smorian*, to smother.

The devill sa devit wes with thair yell,
That in the depest pot of helle
He *smorit* thame with smuke.
(Dunbar.)

A credill of iren for hir he makes,
And hinged it up on iren stakes,
Under it gert he make grete fire,
And kest in oyle to make it schire,
Sethin toke þai hir with bitter brayd.
And in þat credel allone her layd.
To *smor* hir in þe smoke so thik.
(MS. Harl. 4196, fol. 164.)

We war in a hus bath wonnand,
At ans bath wit child we war,
At ans bath barns bar;
In wanes war we stad unwide
And laid ur barns be ur side,
Bot wailawaa it sua bitide,
Mi felaw *smord* hir barn in bedd.
(Cursor Mundi fol. 49.)

*Snaip, to curse.

Snaw, 1440, 6661, snow. A S. *snáw*.

Socur, 5861.

Sodanli, sodanly, 1282, 1989, 4476, suddenly.

Sodayn, sodayne, 1951, 4331, 5129, sudden.

Soft, 1004, easy, pleasant.

Soght, sought, pret. of *seke*.

Solace, 3245, 3729, 6036, pleasure.

Son, 687, 1018, 4702, 5128, sun.

Son, 4971, 5044, sound. A. S. *son*.

Sonder, *vb.*, 4789, to sunder.

Sonder, 'in *sonder*', 888, 1787.

Sone, 68, 4161, soon. A. S. *sona*.

Sotelle, 9271.

Soth, 7687, sooth, truth. A. S. *sóth*.

Sothefast, 5532, true. A.S. *sothfæst*.

Sothly, 6175. see 'Suthly'.

*Sotthede, folly.

Sonche, 788, to suspect.

Souke, 6767, to suck. A.S. *súcan*.

Sounes, *vb.*, 4678, sounds, see 'Son'.

Soverayne, *sb*, 5579; *adj.*, 3074.

Soverainly, 8777.

Space, 3933.

Spare, 3928, to treasure or hoard up. A.S. *spárian*.

Great heaps of gold by *sparing* gan I save.
(Surrey, Ed. Bell, p. 111.)

Some time we seek to *spare* that afterward we waste.
(Ibid, p. 115)

Specialy, specyaly, 3603, 3654, 5648, 6412, specially.

Speciel, 3696, special.

Specify, 6590.

Spede (pret. *spedde)*, 5, 2682, 3585, 3725, to hasten, to succeed. A.S. *spédan*.

Spede, 2882, success.

Sped, 6258, hastened.

†Spelling, teaching.

Spended, 5968, spent.

Sper, 3835, to lock, fasten. A.S. *sparran*. O.N. *sperra*.

Þe yhates þan he gert þam *sper*,
And sat and et at all laser.
(Barbour, p. 116.)

Spere, 4887, sphere.

Spere, 5292, spear. A.S. *spére*.

Spille, 1320, to destroy, ruin. A.S. *spillan*, to spoil, destroy.

Spilte, 5558, destroyed, pret. of *spille*.

Spowse, 8844.

Sprawel, 475, to sprawl.

Sprede, 649, 6335, to spread. A.S. *sprædan*.

Sprent, 6814, to leap, scatter, pret. *sprent*. A.S. *sprœncan*.

Þair speris in splenderis *sprent*.
(Syr Gawayne.)

And Salamon sais to understand,

þair mowthes er like a pot welland,
Wharof hate dropes ay *sprentes* out
And skaldes þam þat er obout.
(MS. Tib. E. vii, fol. 70.)
— — —abak he dreuch
As quha onwar tred on a rowch serpent
Lyggyng in the bus and for feir bakwart *sprent*.
(G. Douglas, p. 96.)

Spycery, 6278.

Spylle, 7600, see 'Spille'.

Spyttyng, 655.
His neys smellid of the Iewes snot and foul *spitting*.
(Castle of Love, p. 147.)

Stak (pret. of *stik)*, 5602, to stab.

Stalworth, 689. A.S. *stæl-weorth.*

Stalworthly, 9084.

Stan, stane, 3076, 4784, stone. A.S. *stán.*

Stang, stayng, 5293, pret of *sting*, to pierce, stab; p. p. *stungen*. O.N. *stinga*, to prick, stick. Germ. *stechen*.

†Starck, stubborn.

Stare, *vb.*, 7426, to look sternly upon.

Stature, 4980.

Sted, stede, 457, 1168, 3723, 5001, a place, stead. 6170, *vb.* A.S. *stede.*

Stegh, stey, 4306, 4557, 4603, 5134, 7692, to ascend, pret. *stey*, *stegh.* Hence O. E. *stegh*, a ladder. A.S. *stigan*, to ascend.

Sterne, 996, 4120, star. A. Sax. *steorra.* O. N. *stjarna.*

Sterned, 993, 7567, starry.

Steven, 4559, 5044, a voice. A S. *stefen.*

Stey, 5132, to ascend.

Stille, 1388, secretly. As a phrase 'loud and *stille*', 3782. O. Eng. *stilly*, secretly.

Stille, 3737, continually.

†Stilli, secretly.

Sting, (pret. *stang* and *stanged*, p. p. *stungen)*, 5293, to pierce, stab.

Stok, 676, stock. A.S. *stoc.*

Stonde, stounde, 3329, a space of time. A.S. *stund.*

Stopp, 7359, to stuff, stop up. Du. *stoppen.*

Stoupand from *stoup*, to stoop, 777, stooping.

Stour, stoure, 1820, 5812. conflict, batele.
For þe best and þe worthyast,
þat wilfull war to win honour
Plungit in þe stalward *stour*,
And routes rud about þam dang.
(Barbour, p. 38.)

Strake, 7355, pret. of *strike.*

Strang, 881, 6562, 6563, strong, violent. Phrases '*strang* payne', 6690; '*strang* stynk', 6692.

Strangelle, 8408.

Strayt, 2376, 5613, 6000, 6136, strict.

Straytely, 7181, severely.

Straytest, 4736.

Strek, 3388, straight, direct.

Strenth, strenthe, 5898, 6703, strength.

Strenthi, strenthy, 5075, strong.
He [Crist] es a *strenktthy* swayne.
(MS. Harl. 4196, fol. 209.)

Stresced, 8546.

Streyned, 7181.

Strik, 2624, direct, straight. Icel. *strik.* A.S. *stræc.*

Stryfe, 7376, to strive, pret. *strafe.*

Strykly, 3288, straight, direct.

Study, 7204.

Styk, in phrase '*styk* fast', 7633.

Styk, 5337, to stab, pierce, pret. *stak.*

Stynk, *vb.* 566.

Stynt, *vb.*, 1630, 6093, 7299, to stop, cease. A.S. *stintan.*

Styntyng, *sb.*, 7016, a stopping.
Styr, 7091, move, instigate.
Styther, comp. of *stythe*, 3173, stiff, stubborn.
Subieccion, 4064.
Suffishaunt, 3874, sufficient.
Sugette, *adj.*, 4052, subject.
Suld, 3705, should.
Suppose, 3776.
Suthefast, 6128, true.
Suthfastnes, 4268, truth.
Suthly, 6175, truly.
Sutille, sutelle, 5904, 7687.
Sutilté, 5903.
Swa, 28, 231, 3550, so. Compound *how-swa*, *wha-swa*.
Swelge, 6232, to swallow. Sc. *swelly*. A.S. *swelgan*.
Swelt, 5212, to die. A.S. *sweltan*.
Swet, 1781, pret. of *sweat*.
Swete, 4915, sweet.
Swetter, 3699, comp. of *swete*.
Swilk, 155, 273, such A.S. *swilc*.
Swinacy, 2999.
Swithe, 5713, quickly. A.S. *swith*.
Swipp, 2196, to pass quickly, to *whip*. O.N. *swippa*.
Swowne, 7289.
Swynk, 755, labour.
Swynsty, 9002, a pigsty.
Swythe, 1390, 3424, see 'Swithe'.
Syde, 1534, long. A.S. *sid*.
Syght, 2218, vision, appearance.
Syker, 1372, sure, certain.
Sykerly, surely, see 'Siker'.
Sykernes, see 'Sikerness'.
Syn, see 'Sen'. Scotch *syne*.
Synging, *sb.*, 3702.
Synoghe, 1917, sinew. A.S. *sinu*.
Sythen, *adv.*, 1) 25. 731, afterwards. 2) 4138, 6014, since.
Sythes, 1272, 3496, times.

Ta, tan, tane, 972, 1375, 1856, 2264, the one.
Taa, 1910, toe.
Tade, 1910, 6900, toad.
Taken, 359, 1328, 2093, 3972, token, miracle.
Takenyng, *sb.*, 1335.
Tald, talde, pret. of *tell*, 1) 213, 4040, told; 2) 436, reckoned.
Tale, 7702, reckoning, number.
Tan, tane, 58, 964, taken.
Tariyng, *sb.*, 1172, delay.
Tary, *vb. tr.*, 1180, 3921, to provoke, annoy, mock. A.Sax. *tirian*, *tyrgan*, to provoke, vex. Pl.D. *tarren*, to tease. Dan. *tirre*.

For speches of God gremed thai
And *taried* rede of heghest ai.
(Ps. cvi, 11.)

Summe he temptes alswa and namely solitary men and wymmen be dredes, and ugglines and qwakynges and schakynges, outher aperand to þam in bodilé liknes, or elles in ymagynynge, slepand and wakande, and *taryes* þam swa þat þei may unnethes have any rest.
(MS. Harl. 1022, fol. 27, see King John, act. iv, Sc. 1.)

Tas, 275, 3865, takes.
Taes, tas, 685, toes.
Tattird, 778, rough, shaggy. Ph. '*tattird* as a fole'. Sc. *tatty*.

Þan þe angelle shinand bright
Schewes þam a ful grisely sight,
A fende blacker þan any cole,
And *taterd* als a filterd fole.
(MS. Harl 4196, fol. 175.)

Teche, 5548, teach, pret. *taght*.
Tempest, 4940.
Tempre, 7612, to moderate.
Tend, 3990, 4794, tenth.
Tene, *sb.*, 7327. A.S. *teón*.
Tent, 7615, to take note of, attend to, pret. *tent*.

'To tilth he *tent* and tend [tenth]
gaf lele, 1804
(MS. Vesp. A. iii, fol. 57.)

Þa, 9087, these, *dem. pron. pl*, 1253, those, used either with or without a following substantive,

Þair, 4329, their.

Þam, ward, 7281.

Þan, 4712, then.

Thankyng, *sb.*, 7842.

Þar, *rel. adv.*, 361, where.

Thar, *vb. imp.*, 2167, 2173, 2963, behoves, need, pret. *thurt.* A.S. *thearf*, imp. *thorfte.*

Tharlles, 1064, slaves. A.S. *thrall*, a servant.

Tharn, *vb.*, to lose, be in need of, want, 8509.

And alle þat mercy here wille warn
Mercy of god sal þai *tharn*,
So he turnes þe defe ere to þam
þan,
Þat turnes þaires to þe pore man.
(MS. Tib. E. vii, fol. 37.)

Tharnyng, *sb.*, 7300, want.

Þartille, 6307, 6828.

Þas, þase, 491, 7236, those.

Þat, 3781, what.

Þeder, 140, thither.

Thef, thefes, 1237, 5210, thief, thieves. A.S. *théf.*

Þer, þere, 1259, these.

Therst, 6775, thirst.

Þeþen, 2721, 5831, thence.

Thewes, 1883, 5548, manners. A.S. *þeáw.* 'Maner or *thewe*' Mos. P. P.

His resoun and his wise *thewes*
Þat he was Godd ful graitheli
schewes. (M. H. p. 3.)

Þider, 1417, 3731, thither.

Þiderward, 7539.

Think, 306, pret. *thought*, to seem.

Þir, 1281, 4151, these.

Þof, þogh, þoghe, 1713, 6288, 6308. 7721, though.

Þoght, 278, thought.

Thole, 3542, 4352, to suffer. A.S. [*tholian.*

Thraldom, 8005.

Thralle, 8001.

Thrang, 4704, 7364, throng, pressure. A.Sax. *þringan*, to press, push.

Thrast, pret. of *threst*, to thrust.

Þan þai gederd thornes kene,
And made a corowne þam bitwene,
And on his hevid þai it *thrast*,
On ilka side þe blude out-brast,
With staves of rede þai set it doun,
And clapped it fast untille his
crowne,
So þat þe thornes went in þan,
Tille þai perced þe hern-pan.
(MS. Harl. 4196, fol. 76.)

Thraw, 2099, throe. A. S. *threáy, threá.* Icel. *thrá.*

Thred, 354, third.

Thredend, 4804, thirteenth.

Threp, threpe, 5407, to dispute. A.S. *threapian.* O.N. *threfa.*

Give ear to my suit, Lord! from-
ward hide not thy face
Behold! hearken, in grief lament-
ing how I pray:
My foes þat bray so loud, and
eke *threpe* on so fast,
Buckled to do me scath, so is
their malice bent.
(Ps. iv, Surrey's works, Ed. Bell,
p. 128.)

Threst, 3254, 6734, to thirst.

Threst, 8591, to thrust, pret. *thrast.* A.S. *thræstian*, to twist.

Thrested, p. p. of *threst*, 5296, to thrust.

Thresty, 6165, 6777, thirsty.

Threttende, 7173, thirteenth.

Threty, thretty, 4588, 4987, thirty.

Threttyng, *sb.*, 2230. A.S. *threatung.* 'Manaisse or *thretynge*'.
(Pr. Pm.)

Thrist, 6118, 6204, thirst.
Thunder-dyntes, 5418, thunderbolts.
Thurgh, 1428, through.
Thurt, 6229, pret. of *thar*, to need.
Thynk, *vb.impr.*, 2094, seem, pret. *thoght*. A.S. *thincan*.
Til, tyl, 85, 1302, to. O.N. *til*, to.
Tilles, 1183, leads away, and hence entices, from O.N. *til*, to. A.S. *till*, end, object. This must not be confounded with *tolle* or *tulle*, to entice, deceive.

For ille felawes hafd sli maistri
To *tille* this ȝong man to foli.
(Met. Hom., p. 113.)

It is not always used in a bad sense.

For þaim we au to *til* and drau
Wit god ensaumpil til godnes.
(Met. Hom., p. 103.)

*Tinsel, perdition.
Tirauntes, 5526.
Tite, *adv.*, 471, 1914, 4979, quickly, comp. *titter*; superl. 405, 3703, *titest*. O.N. *titt*, frequently. Cf. A.S. *tid*, *tidlice*. Sw. *titt*, ready. Ph. '*als-tite*', 2901, as soon, at once, immediately.
Titte, 1918, a tug, pull. It is used by G. Douglas and Dunbar. See 'Tytt'.
Togider, togyder, 1841, 1858, together.
To-gnaw, 863, gnaw away.
Toke, 5196, took.
Tokenyng (= takenyng), *sb.*, 1322, token.
Tome, 6248, leisure. Sc. *tume*. A.S. *tom*. O.N. *tómr*.

Ga yee to fest, for sua yee do,
Haf I na *tome* at ga þarto.
(Cott. MS. Vesp. A. iii, fol. 80.)

It also signifies empty, and hence idle.

And efter none ogain he ȝode,
And other ȝet in þe marked stode;
Unto þam fulle even he come,
And said whi stand ȝe al day *tome*.
(MS. Harl. 4196, fol. 38.)

To-morn, 4666, the morrow.
Tong, 7315, tongue.
To regard of, 5516.
Tother, 384, 552, 3592, the second. that other.
Touch, 3969, to concern.
Tour, 4783, tower.
Trace, 4349, 6037, 7076, track, path, example. Fr. *trache*.
Traist, 1359, to trust, confide in.
Transyng, trance.
Travaile, travayle, 1) *sb.*, 545, work, labour; 2) *vb.*, 539, 542, 1378, 2657, 5942, 6401, to labour.
Trayst, trayste, 1091, 6297, 7339, see 'Traist'.
Trecherous, 4232.
Tregettour, a magician.

A *tregetur* I hope [expect] he be,
Or elles Godds self es he.
(MS. Vesp. A. iii, fol. 68.)

Tremblyng, *sb.*, 6108.
Tresor, tresore, tresour, tresur, 1266, 3819, 3837, 3882, 4115, treasure.
Trespas, 5262, 6361, fault.
Trewely, 6297.
Trey, 7323, sorrow. A.S. *tréga*. Phrase '*trey* and tene'.
Tribulacion, 4133, 4353.
Troble, 4319, to trouble.
Trofel, *sb.*, 183, (a lying) tale, story, fable.

Iogeloures grete avantage gettes
Thurgh fals *trofels* and tregetes.
(MS. Tib. E. vii, fol. 35.)

'to *tryfle* or jape or lye' (Ortus), 'iape or *trifull*'. (Palsgrave.)

Trouthe, trowth, trowthe, 4228, 4388, belief, opinion, from *trow*, to believe, think. Ph. '*false trowth*'.

And þat fals Crist as I telle þe
In þe flum sal baptist be,
To save man saules he salle be send.
And alle *fals trowth* he salle defend.
(MS. Harl. 4196, fol. 78.)

Trow, *vb.*, 3776, 7504, to believe, think. A.S. *trúwian.*

Trowage, 4053, fealty.
For alle kinges yald *trouage*
Till Rome, and servis and homage.
(Met. Hom. p. 61.)

Trowyng, *sb*, 789, opinion, belief.

*Tuin, combination.

*Tun, town.

Tung, 783, 4294, tongue.

Turment, 1) *sb.*, 4260, 4383; 2) *vb.*, 4385.

Turrettes, towers.

Twa, 374, two.

Twelf, 6046, 6047, twelve.

Twelfte, 4802, twelfth.

Twin, twyn, 1) *adj.*, 3594, 5842, two; 2) *vb.*, to separate.

Twinyng, *sb.*, 1864, separation, division.

Tyde, 379, 6142, time.

Tyn, tyne, 1) to lose; 2) to destroy, 1457, 2027, 2322, 5274, pret. *tynt.* O.N. *tyna.*

Tynt, 4854, destroyed, pret. of *tyne;* 6094, taken away from; 1631, lost.

Tyraunt, 4149,

Tyrauntry, 1601, 4392.

Tysyk, 701.

Tyte, tyttest, 322, see 'Tite'.

Tytt, *vb.*, 7216, to pull suddenly or with great violence. A.Sax. *tihtan*, to draw.

Ugge, 6419, to frighten. MS Harl. 4196, reads *ug.* Cf. *ughe*, Liber Cure Cocorum p. 47. *Uggi* (Ancren Riwle). O.N. *ugga*, Hence O.E. *ugsome*, see Surrey's Ed. Bell, p. 174.

Uglines, 2364, horror, see 'Ugge'.

Ugly, 6683, 7182, horrible.
'*Ugly* Furies', Surrey, p. 194.

Uglynes, 917, 6832, horror.

*Umbélai, to lie with.

Umlapp, 6937, envelop.

Umset, 1250, 5420, surrounded.

Unbowsom, 8596; unboxom, 1599. disobedient.

Unchastide, unchastyd, unchastydde, 5434, 5544, 5985.

Unchaungeable, 8232.

Uncomly, 1542.

Uncristen, p. 76, unbaptized.

Uncurtays, 2056.

Underlout, 1) *sb.*, 3877, underling, inferior; 2) *adj.*, 4052, see 'Lowt'.
Underlout to Laverd thou be,
And bid [pray to] him, for best es he.
(Ps. xxxv, 7.)
And *underlout* til thaim was he
Als god child au til elders be.
(Met. Hom. p. 109.)

Understanden, 1681, 2135, understood.

Undiscussed, 5697, not investigated.

Uniustifyed, *adj.*, 5871, not done justice to, wronged.

Unknawen, 337, unknown.

Unknawyng, *sb.*, 194, 5741, ignorance.

Unkunnand, 152, ignorant.

Unkunnyng, 169, ignorance.

Unkynd, unkynde, 122, 5855, ungrateful.

Unkyndness, 6219, ingratitude.

Unlered, 5947, ignorant.

Unnethes, 476, 890, hardly, scarcely, from *un*, not, *eth*, easy.

Unproperly, 8130.

Unredy, 1990, unready.

Unrekend, 2462, 5652, untold, unaccounted for.
Unresonable, 599, without reason.
Unsemely, 5009, 5023.
Unsiker, unsyker, 1089, uncertain, not secure.
Unsykerness, 9049, insecurity.
Unskylwys, *adj.*, 166, not possessing, '*skill*' or reason.
Unsleghe, 1938, unwise, see 'Sleghe'.
Untaght, 5872, untaught.
Untald, 7447, untold.
Unthewed, 5873, rude, ill-manered, *theud*, well behaved, occurs in the Cursor Mundi fol. 47—

Þe child es *theued* and milde o mode,
Lok þat he haf maister god.

Until, 182, unto.
Unto, 3319.
Unwroght, 5976, undone.
Uppas.
Upcalle, 4963, to call up.
Upraise, uprayse, *vb. intr.*, 4985, uprose.
Uprise, upryse, 4979, 5046, 5047, to rise up.
Upstand, 4762, to stand up.
Upstegher, 4180, see 'Stegh'.
Upswadoune, 7230, upside down.
Uptane, 5142, uptaken.
Uptrust, 5567, stored or *trussed* up, from *up-trus*, root, *truss*, see T. M. p. 287—
In the southern dialects *truss* signifies 'to bind in bundles', while in the North it means 'to *store-up*, house.

He had so grete plenté of corn,
He wist noght whare it might be laid,
And to himself þan þus he said,
'How salle I do now of þis thing,
I se þat I ne have no howsing,
Wharin þat I my corn may *trus*',
And eftsones þan said he þus.

Usage, 3790, custom.
Use, 6071, 6078, to practise.
Utter, 4815, 7194, extreme.

Vaile, vaille, 3646, 3942, avail, help.
Valeis, 4796, valleys.
Vany, 955, vain.

Sins þat cumes of werldly dede
And of þe body er þise to rede,
Dronkenes and glotony,
And manslaghter and lichery,
Sacrelege, thift, and ravyne,
And symony, a wikked syn;
Oker gretely God mispays;
Brekeing of dere haly days,
Forsaking of order þat men mase,
Taking of howsel unworthily,
Unreverence unto goddes body,
Bisynes for vanie reverise.
(MS. Tib E. vii, fol. 28.)

Vanyst, 2269, vanished.
Vanyté, 7228.
Variance, variaunce, 1423, 1446, change.
Variand, 1413, changing.
Vedir, 1415, weather.
Velany, 1528, 7148, crime.
Venemus, 6751.
Vengance, vengeance, vengeaunce, 4852, 6101.
Venge, 5533, avenge.
Veniel, 3175, 3902, venial.
Venym, 4185, 6756, poison.
Veray, true.
Verdite, 2952, verdict.
Vermyn, 916, 6574, vermin, worms (all creeping things, large and small).
Verray, 4310, true, very.
Verrayly, 9239, 9240.
Vers, 6624, verse.
Vertow, vertu, 3821, 9198.
Vertuouse, 9072, valuable.
Vicar, 3837.
Vilan, 4412.

Vilany, see 'Velany'.
Voce, 4555, voice.
Voyde, 390, empty.

Wa, 1) *sb*, 4207, woe; 2) *adj.*, 1452, ph. 'fulle *wa*', 7320, very sorrowful', '*wa* worth the, 7396.
Waghe (=waw), 6619, a wall. A.S. *wáh.*
Wowe or wal, murus. (Pr. Pm.)
Wake, 1970, to watch. A.S. *wæccan.*
The ship-boy and the galley-slave, have time to take their ease;
Save I alas! whome care, of force doth so constrain,
To wail the day and *wake* the night, continually in pain (Surrey).
Walaway, *interj.*, 2434, an exclamation of sorrow = '*well-away!*' '*well a day!*'
Wald, 15, 6193, would.
Wam, wambe, wame, 463, 515, 4161, womb. A S. *wamb.*
*Wan, deficiency, want.
*Wan, pret. of *win*, to go.
Wand, wande, 5876, 5880, rod, (birch). It also has the meaning of branch, twig in O.E.
Wanhope, 2229, despair. Cf. O.E. *wantrust*, *wanthrift* &c.
Want, *vb.*, 6198, to be without, to be absent or missing.
Wantyng, *sb.*, lack.
Wapen, 1707, weapon. A.S. *wæpen* Du. *wapen.*
War, 2022, 2676, cautious, careful. A.S. *waér.*
David es his name
And for þat he es *ware* and wise,
I have him chosen to þis servis.
(Cott. MS. Vesp. A. iii, fol. 42.)
War, 1903, 1905, was.
War, 583, were.
Wardes, 9089, outworks.
†Warlau, wizard, sorcerer.
Warn, warne, 7985, to deny, also forbid. O.N. *varna.*
Warne, 2342, 7264, unless.
Þai said 'Sir bind þe nedes us bus,
And lede þe unto Iams with us,
And to Philet þat fra þe fled,
And *warne* it war us forbed,
To do þe harm, or hurt þe sare,
Þou suld far ille or þon com þare.
(MS. Tib. E. vii, fol. 165.)
War[ne]d, 3058, denied, pret. of *warn* or *wern*, to deny.
—God schewes in his godspelle
[Of] þe riche man and lazarus,
How þat he *warned* him almus
Þarfor god *warned* him agayne,
A drope of water to sloken his payne
In þe fyre of helle when he was þan.
(MS. Tib. E. vii, fol. 37.)
Wast, waste, 4864, 4883, to destroy, do away with.
For he [Crist] sal wit the hali gaste,
Batiz you and your sinnes *waste.*
(Met. Hom., p. 11.)
Wat, wate, wayte, what, 5372, to know. A.S. *witan* [*wát*].
Wate, *sb.*, 7611, wet.
Wathe, 1) danger, harm; 2) torment, 4558, see 'Quathe'.
Sorwes of dede umgaf me ai
And *wathes* of helle me fand thai.
(Ps. cxiv, 3?)
In the Cursor Mundi it occurs as an adjective.
Allas! þat i [Jacob] him outher out-sent
Þat way þat was sa *wath* to wend.
(MS. Vesp. A. iii, fol. 25.)
Watter, 4777, water.
Wawes, 148, waves. A.S. *wæg.*
Wawe of the water, flustrum.
(Pr. Pm.)

Wax, 4039, to increase, become (pret. *wex*).
Wayke, 6157, weak. A.S. *wæg*.
Wayknes, 9026, weakness.
Wayt, wayte, 1186, 1243, to watch for in order to harm.
He *waites* in hidels als liouns in den,
He *waites* to reve þe pover in dim,
To reve þe pover while he to-drawes him.
(Ps. ix, 30.)
Waytyn, to harmyn, Insidio. (Pr. Pm.)
Wayte, see 'Wate'.
Weder, wedir, 1424, weather.
Wederward, witherward.
Wedlayk, 8z61. wedlock.
Weght, 7690, weight.
*Weild, power.
Weld, 7361, move, stir.
Weld, welde, 5777, 6149, to rule, govern, posses, use. A.S. *wealdan*.
Wele, 131, 1452, well.
Wele, 1002, weal. A.S. *wela*, weal, wealth, *pl.* riches, property.
Welk, 4248, pret. of *walk*.
Welk, 707, wither, fade. Sc. *wallow* A.S. *wealwian*. Germ. *welken*.
þe *welkid* tre þir appels bare
þat has bene ded þre yere and mare.
(MS. Harl. 4196, fol. 96.)
Welland, 7126, boiling, from *welle*, *walle*, to boil. A Sax. *weallan*, to boil.
Welthe, 1307, prosperity, riches.
Welthes, *pl.*, 1319, riches.
*Wem, spot, blemish.
Wend, wende, *vb.*, 3557, 6028, to go. A S. *wendan*.
Wene, 2154, to think, suppose. A.S. *wénan*.
Were, 2296, doubt. A.Sax. *wær*, caution.
Were, 4088, war. A.S. *uuerre*.
Weried, cursed, see 'Weryed'.
Werk. 4683, 5977, 6905, work.
Werray, 7268, true.
Werray, 4477, to make war upon.
Wers, 61, worse.
Werst, 4456, worst,
Wery, 7422, to curse.
Weryed, *adj*, 6186, 0392, 7393, cursed. A.S. *werigan*.
Wete, 1438, wet.
Wethen, 90, whence.
*Weve, a piece.
Wex, (pret. of *wax*), increased.
þe water *wex* þan cald and lyth.
(Cott. MS. Galba E. ix, fol. 37.)
Wha, 900, who.
Whake, 5411, to quake.
'*Whakyn* or *quakyn*. Tremo. (Pr. Pm.)
Wham, 3868, whom.
Whar, 357, where.
Wharfor, 3702.
Wharwith, 3835.
Whas, whase, 23, 892, whose.
Whaso, whaswa, 4153, whoso.
What, 2666, see 'Wate'.
What-kyn, 856, what kind of.
What-swa, 885.
Whethen, 5205, whence.
Whider, whyder, 2115, 2935, whither.
While, *sb.*, 632, 1418, time.
Whiles, whilles, whyles, 3645, 3930, 5715, 5778, whilst.
Whilom, 4202, formerly.
Whilk, wilk, 144, 204, 244, 3950, which.
Whine, 7423, see 'Whyne'.
Whit, see 'Wite'.
Whyderward, 5401.
Whylles, see 'Whilles'.
Whyn, 3887, obtain, see 'Wyn'.
Whyn, whyne, 1207, 6228, utinam, = whi + ne = why not. But *whi ne* as separate words take a negative in the same clause.

Whine bad he eghen, in ilk hows,
Whine might his sight be set ay-
ware!
Than suld his sorow be mekill
mare
(Cott. Collect; MS. Galba E. ix.)

Wiche, 4214, a witch (not confined to *females)*.
Wytche magus, sortilegus.

*Wiers, protectors. (Pr. Pm.)

Wight, creature.

Wight, 1874, active, see 'Wyght'.

Wille, *sb.*, 7288, desire.

Wille, *vb. tr*, (pret. *wild)*, 8340.

Wirk, 3685, 4877, 6905, to work, operate, perform.

Wirkyng, *sb.*, 4907, operation.

Wisit, 6158, visit.

Wisse, 9304, to show, direct. A.S. *wisian*.
Wyssyn, dirigo. (Pr. Pm.)

Wist, wyst, 9516, knew.

Witandly, 5727, wittingly.

Wite, whit, witt, witte, wyt, wytt, wytte, 1) *sb.*, 4093, 6847, wisdom, knowledge; 2) *vb.*, 4734, 6118, to know; 4664, discover.

†Witherwin, an enemy.

With-outen, without.

Witness, 6769, to bear witness.

Wittes (five), 5518, the senses.

Wittles, 6864, out of one's wits or senses.
O caytyve *wytles* knaip!
Quhat! wenyt thou our handis to
eschaip?
(G. Douglas v. ii, p. 562.)

Witty, 880, 6280, wise.

Wlatsom, 459, 656, hateful, lothsom. The verb *wlate* = hate occurs in Ps. v, 8.
Men slaers and swykel Laverd
wlate sal.

Wode, 99, 1608, 2224, 6864, mad.

Wodeness, 6915, madness.

Wolwarde, 3514, plagued, miserable A.S. *wól*, plague, severity. Cf O.E. *wle* (= wol) bad. (Owl and Nightingal l. 35.)
Wolleward and weetshoed
Wente I forth after,
As a reccheles renk.
(Piers Ploughman, p. 368.)
Thei shulden delven and dyken,
And werchen and *wolward* gon
As we wrecches usen.
(Ibid. p. 497.)

Wolwes, 1228, wolves.

Won, wone, 13, 16, 1001, 4221, to live, dwell. A.S. *wunian*. Germ. *wohnen*. O. Fris. *wona*.

Wonand, 997, 6831, dwelling.

Wonde, 5337, *wound*. A.S. *wund*

Wonder, *adj.*, 1786, 4321, wonderful.

Wonderly, 7619, 7641, wonderfully.

Wonnyng, wonyng, *sb.*, 980, 6827 a dwelling.

Wonnyng-sted, 1372, a dwelling place.

Worldisshe, worldesche, 1065, 1066, temporal, worldly.

Worow (= worry), 1229, to strangle. Sc. *worrey*, *wirrey*, choke, kill. Germ. *würgen*.
Worowen, suffoco, strangulo.
(Pr. Pm.)

Worschepe, worshepe, 6217, honour.

Worthynes, 3757.

Wrahte, 5406, wrath.

Wrang, *sb.* and *adj.*, 193, 5488, 5992, wrong.

Wrangwysly, 3865, wrongfully.

Wrathe, *adj.*, 5479, angry, wroth.

Wreched, 557, wretched.

Wrechednes, 6102.

Wregh, *ob.*, 5460, 5462, to betray, accuse.

Wreke, 5538, 6101, vengeance.

Wrenk, 1360, trick, stratagem. Ph. 'wyle and *wrenk*'. A.S. *wrenc*.

Sa quayntand crafté mad thou itte,
That al bestes er red for man,
Sa mani wyle and *wrenk* he can.
(Met. Hom. p. 2.)

Wreth, wrethe, 1) *sb.*, 787, 1552, 1556, 5081, 5091, 6102, wrath; 2) *vb.*, 1551, 5606, to make angry.

Wrethful, 5107, wrathful.

Wrynchand, 1538, wriggling, twisting. MS. Harl. reads *wrythand.* MS. Lands. 348 has *wrickyng.*

Wydenes, 7576.

Wyght, *adj.*, 689, Sw. *vig*, active. '*Wyghte* or deliver, agilis.
(Pr. Pm.)

Wyghtes, 6186, creatures. A.Sax. *wiht.*

Wyk, 6694, horrid, bad. A.S. *wæc*, *wac.* Germ. *weich.* Prov. Germ. *week*, soft, mean. Cf. *nasty*, O. Eng. *nasky*, from *hnesc*, soft; and O.E. phrase '*wikke* clothes'. Germ. *weichen.* Prov. Germ. *wiken.* A.S. *wican*, to be weak.

Þe wind began rudely to rise,
And þe see to bolne on wunder wise,
Grete stormes wox with weders *wik*,
And þe wawes went wunder thik.
(MS. Harl. 4196, fol. 154.)

Wyle, 1360, trick, artifice. A.S. *wile.*

Wyn, wynne, 1) 2769, 3880, to obtain, (pret. *wan*, p. p. *wonnen).* 2) 2871, 3263, 4462, 5057, to go.

Wyndyng-clathe, 840.

Wynter, 7652, *pl.* = years.

Wys, wyse, 3622, manner.

Wyst, see 'Wist'.

Wythen (= witen), 5355, to give or bear witness.

Wytnes, wyttenessyng, *sb.*, 3612, 3366, witness.

Wytte, *vb.*, 3763, 4788, to know. A.S. *witan.*

Ydous, 2911, hideous.

Yhate, 2130, gate. A. S. *geát.*

Yhe, 68, 400, 4046, ye.

Yhed, pret. of *ga*, 4851. It is sometimes written *yhode.*

Yheld (pret. *yhald)*, 3864, 3987, to pay, render, give up, yield, reward. A.S. *geldan.*

Yheldyng, *sb.*, 7846, bestowal.

Yhell, 7341, to yell. A. S. *geallian.*

Yheme, 5792, to protect. A. Sax. *gyman.*

Yheme me laverd stedfastly,
For þat in þe hoped I. (Ps. xv.)

Yhere, 741, 3933, 4526, year.

Yhern, yherne, 1649, 2176, 2182, 4663, 6725, to desire, yearn, ph. '*yherne* it ete', 6705. A.S. *geornian.*

Yhernyng, *sb.*, 1127, 1579, desire; 6632, lust.

Yhet, yhit, yhitte, 22, 105, 930, 2207, 3652, yet, also.

Yhister-day, 8083, yesterday.

Yhode, pret. of *ga.*

Yholden, p. p. of *yheld*, 6672.

Yholke, 6451, yolk. A. S. *geolca.*

Yhong, 3785, young.

Yhou, yhow, 3560, 5143, you.

Yhour, 5210, your.

Yhouthe, yhowthe, 5972, youth.

Yhouthede, 5713, youth-hood.

Yhong, yhung, 5712, 6011, young.

Ymages, 4323.

Ymagyn, 6685.

Ymyddes, 6450, amidst.

Ynogh, ynoghe, 1466, 1759, enough.

Ynwitt, 5428, conscience.

Ypocrisy, 4240.

Yren, 6572, iron.

Yse, 6644, ice.

Yvel, 698, 3001, 5347, evil, disease.

CORRIGENDA.

Page 11, note for 'MS. Addit.' read 'MS. Addit. 11305.'
Page 13, l. 450 for 'inquitatibus' read 'iniquitatibus.'
Page 18, l. 620 for 'cansideres' read 'consideres'.
Page 40, note for 'MS. Harl.' read 'MS. Harl. 4196.'
Page 41, l. 1478 for 'pus' read 'þus'.
Page 56, l. 2010 for 'fayles' the sense requires 'flayes'.
Page 68, l. 2496 omit 'non'.
Page 69, l. 2516 for 'men' read 'man'.
Page 74, l. 2727 for 'þayn' read 'payn'.
Page 77, l. 2823 for 'fldelium' read 'fidelium'.
Page 88, l. 3215 for 'allen' read 'alle'.
Page 91, l. 3333 for 'par' read 'pas'.
Page 93, l. 3426 for 'þat' read 'þai'.
Page 124, l. 4578 for 'ma' read 'man'.
Page 165, l. 6117 for 'nan' read 'man'.
Page 189, l. 6991 for 'knaw' read 'gnaw'.
Page 190, l. 7034 for 'here-ol' read 'here-of'.
Page 208, l. 7727 for 'couth clerk' read 'couth na clerk'.
Page 217, l. 8040 for 'po' read 'þe'.
Page 229, l. 8509 for 'þat' read 'þai'.
Page 253, l. 9408 for 'pai' read 'þai'.
Page 296, l. 43 for 'ferse' read 'fersc'.
Page 300, l. 31 for 'heribyrigan' read 'herebyrigan'.

CONTRACTIONS USED IN THE GLOSSARY.

A. S. Anglo-Saxon.—Dan. Danish.—Du. Dutch.—E. English.—O. E. Old English.—P. E. Provincial English.—Fris. Frisian.—O. Fris. Old Frisian. Icel. Icelandic.—Jam. Jamieson's Scottish Dictionary.—Met. Hom. Metrical Homilies.—Pr. Pm. (P. P.) Promptorium Parvulorum.—T. M. Towneley Mysteries.—W. C. Wyntoun's Chronicle.

Words marked by a * occur in the *Notes;* those marked by a † are in the *Introduction.*

CPSIA information can be obtained
at www.ICGtesting.com
Printed in the USA
LVHW110806120522
718525LV00003B/47

9 783375 004477